'It's a disease, yo[...] air, which is wh[...] bombs and smoke and things – and it star[...] years ago, and we call it MERS. You're not old enough to understand yet, but that's Male Embryo Rejection Syndrome. It's very sad, Harri, and we're going to find a cure. But nobody's killing baby boys. They just aren't happening. Baby *girls* are, but – '

Moma took one of Harriet's hands, found the other, held them both together. 'What your father isn't telling you, precious, is that it's all part of God's wonderful plan. Giving it letters and calling it a disease and talking about cures won't change that. God the Mother has watched the world for hundreds of thousands of years, and She's seen how mean and wicked men are, and what they did to Her son Jesus, and now She's decided to even things up. In Her mercy She's sent us this afflic- tion. We may not like it, but Her will be done. I'm sure you can understand that. The world's going to be a very different place, Harri . . . '

Also by D. G. Compton in VGSF

RAGNAROK
(with John Gribbin)

D.G. COMPTON

NOMANSLAND

VGSF

First published in Great Britain 1993
by Victor Gollancz Ltd

First VGSF edition published 1994
by Victor Gollancz
A Cassell imprint
Villiers House, 41/47 Strand, London WC2N 5JE

A catalogue record for this book is
available from the British Library.

ISBN 0 575 05714 9

Printed and bound in Great Britain
by Cox & Wyman Ltd, Reading, Berks

For John Gribbin

With affection, and gratitude for all
his encouragement and help, without which
this book would never have happened.

CHAPTER ONE

The Attrition. Year 40: late October.

I didn't believe what I was hearing. I did believe it. And Dr
Marton's performance was so shameful and so shameless that for
once words failed me. He smiled, he spread his hands, he stared
at the cedar-panelled ceiling, he elaborated his argument. He
cheated. Watching him operate, seeing him behind his priceless
antique desk, his hi-tech desk lamp, his array of screens and
telephones, his machinery of power, I was suddenly afraid of
him. Oswald Marton was the Minister's aide. People said she
listened to him.

I folded my hands in my lap. My knees were together, the hem
of my white lab coat pulled down over them, and my back was
straight. I waited coldly, letting him run on. I wasn't some
snivelling clerk. I too had friends and position. Maybe my
silence, and all his words, would embarrass him.

Him? Marton? Embarrass Oswald Marton?

The ironic thing was, I'd asked my secretary to make this
appointment entirely as a matter of courtesy. There'd obviously
been a clerical error somewhere, and I'd decided it would be
tactful to clear it up in person, have a quiet chat with someone,
and save departmental face. I knew how government departments worked. It wasn't easy, but Maggi eventually fitted this
meeting in between a voice-over session with the bloody TV
dubbing people and some computer time I'd already booked on
the Institute's mainframe. She allowed me seventy-five minutes:
thirty minutes travelling each way and fifteen minutes in which
to sort out the mistake over my application.

Fifteen minutes, it now turned out, in which to be made to feel
like a snotty-nosed schoolgirl.

Marton had stopped speaking. His silence joined mine. The
room was elaborate, cedar-lined with rich period fretwork, more
like a private study than a government office. I noticed distant
sounds of traffic, then the slow tapping of one of Marton's fingers
on the red leather of his desk-top as he returned my gaze. I didn't
speak and neither did he. He was insultingly unconcerned.

Finally, the point made, he cleared his throat and produced another of his smiles. 'Tea, Dr Kahn-Ryder?'

I shook my head. It was a tiny movement but he caught it instantly. Marton never needed telling twice. I'd expected some girl, some clerk; I'd got the Minister's aide himself. This was Chief Secretary Marton. A man. In those days, forty years into the Attrition, only the top echelons were men. They might be a dying breed, but they clung to power.

Marton didn't press the matter of tea. He started a reprise.

'Frankly, Dr Kahn-Ryder, your presence here surprises me.' It had surprised him for the last ten minutes. 'The Minister's memo was explicit. Regretful, of course – nobody likes saying *no* to a scientist as distinguished as yourself – but quite explicit. And in any case – ' he fingered my application file yet again ' – in any case, I'm surprised that you yourself should wish to go public. Your team's research is clearly incomplete. It does not support your conclusions. The International Patent Office would laugh at us. Premature publication is – '

'That's for the IPO to say, Dr Marton. Not you – and certainly not on the basis of the summary you have there. Do you really imagine the World Health Organization would have invited me to Paris in December if – ?'

'The Department doesn't operate in a vacuum, Dr Kahn-Ryder. We consult.' He sat back, rubbed his eyes wearily. 'We have advisors. We take the scientific temperature. We – '

'Advisors? What advisors?'

'Respected people, Dr Kahn-Ryder.' Again the spread hands. 'People working in your field. I don't have to tell you how big Syndrome-related research is these days. You have no lack of well-informed colleagues.'

'No lack of rivals, you mean.'

'Oh, come now, Dr Kahn-Ryder . . . '

That had been a mistake. I took a deep breath, counted to ten. I was handling this badly. They were trying to take away my scientific freedom and I was letting myself sound paranoid.

I began again. 'I'm sorry, Chief Secretary Marton, but within the broad spectrum of MER Syndrome research my own area is unique. There are *no* respected people working in it. And that's not just my vanity – you know it's true as well as I do.'

He tried to interrupt but I talked him down. 'And what's more,

6

even if there *are* people working in it, I cannot believe that any of them – on the basis of the data you have there – would dare to give an opinion on the adequacy of my research. That must wait on the full text of the paper I plan to publish. And the responsibility for that paper is mine, Chief Secretary. It has to be. Not yours, not the Minister's, not the Department's – mine. It has to be.' I was on my feet now, angry again, leaning forward across his desk. 'It has to be, because it's my reputation that'll be at stake, Chief Secretary. Not yours, not the Minister's, not the Department's – mine.'

He stared up, carefully observing me. Now, with winter begun, at five in the afternoon the uncurtained window behind his chair was bright black glass, a mirror. In it I could see myself, leaning forward, just as Dr Marton could see me. I was too vehement. I was shrill, my hair was cut too short, my white lab coat, straight from the Institute via the recording studio, no time to change, was too crisp, the priority bleeper on my lapel was too prestigious. At five o'clock on a Thursday afternoon, with two hours of his official male workday still to go, Chief Secretary Marton would detest me. I was the New Woman. Very soon, if the Syndrome wasn't checked, I would inherit the earth. Until which time, for as long as he lived and breathed, Chief Secretary Marton would do everything in his power to humiliate me.

I saw all this, how mighty issues can hang on matters of clothes, hair, vehemence, executive accessories, in the polite half-minute he waited to be sure that I had done. I saw it much too late, of course.

I'm still not good with people, and then I was terrible. Thirty-six years old and I'd learned so little. My husband Mark, with his journalist's eye, had summed Marton up in one brief meeting. A small man, and probably not out of quite the right drawer, Dr Marton had been ambitious enough, and intelligent enough, to avoid over-compensating for these handicaps. He moved slowly, spoke softly, and dressed with low-key elegance. And he'd chosen an office chair over the arms of which he could drape his short legs as if they were long, displaying slim handmade shoes and smart amounts of grey silk sock. And while the premature silvering of his hair was probably natural, the irises of his eyes, very brown and bright, showed the tiny scars of recent corrective surgery. Image mattered.

Mark had seen in a flash that Marton was a force. He had taken himself, and the world, firmly in hand. He was impressive. Dangerous.

But how else could I have handled him, that day in his cedar-smelling office? Insulted us both with silly frills and simpering?

'The trouble with you scientists,' he was telling me, 'is that you lack a sense of proportion. For all your great abilities you remain – forgive me – strangely naïve. Which is all the more strange in your case, considering your husband's profession. I would have expected a science writer – ' he paused fastidiously ' – that *is* what Mr Kahn does, I believe? – to have his feet pretty firmly on the ground.'

'Mark's away. I haven't discussed this with him.' I too paused. 'Yet.'

Marton could take that as a delicate threat: a fair response to his delicate scorn. He chose not to.

'You should take his advice. I'm sure he'll say the same as me. Basically the Minister has your interests at heart. There's plenty of time. Premature publication would do none of us any good. What's wrong with an additional test program along the lines suggested in our memo? Three months, six months . . . surely, Dr Kahn-Ryder, it's better to be safe than sorry?'

'What's fucking wrong with an additional fucking test program, Chief Secretary, is that it's not fucking necessary.' I'd lost. And I was wasting my time – I'd lost long before I'd even got there. 'And what's more, Chief Secretary, it's none of your fucking business anyway. *Scientific freedom*, Chief Secretary – it's written into my fucking contract. I was to have complete scientific freedom.'

He rested his chin on his steepled fingers. 'Ah yes, your fucking contract . . . ' His repetition annihilated me. He'd reduced me to just another foul-mouthed woman. 'And while we're talking of contracts, it seems I must remind you of another. You signed the National Security Protocol, I believe? Including the '97 Amendment?'

'It was a formality. You told me yourself, Chief Secretary. All civil servants have to. It was a formality.'

'It was indeed. But on the authority of such simple formalities heads have often been severed from bodies, Dr Kahn-

Ryder. I speak historically, of course – ' he sighed, to show he wasn't joking ' – but I'm sure you take my meaning. It would be very unfortunate indeed if you were to disregard the Minister's recommendation.'

'Recommendation? Is that all it was? I must admit I thought it was something rather more . . . rather more . . . ' I tailed off. I couldn't think why I bothered.

Neither could my companion. He glanced at his watch.

'You force me to be frank, Dr Kahn-Ryder – '

'Yes.' I came in quickly. 'Yes, I do. For the good of your soul, Dr Marton. Just for once – to see how it feels.'

I'd raised a spark. He heaved himself to his feet, lifted my file, angrily stabbed the air with it. 'Frankly, ma'am, if one word of the material in this proposal were to get out, you'd be in serious trouble. And I don't just mean instant and total withdrawal of government funding . . . The smallest leak, even if you were to find some journal willing to take the risk, would bring down the full weight of the law upon you. The Security Protocol is not to be taken lightly, Dr Kahn-Ryder. You accepted that when you chose to work for the state.'

I had chosen to work for the state principally because I believed – foolishly, it now seemed – that political restrictions would be less offensive than capitalist restrictions.

He flung the file down. 'Go back to your department. Take my advice and stick to what you know. Research is what you know. Stick to it. Resubmit your proposal, properly supported, in six months' time. And until then – ' He checked, stared at me thoughtfully, lowered his voice. 'Believe me, my dear, one day you'll thank us for saving you from making a fool of yourself. Time is on your side. Get your stuff right and it's Nobel material. My minister realises that. Do your homework properly and you'll have her fullest possible support.'

I stood up also. The man was too obvious – first the stick and then the carrot. Scare the little lady to death with dire threats, then send her away with promises of fame and fortune. The trouble was, I'd already done my 'homework' – my 'stuff' already was right. Our team at the Institute had been confirming its findings for the last year and more. Nothing remained to be done – I was ready to publish.

I was going to publish.

I eased back, away from Marton. I had to be careful. He wasn't dumb – he'd see through too easy a capitulation.

'In six months' time, Dr Marton, the Minister's support will probably be too late. It's being first past the post that matters, and in six months' time, for all I know, someone in the private sector will have pre-empted us. The patents rights will have gone elsewhere, to Brandt or Unikhem. What will the Minister tell the taxpayers then about the millions of their money she's poured into my work?'

He was putting my file away in a desk drawer, making a production out of locking it. Now he came round the side of the desk, laid a fatherly hand on my shoulder. He'd won: he could afford to be generous.

'You're a scientist, my dear. Leave the politics to us. And trust our connections – we'll be the first to hear if anything of that sort threatens.'

He turned me round and we started the considerable walk to the door. I said. 'I hate being muzzled like this. I have to warn you I'll be seeking expert legal advice.'

He smiled tolerantly. 'Please do. I'm confident that any lawyer will confirm what I've told you.'

'And what am I to say to the WHO's Paris organisers? They've invited me to deliver a paper in December. What am I to tell them?'

'Tell them you'll go. It's a great honour. And I'm sure you can cobble up something.'

Cobble up something . . . he made me sick and I moved sideways to disengage myself. His hand lingered briefly on my neck, then fell away.

'No hard feelings, my dear?' Still smiling. 'It's part of my job sometimes to have to play the heavy father. I promise you I don't enjoy it.'

I didn't believe him. He loved it. As I turned in the doorway my smile was similarly false. 'Fathers seldom do enjoy it,' I told him, hurt more than I knew. 'My own enjoyed it so little, all of it, that he killed himself. Destroyed his trachea. Drowned in his vomit. You've read my file, you already know that.' I glanced at my watch. I was a busy lady. 'Thank you for giving me your time, Dr Marton. At least I know where I stand now.'

His hand still hovered. Already ashamed of myself, I shook it.

Dragging in Dada's suicide was cheap. It had hardly been Oswald Marton's fault. Why, after seventeen years, did it rankle so?

We parted. If he'd intended to deliver a final warning, my briskness told him he'd made himself sufficiently clear. He closed the door behind me and I hurried away, my flat heels squeaking faintly on the marble floor.

I seethed. Solemn portraits of presidents glided by, and the occasional range of national mountains under optimistic pink snow. The pink snow cheered me. I was going to publish. I'd made up my mind. With or without the Minister's permission, if not at the Paris seminar then by some other means, I was going to claim my right to scientific freedom. What could they do? Once I'd gone public the Minister wouldn't dare prosecute. World opinion would be on my side. I wouldn't even need their bloody funding – the big pharmaceuticals, Brandt, Unikhem, would be trampling each other in the rush. I could take my pick. I could go for the Swiss. They paid best.

Out in the foyer I found a telephone. I wanted to talk to Mark, to tell him about Marton, and I called home but he wasn't there. Yvette answered, very much in the middle of giving Anna her supper. Mark wasn't at *Science News* either – the switchboard said he was away on a job, not bleepable.

Of course he wasn't there. He was out in the farmlands, researching his piece on UV radiation. He'd told me that morning where he'd be, and that we weren't to wait supper.

I leaned my head against the inside of the phone hood. My brain was buzzing. I needed to talk to someone, confide in someone I could trust. Someone who would advise me. I needed to let out my anger and be told I was right.

The clock in the Ministry foyer said I was already hopelessly behind schedule. I ought to contact the Institute, tell them to release my computer time. There were always people hanging round in the hope of a cancellation.

I had a brainwave – I'd call my brother. It was a brave thought: we weren't exactly talking, but we weren't exactly not talking either. And he worked in security so he'd be able to advise me. He was in the private sector but he'd have a good idea of the guns at the Minister's disposal.

I called for his number on my datastor. I didn't ring him often enough to remember it. Often enough? Once, in maybe the last four years . . . In any case, he was stationed out of town these days, at NatSekur's headquarters down in the South Forest, so the area code alone was as long as the number of miles to the moon and back. I read it off the display, fed in my card again. The screen in the booth was small and scratched, but I paid the extra. I wondered how Danno was doing. He'd been running to fat, four years ago.

We weren't close. Well, we *were* close but nobody'd have known it.

Danno wasn't in his office. Once I'd got past the computer the young woman at NatSekur put me on hold, Fingal's Cave and seagulls in long-shot against an improbably blue sky, while she ran Colonel Ryder to ground. Once again I thought about the distances between Daniel and me. Once again I decided they weren't because of anything I'd done. Except to grow up, maybe. I'd always been the clever one, but oddly that had never bothered him. In fact, he'd been proud of that in the old days. So what happened?

'Harri? I've run all the fucking way, Harri.' He lurched into focus. 'Don't tell me. Someone's died. That's it. Who then? It's that fucking canary of yours.'

'We don't have a canary,' I told him. 'Annie's got a cat. For his sins, Elvis.'

'So who is it then?' He peered into the camera: the same square, simple, wary man, still unlined, a little less puzzled now, at forty, but the same Danno. '*Someone* must have died. I don't rate phone calls for the fun of it.'

And the same bitterness. But it wasn't only *I* who hadn't called *him* – *he* hadn't called *me*.

'I might just want to talk to you, Danno.'

'I'm listening, Harri. Talk on . . . how much?' He reached for his wallet inside his dark blue uniform jacket. 'I always was a sucker for a pretty face.'

Bugger it. I needed his help, but not this much. I'd never gone to him for money. Before today I'd never gone to him for anything. 'Forget it, mate. Just forget it.' There was a small office behind him, its door open, beyond it racks of guns. 'Get back to your noisy toys, Danno. I can see I interrupted you.'

I reached for the cut-out.

'Hang on. Hang on there . . . Harri, I'm sorry. I was only joking. It was only a joke.'

It was never a joke. But I recognised my own short fuse and its reason. Guilt. Why else was I calling him, four years late, except because I wanted something? 'I'm sorry too, Danno. It's been a bad day . . . I really need to talk.'

He settled himself on the edge of the office desk. 'Fine. Fine . . . ' His waist was thick, but it wasn't life-threatening. 'I've given my girls five but they'll be happy to take fifteen.'

'I don't see any girls, Danno.'

'You've caught me down on the indoor range. I'm passing out a group of recruits on their marksmanship tests.' He held up a pair of ear-muffs to prove it. 'Between you and me, Harri, there's not one in five can shoot worth a damn. And that's not sexism, that's what's called virgin card. Targets unpenetrated. Ten zeroes out of ten. It's hard to believe.'

He was establishing himself: after four years, hitting me with his macho profession. Challenging me to disapprove, which I always had. Secretly. Maybe not so secretly.

'I'm in trouble, Danno.'

'I tell you, for half of them a handgun's a fucking fashion accessory.'

'I need advice, Danno. Your sort of advice. Legal. You see, I've done some research, and I want to publish it because it's important, and they won't let me.'

I watched him reel himself in. 'Who won't let you?' He frowned. 'Who're you working for these days? I see you on TV, sounding off, my sister the famous scientist, but – '

'I work for the Government, Danno. For the Science Ministry. And they're throwing the Security Protocol at me, and some amendment that – '

'Ninety-seven? Well, they would. I mean, working for them, you signed it didn't you?'

'I must have done. I signed a lot of stuff. But in any case, what can they do? Once I've published it'll be too late. They can arrest me, I suppose, but . . . Don't I have any rights, Danno? If not as a scientist, then just as a citizen? Won't the European Court be – ?'

'Wait a minute, Harri. Stop right there. I fucking mean it. Whoa.'

The screen went blank. I waited. We hadn't lost the connection – I was still getting audio. He'd covered the lens, maybe hung his cap on it. I waited. Around me footsteps hurried in the Ministry foyer, telephones rang, lift doors hissed open.

The picture returned: Daniel, the door behind him now closed. 'Harri? First thing, Harri, if they go for '97 that's the end of your rights. You don't get none. They've got you tied up tighter than a nun's – '

He broke off. Self-censorship? On my account? On my account, no twats? Was that how much we'd changed together?

'Second thing, Harri, I reckon you're calling from a booth, and you're using your card.'

'Of course I am.' The censored twats upset me. 'How else would I get through to you? I'm still on your access list with NatSekur, obviously, and my card matches, so of course . . . '

So of course . . . the penny dropped. The eurocoin descended. He was telling me that if NatSekur could match my voiceprint with my eurocard in a nanosecond, then so could the Ministry's watchdogs. He was telling me that from now on I was marked. Telephones were out, even from home. We'd been paying by eurocard for years – it simplified accounting. It was also great for pulling in automated phone taps. The card woke up the computer and the computer woke up the tap.

The Ministry would have Mark's card on file. I needed to warn him.

'So if you want my advice, Harri, it's calm down.' He gave two fingers to an imaginary someone off camera. The listeners. They didn't tap the video yet. 'Forget the European Court. If the Ministry says no, chances are the Ministry knows best.'

'You think so?'

'You asked my advice. That's my professional advice.'

'OK.' It stuck in my throat, but I needed to be believed. 'I'll do as you say. I'm not the martyr type. Besides, what would Annie do, with her Moma in jail? And Mark . . . '

'What about my career prospects? Famous scientist I survive. TV Green I survive. Jailbird I don't survive.'

I laughed. I couldn't help it – the mimicry was terrible but we watched the same Jewish TV comic.

'Thanks for the advice, Danno. I'll be good.'

'Fine. Fine . . . After all, they'll have you tagged.' Tagged? Not

14

so soon – tagging was for criminals out on licence, and needed a magistrate's order. But so did phone taps. He was saying they'd got me all ways. 'You sign the Amendment, Harri, you stick to it . . . How're you keeping otherwise? How's Mark? And little Annie?'

'We're in good shape. Annie's not so little. She's coming up fifteen. And how're you?'

'Never better.'

'And Bert?'

'Bert's going along.'

Bert Breitholmer was a NatSekur officer also. They'd shared a flat ever since Danno first joined. I'd never met him but I'd seen him once in the street. He was older than Danno, a powerful presence, and I'd imagined there was something sexual between them. Mark said matchmaking was part of women's need for continuity, but if Bert was still around, maybe I'd been right.

We waited. There was a chance now for one of us to say something real. I could have told him how I'd dragged up Dada's suicide and wished I hadn't. He could have told me about his life with Bert. We could have exchanged news about our crazy moma in her island convent. We could have talked about why we never talked.

'Well, Harri . . . time I got back to work.'

'Of course. It was good to chat.'

'Yeah.'

'We don't do this often enough.'

'You're a busy lady.'

'That's no excuse.'

'Fuck excuses. If you need excuses, that means there aren't any.'

'Who said that?'

'Search me. I did. 'Bye, Harri.'

'See you, Danno.'

He cut the connection. We both knew very well who had said it. Dada had.

I stood for a moment in the booth, brooding on the sad things that happened to families. Then I ducked out, and away across the Ministry foyer. I half-expected the guards to stop me under the '97 Amendment but they let me through.

Out on the pavement a news-stand was flashing another karate

15

killing, the sixth, a sixth young woman with her throat smashed in. Janni Wintermann. The killing wasn't news – women died violently often – only the method. Every now and then, no pattern, a throat smashed in. A karate blow, allowing the media their cheap glib phrase, *karate killers* . . . Poor Janni Wintermann. I saved my money, thinking of Anna and glad that few of the killings had been here in the city.

I turned up my collar against the cold, hurried across the street, and flung myself on a tram that was going in my direction. I rode it to the bottom of our neighbourhood, twenty minutes of soothing rubber tyres on rubber track. I set my mind in neutral. It was a useful trick. Time enough to think about what to do next when I'd talked to Mark. For the moment I considered the coming winter and the cross-country skis we'd promised Anna.

Our house is in what I have to admit is a classy area. It's a big last-century house, traditional, painted black and red, L-shaped, with a broad raised porch filling in the L, its upstairs windows tucked deep in under wide eaves and curlicued barge-boards. That October we'd just repainted all the window shutters and put up the storm screens round the porch, ready for the snow. The house stands on a low grassy mound, hidden from its neighbours by mature pine trees and silver birches, and it has a double garage left over from the oil-rich years. There was a single small Saab-Honda in it then. We're professional people, Mark and I, and we've done well. If I feel any need to apologise for the house and the classy area, it's because of the area. It's too rarefied. There isn't the sort of security screen some areas have, but there might very well be for the amount of contact most of us have with flesh-and-blood living. I didn't like bringing up Anna so fancy, and neither did Mark, but we didn't want her growing up in the real, angry world of the Attrition either.

I ran up the steps to the porch, eurocard ready in my hand. I hadn't yet telephoned the Institute about my unused computer time and I needed to discuss it with my program director. Natalya Volkov was with me for her obstetrics experience, a big sensible woman from the Russian Federation, but she'd shown a skill in statistical analysis that made her doubly valuable. Perhaps she had something going that she could take over to use up what remained of my mainframe time.

Yvette was finishing in the kitchen and Anna was upstairs, washing her hair. They were both going out, Yvette for a meal in town with her latest elderly boyfriend and Anna to a girl just up the road – she and Jessica did their physics homework together. Jessica's father was a British psycho-engineer we were on dinner-party terms with. Mark wasn't home yet.

I called Natya and we fixed something. I can't remember what, and it doesn't matter. What happened later that evening was so unexpected, and so horrible, that I remember very little of the time immediately before it. I played the piano for a while, to unwind, then Anna came down and we sat and talked about ordinary things, and I thought how unusually beautiful she was that night. Her father was black and she'd inherited his lustrous dark eyes, with my Nordic bone structure: her gold skin glowed with good health and her hair, newly washed, took the best from both of us, blue-black and in shining waves to her shoulders. I know I seem to boast about my daughter, as if I was responsible, but I've worked in genetics too long for that. It's not pride, it's more like cele-bration – the delight of a lottery winner who can't believe her good fortune.

So we talked, and I thought how beautiful she was that night, and Elvis arrived in his stately fashion and settled on her lap – a terrible name for a cat, but Anna's choice, back when she was seven and the video firms were hyping vintage Presley – and then it was time for her to go up the road to her friend.

We know an amazing amount about the generations im-mediately before us, back to Presley and beyond. A hundred years of their lives, sometimes in the minutest detail, their rituals preserved, their fears articulated, their aspirations easily inferred. How sad it is that their experience is of so little use to us.

But I'm putting off what happened next. I'm afraid of it and I'm putting it off. What happened next is that Yvette left for the city, and Anna went up the road to her friend, and I ate the supper waiting for me in the oven, and the front doorbell rang. And when I checked through the spyhole there was a young woman standing on the step, a short-haired blonde, about my age, in a neat, not unfeminine grey-green woollen suit, holding up a card with her picture on it, the big letters SPU, a lot of other writing, and the state coat of arms.

'Sergeant Milhaus,' she said through the answerphone. 'Special Police Unit.'

My first thought was that something had happened to Mark. I let her in.

'I'm on secondment to the Science Ministry,' she told me. 'Is your husband at home?'

I shook my head, relieved.

'And your daughter?'

She had a nasty voice, ugly vowels, sharp and demanding.

'She's out too.'

She caught the question in my expression. 'It's just that I don't want us to be interrupted. Can we have a word?'

I led her into my own little sitting-room, of all places, where I'd been before with Anna. Elvis eyed her from the sofa, but didn't get up. A policewoman from the Ministry so soon after my conversation with Dr Marton: there had to be a connection. Well, my conscience was clear. So far.

'Sit down, do.' I gestured lightly. 'Park your bum.'

Or perhaps she was the result of my phone call with Danno. If so, then they'd acted very promptly – we'd signed off less than two hours ago. But in either case I still had an easy conscience. Whatever my dark intentions, I'd done nothing wrong.

Sergeant Milhaus chose the far end of the sofa from Elvis. I sat in the armchair opposite.

'Nice cat,' she said, and took a folded document from her inside jacket pocket. 'I'll get to the point, Dr Ryder.'

'Dr Kahn-Ryder.' The *Kahn* is Mark's name, of course. I don't usually insist on it, but faced with this woman's vowels I needed all the double barrels I could get. I wasn't taking her seriously, you see. 'Dr Kahn-Ryder.'

She ignored the correction. Unfolding the document, she held it out. 'This *is* your signature?'

I looked at it. It seemed to be mine. 'Yes.'

She rattled through the document, held it out again. 'And this?'

'Yes again.' I knew now what she/the Minister was up to.

'And you know what this paper is?'

'It's the National Security Protocol. And its '97 Amendment.'

'Exactly so. Exactly so.' She refolded the protocol and put it

18

back in her pocket. 'The Minister was afraid as how you might not recognise it, Dr Ryder.'

She pronounced the word *reckernise*. But that was none of my business. I gently reminded her, 'Dr Kahn-Ryder,' and waited.

'The Minister was afraid as how you might of forgotten all about it.'

'Not at all. And if I had, her Chief Secretary this afternoon kindly reminded me.'

'That's nice. That's very nice. I'm glad to hear it.' She moved one hand along the sofa cushion towards Elvis, scratching the lavender chintz encouragingly with her blunt, sensible fingernails. He widened his eyes, stretched a tabby paw to investigate. 'Nice cat,' she said again.

No woman who liked Elvis could be wholly bad, I thought. 'He's my daughter's,' I told her.

'Yes. Her name's Anna, I believe. I don't have no daughter.' She reached for Elvis, gathered him on to her knee. He went without protest, floppy like an old fox fur. 'Nasty things can happen to daughters these days,' she said conversationally, rubbing under his chin. His best place. Sergeant Milhaus knew about cats, no doubt of that.

'We're careful,' I said. 'And out here in the suburbs there's not much danger of – '

'Very nasty things, if their mothers don't behave.' She looked across, meeting my eye. 'The Minister wanted you to know that.'

Suddenly I felt sick. So that was it. 'The Minister's threatening me?'

'Not at all. That would be against the law. A fair warning, more like. The thing is, where state security's concerned, sometimes her servants gets what you might call over-zealous. They take state security very seriously, Dr Ryder. Dr Kahn-Ryder. And it makes them over-zealous.'

Elvis's head was raised in ecstasy to the ceiling. There was a faint click and a knife blade appeared in Sergeant Milhaus's other hand. Quickly, with both her sleeves well back from her wrists, before I could move or make a sound, she cut his throat. Blood sprayed across the carpet. She held him tightly as he shuddered and gasped. Blood pumped steadily, not a drop falling on Sergeant Milhaus. I watched it in silence, paralysed, dying with him. Finally it stopped. There'd been a surprising amount for one not-very-large cat.

Still holding him carefully away from herself, Sergeant Milhaus leaned forward and, using her muscular thighs, stood up. I watched her, in shock, genuinely curious about what she'd do next, as she squatted on her heels and quite gently laid Elvis down in the pools and thick spatterings of his blood.

My hands were shaking. She reached out, took one of them and turned it over, examined the palm. 'Parents can be careful,' she said, 'but they can't be careful all the time. And never careful enough.' She folded my hand, patted it, and gave it back. 'I'll see myself out.'

She straightened, stepping carefully, and walked to the door.

'Sorry about the carpet. I'll see the bill gets passed if you send it to the Ministry.'

She went away. I heard her deal efficiently with the automatic locks on the front door, then it closed behind her and the house was silent.

CHAPTER TWO

The Attrition. Year 10: early September.

' . . . *God so loved the world, that She gave Her only-begotten son, that those who believe in him shall have everlasting life* . . . '

Asked in a recent interview if she could isolate a particular event in her childhood that had started her on her remarkable career, Dr Kahn-Ryder paused for thought, characteristically, and then replied that it had probably all begun some thirty years before, on a September morning she vividly remembered, in Year 10 of the Attrition, in her parents' harbourside cottage on the west coast where she'd been born, a couple of miles down the Windstrohm River from Brandt Laboratories, as they were then called. Unprompted, she went on to say that she believed the shape of her brother Daniel's future had been fixed at roughly the same time, perhaps even on the same day.

. . . The time was eight fifteen and the TV set, tuned to the religious channel, stood in its usual morning position in the middle of the breakfast table, its back to the window. The two children were having breakfast in front of it: Harriet – then just plain Ryder – was six, Daniel ten. Their father, Johan Ryder, had finished eating and was behind his newspaper. Their mother Bess leant against the sink at the back of the low-ceilinged kitchen, watching the TV preacher. The cat Memphis dozed on the draining-board beside her. Domestic accord, which was fragile in the Ryder family, seemed to be holding.

' . . . *Her only-begotten son, dear friends and comrades. A man. A man . . . and what was done to him, to this man? We know what was done to him, to this man. Other men crucified him. They killed him. They were afraid of the message of love that he brought, of love for God the Mother, so they did away with him . . .* '

Her muesli breakfast eaten, Harriet was gazing absent-mindedly past the television set at the view outside the window, little brown varnished sailing-boats at anchor across the sparkling water of the harbour. She was so used to the tanned TV face of the preacher, and to the woman's sugary preacher's voice, that she no longer noticed them. The sailing-boats too, this morning, made little impression: they'd been there all her life, a decorative frieze outside the kitchen window and the square wooden bays of the living-room upstairs and her parents' bedroom above that. Her eyes were on the harbour, and its image in later years would dominate her childhood memories, blue as the sky in summer, ice-bound in the northern ocean's winter, but her thoughts that September morning were on pink brylon hair ribbons. Moma said they were common and old-fashioned, but that wasn't fair. Her best friend Karla Beck wore them, and Karla wasn't at all common or old-fashioned.

' . . . They crucified this man, dear friends and comrades. Other men, in the baseness of their male nature, crucified the Lord Jesus. Who was, like them, a frail male vessel . . . '

Harriet's mother, leaning against the sink, drying a long-dry dinner plate, had come to realise that she was wasted on her family. Golden-haired, with flashing, dramatic features, she should have been a professional actress. She'd been accepted at the state drama school, but then she'd come on holiday here and had met Harriet's father on the Town Quay. Johan Ryder was local, up at university, doing a holiday job in a tight blue fisherman's sweater, selling boat trips round the harbour. Neither of them had believed in condoms: if you couldn't trust the person you had sex with, who could you trust? Now Johan was a lab technician up at Brandt Laboratories. And Bess? Bess Ryder worked part-time in the Ritz video library along on Front Street – she called it the House of Illusions – smoked black Russian cigarettes, rehearsed Ibsen three evenings a week with the Town Players, and was helped to make sense of a troubled world by her new-found belief in God the Mother.

' . . . Like them, dear friends, a mother's son. And yet – and yet, vitally, world-shakingly, not like them at all. For the mother on earth of Christ the Lord was intacta. Mary, the agent on this earth of God the Mother, was a virgin. Make no mistake. On that, dear friends and comrades, the Gospels are agreed . . . '

Daniel, at ten, was the sharpest of his mother's troubles. Until recently he'd worried about this, not knowing why. Now, after Mr Barendt's talk at the beginning of term, he didn't care. He sat beside his sister, elbows on the table, glaring at his muesli. Life was a bitch. He'd given himself a big second helping, and now he was full and couldn't finish it, and if *that woman* saw it she'd be pissed off, and of course she would see it, and she'd rabbit on about wicked waste, getting things straight she called it, and he wished he was dead. His only hope was that, if she was the way she was some mornings, stoned out of her mind with God the fucking Mother, he could secretly swap his bowl with Harri. His sister wouldn't mind: she got away with murder.

'Nearly time to go, offspring. Have you finished your cereal, Daniel?'

He closed his eyes. He couldn't bear it. She could see bloody well he hadn't finished.

'You haven't finished. You haven't finished, Daniel, have you?'

Other people called him Danno, but never she. She knew he wouldn't answer if she did.

'You know about wicked waste, dear. Eat it up now. If you didn't want it you shouldn't have taken it.'

He opened his eyes. Nothing had changed. The kitchen was still just the same. His bowl was still nearly full. He wasn't silly – nothing ever did change, he'd never thought it would.

'Oh Daniel, Daniel, what are we going to do with you. What the hell are we going to do with you?'

Harriet drummed her feet against the legs of the table, hating the coming row. Memphis fled upstairs. 'Moma? Can I have a pink hair ribbon, Moma? Shiny brylon? With a bow?'

'Please don't do that with your feet, Harri. You know it only encourages him.'

Daniel glanced sideways at his father's newspaper. Had it moved? One of the worst things that woman did was talk like that, as if he couldn't understand, as if he was an idiot. He reached for the tomato-pickle bottle, opened it, and poured pickle carefully, in a spiral like ripple ice-cream, into his muesli. Then he stirred it.

His mother unstuck herself from the sink and drifted forward. 'Do you think that will make it nicer, dear? I hope you're right.'

'There's ribbons in your drawer,' Harriet persisted. 'Can't I have one?'

'There are more beguiling things in life than ribbons, precious.'

'Karla has them.'

'Poor Karla. Still, she can't really help it. Mrs Beck doesn't have taste enough to fill a thimble. Daniel child, do please hurry up.'

' . . . And that, dear friends and comrades, is the true significance of the Annunciation. We know now how often the evangelists gave in to their sexist prejudices – men have rewritten history to their own ends all down the ages – but on the matter of the virgin birth they dared not lie. No masterful sperm, no penetration. They tell us bluntly, Mary "knew no man" . . .'

'What's wrong with ribbons? It isn't fair.'

Her father looked round his newspaper. 'Shirley Temple wears them,' he suggested.

Bess sighed, smoothed the curve of one eyebrow expressively with a forefinger. 'And who bought her the wretched video? Honestly, Johan, do you really want your daughter done up like some Hollywood antique?' She looked down at Daniel. 'And do hurry up with that. There's a dear.'

Daniel took a decision. He picked up his bowl and tipped its contents down the back of his sister's school tunic. That woman had to be stopped. She'd go on like this for ever, not getting cross. Getting cross was against her fucking religion, just going on, calling him dear and going on and on for ever. And then he'd be late for school, and she'd send him in without a note, saying it was all his fault. Fucking hell, he hated women. Women were killing all the boy babies. Mr Barendt had said so. All the boy babies. And he was ten now, Mr Barendt had said, so he was old enough to know.

'Daniel – you bloody child, how *could* you?'

She reached forward to clout him. Cross at last. Ha. He evaded her first swipe, slipped down from his chair, faced her for the second. It checked in mid-air. He looked up at her, a daunting gaze. She was helping the other women to kill all the boy babies and he knew. She lowered her arm, glaring, her face red and blotchy with bottled-up anger, and held the side of her chest. Breast. Held the side of her breast. Women had breasts. His mother had big blobby ones. Knockers. Only men had chests.

He discovered he was still holding his empty breakfast bowl. He put it back on the table, carefully straightened his chair, then walked stiffly out of the kitchen and upstairs to the hall. He heard Dada call after him, expected to by that woman. He didn't answer: when they were ready to take Harri to school he'd be ready too, waiting by the front door with his books in his satchel and the car he wanted to show Petr.

Down in the kitchen Harriet had taken over. Danno's breakfast had trickled down into her knickers, cold and horrid, and her school tunic was a disaster, but Moma would let her have a ribbon now to make up for things, so she didn't make a fuss. She turned off the TV – Moma was looking away, lighting a cigarette from the pack in the pocket of her video library overall – and tidied up Dada's paper from where he'd dropped it, one corner in the milk. She tried to fold it but the pages were too large for her to manage properly. The rustling was companionable, though, and filled the silence.

Moma's hands were shaking as she smoked. She moved Danno's chair back from the table and sat down on it. She spoke to Dada. 'That boy needs counselling.'

'They all do.' He squared up his knife and fork on his eggy plate. 'All the boys in his class need counselling. Probably in the whole school.'

'No. Daniel's worse. I know. Remember – I talk to the other mothers.'

'Perhaps the other mothers don't like to admit it, Bess. Do you?'

'Me, old friend? I brag about it.'

Dada winced. 'I'll talk to him.'

'*You?*' She checked, remembered Harriet, closed her lips in a tight line. She turned. 'Harri, that tunic is a disaster. How *could* you?' She shook her crossly. Harriet was pleased at the injustice, wished Danno had been there to see. 'I must get you changed, my girl. And fast, or we'll be late for school.'

As she was dragged out of the room Harriet heard her father quietly tell the coffee-pot, 'I *will* have a word with him. I really will.'

Dada often talked to the coffee-pot, when he thought no one was there.

Moma took her into her dark little rosy-papered room at the front of the house, below the level of the street, its window looking out on white bricks and a rusty grating people walked on. Spiders lived in the bricks.

'That boy needs counselling.' Bess hauled the tunic up over Harriet's head, hurting her ears. 'We can't go on like this.'

The milk and tomato-pickle mixture had soaked through on to

25

her vest. That had to come off too. And this would go on for years. Seven, in fact, until Daniel left home and joined the army.

Harriet was transferred to the bathroom next door. She stood by the basin, banged about from side to side as her mother changed her clothes and washed her. She didn't complain – the case against her brother was bad enough already. But she didn't like being dressed. Being banged.

Upstairs by the front door, needing to leave for work, Johan had encountered his son. Neither was ready. They pressed themselves against the rough wooden walls, uncomfortably close in the narrow hall. Dada was too big, Daniel suddenly realised, to live in such a steep little house. And that woman said his clothes were a mess five minutes after he'd put them on. In his mind Daniel reached out and hugged Dada's big thick thighs. A diesel delivery van went by outside in the street, sounding as if it was coming in. It was Wednesday. Vans were allowed down in the town only on alternate weekdays.

'I think I know how you feel,' Johan said at last. 'Me, I've always got my paper. To hide behind, I mean. But you . . . The thing is, Moma loves her morning TV. It's made all the difference – you wouldn't remember. And who's to say that preacher isn't right, anyway?' He rubbed his bearded cheek with the back of one hand. 'Perhaps you should get yourself a book, Danno. Something you could read at breakfast, something you could hide behind too.'

Daniel hunched his shoulders, looking awkwardly down at the car he was holding. It was an armoured personnel carrier the size of his hand, painted in United Nations colours. He didn't mind the TV preacher. She was part of breakfast, just a face and a noise.

'Danno? I have to go to work now.'

A reply was expected of him. 'Sorry, Dada.'

His father sighed, his feelings clear in his face, disappointed and angry at the same time. He reached past Daniel for his anorak, hanging on the wall behind the door, put it on, and leaned down the stairwell.

'I'm off now, Bess. 'Bye, Harri. Work hard. Learn a lot.'

Daniel's lips moved with his, shaping the familiar words. Johan glanced down at him, then opened the door and went out on to the narrow strip of cobbled pavement. Exhaust fumes from the van drifted in, trapped between the tall wooden houses.

Their side of the street was in shadow, but the upstairs of the pink-painted house opposite was in full sunlight. Looking out, Daniel saw his father's head and shoulders in dark silhouette, immensely tall and distant against the flat bright pinkness.

The door closed, then opened again, just wide enough for the left half of his father's face. 'Don't be sorry,' Dada said. 'Either do a thing or don't. Never be sorry.'

Half a face. It was as if he wasn't really there. And when he let go of the door and it swung wider, he wasn't. The street was empty, footsteps retreating. Daniel slammed the door shut, kicking at it angrily. He was going to be late for school if that woman and Harri didn't get a move on.

A minute later they appeared, went past him in a rush and on upstairs, right to the top by the sound of it, and when they came down again Harriet had her bow. Bess opened the door and the three of them set off along the street.

Harriet loved the house next door: it was one room thick and you could see the harbour through the net curtains at the front window and out the back. And you could see old Mrs Bolger, who was ninety, sitting in her chair. The houses on both sides of the street here were joined togther, with black slate roofs, wide eaves and flat wooden fronts, but different heights and colours and sizes. The street was level for a couple of hundred metres, then climbed steeply past the magazine shop with its tattered billboard: MINISTERS VETO SPERM DONATION CENTRES. Dada had gone the other way, down to the Town Quay to catch the bus that went up-river to the Brandt Laboratories. He said he was in charge of thirty thousand oysters this month, making them stand to attention.

A short way up the hill they turned left into a narrow alley between two white clapboard houses. Moma was chatting brightly, but Harriet didn't hear her. She was brooding: her bow wasn't brylon – Moma didn't have any – but velvet, and she wasn't sure if velvet would do. The alley quickly became a staircase of worn stone steps with grass on either side and an iron banister, polished by hands, clamped to one wall. They climbed quickly, used to it, Daniel lagging behind. Harriet looked back at him. She wished she could make him happier. Older brothers' moods were a disaster. A lot of the girls had older brothers, and they all had moods. Poor Danno. She reached back to take his hand but he was using it to tuck in his shirt.

'Harri? You're not listening, child. What did I just say?'

Moma kept on climbing. Harriet peered up at her, at her bare sun-tanned legs working like levers beneath her yellow overall. Distracted, she tripped on the next step, grabbed at the overall, saved herself.

'I could as well be addressing the birds of the sky. Do you know that? For the amount of attention you and your brother take I could be doing my mad Ophelia. And Daniel's ten. Which I would expect to carry certain responsibilities.'

Harriet felt cheered as she hurried to keep up. Whatever Moma was going on about, Danno's inclusion in it meant he was on the way to being forgiven. She hated him to go off into school, still in disgrace.

Iron safety rails marked the upper end of the stairs, overlapping and a foot or so apart so that you went between them sideways, and beyond them there was immediately another street. School Lane was crowded now with bicycles and fibreglass trailers. The school was almost at the top of the town, and in summer parents from inland were able to bring their children by pedal power. Protected from the winds off the sea by a final rise and a row of modern houses, the school faced east, over the cranes on the clay jetties and back along the steep cleft of the winding tidal river valley. Down among the trees in the distance were the shining roofs of the Brandt Laboratories.

Bess gathered her children just past the rails. 'Now listen, offspring, and listen good. I'm working late this afternoon in the House of Illusions so I won't be here to fetch you after school. I'm putting Daniel in charge.' Faintly, from along by the school, came the familiar sound of men's jeering voices. Bess squatted down on her heels, drawing Harriet and Daniel protectively closer. 'Go straight home after school. I'll be there around five. Dada may be home sooner. You've got the key?'

Daniel nodded: it was in his trouser pocket, on a piece of string tied to his belt. The men's shouting grew louder, interspersed with coarse angry laughter.

'The loonies are in good form, I hear.' Bess sighed. 'Oh well. They're only noise, and they probably won't be around this afternoon. And anyway, if I'm not there you'll be fine. I've told

28

you before, it's knockers that rouse their loathly passions. So listen to what I'm saying. Do what your brother tells you, Harri. And Daniel – I'm counting on you.'

He nodded again, his eyes straying past her, looking for his friends.

'I'm sorry I'm working late but it can't be helped. Keith the Teeth is having the afternoon off to visit his boyfriend. He's in hospital. AIDS, poor sod.'

Both children were fidgeting. Bess gave them a brief shared hug, stood up, went with them along the road the short distance to the school. The usual crowd of parents was standing around, most of them mothers, and across the road were the usual loonies, men with wild hair, in jeans and shabby jerseys. Harriet went past the loonies with her head turned away, not looking. They weren't dangerous, but they were angry, and they made ugly gestures and ugly noises, and sometimes they threw things at the mothers. Usually a policeman was there, but he couldn't always stop them. Harriet put her face up for her mother to kiss, then ran off across the playground to her classroom, her satchel bumping.

'Bloody dykes,' she heard behind her. 'Pleased with yourselves, aren't you? Bloody fucking tossers.'

Nearly all the girls had already gone in. Harriet felt her bow move in the wind of her running. She began to have doubts again about velvet.

Daniel hung about. He'd evaded that woman's kiss and now he dawdled across the playground. They'd be closing the door soon, and Petr was mouthing *come on* from their classroom window, but the loonies fascinated him. For one thing, the name 'loonies' was only that woman's idea. Dada said they weren't loonies at all, just unemployed and of low intelligence. And if any of them were brown they were probably Muslims, which Dad said made a sort of sense. Daniel looked back over his shoulder. Two of them were very brown . . .

And for another thing, they used words other people didn't. Men's words.

He stopped in the middle of the playground, turned properly round, looked at the men through the high school fence. He held his UN armoured personnel carrier very tightly, feeling its strong, square edges. One of the men noticed him and gave him a cheer. This attracted the attention of the others, and they all cheered. Daniel thought they might be laughing at him. He backed away, reaching the school door just as Mr Barendt was closing it. He waved to the men, showing he wasn't afraid, and went in.

The day when it all began? Was this when the shape of Dr Harriet Kahn-Ryder's life was set, and Daniel's? An ordinary September schoolday thirty years ago, when she was six and he was ten? As described so far it hardly seems a day for dramas: no catastrophes in the making and no triumphs either. Just an ordinary September schoolday, more or less what might be expected for Year 10 of the Attrition. In short, surely no great life-shaper?

For those of us with the benefit of background knowledge, maybe not. But Harriet, for one, wasn't so advantaged. She came to it new. Lamb-like.

Work hard, Johan Ryder told his children in the morning. *Learn a lot.* And in the evening, the half-jocular question, *And what did you learn today?* To which both children, although in many ways so different, would similarly squirm, and mutter *Nothing,* and mean it.

And by so saying would do both themselves and their teachers an injustice.

In formal school terms, on that day in September thirty years ago Harriet Ryder's education was advanced by two pages of *Jinks and Jenni on a Train,* and a video told her that Stone Age boys and girls fetched wood for the fires on which their mothers cooked meat and a sort of porridge. And in informal terms, when the class acted a Stone Age day and Miss Astrid had to choose the girls who would play the boys and men, Harriet's education was advanced when – even though for the third time that term she had got all the answers right in the Comprehension Quiz – for the third time that term she wasn't chosen.

Daniel Ryder's progress that day was less cut and dried. Formally, he multiplied fractions on his calculator and got three out of ten right, which confirmed his opinion that fractions were silly, and Mr Barendt gave him several facts about Joan of Arc which he never forgot. And in the broader sense his education was advanced when Petr and he chased girls from their class round the playground, pretending to look up their skirts, and this caused a fuss even though they'd seen the girls' boring knickers a million times before in PE.

When school ended that day Harriet and Karla were among the first out down the path to the gate, holding hands and trotting busily. Neither wore a hair ribbon. Karla had come to school that morning without one, having lost interest, so Harriet had quickly slipped hers off and stuffed it down behind a radiator. Karla's mother, Mrs Beck, was waiting at the playground gate, with her sister Buzz in a push-chair. While they hugged and Mrs Beck pulled up Karla's socks, Harriet looked wildly round for her own mother, panicked when she couldn't be seen, and then remembered: Danno was taking her home.

Mrs Beck tore off with Karla and Buzz – they lived at the far end of town, by the new railway station, and she was always in a hurry. Harriet hung about as the crowd of mothers and children thinned. Danno was always one of the last out. There were no loonies and she wasn't worried. A wind gusted in sometimes from the sea, threatening winter, but the sun was still bright and the day warm. She hung on the fence outside the Upper School and peered at the window to Danno's classroom. If she closed one eye and lined up the fence post, it exactly filled the left-hand pane. Perhaps Danno was being kept in again for cheeking Mr Barendt.

After a while she unhooked herself from the fence and drifted away. She didn't want one of the teachers coming out and asking her what she was doing. On the high ground above the school, before the row of modern houses started, was the children's adventure playground, bridges, castles, an overhead cable, slides and roundabouts and swings. The grass beyond the playground fell away sharply to the edge of the cliffs and the sea beyond, with a strong fence in between, and when you swung on the biggest swing there was a moment when all you saw was the sky and the sea, and you seemed to be flying right out over the edge. It was frightening the first few times it happened, and Harriet was only just getting used to it. She ran up the hill to the swings. Danno would know where to find her.

The playground was windy, and deserted except for the life-size bronze statue of a boy and a girl, standing on a sort of rock. The boy was pointing out to sea, showing the girl something, and she was looking along his arm. The statue was part of the

31

playground. Children had splotched it with paint, which Harriet's father said didn't matter and her mother said was a disgrace, and the boy's arm was strong: you could hang from it with your feet off the ground. Harriet liked the statue, and once she had finished swinging – it was cold up there and the empty playground felt creepy – she ran over to it.

She tried to see along the boy's arm, to find out exactly what he was pointing at, but as always the girl's head was in the way. There were green headlands along the coast in either direction, and lumpy cliffs, very clear and close in the afternoon sun, but he seemed to be pointing at nothing, just out at the sea. The wind rushed round them, hissing in the space between the two carved heads. There was a beard painted on the boy's bronze chin but Dada was right, it didn't matter. She loved the boy. She wanted to touch his cheek, the side of his nose, his wide bronze eyelids, but dared not. He was magic and wouldn't let her.

Suddenly she felt very sad, and ran away, back down the lane to the school.

'Stupid kid.' Daniel was by the school door. He'd only just come out. 'I've been looking for you everywhere.'

'I waited for ages, Danno. Where were you?'

'I couldn't get away.' He'd been looking at car magazines in the toilets with Petr and some other boys until Mr Barendt chased them out. 'Come on then, now you've condescended to appear.'

'If you'd really looked for me everywhere you'd have found me. You couldn't not. If you really looked everywhere.'

'Silly cow. Come on then.'

'Cow yourself.'

She started off.

'Not that way. We're going round, and down Harbour Street.'

'That's miles. Moma said we were to go straight home.'

'Moma said you were to do what I said. Right?' He walked away in the opposite direction. He'd been genuinely worried when he'd come out and Harri wasn't there. Now she was a pain in the neck.

Harriet looked from his retreating form, back along School Lane to the iron rails at the top of the alley steps. She could easily go home on her own. She knew the way. But she didn't have a door-key to get in with. Besides, she was fed up with the same old boring walk, and the change would be Danno's fault – Moma had told her to do what he said. And he was going home the long way round only because he wanted to look in the window of the Harbour Street toyshop. She ran to catch up with him. She didn't understand the sadness she had felt up by the boy's cold statue, but it hurried after her now, refusing to go away.

They tacked along School Lane, Daniel a few steps in front of her, his hands in his pockets, kicking a stone. The lane was very quiet now, all the other children long gone home. Ahead of them a woman eased her baby's pram down the steps from her front door, out on to the pavement to make the most of the sun.

Daniel walked just fast enough to make his sister trot.

'Danno,' she called, 'what's counselling?' He pretended not to hear. 'What's counselling, Danno?'

He stopped walking, turned, allowed a derisive pause. 'Counselling?'

'Moma said you needed it. Counselling. She said you – '

'Bloody women.' He didn't know the word. 'I really hate them.'

'That's stupid.'

'No it's not.'

'Yes it is. Hating people's stupid.' She hunted for her father's word. 'Counter-productive.'

'Not when there's a reason.'

'What reason?' His reason was he hated Moma. She mustn't let him say it. 'You haven't got a reason. What reason, Danno?'

He swung round and started walking again, faster than before. Mr Barendt had said he was ten years old, old enough to know. Harri was only six.

'What reason?'

He shouldn't tell her. The lane tilted downhill and he increased his pace.

Harriet was running, shouting after him. 'You haven't got a reason. You're stupid. You haven't got a reason.'

She was chasing him but she was also pursued: by the little boy, by her sadness. They were like water going down a drain, she thought. Nothing could stop them. The lane steepened, joined Harbour Street at an angle, on its way down to the Town Quay. When Harriet rounded the corner, slipping on the stones, she saw Daniel standing outside the toyshop, looking

33

in. The shop was stepped into the hillside, one end of its window level with the pavement, the other end above his head.

There was a sale on: guns and war toys were under half-price.

She joined him, out of breath. 'What reason, Danno?'

'Shut up. You're so boring.'

It was Moma's worst accusation. He didn't even look at her. She withered. He cupped his hands round his eyes and peered through the glass. His birthday was coming up in a couple of weeks and he didn't yet know what he wanted. Harriet leaned beside him. Her hand went out, hovered by his arm, then fussed with the electronic latch of his satchel instead. It had buttons you had to press in the right order.

Daniel started to tell her. He didn't know why. He thought he'd decided not to. He stopped. His throat was tight so he cleared it and tried again. 'Don't you ever wonder why there aren't any boy babies?'

Harriet was puzzled. 'Of course there are.'

'Show me one.' She seemed so positive he had a moment's doubt. 'Go on, show me one.'

'How can I?'

He looked around. There was a woman coming up the hill with a baby in a harness round her neck. 'Come on.' He dragged Harriet after him. 'Excuse me – could you please tell me your baby's name?'

The woman looked down at him, amused. Her baby's name was Mai. Another baby was coming out of a shop across the street. Daniel asked its mother – its name was Frieda.

'Come on.' He tried to pull Harriet on down the hill. She resisted. He was making her cry.

'Why aren't there any boy babies, Danno?'

He glanced back at her. She was such an infant. 'I'm hungry,' he said. 'Race you home.'

They tore down Harbour Street, their legs rushing to keep up with the slope, round the corner past the Millennium Clock at the entrance to the Town Quay and right into the Parade, where they lived. She couldn't win but he let her stay close behind him. He unlocked the door while she jigged impatiently, and then they tumbled downstairs into the kitchen. If they'd gone down any further they'd have been in the harbour.

There was milk in the refrigerator and their favourite yellow

34

cheese. They spread it on crispbread with strawberry jam. They were still breathless and clumsy and banged into things, flinging their arms and legs about. Memphis heard them and came slinking down from his nest on the living-room sofa. Harriet gave him a knife-scoop of the cheese, which he loved, to lick off a plate.

'I know why there aren't any baby boys,' she said cheerfully. She'd suddenly realised. 'It's the same reason there aren't any boys in my class.'

Daniel was horrified. He sat very still, a tingling at the back of his neck. She never gave up. 'Don't say it.' He felt that if she knew, then it was all the more dreadful. 'Don't say it.'

'I'm going to. Why shouldn't I? I worked it out months ago. There aren't any boys in my class because boys are different. They're born older. Eight. Or nine maybe. They weren't always, but now they're just born older.'

For a moment the explanation worked. He thought about it. Then: 'That's stupid. Big as that, how could they get out of women's wombs?'

'How do babies get out anyway?'

He stared at his sister across the kitchen table. It was a good question. He'd seen her pee-hole a million times and he couldn't imagine.

'There aren't any boy babies,' he told her, 'because all the women started killing them ten years ago.' He reached for more cheese. 'Mr Barendt said so.'

'He didn't.'

'He did.'

'He couldn't have.'

He didn't bother to answer. She was so stupid. And boring. He'd been going to tell her all along, so now she knew.

She knew. She lowered her head, close down over her plate. She crouched, believing him, her elbows close in by her sides. There'd always been something wrong, a loss, a sadness, for as long as she could remember. Nobody talked about it, and now she understood why. Not Moma – of course not Moma – but all the other women. It was too wicked to talk about. Mrs Charkas in the magazine shop, and Miss Astrid at school. All the other women. It was too wicked to talk about.

She crouched, letting her store of loss and sadness burst open, that day's and all the others', for the dead boy they'd made a

35

statue of, for his dead brothers, and for herself. There were no pictures in her mind – those would come later, in her dreams – just an unbearable grief. She wept without anger, as young children seldom do, in the shadowed kitchen above the sunlit harbour. It was like the loosening of an iron band. She knew now. No more Jinks and Jenni. The Stone Age was long ago. The babies on Harbour Street were called Mai and Frieda.

'Harri . . . ? My precious child, what is it? What's the matter?' Bess Ryder loomed in the doorway. 'Daniel? You obnoxious little cretin – what have you done to her?'

He looked up at her, terrified but calmly chewing. 'Nothing.'

'Nothing? Christ, what a liar you are.' Her first moment of shock past, she swooped on Harriet, enfolding her. 'Did he hurt you? What happened? What did he do to you?'

Harriet's throat and face were too swollen for speech. She shook her head wildly, tears and mucus trailing.

Daniel said, 'I didn't do anything. It's some idea she's got.' But he knew he'd be found out as soon as she could speak. Eyeing the distance to the door, he eased himself down off his chair.

'Nothing? Your sister's in this state for nothing?'

'Does it always have to be me done it? *Did* it? Always me? Couldn't it be someone else?'

Bess was fumbling in her overall pocket. Daniel wasn't worth answering. She found a wad of tissue and prised Harriet's face out from the hollow of her shoulder. 'That's enough now, Harri. Nothing's as bad as all that, child. You must tell me what happened.'

But she choked and couldn't, and it was Daniel finally – what the hell – who told Bess what he'd said. Defending himself, what Mr Barendt had said.

He'd been right to be afraid. Suddenly his mother was vast, spraying saliva, red and ugly, far angrier than he'd ever seen her, with a laser-saw voice and hard flailing hands that shook the teeth in his jaws and made his head ring. And she was between him and the door, Harri pulling at her arm to stop her, and the kitchen was like a cage with wild animals in it, and he was sure afterwards that she'd have killed him if his father hadn't come down the stairs at that moment.

'Hey there. Hey – I could hear you lot out in the street.'

It took more than Dada's *hey there* to stop her. Dada had to hug her from behind, and grope for a chair to sit on, and put her on one of his knees and Harri on the other, his arms round both of them, holding them tight. Only then did the kitchen stop juddering in spikes and fierce bright lights. And then he had to hear from her, from that woman, what his son had done.

Either you do something or don't, Danno thought. Never be sorry.

'I expect you wanted to upset your sister.'

He nodded.

'*Upset*, Johan? The little monster wanted to destroy her.'

'You shouldn't have done that, Danno. But then you know that.'

He nodded again.

'Christ Almighty, I don't believe it. Is that all you're going to say?'

'You got one thing badly wrong, Danno. Nobody's killing babies. Your teacher would never have said that. Nobody's killing babies. You've got to believe me.'

His nod was doubtful.

'Go up to your room now. I'll come up later. You've been very cruel and silly. But just remember, you've got things wrong, Danno. Children do. It's not your fault. Just remember – nobody's killing babies.'

Daniel went round them, edging sideways, and out of the room. He climbed the staircase, the silence singing in his ears. Nobody was killing babies. Maybe not. That woman would have killed him, but he wasn't a baby. Harri was, though, blobbed on to Dada's knee there. Soon Dada would have to come up after him and blitz him. Christ, he hated women. He hated women, but most of all he hated that one.

Down in the kitchen the bits of Harriet's life that had seemed to be flying apart were coming together again. Things no longer presented themselves in fragments, a table edge, the sleeve of a yellow overall, Danno's eyes tight shut. She looked round for Memphis but he had sensibly gone away. Dada was talking to her.

'You heard what I said. Danno got it wrong. Nobody's killing babies. It's more complicated than that. But he's right that there aren't any more little boys. Not here, not anywhere in the world.' He moved his hand up to stroke her cheek. 'The tiny seeds, Harri

– tinier than grains of sand – the seeds that would grow into boy babies inside their mothers just aren't making it. They're sick, or maybe their mothers are sick, something to do with the immune system, we just don't know. It's a disease, you see – maybe something in the air, which is why we're so careful now with bombs and smoke and things – and it started ten years ago, and we call it MERS. You're not old enough to understand yet, but that's Male Embryo Rejection Syndrome. It's very sad, Harri, and we're going to find a cure. But nobody's killing baby boys. They just aren't happening. Baby *girls* are, but – '

Moma took one of Harriet's hands, found the other, held them both together. 'What your father isn't telling you, precious, is that it's all part of God's wonderful plan. Giving it letters and calling it a disease and talking about cures won't change that. God the Mother has watched the world for hundreds of thousands of years, and She's seen how mean and wicked men are, and what they did to Her son Jesus, and now She's decided to even things up. In Her mercy She's sent us this affliction. We may not like it, but Her will be done. I'm sure you can understand that. The world's going to be a very different place, Harri . . . '

Harriet looked at her hands, crumpled up together in her moma's. It was very simple. Diseases were for curing, and when she grew up she had decided that she would be the person to cure this one. She'd go to school, and then to college, and she'd learn how to cure it. She uncrumpled her hands and got down off Dada's knee. She was going to find Memphis and take him up to Danno. Nobody could object to that. She and Danno and Memphis were friends.

CHAPTER THREE

The Attrition. Year 40: late October.

After Sergeant Milhaus left, I'm not sure how long it was before Mark got back. Not long, half an hour maybe. I wasn't looking at clocks. I'm also not sure what I did in the interval, other than not look at clocks. Mark says I was playing the piano – Satie – in the study, no light on, when he came in, so maybe I'd been doing that since Sergeant Milhaus left. Playing Satie in the dark. It's possible. I do go through composer crazes, and I remember it was Poulenc and Satie that year. So French and innocent.

Apparently it was a while before I could tell Mark what had happened. It seems odd that I should have been so upset – I was a doctor, for God's sake, I knew about blood – but that night it was Anna I kept seeing with her throat cut, not our cat. Sergeant Milhaus would have been pleased to know that.

By the time I was making sense Mark had sent for the doctor. He'd left the police, thank God, for when he'd have some clear idea what to tell them.

Dr Vrieland is a gentle Dutchman, slow talker, fast thinker, and he's been my doctor and friend since before Mark and I were married. I'd met Hannes Vrieland when I was serving my time on Maternity at the City Hospital, but we were neither of us people who rushed into relationships. Our friendship had grown over many meetings, social as well as professional, and included Mark when he came into my life, so that by the time he and I were planning a wedding old Hannes was at the top of our guest list. He wasn't old, of course, then only in his early sixties, but he's played quaint ninety-nine, over gold-rimmed half-spectacles, since his intern days. He thinks it helps people take him seriously. It hinders them, but they take him seriously anyway.

While we were waiting for Hannes, Mark made me the traditional hot sweet tea and I began to come out of my withdrawal. I wanted to forget the whole Milhaus thing, pretend it had never happened, but that much blood on the carpet would raise awkward questions. Junk the carpet and we'd still have to tell people something. Certainly Yvette would want to know, and

Anna. And an explanation was needed for the disappearance of Elvis.

We decided to stay close to the truth. I'd say I'd been threatened by a psychopathic intruder – Sergeant Milhaus was that, no question – and she'd killed Elvis in order to shock me into telling her the combination of the safe she'd seen in the study. The safe was empty but the woman hadn't known that. In any case, Mark arrived before she could find out. She fled the way she'd broken in, through the garden door at the back and off into the woods. Mark had just enough time to fetch his laser saw from the garage and cut round the door-lock to make the break-in plausible before Dr Hannes drove up in his ancient Volvo.

Thieves come equipped with saws these days. The lack of young men has dented violent crime statistics, as has psycho-engineering, but there are enough greedy and reckless young women around to make armed robbery still a problem.

I took Dr Hannes into our big front living-room. There was no need for a serious medical examination, I could diagnose my condition as well as he. But he sat me down and listened to my story and checked my vital signs as attentively as if I'd been presenting as a new patient. He's one of those doctors who pay proper attention. It's not so much the time he gives you as the quality of that time. In his whole life, I think, at the bedside or away from it, he has always looked and listened with his entire attention.

As he was finishing Mark came in from putting away the saw. They went together to inspect my little sitting-room. On his return Hannes was thoughtful. He peered at me over his last-century spectacles.

'Harriet my dear, you are in mild shock. This I do not need to tell you. And my prescription I do not need to tell you either – rest, calm thoughts, a good night's sleep. Assisted perhaps by a light hypnotic . . . ?'

He tailed off, mumbling. He hadn't finished.

'I also prescribe, before the police arrive, untidier clothes – even to the extent of a torn sleeve if you can bear that. A good night's sleep does not need police suspicions . . . Oh yes, and I suggest a sprinkling of earth and pine needles on the floor. Criminal intruders do not wipe their feet.'

I stared at him, embarrassed. Mark and I were bloody awful conspirators.

Mark said, 'I'm sorry, Hannes. We should have told you the truth. It's insulting not to. But you see, what really happened is so – '

Hannes stopped him with one big square hand, like a traffic policeman. 'What I do not know I cannot hurt you with, if I am questioned. And for the rest, you are my friends and if you have need to deceive the police I trust your reasons.' He hunched his shoulders. 'There is a sick mind at work here. I wish only to help you.'

I stood up, hugged him. 'You do help. We're very grateful.'

'Grateful I do not need.' He hugged me back, tweedy and comfortable. 'You are dear people. Only I need that you do not come to harm.'

We wanted him to stay, have a glass of wine, biscuits, some fruit, but he said it was past his bedtime. Past mine too, he said, after the evening's trauma. If we were going to report the break-in to the police we should do so quickly.

He paused by the front door, fussing with his old-fashioned doctor's bag. ' . . . Make sure, Harriet, that when you give a description of your intruder, it's not too much and not too little. And is what you want the police to hear.' He shook Mark's hand. 'And those flakes of scorched white door-paint on your jacket, my boy – ' Mark looked down guiltily ' – I suggest they get there when you shut the door on your return from chasing away the intruder. Don't you think so?'

Mark grinned. 'I do think so.'

Hannes had retained his hand. 'I do not joke. Deceiving the police is a serious matter. It must be undertaken seriously.' He turned to go. On his way down the steps, over his shoulder, 'I shall worry. Call me in the morning. That will not be suspicious, to call your doctor . . . '

We watched him into his car, then closed the front door.

I was worried. 'We should have told him what happened. What's he thinking now?'

'He's thinking we know who the intruder was.' Mark went through to the telephone in his study, fed in his money card. 'It was a friend maybe, and we're covering for him or her. Which is more or less the truth.'

I'd followed him through as he dialled. 'Sergeant Milhaus is no friend.'

He reached out and stroked my cheek. 'I guess not.'

I heard the ringing tone. Eventually someone on the police desk answered.

'What're we going to do, Mark?'

'Do? Not give in. You're going to publish. We'll think of something. That's what we're going to do.'

Sturdy. Comforting. I'd been put to bed and he was sitting on the duvet beside me, sturdy and comforting.

'But is it worth it? If that Milhaus woman was serious about the danger to Annie, then – '

'Of course she was serious. For God's sake, Harriet, she didn't slaughter Annie's cat just for fun.'

Sturdy, yes. Comforting, no. I was a big lady now.

The police had come and gone, a district inspector because I was who I was, and his woman junior. They recorded the details and, because I was who I was, they seemed to take them seriously. But Hannes needn't have worried. The killing of the cat was admittedly bizarre but no great harm had come of it, the break-in was commonplace, nothing had been stolen, and District Inspector Voisin and his junior had better things to do with their time. They noted my distressed appearance, examined the damaged door and the pine needles on the floor, and went away. Inspector Voisin promised further enquiries, but with a lack of conviction that I knew would be reinforced if Oswald Marton or his minister got to hear of them.

Anna had come and gone also, mercifully after the police, so that the cat's poor corpse had been gathered up and decently composed in his basket. Without it the bloodstains on the carpet, a dull red-brown now, looked much less incontinent and shocking, and Anna, from the door, gave them hardly a glance. There had been tears over the basket, and anger, but her concern for me loomed larger. She made sure I got to bed, and didn't fret about her, and took the pills Dr Hannes had left for me.

Soon after that Yvette had got in from her dinner date and the two of them were downstairs now, in the kitchen, talking quietly, a little afraid. Mark had jammed the damaged door, but they still felt vulnerable.

I lay back on the pile of pillows Annie'd given me. I was already drowsy from the pills. 'Is publishing worth the risk, Mark? Scientific freedom and all that – is it worth the risk?'

I wanted him to say yes. I was terrified of the consequences, but I wanted him to say yes and explain how easy it would be for me to publish my paper without danger to Annie.

He didn't.

'What's really interesting,' he said, 'is why the Minister's prepared to go to such lengths. It's surely not just the principle of the thing, putting an uppity scientist in her place?'

I peered at him sideways, at his brisk brown-bear hair and beardery, and the alert, bouncy way he sat on my bed. He made me feel exhausted. He hadn't said yes and explained how easy it would be, and now life was too complicated. It had been a long day and I was worn out.

I said, 'Does it matter? Marton said the Minister wanted to save me from myself. Couldn't that be true?'

'I'll believe that when the Sahara freezes over. Maybe there's a political reason . . . ' His journalist's curiosity was roused. He frowned thoughtfully, the bedside light shadowing his eyes. 'How about next year's election? Maybe the Minister wants to look good for that, so she'd like an announcement from you closer to the date.'

'I'm sure you're right.' I yawned. 'Vote for the government that gave you Dr Kahn-Ryder.'

'I'm serious, old buddy. You'll be big news.'

'Never anything bigger . . . ' I closed my eyes, turned over on my pillow. 'A cure for MERS. Us women safely back in our place before we've ever really got out of it. Patriarchy lives again.'

But Mark's thinking had moved on. ' . . . Unless of course they're planning to keep it to themselves. How about that?' He shook my arm. 'Develop it in secret. For Christ's sake, the nation with a stock of young men ten years ahead of the rest would have one hell of an advantage.'

'Such chauvinism . . . '

But I was half-asleep and he sensibly ignored me. If the years of the Attrition had taught me anything, it was that there were things men undeniably did better than women. And the things weren't all bad. Play, for instance. Men built the best kites. They knew about fun.

'All right, so the Ministry could never keep an operation like that quiet that long. But even a year or two's start would be worth something. And what we're talking about here, Harriet, is people acting out of a sense of patriotic duty. Righteousness. And that rates higher than any number of Annies and Elvises.'

He'd woken me. I sat up, scared again, looking for reasons not to be. 'First they'd need to run a full-scale program of human test pregnancies.'

'No problem. And it'd be in secret, so they could forget health and safety. There'd be no lack of volunteers.'

It was getting more real. 'They haven't got the data,' I protested. 'Nothing detailed about the therapy. It's more than just popping a pill. And none of the primate test findings.'

'That's all they've got? How do we know that?'

'Because it's all I gave them in my application. The rest is either under lock and key or on my-eyes-only computer access.'

'Lock and key? Your eyes only? Yours and how many? Be honest, Harriet – security at the centre's a joke.'

'Rubbish. I'm not a child, Mark. I do know about industrial espionage. Only people I trust have the codes and combinations.'

'And how many's that? Six? Sixty?'

I thought about it. 'Four. Close colleagues. Friends. The four who couldn't do their jobs properly without.' I counted them on my fingers. 'My project director, the lab manager, Karen who runs the clinic, Liesl who – '

'Those were the good old days. As of now, Harriet, things have changed. For one, pending publication your research is more or less on hold, so – whether you trust them or not – those people no longer need it. And for another, there's a chance now that the Minister herself may be after your records.'

I pushed back the duvet. He was making sense. 'So I change the codes.' I grabbed his arm. 'And quickly. Look how soon Sergeant Milhaus got her act together.'

'No rush. If you're too late, old buddy, you're too late.' He leaned forward, tucked me in again. 'Tomorrow'll do. The Department's known how advanced your research is ever since you banged in your application to publish. And that's weeks ago.'

I lay back and let him settle me in. There was nothing really to worry about. My records weren't even all at the Institute. I wasn't sure myself where they all were. I'd rented lab facilities down at Brandt, for instance, and had a file in their store. Collecting it all from wherever would be a big job.

My mind began to drift again. Maybe Mark and I were too easily believing the worst of people. Colleagues, friends, politicians, we were letting all of them find good reasons to cheat and lie and steal, and maybe kill. But with the example of Sergeant Milhaus, what alternative did we have? There was never a lack of Sergeant Milhauses, nor of the people who employed them.

This bleak thought reminded me. 'Mark? Mark, you never answered my question.'

'The risk to Annie? For the sake of scientific freedom?'

I nodded. Whatever else Mark did, and he was an ill-tempered workaholic on his bad days, he always listened.

'To be honest, Harriet, if we're looking for reasons maybe for dying, abstracts like scientific freedom bother me. But in this case we're not talking about abstracts, we're talking about a particular therapy, about making it universally available. I don't care a damn about the abstract principle. We're talking about a cure for the Syndrome, for Christ's sake.'

I reached for his hand and pulled him down beside me. 'We'll be able to keep Annie safe, won't we?'

He was eight years older than me. We were both grown-up people, but I liked him sometimes to be the dada, and I the child.

He didn't fail me. 'Nothing's a hundred per cent,' he said. 'But it'll take an awful lot of Milhauses. They'll have to get past me first. I promise you that.'

I tried to be sensible. 'We'll have to tell her what we're doing. It's her neck we're risking. She's old enough to be given the choice.'

'What choice? She loves you, old buddy. She knows how important your work is.' He kissed me lightly. 'She'll be first at the barricades. Me just behind her.'

I made it early to the Institute. Mark and I were awake by six and it was no morning for staying in bed. He'd decided to take the day off. He was working on high UV levels over the low-rainfall farmlands south of the city and they could wait. He'd been kept out late yesterday, interviewing doctors at village cancer clinics and now he was stalled anyway, waiting for information from a symposium being held over the weekend in Bristol, England. Instead he'd spend the morning sounding out magazine outlets for the research paper I now had to sit down and write.

We were impatient. My invitation to Paris was too far off. And when the time came I probably wouldn't be allowed to go.

I escaped from the house before Anna was up. Telling her the truth shouldn't be rushed. Mark and I would tackle it in the evening.

It was an unusually bright morning for October, and cold. I rode the tram on the city ring track and was at work by seven thirty. The fourteen floors of the Institute – only two were mine – were dazzling in the low sunlight, but the grass by the entrance was already brown and winter-chilled, with that scraped bald look you think no spring will ever cure. I entered by the side door, stamping my feet. The front entrance to our part of the building was for patients and donors, the people who paid most of our salaries. Karen – Dr Karen Bakst – ran a small gynae wing there, and we harvested ova from donors for just about every research project in the country. With minimum drugs, these days we were averaging around sixty ova from each ovary.

In the research area I was the first to arrive. I went straight to my office. It was a pleasant blue-grey room, large enough for team conferences, looking out on the building's central court-yard, a Zen garden of raked pebbles and round, wind-smoothed boulders. When I reached it the door was properly locked, my terminal was cold, no safes hung open, no rifled folders lay scattered on the floor.

I called up a print-out of the application to publish that I'd sent to the Minister. It would be the starting-point for an account of my last five years' work, beginning at that boozed-up old quack – doctor he never was – in his crumbling roach-ridden house in Erzurum, up in the mountains near the Turkish–Iranian border. A town of mud as I remembered it: roofs plugged with mud above mud-brick walls, mud sidewalks along mud roads, mud-spattered awnings above them and mud-soaked duckboards underfoot. And of course rain. Aku Fateya, his name was. Dr Fateya, if you believed the board by his door.

Thanks to Maggi, my papers in the safe were in well-kept blue plastic folders. A surprising number of them, considering the mainframe capacity available. It had often been quicker to file my scribbled research-in-progress notes direct, than write them up at a keyboard. That was one of the advantages of being project boss. You missed the discipline writing-up forced on you, but you saved a lot of time.

I started on the folders, looking for I'm not sure what . . . signs that they'd been tampered with, whatever those might be. And picking out the research I might need. Much of the stuff had been duplicated, or proved wrong, the sort of three-in-the-morning misreadings of data that most of us are capable of. I felt sorry for any thieving spy trying to make sense of them.

But it wouldn't be just any spy. It would be one of the four with a key to my office, and the safe combination, and a familiarity with my work.

I was half-way down the pile, sorting and classifying, when Gusso looked round the door. Gustav Polder called himself the token male on my team. He ran our genome project plus the lab, everything from culture dishes to electron microscopes. He was older than any of us, nudging fifty, and in a very successful single marriage to a *hausfrau* type who was delighted to stay at home and look after their three daughters. He was an exercise-hater and keep-fat freak, with a big smile and no right to the healthy physique his genes had gifted him with. He'd come to me via an excellent microbiology degree and fifteen unhappy years in cosmetics. I'd been able to offer him half the salary but worthwhile work and his own department.

He leaned on the door-jamb. 'Happy Friday, boss. Did you fit in that RNA breakdown?'

I stared at him blankly. Then I remembered. I'd been going to do a small job for him yesterday in part of my hour on the mainframe.

'Gusso – I'm sorry. I had a meeting at the Ministry and . . . it ran on. I never made it back here afterwards.'

'*N'importe rien.* I was thinking of coming in tomorrow anyway.' He had unusually wide-apart eyes. He narrowed them now and peered at me as if through a haze. 'Nothing wrong, was there? At the Ministry?'

'A snag or two.' They all knew I'd applied to publish. I shrugged. 'Just a snag or two.'

'Bastards. *Bastards* . . . ' But he took the hint in my vagueness and didn't press me. 'We'll sort them.'

'I hope so.' I eased my cramped shoulders. Desk work always gets me down. 'I'm having a family meeting here at noon. Progress report. That sort of thing. I hope you can make it.'

'Sure thing.' He leaned there for a moment, then struck the door-frame bracingly with his palm. '*A bientôt*, then.'

Maggi, at five to nine, was the next one in. She looked round the door, saw I was busy, and settled at her WP in the outer office. As I listened to the faint plastic clattering I realised that my secretary must be added to the number of my friends and colleagues who knew the codes and combinations. If not officially, she could easily have acquired them by just being around.

Maggi Frik is a perky young gay with a rather stodgy lover in the state sperm-collection service. The lover worked shifts at that time and often turned up at the end of Maggi's day to accompany her home. They had left-wing ideals and lived in the run-down area by the disused football stadium. Maggi wore her hair in spikes and her skirts to the ground, and I couldn't have survived without her. We'd both become civil servants on the same day, I from Unikhem and she straight from secretarial school.

I remembered to call Dr Hannes. Yes, the police had been very helpful. Yes, Anna was fine. Yes, I was fine too. He didn't chat, he had a full surgery. He may have guessed I was talking for a phone tap. We parted fondly.

By ten forty I'd finished with the folders. I returned them to the safe, the relevant half-dozen or so on top, and locked it, spinning the dial. If the combination was to be changed, Maggi would know how. I was about to call her in when I heard Natya approaching. One does tend to hear Natya before she arrives. She's a big broad Russian woman with a big broad Russian voice, your joke Russian female shot-putter. She also has your joke Russian heart of gold. Combined with outstanding organisational ability that was no joke at all in a group like ours, of work-obsessed professionals. Married, in a rare meeting of minds, to an archaeology professor at the university, she was almost as old as Gusso and had been a refugee from the most recent round of Russian upheavals. Dr Natalya Volkov was my project director. I'd poached her from the city hospital where she'd been totally wasted.

She entered the outer office, towing an angry young woman in shabby military chic. ' . . . Very well. Very well, Miss Rabble-rouser. So here she is. Here's Dr Kahn-Ryder. But I can promise you, if Dr Kahn-Ryder has anything to say to the press, it won't be through you.'

She stopped in front of my desk, released the young woman's arm. 'A reporter from the *City Journal*, Dr Harriet. She was making a nuisance of herself at Reception.'

The girl was tugging her uniform jacket back into some sort of shape. Its green lapels were glazed with too many ironings and its cuff-edges were visibly threadbare. The *City Journal* was a tiny, very radical paper, and clearly no great payer.

I sat back, gave her the full authority figure. 'Can I help you?'

I could, I could make her career, but I wasn't going to. She was trouble, hand-picked for a ministerial leak, and more trouble wouldn't be far behind her. For someone (the Minister?) wishing to cripple my freedom of movement there was no better way: for a while now I'd be knee-deep in reporters every time I put my face outside the door.

She stamped her army boots, straightening her gaiters. 'The name's Hansen. Yesterday you had a twenty-minute emergency meeting with the Science Minister.'

'Not so.'

'Her aide, then. Your immediate boss.'

'I meant there was no emergency.'

'Voices were raised.'

'Voices were not raised.'

Presumably this was going down on her recorder. It would be unrewarding.

'Perhaps you'd like to tell me about it.'

'Certainly. We were discussing my holiday arrangements.'

'I'm afraid I don't believe you.'

'That's your privilege. Now, you know the way out, I think, so – '

'Dr Kahn-Ryder, this operation of yours absorbs huge amounts of government money. Of the people's money. Don't you reckon it's time they got something back for it?'

'I suggest you ask the Minister that question. She's their elected representative.'

'Dr Kahn-Ryder, were you asked to resign yesterday?'

'In my experience, Hansen, ministers don't ask, they tell.'

'That's no answer.'

'It's all you're going to get.'

'Dr Kahn-Ryder, doesn't it worry you that – '

'You heard her, Hansen.' Natya's massive hand reclaimed her arm. 'That's all you're going to get. So either you go away nicely or – '

' – Or my paper gets served with trespass and harassment charges. In short, another government cover-up.'

Neither of us argued. Hansen looked from Natya to me: we weren't going to.

Natya nodded towards the open door. 'Dr Kahn-Ryder's secretary will see you out.'

Hansen went. Natya closed the door after her, stood with her back to it, arms folded. 'No good news with the application, I see.'

I shook my head. 'They say our tests are inadequate.'

'They're wrong. What are you going to do?'

'More tests, I suppose.' I told myself lying to her was for her own protection. 'I saw the Minister's aide and he suggested resubmitting in six months' time.'

'Dr Marton is a difficult man. And in this he is wrong. He does not labour in the fields. He does not know what every month more of the Syndrome means to village women. I shall call him and tell him so.'

I smiled. She probably would too – but out of loyalty to me rather than with any real hope of changing his mind.

'I'm taking a break, Natya.' I stood up. 'Spare me a minute back here around noon, will you? We're having a family meeting.'

On my way out I asked Maggi to phone Liesl about the meeting, then I went for a short tour of inspection round the clinic. I needed to stretch my bones.

Fridays were slow, we only had a couple of our donors in that morning, and Karen was alone at one of the nursing stations, catching up on her paperwork. I told her what I'd told Natya about my application, and that we'd be discussing it in my office at noon. Karen was the group cynic, unsurprised now at the Minister's decision.

'Always the bloody safety play,' she muttered, the cigarette on her lower lip flapping. 'Where would our leaders be without it?' And went on pecking two-fingered at her keyboard.

Interestingly, Dr Karen Bakst had been in government service longer than any of us. She'd run the donor clinic since it opened twelve-odd years before, and I'd inherited her as part of the new enlarged MERS research establishment I'd taken over. A hollow-chested rail of a woman, twenty a day on tobacco and unrepentant, she used herself up relentlessly. Tireless with patients and donors and their problems, a listening bedside presence at all hours of the day and night, she'd never to my knowledge had a day's illness. She lived for the clinic, and had supported me in my research work every step of the way.

I watched her at her keyboard for a couple of minutes, terrible posture, legs cranked back impossibly, knees and ankles like broken twigs wound round her chair pedestal, saved my breath and wandered back into the main building, up to the top-floor canteen. It seemed a long time since breakfast.

We'd agreed Mark couldn't phone. He found me at a table by the canteen window, looking out across suburban dereliction at the ruined granite walls of the original medieval state capital on its cliff-top in the city centre. Granite castle, grey city roofs, black leafless trees, the mountain peaks beyond already streaked with snow . . . even under the pale October sunlight the prospect was bleak.

The news Mark brought was bleak also. He'd been calling round the serious science magazines and TV outlets for the last three hours, using the secure media computer network, and not one of them would touch my paper. Harriet Kahn-Ryder, scientist and animal rights campaigner, fine! Harriet Kahn-Ryder, scientist and maverick government researcher, no way! Mark had also tried the provincial university presses, those within the network. Someone had got to each of them first.

'They're on the list, old buddy, and they've all been frightened off. The '97 Amendment touches nerve-endings other protocols don't reach.'

It was bleak, but it was what we'd expected.

'I'll try abroad,' Mark went on. '*Natur* in Germany, for example. But it'll take longer and there'll be problems of authentication. Your name alone won't do it. Especially as they won't be able to meet you, or even talk to you in person.'

Not meet me? 'We've got airports, Mark. A coastline, twenty-five hundred k's of land frontier. We're a part of One Europe, for heaven's sake. Couldn't I really get out?'

I had a half-full mug of coffee in front of me and an unfinished open sandwich on a plate. Mark reached for both. He'd been tidying up after me since we first met. Now he no longer asked.

'Tell me something,' he said, chewing. 'At your interview, did Marton touch you? I mean, his hand actually on your flesh?'

I thought back. 'We shook hands at the end, of course.'

'Not enough. Palms get too much wear.'

'Oh yes – and he touched the back of my neck. He'd had his hand on my shoulder and on the way down it brushed the back of my neck . . . When I rang Danno he said I'd be tagged, but would that contact be enough?'

I knew about electronic tagging in principle, of course, but I'd always imagined a surgical implant of some sort.

Mark started on the coffee. 'These days, plenty enough. The security people don't exactly advertise it, but an electrostatic molecular film does the job. It virtually bonds on to your skin. Doesn't wash off and it's resistant to friction. A ten-centimetre strip tuned to a very narrow radiation band. You can't see it or feel it, but today's detectors will sense it at ten or more k's.'

He lifted the mug. 'Your very good health, Dr Harriet Kahn-Ryder. I'll set up a scan when we get home, but I'm willing to bet that's what Marton laid on you.'

The canteen clattered around us. I felt the back of my neck – as Mark had said, nothing. I didn't bother to mention the legal requirement for a magistrate's order. I was learning what the '97 Amendment meant. According to Danno it was as tight as a nun's twat. Tighter. I felt I couldn't even pee without the SPU knowing.

The *SPU* . . . Christ. 'Sergeant Milhaus touched me,' I said. 'The back of my hand.' I clawed at it with my nails.

Mark nodded. 'That'll be the back-up. They like to work them in pairs.' He looked across, saw what this was doing to me. I was frantic. They'd made me into a walking radio beacon. 'Hush now, old buddy. Hush . . . '

He pushed the plate and mug to one side and folded my hands in his. 'We can lift them off. I've got the solvent . . . But I don't recommend it. They quickly find out, and then you look like someone with something to hide. At least this way they keep an eye on you without you having their bad breath over your shoulder.'

'How soon could they find out? Maybe I could make it across the frontier. They can't be watching all the time. They haven't the staff.'

'That's the chance you take. Maybe you'd make it. You never can tell. That's how the system works.'

'That means you have to know you've been tagged. I thought the point of all this was that you didn't know.'

'Oh Harriet, *Harriet* . . . not clever people like us, Harriet. Clever people like us always know.' He lifted my hands to his lips, looked at me over them. 'The game they play is to make knowing just hard enough, so that we won't think they know we know.'

This was our government. Bleak? How bleak could you get?

Mark went on, his tone lighter. 'The good thing is, as far as Anna is concerned, is that none of this matters. They'll have tagged her too by now – somebody will have bumped into her, knocked her down, helped her up, you can guess the drill – but it doesn't matter. We're going to have to hide her anyway, so we simply wait till everything's ready, then lift the tag and – hey presto – she disappears.'

He made it sound as easy as his last night's *an awful lot of Milhauses will have to get past me first*. But I was awake now. And older.

Did I want it? All this bloody rotten mess, this lying, distrust, danger. Did I want it? My colleagues downstairs, it was sick to imagine that one of them might be cheating me. It was sick to imagine that Dr Marton was anything other than an over-cautious civil servant. It was sick to imagine that Sergeant Milhaus – no, at her my mind fused. Nothing, nothing was as sick as the imagination that animated Sergeant Milhaus. But did I have to fight it? Why not wait six months as the Minister suggested? Her support, the love of a grateful nation, fame and fortune, a Nobel prize, Anna not in danger – all that, or all this?

I wasn't sure.

The bright canteen didn't help me, nor the view from the window. Nor Mark's broad, generous face with its bright brown whiskers, nor his hands holding mine. I wasn't sure.

'Can we really make Annie disappear, Mark?'

'I know we can. I've a couple of schemes in mind. Trust me.'

'And disappear for how long, Mark? When will it be safe for her to come out?'

'Two weeks. Three. Once you've published and the media circus is under way. When the cameras are rolling. And anyway there'll be no point. With the damage done there'll be no point.'

'A warning? For next time? *Pour encourager les autres?*'

'What *autres*? There aren't any *autres*. And if there were, believe me, the Minister will be so busy belatedly climbing on the bandwagon that you won't see her nether garments for dust.'

Perhaps. Two or three weeks. No real risk. Perhaps he was right.

I glanced at my watch. 'I must go down now, Mark. I've got a meeting in my office at twelve. I was planning to tell them why I was changing all the codes and combinations.'

'No problem there.' He had missed, unusually, the indecision in that *was planning*. 'Now that your application's in, that's basic security. And you can tell them the Minister's delaying her permission while she takes expert advice.'

I didn't argue, but I was glad it was already too late for that particular lie. 'See you later then.' I stood up. 'And don't do anything definite, Mark, till I get home.'

'Definite? You must be joking. Setting up *Natur* will take at least a week. And then it'll be up to you to provide the meat and bones.' He saw my expression. 'Be brave, old buddy. For evil to triumph all it needs is for good men to do nothing.' He blew me a kiss. 'And good women.'

But I wasn't sure.

Downstairs Liesl had arrived early for the meeting. She was waiting in my office. I looked at her – a spy? – and absently rubbed the back of my hand where Sergeant Milhaus had touched it.

'I heard your news,' she said. 'The Minister's a stupid cow.'

I nodded, sat down at my desk. I wasn't ready to talk to her. For something to do I spun my chair round to the safe, opened it, and took out my top half-dozen folders. I wanted them in front of me. They were an important part of what my problem was about.

Liesl fidgeted, tried to pull her skirt down over her knees but it was too short. She was our virologist, the heart of our team, Dr Liesl Wronowicz, trained in the USA, medical degree at Harvard, doctorate at MIT. She was always a little anxious, always trying to make herself neater, brighter, prettier, better at whatever it was, from double dummy plays at bridge to DNA splicing. I'd headhunted her, surprisingly, from Brandt International. There'd been a personality difficulty, she said. Two weeks working with her told me they wouldn't have been able to stand her perfectionism.

I sorted idly through the folders. Three down from the top there was one that hadn't been there when I put them away. It contained some accounts of old-fashioned DNA amplification as a way of sexing human blastocysts. Not valuable, not even useful, but someone had thought it worth borrowing, maybe overnight, and then had opened the safe and replaced it during the last hour, while I was out of the office. And I'd never have known a thing if I hadn't come in that morning earlier than whoever it was, and started sorting my papers.

Three down – that was the killer. Why replace a folder three down, if not in secret, to make it unremarkable?

Someone.

Gusso Polder arrived, leaned round the door. I raised a finger to hush him, pointed to a chair, and rang through to Maggi.

'Any phone calls in the last hour?'

'None on the machine, boss.'

'You weren't here?'

'I had to go over to the library. Got back only just before you. Any sweat?'

'No sweat, Maggi.'

I rang off. No sweat at all. An empty office, an unguarded safe, and five people, five colleagues, friends, Maggi, Gusso, Natya, Karen and Liesl, who knew the combination. No fucking sweat at all.

The others arrived. I waited till they were settled, and Karen had lit up, and Gusso had groaned, and then I told them that, now that my application was in, I was changing my personal codes and combinations in the cause of good security. And I asked them, given the Minister's unhelpful reaction to my application, to put together a team proposal for a volunteer human test-pregnancy program, that being the only 'home-work' left that we could do for her.

Personally, I told them I needed a morale-booster, so I was taking a couple of days' holiday. Maybe more.

Meeting over. No explanations. I doubt if I was recognisable. I didn't care. The trouble was, for the sake of one I hated them all.

CHAPTER FOUR

The Attrition. Year 20: mid-June.

Harriet spread her fingers, stretching them till the ligaments creaked in the back of her hands and wrists. Such young hands, Julius told her. Sweet sixteen and never been kissed. You'll never have them so supple again.

She turned the page back, started from the beginning. The Prokofiev was percussive, fast thick chords, a lot of movement within them: after half an hour at the keyboard her arms were aching. She loved it, but by now she was concentrating on the shape of the movement, hoping the details would take care of themselves.

'Enough!' She heard Julius's protest above all the banging, and stopped. 'You're getting tired.'

'No.' She leaned forward to peer at the music. 'It's just that I can't seem to – '

'*I'm* getting tired, then.' He got up from the stool beside her. 'Time for tea.'

She came up here to the Eckett for lessons after school – it was a long walk home but she always stayed for tea, even today when she was restless, looking forward to seeing Daniel again. She treasured every moment spent in Julius and Anka's shabby old house, stone-built on a stately pre-First World War square, named the Eckett after its designer, tree-lined and shady in summer, a once-exclusive development on high ground above the harbour, now shabby and down on its luck, separated from the town by an ugly sprawl of public housing. It was her refuge from the world.

The Stollmans' living-room, where Julius gave his lessons, was everything her mother's wasn't: high-ceilinged, the Flemish plasterwork up there grey and cobwebby, it was big enough for Julius's enormous Bösendorfer and all his electronic keyboard gear as well as black velvet chairs and sofas with huge down-filled cushions, and black coffee-tables, all terribly eighties, beneath them a vast red-patterned Turkey carpet creased and dusty and threadbare enough to have come with the house. In one corner a post-Millennium laminated elm circular staircase led down through a hole in the floor to a murky semi-cellar and the kitchen. The pictures on the peeling metallic black-and-silver walls were mostly fiery abstracts, hot lumps of paint in ragged discs and oblongs: beside the antique marble fireplace the Stollmans had hung an above-life-size photographic blow-up, sepia dots and smudges, of Anka Stollman in her singing days, and a monumental gilt birdcage, at present empty, its door open, dangled from a chain by the french windows at the back. These opened on to a rickety balcony with fussy wrought-iron railings, once white, that led down to a jungle of a garden, hardly a flower in it, long grass and evergreen trees and shrubs lapping round the balcony like waves.

It was a room, a way of life, that Harriet's mother, on her first and only visit, when arranging Harriet's lessons, had found scandalous and threatening. 'A lot of nonsense is talked about the artistic temperament, child. If one has nice things, one has a responsibility to look after them.'

In Anka Stollman's place, Harriet knew very well, her mother would have looked after the things very differently. When undressing to go swimming, for example, Bess Ryder would first carefully remove her three modest rings – thin gold wedding-band and a first-anniversary gift from Johan, with genuine diamonds, and an eighteenth-birthday scarab from her mother. If you drowned, she said, and your body was recovered, often as not your rings were stolen, so she always left hers in one of her shoes on the beach. Danno had 'stolen' them from there on several occasions, just to see her face, but he'd always given them back. Bess looked after things.

Julius went down to the kitchen to make the tea, ducking his head under the curve of the stairs as he disappeared. Harriet peered at the music again, played a few half-hearted notes, then quit. She'd have plenty of time during the week, if she went straight home after school, in the hour before Moma got home from work. In the house on the Parade the piano, a Japanese upright, was squashed in behind the sofa in the upstairs living-room. Moma never actually complained about the noise, but she sighed sometimes and Harriet couldn't blame her. There was nowhere in the house you could get away from it.

The tiny house had bothered Danno too. He hadn't been home for six months, but maybe that was the army's fault. He'd be arriving some time that evening on a weekend pass, probably latish – it wasn't far to come, but they didn't let him out of barracks till after five. She was looking forward to his visit very much. She wasn't sure why, he was a stranger these days, but she'd thought of little else since he'd rung to say he was coming. She wanted to see him: he was her brother. Also there was a disco on Saturday and maybe he'd take her. The competition for any man under forty was impossible, and she was sick of dancing with girls.

Danno had been in the army a couple of years now. The quarrels between him and Moma had become so foul it was no wonder he'd got away as soon as the army'd have him. Dada hadn't been pleased, but he saw the need.

Julius's head and shoulders appeared above the floor. 'How's the chemistry course?'

'Hard, Julius.' She grimaced. 'It's all so interdependent. And it's getting in the way of the practice.'

'I thought something was. Are you losing heart?'

'What with? Medicine or music?'

He came up a step, leaned on his forearms. 'I was reading the other day, Harriet, that there are perhaps a million spermatozoa in just two cc of ejaculate. That's a great many people. And it's still a long time till the last old dodderer can't manage it any more. Thirty years at least. By then, at present rates of collection, we'll have people on ice for just about for ever . . . What I mean is, why bother with finding a cure?'

'Not *people*, Julius. Only women.'

'Is that really so bad? On balance the world's already a gentler place. And losing male embryos is cutting the population.'

It was a game he played with her. Devil's advocate. Today she couldn't be bothered. Perhaps he was right.

'Perhaps you're right.'

'Perhaps I'm not.' He raised one of the straggling eyebrows he was so proud of. 'What about music, then? There's more of that stored away than all them sperm. Who needs more pianists?'

'Did I tell you Danno's coming for the weekend?'

He grinned. 'All right. Point taken.' The kettle downstairs in the kitchen began to whistle. 'In point of fact there's room for both. Plenty of excellent scientists are – '

She joined him. ' – Are excellent musicians too.'

They both laughed.

'*Oy veh* . . . so I repeat myself. I'm also the sort of old fart who asks young people how they're getting on with their chemistry at school. It's the price you pay for contact with a dying life form.' He disappeared down the stairs. Surfaced again. 'Even that isn't true. There'll be plenty of old men to last out your days. It's the young you won't be seeing.'

He went back down and the whistling stopped. Harriet uncurled her feet from under the piano stool, got up, and wandered over to the open window. She realised, shockingly, that she was bored. She shouldn't have stayed. Waiting for tea that you didn't really want was *boring*. She looked out at the jungly garden. A diversion occurred to her.

'*Polly?*' she called in her most basso, Julius-like voice. And then, on two rising notes, '*Pol–ly?*'

Nothing happened. It never did when she called. But there was no harm in trying.

Young people, he'd said. She didn't feel like a young people.

Julius came up the stairs with a loaded tea-tray. Dented silver pot, odd bone-china cups and saucers. 'As I was saying. All the young men . . . but the trouble is, I don't grieve for them. I should of course. It would be easier if I were gay. One famous old literary queen, I refuse to remember who, once said he could forgive young men anything because they were so beautiful. I envy him.' He came forward, put the tray down on a coffee-table. 'Harriet, do *you* find young men beautiful? You seem to be female, and sexually arrived, and not noticeably gay – do *you* find young men beautiful?'

She thought about it. 'I expect he meant *attractive*.'

'A literary gent, Harriet. I think we should credit him with meaning what he said.'

'Then I can't answer. Not about men. They may be beautiful, I don't know. At my age sex gets in the way.'

Julius was delighted. 'Obviously it did for him too. Whoever he was.'

But Harriet was still thinking. A serious question, a serious answer. 'I wonder what he felt he had to forgive them for. Young men, I mean. Isn't it the old ones that do the terrible things?'

She looked at him, standing over the tea-tray. He was an old man himself. But he wouldn't take her words personally. Not Julius.

He didn't. 'You're right, of course. I'm afraid my anonymous aphorist and I were being facetious. Young men's crimes are restricted to pimples and an over-eagerness to follow leaders.'

Harriet turned away to the window. She accepted that Julius loved showing off, but she wished he didn't make her feel so heavy sometimes. So juvenile. Not young – *juvenile*.

'Call Polly for me please, Julius.'

He went past her, out on to the balcony. '*Polly?*' His cry was operatic, and deafening. '*Pol–ly?*'

An answering squawk came from the trees at the far end of the garden, and eventually a grey parrot lurched out from among the leaves. An outdoor bird for the brief summer months, it flew clumsily, landing with a clatter of claws on the balcony handrail. It twitched its back feathers, settled them, then glared at Julius, first with one eye and then the other, its head bobbing in fierce scooping movements.

'A visitor for you, Polly,' he said. 'A visi-it-or.'

The bird made considering noises. It was a dusty, very plain little parrot, of undiscovered sex (it had never laid an egg), with pinkish feet and bright orange irises to its skinny, double-lidded eyes. Harriet, as always, was both fascinated and repelled. She went back into the room and sat on the edge of the sofa, cautiously, to avoid disappearing into the cushions, close by the tea-tray with its plate of English biscuits. Polly climbed down a handrail support and followed her, swinging laboriously from foot to foot. Harriet broke a biscuit and held out a piece. Polly took the piece in one claw and transferred it to her formidable beak, jointed like medieval armour. As it opened, a thick dry purple tongue was briefly visible.

Julius sat in the chair opposite, angrily punching it into a more bearable shape. 'Bloody thing . . . Your brother's home this evening, you were saying?'

The parrot sidled closer. Harriet didn't take her eyes off it. She nodded. 'Late this evening.'

'I seem to remember he's liking the army.'

'Very much.' Danno would have liked anything that got him away from Moma, but she wasn't saying that. Not even to Julius.

'He likes something to belong to, I think. And the smartness. Regimental tradition – that sort of thing.'

'How old is he – twenty? It's just the right age.'

'He'll make it his life.' She suspected Julius of patronising her brother. 'He's taking a course in advanced weapons systems.'

'Dear God.'

Polly had opened her beak wide enough to get a careful grip on Harriet's right shoe. She felt she was being attacked on two fronts. She didn't like talking to people about Danno. And Polly hung on now, crunching her big toe slightly, staring up at her with one baleful eye.

'You asked about school, Julius, about chemistry. It really is hard. But science is what I want to do. What I must do.'

'Of course you must. I wasn't thinking. I'm sorry.' He had observed both her predicaments. Having released her from one, he heaved himself forward in the chair, grasped Polly firmly, unhooked her from Harriet's shoe and took her away to her cage. He closed the door on her and latched it. For so small a creature Polly was curiously intimidating.

Julius turned back to her. 'Hard, you say? Hard enough for the exam to be a worry?'

'Not really.' Exams were at the end of July, six weeks away. 'I'm a year ahead. It's just these neurotic teachers, wanting you to be best, to make up for them being less.'

'That's harsh, Harriet.'

'It's true. They know I'll pass. So why else isn't that enough?'

Julius sat down again, poured the tea, eyed her thoughtfully not because he didn't have an answer, clearly, but rather because he had several and was choosing. A melodious, *I'm here* sort of whistle from the front hall spared him the decision. The parrot repeated it exactly – this was its only attempt at mimicry – and climbed excitedly sideways up and down its bars.

The front door banged shut and Anka appeared in the living-room, sun-hat low over her eyes, laden with shopping bags.

'Tea-time,' Julius told her. 'I was so sure you'd make it I've laid a cup.'

Anka hung her hat on the doorknob, stacked her bags by the head of the stairs, took a plum out of one of them and stuffed it warily between the bars of Polly's cage. Much as the parrot loved her, it loved taking pieces out of people's fingers more. Anka whispered something to it that Harriet didn't catch.

Anka Stollman had no voice. If she wanted to attract attention she whistled: thereafter she whispered. She had a voice synthesiser which she hated and never used. The noises it made were derived from her singing on nineties pop CDs, with an ageing element factored in. Julius said they were plausible, but she still hated it.

Harriet could see why. The voice wasn't *hers*, not the way her whisper was. If you paid attention, Anka Stollman's whisper was the most expressive in the business. She could have had an amplifier for it, but she rejected that too: she said it made her sound like the ghost in Hamlet.

Anka had lost her voice as the result of an early botched bioengineered implant. A radio mike. She'd been big for a while, fifteen years or so before the beginning of the Attrition, and she'd met Julius at a recording session. He was on keyboards, a refugee from a classical concert platform shrunk to virtually nothing by world recession, ambient multiphonics, populist government, you name it. They moved in together three months later, and six months after that her implant went sour. The bioconnections started growing in places they shouldn't, and by the time it was spotted they could only be removed by cutting out most of her own vocal apparatus along with the mike.

Julius taught piano and keyboards for a while in the city, then they came down here. She'd had the sense to put a bit away in her golden days, and in the first year after her voice went she sold more than ever before. Almost as good as dying of an OD, her agent had said. But it hadn't lasted. She painted now – the abstracts in the room were hers – and she'd learned signing so that she could teach art at a school for the profoundly deaf a few miles down the coast. Harriet thought she was marvellous.

Julius she was in love with, but Anka she thought admirable and marvellous.

Anka sat down neatly on the sofa beside her. Its cushions never bothered Anka: she'd long since subjected them to her superior will.

'Harriet – I'm glad I caught you. I want you to have a word with your mother for me. She still runs her Saving the Babies Fund?'

Harriet nodded.

'And it deals with education, not just picking them off the mountain or whatever?'

' . . . It tries.'

Anka saw her hesitation. 'Obviously it won't stop Chinese mums dumping their girl babies the first time it tells them there won't be any more boy ones. But at least it tries . . . I gather Muslim mums are at it too.'

'Not really. There it's the men.'

Anka sighed. 'Well, if one has to have a religion I must say I think your mother's picked the right one.'

'Now then, Anka.' Julius filled her teacup. 'You know you don't mean that. Last-century sexism's bad enough, without bloody God the Mother putting Her oar in.'

'At least she sent down Jesus as a role model.'

'Yes – with his "Woman what have I to do with thee?"'

'Not fair,' Harriet protested. 'Moma says that was written in later.'

'Frankly, if the Bible's God's word, I'd have expected Her to do a better job of keeping it on the rails.'

'*Please*.' Anka's smile softened the sharpness of the sibilant. 'Could we get back to Mrs Ryder's fund, Julius?'

Talking to Anka involved a lowering of your volume. Living with her mother, Harriet liked this but it gave a hushed urgency to the most ordinary conversation.

'The artists at college – ' Anka never called them her students: she claimed she was as much a student as they ' – want to mount an exhibition, raise money for the Fund. One of them read the piece your mother had in the local paper.'

Harriet fidgeted. Moma's good works were a trial – mostly because they made her hard to ignore. Harriet loved her, and they rubbed along, but she'd rather have been able to write her off as a bit silly. 'I'll bring along one of the Fund's hand-outs next time I come.'

'Which reminds me,' Julius put in, changing the subject. 'For your lesson next week give the Prokofiev a rest. It's becoming all fingers. Work on the Ravel instead. And some free-association chording. It's too easy to get your ear trapped. Wouldn't you agree, Anka love?'

They talked about music. Anka remembered something, darted over to her shopping bags, came back with a recording.

She was tiny these days, and moved like a squirrel. She put the recording on the player.

'I specially wanted Harriet to hear this. I ordered it weeks ago – it's only just come in.'

The room was filled with a Palestrina motet, sung with exquisite lightness, the choir lifted on the thin, strangely breathy sound of the upper voices. It was like nothing Harriet had heard before. The music was achingly beautiful, crystal-bright, unearthly yet passionate. Realising that the recording must be historic and that the singers were boys, she felt an acute sense of loss. She had felt other Attrition losses, had wept watching films of teenage love on TV, but this was a loss of a different order. A loss that wasn't even in one sense real – she could hear this music again, and for always – yet a loss that showed her, for the first time in her life, how the old world, the world before MERS, how the old world had ended.

They played the recording through to its end. Palestrina, Monteverdi, Tallis, Vivaldi, she would have had it go on for ever. But the time was after six and she must go home.

She gathered her sheet music from the piano. Out in the hall Julius fetched her sun-hat from the ornate pine newel post at the foot of the stairs. 'Skip the Prokofiev,' he reminded her. 'Enjoying your clever fingers is fine, but you must ask more of yourself.'

He opened the front door, kissed her forehead lightly, and she ran off down the path. The magic of the singing was over. What rubbish he talked. The Ravel asked far more of her fingers than the Prokofiev.

It was early June, the sun still high in a clear sky. Even up there above the harbour not a breath stirred. Harriet slowed her pace, walking in the shade of the ornamental cherry trees that lined the square. There were smells of privet, and alyssum, and mown grass. She walked softly now, heel and toe. The silence was precious. It could be felt, a tingling on her face.

At the end of the square there was an opening out on to a crossroads, an area of graveyard, and then the public housing began. On winter evenings Julius went with her down through the dark maze of identical three-storey blocks, brown brick with yellow clapboard panels, flat minimalist porches over flat minimalist doors, lanky grass beneath cracked windows, dustbin shelters overflowing with broken plastic toys, snapped-off horse-chestnut saplings still tied to their stakes, and the occasional group of lock-up garages, empty now of cars but not of unofficial residents, set around crumbling concrete yards. Streetlamps were infrequent, many broken, and you heard of violence there, rape and robbery. Girls' faces were slashed. Terrible things.

There was violence in the summer too, but it waited for night, so Harriet was allowed to cross the estate alone after her lessons. She had never been bothered, but she trod warily. Often there were young people hanging around, but they didn't interfere with her.

Today they did.

'Hey – Blondie . . . tell us the time then.'

She'd seen them ahead, sitting in a bus shelter, swinging their legs, and hadn't looked. Behind the bus shelter a row of garages backed on to the road.

'What's the matter, Blondie? You deaf or something? Tell us the time.'

Three boys, two girls, the girls giggling. She could walk on past. None of them had moved. But walking on seemed snobby. She turned and faced them.

'It's twenty past six.'

'Ta.'

The boys weren't boys at all, of course, older than Danno, in their twenties, grinning at something she didn't understand. Them in the bus shelter, a space, and then her out on the pavement. She still felt snobby, the space in between, she in her sort of clothes and they in theirs. The girls were just girls, hanging out after school, but the boys were old enough to have something better to do. Jobs? These days, for boys? Certainly.

She realised she was still thinking of them as boys. Was that snobby? She turned to walk on.

'Hey, Blondie – shouldn't you be wearing your you-know-what?'

She didn't understand that either, except that there was a threat in it somewhere, and it decided her. She walked away briskly. Soft-soled feet approached fast, and more giggling.

The boys ranged themselves in front of her, the skinny one leaning absently against a blank garage wall, the fat one scuffing his feet in the gutter, the boss one facing her in the middle. And the two girls stood behind her, quiet now. She stopped. She had to.

'What d'you want?'

The boss one: 'I said, shouldn't you be wearing something?'

'And I said, what d'you want?'

She refused to be afraid. It was broad daylight and there were house windows opposite, with ornaments and open shutters. Being afraid was as snobby as being snobby.

The boss boy laughed. 'What do we want? What do most people want? To be fucking needed, I'd say. Wouldn't you say most fucking people want to be fucking needed?'

What was he after? They hadn't stopped her in the street to talk about the meaning of life. The plan was to make her look foolish. She didn't answer.

'Which is why I asked you if you shouldn't be wearing you-know-what. My name's Brak, by the way. That's without no "c" – b-r-a-k.'

He held out his hand. She shook it.

'Harriet Ryder.' Her own name always made her cringe. 'So what should I be wearing?'

'You'll have noticed, Harriet Ryder, that this is not a nice fucking area. Frankly, an undesirable area. A highly undesirable area.' He enjoyed the words he chose. She liked that – she too enjoyed language. 'Not an area conducive to personal fucking security. Which is where us wanting to be needed come in. Only first you got to be wearing the button.'

'The what?'

'The button. Know what I mean? The trust button.'

Now she did know what he meant. Trust buttons were an idea from the cities. Basically they were a protection racket, but demanding humiliation rather than money. Gangs of men roamed the poorer streets, offering 'protection' to any woman who wore a big dayglo plastic button with two stylised downturned eyes printed on it. These signified what the men said was trust but everyone else knew was submission. Buttons were available in the shops – they broke no law the police could discover – and women who didn't wear them could be said to be asking for trouble. Many did refuse, and they were the women who ended up in hospital emergency rooms. But

67

that was in the city. Harriet had never thought to ask herself what she would do in their place.

'I mean, Harriet Ryder, there's rough types around these days. And if you wore your button, then me and me friends would be needed. We could look after you. I mean, most men're lovely fellers. I mean, a nice girl like you can trust most men. Really trust. So where's the harm?'

He spoke reasonably. He'd seen the way the better villains did it on TV. By now the girls behind her were peeing themselves laughing – a hundred to one they wore their buttons – but Brak and his friends only smiled. Even so, it was all terribly relaxed and low-key.

Out in the street, the sun shining, the windows opposite, ornaments and shutters, even a man in the distance now, walking his dog, and Harriet was scared. Terrified.

But, 'If you're one of the lovely fellers,' she said, 'why would you look after me only if I was wearing one of those buttons?'

'Yeah. Well, I mean, what sort of girl doesn't? Only the slags and the lezzies. They can look after themselves. I mean, what's wrong with a bit of fucking trust between civilised fucking people?'

'Fucking slags.' The fat boy in the gutter looked up from his feet. 'That fucking baby died, you know.'

The boy against the wall joined in. 'My paper had a photo.'

'My paper said photos wasn't fucking allowed.'

'An artist's impression, then. He was a monster. On the front page. He was a fucking monster.'

She realised they were talking about the latest failed SIR conception. They were blaming her. Her biology teacher said suppressed immune response experiments went on all the time. Occasionally a result leaked out. Up to now the immuno-suppressants were so toxic that, although they allowed male foetuses to implant, none had survived for more than a matter of hours.

'That's ridiculous,' she said. 'You couldn't have an artist's impression. He'd have been microscopic.'

'Poor little sod.' The skinny one. 'All the same to you slaggy lot if he hadn't been.'

Brak winked at her. He was on her side against the idiot masses of the world.

'You wear your trust button, Harriet Ryder, because if you don't the nasty men out there are going to get you.'

He reached forward, his gaze still locked on hers, and gently took her music case from her hand. She let it go, mesmerised. He stepped back, opened the case, took out some sheets of the Prokofiev. He looked down briefly.

'Very nice.' His eyes returned to hers. 'I always did like a bit of fancy music. Very nice indeed.'

He tore the sheets in half, then carefully into quarters and sixteenths. When the wad of paper was too thick to tear again he put it into the case and handed the case back to her.

'In case you forget, Harriet Ryder. A fucking reminder. Next time wear your button. Then the nasty men won't get you.'

The girls behind her were quiet now. Brak came straight past her and joined them, followed by Fat and Skinny. He left a faint hint of expensive aftershave. Harriet waited, gathering her strength, as the small sounds of them faded, the scuff of sleeves and trouser legs.

She didn't turn round to see. She couldn't. She could barely stand, so intense had been her fear. Brak was capable of anything. She didn't know what. Anything.

Eventually she walked on, trembling, down the road into town. A ship's siren sounded out beyond the harbour mouth, echoing between the steep hillsides. It made her jump. From where she was, up on the Eckett estate, she couldn't see the harbour mouth.

By the time she'd descended Harbour Street the ship was passing the Town Quay, a smart Japanese freighter gliding up-river to the jetties, a motor sailer with tubular alloy sails, unladen and towering above the local yachts and fishing-boats. The original Working Men's Institute – the words were still carved above the door – had been converted into a state sperm-collection centre, and men came out of the waiting-room to watch. Such ships were rare: the clay deposits inland were almost mined out.

Harriet waited at the back of the quay, under the Millennium Clock, until the ship had passed, and then went slowly forward to the bin by the rail and tipped into it the torn pieces of music out of her case. She understood now why girls didn't tell their mothers when they'd been raped. She wasn't going to tell Moma about Brak. It was too disgusting.

She went home. Danno would be arriving in a couple of hours. It was his first visit since Christmas and she'd been looking forward to it for weeks.

Two years in the army had filled Daniel out. They had taken a spotty adolescent and, in his own words, made a man of him. Joining up had been all his idea, the best he'd ever had. As the little robot train trundled down the single-line track beside the Windstrohm River from the junction, he leaned back agreeably in his seat, yawning and stretching. He observed himself, from one extended olive-drab cuff, along sleeve and down leather-belted jacket to knife-creased trousers and black, highly polished boots. Some guys got into civvies at the drop of a hat. He couldn't see it. It wasn't as if he was ashamed of being a soldier.

He stretched again, his boots pressing against the base of the empty seats opposite, his neck muscles creaking, and felt, inside his soldier's clothes, his absolute reality. He occupied them, filled them, as he occupied nothing else. He was the train's only passenger that evening: the journey along the river, which he'd always loved, winter or summer, was his alone. He had the beginnings of a hard-on. A toss-off would be great. Sort of a celebration. But the waste wouldn't do. Every cc was needed. He should save it for a collection centre.

He retracted his arms and legs, sat forward, and looked out of the window. Flickering glimpses through the pine branches showed him the tide was high, filling the Windstrohm to its banks right up under the trees. The sun was below the western ridge now, the water still and dark and mysterious. As the train rode on, the trees ended, giving him an uninterrupted view of reed-topped mud cushions and a half-submerged hulk close against the far shore. Above it the steep hillside was forested up to the skyline, mostly stunted scrub-oaks black against the glowing opal sky, a line of crooked cable poles in silhouette marking the road. Even through the train window he could feel the stillness out there.

Nothing changed. He'd been up here canoeing as a kid. They'd played on that old hulk, tortured by mosquitoes, and nearly missed the tide. It had a wheelhouse then. He stared, narrowing his eyes. It still had a wheelhouse. Nothing changed. He corrected the thought. People changed. He changed.

The train rode into trees again, then between dank cliffs, taking a short cut across a bend in the river. Giant ferns brushed the carriage windows. A waterfall appeared, white against green moss, and was gone in an instant. The cliffs leaned together, joined overhead. After the darkness of the tunnel the twilight in the river valley seemed as bright as day. A heron staggered by on huge square wings, looking for a place to settle. Daniel breathed his childhood. Like this, it hadn't been so bad. Like this, maybe he hadn't been so bad either.

The train lurched slightly at the junction leading off to the Brandt Laboratories. From here on down to the sea the Windstrohm was dredged and kept free of ice in the winter, and a smart company research vessel, exhaust stacks in the blue-and-white Brandt colours, lay at anchor in the channel. Once Daniel had thought of getting a job with Brandt, like his father. But Dada had a college degree – and even then, look where working for Brandt had got him. You either had to have six doctorates or be in marketing.

There were houses among the trees on the far side of the river. Points of light shone from their windows, and down at water-level coloured lamps festooned the yacht-club jetty, their reflections obscured by the vague shapes of rich men's boats. This was classy stuff, armed-security stuff, classier even than the town yacht club with its two-hundred-year history. Daniel had paddled by close in, envying. The guards had shouted at him, but no one could stop you envying.

His journey was nearly over. The jetties came in sight, brilliantly lit. A freighter with a Japanese flag was tied up alongside, massive hoses discharging into its forward hold. Centuries of research, Dada said, and there was still no better base than the local china clay for a wide range of pharmaceuticals. When Daniel had been a lad a wide area round the jetties was thick with the white dust. It dried your mouth if you scooped it up and licked it. Now, the claypits failing, hardly a grain was allowed to escape.

The train rattled over more points, past the dazzling machinescape and into a final brief swathe of intense darkness before it slowed for the station. Daniel stood up and hefted his kitbag. There'd be nobody meeting him. He'd been able to say he didn't know exactly when he'd arrive. Really, he didn't want chatter spoiling the first moments.

The train stopped. He stepped down on to the platform and strode along it to the station building, stamping his feet. It was after eight and the road outside was deserted, a single methanol-burning taxi waiting by the yellow line. He avoided it and set off into town, his back straight, swinging along, his kitbag on his shoulder.

He was home. These were his schooldays. In the New Century Café a pale young derelict, AIDS by the look of him, was dipping bread into his mug of something at one of the tables and the waitress was behind the counter watching TV. He marched on. Nothing changed. He changed.

Beyond the café the Station Disco was closed, advertising a show tomorrow night, Saturday, starting 8.30, all welcome, positively no alcohol or drugs on the premises. He didn't go to discos much. Not any more. In the army there were better things to do. The army kept you busy.

He went on along Front Street, past the disco hall and the Back Quay, through the town and along the Parade to his house. He put down his kitbag, rummaged for his key, opened the door. He was a man now. The hallway was dark, voices coming up from the kitchen. The house was smaller every time he returned to it. It smelled of damp. Leaving his kitbag, he went quietly down the stairs, peered through the open kitchen door. They were all in there and only the cat, on the refrigerator, eyes wide, had heard him.

He stepped forward. *'Stand by your beds!'*

'Danno – ' Harriet flung herself at him.

His mother looked up from what she was doing at the sink. 'Dear God, look what's here. The Obersturmbahnführer.'

Time stopped.

That woman . . .

His father put down his newspaper. 'You're looking great, Danno. Welcome home.'

The moment passed. Daniel forgot it.

Harriet was hunting in his pockets. 'Where's my present?'

'Should I have brought you one? I thought you'd be offended. I mean, now you're sixteen and all that.'

'Pig. You mean you haven't got one?'

72

'Well . . . '

'Where's your kitbag? It's in your kitbag.'

She tumbled upstairs to find it. It was the least she could do. Moma made her so sad. She'd spent the whole evening since she came in from work cooking Danno's favourite supper, but that was the easy thing. Magazines told you that. Liking your son was something else.

Harriet tore at the arcane fastenings to the kitbag. He'd brought her a present, so she had to.

Daniel followed her up. Was she really sixteen? She had knockers, little ones, he could see them, but she wasn't behaving as if she had. He hugged her from behind, then helped her with the buckles. She was still just a kid. Good old Harri.

Her present was a mouth-organ, what she called a harmonica. It came on a curved bar with a clip that fixed round your neck, leaving your hands free. The idea was for her to learn to play it and accompany herself on the piano and upset her poncy old teacher. She hugged him again and tried to drag him off to try it out at the piano in the living-room but he signalled, nodding, that they ought to go back downstairs to Moma and Dada.

They took the mouth-organ with them and he played it to them later. He'd been practising on his own, and had 'Red River Valley' and 'Ridin' Old Paint' off pat. It was nice. Harri'd learn, of course, but for the moment she couldn't play it at all.

Harriet never learnt. Secretly she hated the noise harmonicas made, and she hid her present at the back of her sweater drawer. It stayed there till she was clearing everything out the following summer, to go to college.

Next morning Daniel lay in. Moma did volunteer work on Saturdays, up at the AIDS family advice bureau, and recently she'd co-opted Harriet to help her. MERS had made women resistant to AIDS, and those already infected had gone into what seemed to be permanent remission. Evidently the mechanism that rejected male embryos rejected the AIDS virus also. And if, in Her wisdom, God the Mother was so merciful, Moma said, then the least Harriet and she could do was put something back in the kitty.

That left Daniel and his father alone in the house. Dada spent a couple of hours writing up his week's lab notes, and then they had respectively an early lunch and a late breakfast together.

They cooked and chewed and told each other about their work. Daniel hadn't been accepted on the advanced weapons course – something to do with being late to apply for enrolment, he said. He was trying instead for a course in specialist anti-terrorist techniques. Everybody in today's army was an expert at something. That was what made it so great.

Johan Ryder's work up at Brandt now was to do with farming lobsters. The current problem was how to stop them tearing each other to pieces when they were kept intensively.

'That's easy, Dada. Just peg their claws.'

'They need their claws. Without them they can't get food and they starve. Think about it, Danno.'

Daniel shrugged. He didn't like being told things. It had seemed to him a perfectly good answer.

Johan stirred his tea. ' . . . Tranquillisers don't work. Lobsters need to be feeling bloody-minded all the time, otherwise they don't bother. They simply fade away.'

'There's guys like that in the army.'

'Quite right. There's guys like that everywhere.'

Daniel stuffed more bread in the toaster. His father had this way of turning things. He could never put his finger on it, but it made him uncomfortable.

Around midday they went out to the bar, the Pelikan, on the Town Quay. A gang of Daniel's friends was there from before he joined up. They talked about town things, which he no longer knew about, and about women. They accepted his father as one of them. The consensus was that the Attrition was fucking great. It was fucking terrible of course, girl fucking footballers, but they'd soon find a cure, and meanwhile the women fucking literally couldn't get enough of it.

By their third pint Daniel saw his father was already un-steady. He wasn't used to drinking at lunchtime. He wasn't used to drinking. Daniel worked out how old his father was. Forty? No, forty-two. That wasn't old. He excused the two of them and took Johan outside. They sat with their tankards on a bench in the sun. The quay was crowded with boatmen and tourists, seagulls clattering noisily overhead. Johan stared at the people. He seemed very low.

'Dada? Penny for 'em?'

'Not worth it.'

Daniel looked away. There were women on the quay. Looking at them, he saw it was true they couldn't get enough of it.

'Danno? I was wondering, Danno. You . . . you planning to have children?'

'One day. Of course.'

'Girls only?'

'Why not? Kids are kids.'

'That's not true.' His father leaned forward. There was sweat on his face. He looked so pissed-off. Daniel wished to God he could help him. 'Of course men love their daughters, Danno. But they hope for sons. It's the sharing . . . I know I did.'

'So you got me.'

'You're finding your way. No man can do more than that.'

'Yeah.' It sounded like an apology. Daniel emptied his glass. That wasn't what he'd meant. 'Did I tell you I'm going on a signals course?'

'Anti-terrorist, you said.'

'That too.' He stood up. 'Same again?'

His father shook his head, then shrugged. 'Why not?'

Sons bought their fathers drinks. It was what sons did.

When he returned with the beer Johan seemed not to have moved.

'Lobsters,' he muttered. 'Working my guts out for bloody lobsters.'

Daniel sat down, gave him a tankard, lifted his own.

'Cheers.'

'Luxury foods for luxury people, Daniel. I mean, it's not exactly helping to feed the starving millions.'

'Join the club, Dada. Look at me. And what did you just say? We do what we can.'

'Did I say that?'

'Near enough.'

'Your father's complacent, Daniel. You shouldn't listen to him.'

Who else, for fuck's sake? 'You're all right, Dada.'

Something might have happened then. Daniel wanted it to. He could just imagine it. Fathers and sons. Something.

But, 'No Daniel . . . I'm wasting my time. We've so little of it left, you and me, we men, and so much to make up for. Doesn't it frighten you?'

75

'What?' Fuck it all. Fuck everything. 'You mean the Attrition? They'll find a cure. They always do.'

'I don't think so. Twenty years of research, the biggest potential moneymaker the industry has ever known, and not a whisper.'

'They're waiting for Harri, Dada. Another couple of years, she'll show them how.' He reached across, punched his father lightly on the shoulder. What a lousy fucking way to spend his Saturday.

But Johan wasn't listening, had gone back to where he'd left off. 'It frightens *me*, Daniel. The life I've wasted. You can do things out of love, and you can do things out of weakness. Between people, I mean. Husbands and wives . . . I don't have to tell you that, of all people. You've lived through it. Haven't you lived through it?'

Daniel glared at him. This was disgusting. This wasn't what he'd come home on leave for.

His father got the message. He leaned back, head against the wall, and stared out across the harbour. 'I'm sorry. Hell, I've had too much to drink too, but that's not why I'm sorry. You'll be used to that . . . No. I'm sorry, Daniel, because I am what I am and I never said her nay. And I called it love. It's as simple as that. Not for your sake, not for anybody's, I never said her nay. *Christ Almighty . . .* '

He shook his head, heaved himself upright, spilling what was left in his glass, and loomed over Daniel, one hand on the back of the bench. 'Three pints it's taken to get me here. How's that for pathetic? And now you're away in the army, and God knows what you think about things, if you think anything. So I'm going home now, and I can manage on my own so you needn't accompany me, and come supper-time none of this will've happened . . . But I'm sorry it did. I really am.'

He put his glass down on the bench and walked carefully away, not a big man, disappearing quickly in the holiday crowd.

Transfixed, his anger shrivelled, Daniel stared after him, as if down a blinding tunnel of years, to a time he couldn't specify, a place he didn't recognise. I'm sorry. *Never be sorry.* Trigger words. He'd heard nothing else. The time was all his years, the place was everywhere. Never be sorry. What he was, what he had become, and why.

Slowly he returned. He wiped his eyes on his sleeve. What was he anyway? A soldier in the finest fucking army in the world, and the last of his kind. Six weeks after him the intake was all girls. Girls, for fuck's sake. Army girls, slags and lezzies.

His father's tankard was still on the bench. He swiped it off on to the ground and kicked it against the wall, smashing it. Then he went back to his friends in the bar and some serious drinking.

Harriet and Bess got home from the AIDS bureau at around two thirty. Danno's room was empty. Dada, unusually, was asleep upstairs on the living-room sofa. A letter for Harriet had come in on the printer. She took it and went down to her room to change out of the clothes Moma thought suitable for the bureau. The letter was from her Gran, Bess's mother. Gran had never married, or had a man regularly around; Johan's parents were both dead, killed in a bomb attack outside a women's hospital the previous year; there were no aunts or uncles. Gran was now Harriet's only living relative outside her immediate family.

Her news was that she was taking early retirement. She'd worked in the library service all her life, but recent legislation had raised the male retirement age to seventy, with a further five years negotiable, and Gran said this left her, at fifty-eight, with no promotion prospects whatsoever. So she was sensibly getting out.

Upstairs in the living-room voices were raised. Harriet folded the print-out along its perforation, propped it on the chest of drawers so she could see the second page while she changed her skirt. Gran was selling her house. She was thinking of going to live on an island off the South Foreland – the island she'd holidayed on for the last three summers. The idea of a small community appealed to her, and there was the possibility of part-time work in the primary school there. Did Harriet think she was crazy?

The noises upstairs increased. Harriet brushed her hair fiercely. She thought Gran was brilliant. Just at that moment an island miles from anywhere appealed to her enormously.

She put on loose slacks and comfortable shoes, ran straight

upstairs and into the living-room. She wanted to get it over. Her parents froze: their crude, exaggerated attitudes were there for ever, even the expressions on their angry, ugly faces.

Julius said the world was gentler. Harriet couldn't see it. The problem wasn't men or women. The problem seemed to be anger – either it translated into power or it didn't.

She said quickly, 'Dada – d'you know where Danno is?'

They moved on. Moma said, 'Your father's drunk.'

He spread his hands. 'I wasn't denying it. My point was, on a Saturday afternoon, was that really so dire?'

Harriet hated them. In particular, at this moment, she hated his *dire*. Laughing at Moma like that with words was so feeble. 'Where's Danno?'

'I left him at the Pelikan, Harri. He may have migrated, of course.'

Her mother sneered. Actually sneered. 'If he can still stand.'

'No fears in that direction, Mother. I get the impression our Danno is a man of some considerable drinking experience.'

Harriet left them, banged out of the house and down the road. *Mother* was another taunt, one of Bess's known dislikes. But Johan never won these contests. Afterwards he saw himself too clearly.

Daniel hadn't migrated. Harriet found him in the Pelikan bar, a glass in his hand but steady on his feet and unfuddled.

'Harri. You found me. Great. Harri – this is Douglas. You remember Douglas? Let me buy you a Coke.'

She did remember Douglas. He was often around. Since leaving school he'd got a job along on the jetties. He had hairy arms and he thought himself the sexiest thing in town.

'Christ, Harri, don't look like that. He's on his best behaviour today. Aren't you, Doug boy?' Doug boy didn't answer. Daniel moved on smoothly. 'Did Dada make it home all right? Pissed as a newt. Just a sniff of the stuff, that's all he's had, and he was pissed as a newt . . . Doug stayed inside. You didn't see him, Doug. Pissed as a newt.'

'He seemed OK to me. He was asleep on the sofa when we got in from the advice bureau.' She said no more. 'And I'd love a Coke.'

She didn't know what she was protecting Danno from. It wasn't Doug being there that had stopped her. Perhaps she

78

was protecting herself. Daniel ordered the Coke, and another beer for Douglas and himself. Douglas didn't take his beer. He hadn't said a word so far, and she realised he was unconscious. On his feet, eyes open, grinning, but unconscious.

'I didn't want to push in, Danno – ' She was there because it was preferable to the house. She improvised. 'I came because . . . well, I just wanted to know if you'd anything planned for tonight.'

Danno eyed her sideways. 'Orgies, little sister. You shouldn't ask. All the prossies in town. Like all good things, they're cheaper by the dozen.' He raised his glass. 'Cheers.'

She drank her Coke. She hadn't improvised, she'd been thinking about tonight since she'd known he was coming. 'I meant earlier, before the prossies.'

He pulled himself together. She wasn't Moma, he didn't have to be getting at her. What would she like best for tonight? Poor kid, there wasn't much for her in this dump. Only the one place, really.

'Because if you're free,' she went on, 'then I thought perhaps we might – '

'Ask some chums in for ludo?'

'Not quite what I had in mind, Danno.'

'Fix each other's hair in front of the TV, then?'

'I hate you, Danno. I swear I never – '

'Drop in for a jig at the Station Disco?' He grinned at her. 'Starting eight thirty? Positively no drugs or alcohol on the premises?'

She hugged him. 'You think you could manage that long without?'

'I could try.'

She was suddenly embarrassed. 'Then I'd like to very much.'

Douglas was beginning to sag. He'd have lasted upright longer, but getting him out was useful to them both as a punctuation. Harriet had been too pleased by Danno's invitation, and Danno'd been too pleased by Harriet's pleasure. They supported Douglas out of the bar, his legs making dutiful walking movements, and laid him down on a bench in the sun. It helped them to move on; to grow up a bit.

Daniel had left his and Doug's pints inside on the counter.

He couldn't think why he'd ordered them. Three in the afternoon was a bloody stupid time for a booze-up.

On the other hand, as Harriet arranged Douglas's feet on the bench she was thinking about her father's poor little attempt at getting pissed. It raised an important question, and now, with Douglas as mediator, seemed a good time to ask it.

'Danno . . . were Moma and Dada ever happy, d'you think? Happy together, I mean? You're four years older than me. You saw them earlier on. Do you remember?'

'Happy?' He'd already sidled off. 'There's a question.'

'I know. And I'm sorry. But it's important.'

'Important.' His eyes flicked round. 'Then why not ask them?' He had to get away.

She saw his pain. 'I'm sorry, Danno.'

'Don't be sorry, Harri. Never be sorry.' It just came out. From nowhere. He looked at his watch. 'What time's supper?'

'Sevenish, I expect. Same as always.'

'See you then, Harri. And tell Moma I won't be late.'

He walked away quickly. Happy? He was drunker than he'd realised. Any minute now he'd spew his ring up. He broke into a shambling run.

Harriet called after him, 'What about Douglas? We can't just leave – '

But she supposed they could. And Danno wasn't waiting. She let him go. Maybe he had his own questions to answer. But if he was taking her out tonight just as a brotherly gesture she refused to feel bad about it. Had there been anything better on offer he'd have taken it. She was sure of that.

She made her way home slowly. Moma would have won by now, and Dada would be penitent. But if they were staying together for her sake, that was something else she refused to feel bad about. When they were apart she loved each of them dearly. Staying together made that harder.

Within a cheap cab ride of Danno's barracks at army headquarters there were five discos. Compared with any of them, this was a joke. He'd changed into his sharpest gear and he could've saved himself the effort. The DJ here was so square you could've marched a regiment across him, the holos were out of sync, the light show was prehistoric, the speakers were mush, and the live band was a disaster. Two years ago he'd have thought it great: now he knew better.

He leaned against a pillar, suffocating in the mix of cheap scent and cheaper deodorants, while Harri danced with some guy old enough to be her father. He didn't have to do this. Ten more minutes and he'd bugger off, find a decent bar. Harri ought to know better – he'd have to tell her. This place was a dump. He didn't like seeing her make a fool of herself.

Then she burst out of the crowd, hair over her face, cheeks flushed, still moving to the music. She reached for his hand through the flashing bars of light and dark. He hesitated. She looked ten years old. What the hell – just for a couple of minutes. He didn't want to disappoint her.

Three hours later he was wrung out. She wouldn't let him go. They seldom touched, but her eyes held his and he'd never seen anything like the life in them. The drive. He'd put a lot of work into his dancing over the last two years, and the women he went out with admired it. Tonight, with Harri, neither of them gave it a thought. Other guys took her off, but not for long, and he waited for her. She was great company. An amazing kid.

At midnight they eased over to the refreshments area, had huge tumblers of the fluorescent green-and-yellow marbled stuff the kids were drinking that year, and went outside for a breather. The night was warm and very dark, the sky overcast, the moon not risen. They strolled the few hundred metres to the Back Quay, where the last ferry across the harbour that night was leaving. They watched the little motor boat's mast-light dwindle and disappear. From now on Saturday nighters from the other side would have to use the Town Quay ferry.

They leaned their elbows on the rail beneath a streetlamp. At half-tide the water seemed a long way down, lifting and falling away in slow, oily eddies. Its lapping was the only sound: that and the faint beat of music from the disco. They were alone, isolated in the bright cone from the lamp overhead.

'Do you think about all this, Danno?' She wanted to find things they shared. 'I know I will. When you're away in the army, what do you remember?'

He shrugged. 'Nothing much.' The army was another world. Doors closed. He looked at her sideways: she wouldn't understand that. She was only a kid. 'I'd only get homesick,' he said, to simplify.

'*Home* sick?' She separated the words. 'I was talking about the *place*.'

She meant she couldn't imagine him grieving for his home. It was an invitation to confide that he didn't take up. She hadn't expected him to.

'How much longer here have you got?' he asked instead. 'Two years? And then what – still college?'

'I have to, Danno. It's the only way to what I want to do.' It was ridiculous that she should have to apologise to him for going to college. And not tell him they'd put her forward and she only had one year. She'd always been cleverer than he. She couldn't help it.

Frankly, she didn't want to help it.

But in any case he missed the nuance. 'My sister the famous scientist.'

They laughed and Harriet moved closer. She linked her arm in his and they stared out at the confusion of lights reflected in the water. He missed so much.

'There's a problem, Danno. It could affect the courses I take. You see, there's two ways into this stuff – the causes or the results. I need to decide which is more important, curing the symptoms or finding out what went wrong in the first place.'

'I read it was a gas from outer space.'

'Nothing's impossible. It could be the increased ultraviolet, or some residue from the oil wars. Or a virus that's always been around, like HIV. The Gaians say it's a natural eco-based reaction to overcrowding.'

'There's the job for you, then. Dig out which one, and you're rich and famous.'

She frowned. He missed so much. She'd said there were two ways in – he should have noticed that, and waited for her to explain.

'But finding causes takes time. Look at cancer. So maybe the most useful work is in getting more babies born. Improving artificial insemination. Sorting out parthenogenesis. Otherwise people may simply run out before – '

'Hang on a minute. Whatto-genesis?'

'Partheno. PTG. Cloning. Virgin birth.'

'I don't fancy that.' He turned away sharply, thought about all those babies being born without the need for any men. 'You reckon it's a starter?'

'It should be. We can do it with mice.'

'People aren't mice. I think it's disgusting.'

And so, she realized, was what she was doing. Sounding out the local peasant, the noble savage, for his opinion because she was unconvinced by the opinions of her career advisors. Little virtue could be attached to being untutored, to labelling your brother a peasant. She'd been playing games. It was worse than her father and his *dire*.

'Parthenogenesis will never be more than a stopgap, Danno. It limits the genetic pool, and in the long run that's very dangerous.'

'Yeah. Well, I still don't think it ought to be allowed.'

Their evening was over. She'd spoiled it with her games. She took a step away from him and held out her hand. 'It probably won't be. More disco?'

'Up to you.'

He didn't want to either. She shook her head. 'I'll just get hot again.'

'No stamina, that's your trouble.'

But he turned to go, taking her hand.

If they'd moved off two minutes earlier they'd have missed Brak and his friends, entering the rear of the quay from Front Street. But now –

'Hullo there, young lovers.' It was a TV catch-phrase. He stepped softly forward into the light, flanked by Skinny and Fat. No girls this time. 'Hot, innit? I mean, for the middle of the night.'

Harriet backed away, into the shadows by the rail. She didn't want to be recognised. Yesterday up in the estate hadn't happened.

Daniel assessed the three men. 'Piss off,' he said. 'When I want a weather forecast I'll ask for it.'

'An understandable response, friend. Sorry if we interrupted something. Only doing our job.'

'That's a laugh. What job's that?'

'My name's Brak. Without the "c" – b-r-a-k. We're your friendly neighbourhood watch.'

'Bloody peeping Toms, more like.'

'Like I said, friend, sorry we interrupted.'

'You interrupted nothing. And I'm not your friend.'

Harriet had relaxed, her gaze switching back and forth between them. She hadn't been recognised, she'd hardly been noticed. It was just macho nonsense. They were like dogs. Sooner or later they would both back down. She wished Danno wasn't like this, but he was.

'We ought to go home now, Danno.'

'Oh, *Danno* . . . ' Brak's imitation wasn't bad. 'Oh Danno, you've lost your chance of a quickie now, Danno. She's asking to go home. Bye-bye.'

'Shut your fucking mouth.' He was angry now, and stepped forward from the rail. Then he decided the guy wasn't worth it. 'You're right, Harriet. It's time we were off.'

He took her hand again and they moved away. Two strides. But Brak had leapt forward, on his toes in his silent, supple shoes, leaving his companions still lounging in the shadows.

'Did you say Harriet? *Harriet Ryder?*' He stopped in front of them, peering. 'Well, well, well. Harriet Ryder, and still without her trust button.'

Daniel pushed past him. 'Piss off. You deaf or something?'

Brak laid a hand on Daniel's arm. The other two had joined him. Crowded by the three of them, Daniel paused.

'We warned her, friend. There ain't no excuse. We warned her and she didn't listen.'

Daniel freed his arm. 'And I'm warning you. Just don't push it.'

Brak looked him up and down. 'Frankly, friend Danno, it's guys like you I blame. Guys like you, consorting with slags what won't take a warning when it's kindly meant. No standards, Danno. See what I mean?'

Aiming upwards, Daniel kicked him squarely in the crotch, lifting him clear of the ground. As his shoulders came forward Daniel's head caught him between the eyes. The attack was so sudden and so totally violent that for a moment Brak's companions hesitated. The moment was enough. Daniel grappled the skinny one, flung him sideways over the rail, then struck like a sledge-hammer at his face so that he toppled backwards over the rail and disappeared. The water received him, drowning his cry of pain.

84

The other guy fell on Daniel from behind, clawing desperately. Harriet had been knocked to one side in the brutal first
struggle. She retreated. Brak was down on his hands and
knees, gasping and cursing. Her brother could look after himself.

The fat guy's hands were tearing at his face, gouging for his
eyes. Ignoring the left hand, Daniel clasped the other and
lunged with it downwards. It checked at full extension, then
there was an audible click as the shoulder dislocated. The guy
screamed, struggling to free himself. Daniel released him and
stepped away. Suddenly the fat guy became very still, his face
set in agony, leaning forward slightly, protecting his shoulder
socket from movement.

Harriet backed away, appalled, flattening herself into the
shadows against a wooden cottage wall. Under the streetlamps
the quay was like a stage, the three young men on it moment-
arily in artificial, melodramatic attitudes. Lights came on in the
overhanging windows of surrounding cottages. She watched.
More must happen – the scene was unfinished.

Daniel moved first, rubbing his knuckles and turning to look
for her. Behind him Brak was crouched and easing forward, a
knife now in his hand, his face below his eyes trailing a long
dark slick of blood. Harriet didn't think to warn her brother.
The action was unreal. She was a spectator, outside it. Once
within striking distance Brak stayed at the crouch, said a single
word, something she didn't catch, enough to attract Daniel's
attention. A knife in Daniel's back would be to kill, and she
understood now that Brak would want to scar, to frighten, to
be seen, above all to be seen.

Daniel swung round to face him. Brak moved the bright
knife-blade for him to follow. It darted and flashed, leaving
brief curves like wounds in the darkness. Daniel ignored it. He
charged, silently, with complete indifference and efficiency, an
action that seemed to scorn their shared flesh and bone and
human pain. He struck at Brak with his entire power, an
astounding onslaught, far beyond mere survival. Brak fell
beneath him, aghast. His knife-hand opened. His eyes, his
mouth, his arms, his whole body opened wide in instinctive
surrender.

Windows were unlatched, and doors. People peered out,

85

murmuring. Under their gaze, and Harriet's, Daniel sat astride his victim, fingers in Brak's hair, flinging his head down with repeated and unhurried savagery against the quay's stone paving. The sound was dull and already sodden. Its insistence required Harriet to understand that the show was over: what her brother was doing was real. And on the stones a pool of real blood spread.

She walked forward. The sound continued. Brak's companion, the fat guy with the dislocated shoulder, had come through the first shock of his injury and was beating at Daniel with his one good arm, shrieking abuse. Daniel ignored him. Down at the bottom of the steps up to the quay the skinny guy was noisily pulling himself up out of the water. People emerged from their houses. Harriet squatted down, level with her brother's face. Again and again he flung Brak's head against the stones.

'Danno?' she said. 'Danno?'

He heard her. Slowly he returned from his dream. He stopped beating Brak's head against the stones, disentangled his fingers from Brak's hair, wiped them on his shirt where they left red smears which he examined. He was unsurprised. He stood up. Harriet ascertained that Brak was unconscious but still breathing, and stood up also. Brak lay face downwards, breathing. The fat guy gaped at them, his chest heaving, his eyes wild.

Daniel swung one leg over Brak's body and walked away. Harriet followed him. The people from the cottages shifted and muttered, but neither they nor Brak's two companions were inclined to interfere.

Harriet caught up with her brother as he left the quay. 'What do you want me to do? Call an ambulance?'

He shook his head. Guys like that deserved everything they got. Now he felt bone weary.

'Nah. I'll go to the police station. Tell them what happened. You too. I bet they have those guys on their list. In any case, three against one, they can hardly accuse me of starting it. The knife helps, of course. Maybe they'll give me a medal.'

He smiled at her. Suddenly she felt chilled.

'You've done this before, Danno.'

'Done what?' He didn't need an answer. 'Nah. Don't think so. Never had a reason.'

86

She didn't believe him. *Reason?* Could there ever be a reason, any reason, for what she'd seen tonight?

He walked on ahead. The guy had wanted Harri. To fuck Harri. A kid like Harri. He'd deserved everything he got.

CHAPTER FIVE

The Attrition. Year 40: late October.

That Saturday morning Mark and I had one of our rows. Fortunately Anna was doing her teenage weekend thing, staying in her bed till it rotted around her, for it was she, ostensibly, our row was about. Ostensibly. Our rows are always ostensibly about one thing while actually being about something much more/less important. The same something usually: what I see as Mark's dictatorial ways.

He'd already taken over organising publication for me: much of the previous afternoon had been spent on the computer link, negotiating with *Natur* in his execrable German, and today he was faxing off my rejected application to them as a teaser. A detailed presentation, written by me and then rewritten by him for the magazine market, could wait, he kindly told me, until the middle of the week. But by then I'd have to have a patent application ready too, for filing with the International Patent Office in Geneva.

For the breakfast moment, however, he'd turned his godlike attention to finding a Milhaus-proof haven for Anna.

I could hardly blame him for this: we'd known all along that nothing could be decided about publication until Anna was safe. The trouble was, I'd come out of my fugue. I was no longer only-a-poor-weak-woman, shocked and biddable. Discovering I had a traitor in my team at the Institute had done that for me. Six years of misplaced trust, of downright bad judgement, rankled. I hadn't decided what to do about it, but in the meantime I was in no mood to listen to Mark telling me how to protect my own daughter.

' . . . One of the *Science News* guys has a weekend houseboat down on the Haskel estuary, Harriet. It sounds ideal. It's at the end of nowhere, and – '

'So ideal that it's the first place they'll look for. Have some sense, Mark – your friends at work are the last people we can use. Their names will be lit up like Christmas trees on the Department's computer.'

We were at the breakfast table in the kitchen. The sky was clear again, a wintry white-blue, and the sun cast long early-morning shadows of the silver birches outside the window. Yvette's weekends were her own, so we had the kitchen to ourselves. This freed us: we'd given her the truth about Sergeant Milhaus's visit and the reasons for it, but the less she knew about our future plans, the better for her.

Mark was finishing the chopped egg and herring roe I hadn't wanted. 'You're talking of maybe two hundred people, Harriet. It's a big organisation, not just *Science News*, and I get around it. You're falling for the popular lie that government is omnipotent. They have their problems. The fact is, surveillance on a couple of hundred people, they haven't the resources.'

'I'm not a fool. They run spot checks. If you're prepared to risk that you're crazy.'

'All right, I'm crazy. So what do you suggest?'

'I'm not sure. Maybe I could book her in at the clinic under another name. List her in our records for an IVF. Hide her in the most obvious place, the place nobody looks.'

Mark pushed back his chair. 'And you say *I'm* crazy. Have you forgotten someone on your staff's working for the opposition? It could quite well be that skinny Bakst woman who runs the bloody clinic.'

I glared at him. I *had* forgotten. 'We don't know which opposition,' I said. 'If it's not the Minister, Annie'd be safe. It could be any of the big pharmaceuticals.'

'And you'd take a risk like that? Anchor your daughter in a bed at the mercy of that Kraut? I'd say that's plain irresponsible.'

'It's easy to criticise.' The trouble with Mark was, he had no idea of a mother's feelings. 'I seem to remember it was you who promised to keep Annie safe. Over your dead body, you said. Or words to that effect.'

'That's vile. Bringing that up . . . ' He got up, strode away to the window. 'That's absolutely vile.' He swung round. 'And anyway, what the hell's it got to do with anything?'

The phone rang. He snatched it off the wall beside him, listened briefly, then held it out. 'It's for you. One of your bloody women.'

At least it wasn't the press, starting early in the wake of the military Ms Hansen. I took it from him, inhaled deeply, counted to ten. He must have been clearly audible on the other end of the line. Thank God our last-century suburb wasn't yet wired for pictures.

'Hello? Harriet Kahn-Ryder.'

'Harrietta. Gila here.' It had to be. Only she and Magnus called me that. 'Your Mark sounds wrong side of the bed this morning.'

'We were having one of our . . . ' Her sensible outside voice was an instant febrifuge. 'We were having a discussion. Nothing important.' I raised my eyebrows at Mark and he bared his teeth in a dreadful grin. 'So, Gila – and how are you, my dear?'

'Fine . . . The thing is, Harrietta, Magnus and I are getting together a little lunch party.' Magnus, her husband, was the blond Icelander Professor Asgeirson, involved with Brandt International's MERS research program. 'Up on the Lakes – we have a sort of yacht there, you know.'

'A lunch party . . . '

'Nothing grand. Just a few friends. The Sunday forecast's good, and it'll probably be the last chance before the ice.'

'Sunday? You mean tomorrow? Ah . . . ' I started to shake my head, saw Mark nodding fiercely.

'I know it's short notice, Harrietta. But we haven't seen the three of you for ages, and Magnus said . . . '

I frowned at Mark. Party chit-chat, just then, I did not need. 'Gila, I *am* pretty busy just at the moment. I – '

'Of course you are. I told Magnus that. He came back with all those boring things about all work and no play making Jill a dull . . . '

Mark was beside me now, listening. He pulled the receiver from my ear, covered its mouthpiece. Gila could be relied on to keep going for a while yet. 'Say yes,' he hissed. 'It's too neat. It can't be a coincidence.'

I took the receiver back. Gila was still talking. I thought about what he'd said. Two days after my set-to with the Minister, a casual lunch invitation from a senior man in Brandt's research? ' . . . Gila? Gila, we'd love to. The break will do me good. Thank you very much.'

The arrangements took another ten minutes. Gila was still talking when I said goodbye and gave the phone to Mark to hang on the wall, telling me how glad Magnus would be that Mark and Anna and I could make it.

90

'We should've waited and asked Annie,' I said. 'What if she's got something on?'

'Then we'll go without her.' Mark returned to the table, gave himself a coffee refill. 'Let's face it, old buddy, it's not Annie the Asgeirsons are after. Nor me neither.'

'So why me? Even if you're right, and Magnus has heard about me and the Minister, he's hardly going to try to woo me away at this late stage.'

'You never can tell. I hear in the trade that Brandt's whole program has drawn a blank. Perhaps he's hoping to call in his marker for letting you use his primate facilities.'

'Brandt got paid, Mark. I don't owe him a thing.'

'Maybe I'm wrong. Maybe it's all just going to be a lovely afternoon out on the water.'

But he didn't believe that; neither did I. We'd known the Asgeirsons for years, from back in my days with Unikhem. They had a daughter, Jenny, who was about Anna's age, and we'd had a couple of summer holidays together down by the sea, and last Christmas we'd all gone skiing together in the Italian Alps, but months went by in between without any contact. They had their lives (Magnus was a Brandt vice-president and lived like one) and we had ours: impulsive lunches on the lakes weren't on the agenda.

I liked Gila's description of their 'sort of' yacht. We'd seen pictures: it was a magnificent twenty-five-metre catamaran, with the latest H^2 gas power-plant.

Mark was smiling to himself. I asked him what the joke was. 'I was thinking of Team Milhaus. With both you taggees out on the water in one boat they'll be having kittens. Lake Marandel's on the frontier.'

Us taggees . . . Yesterday afternoon Mark had borrowed a scanner from his office – I was sufficiently streetwise now to be unsurprised that reporters got tagged often enough to need one – and had checked me, and Anna when she got in from school. I had the two tags we'd already deduced, and Anna had one in the middle of her forehead, like a Hindu third eye. She immediately remembered a woman on the tram, in odd wrap-round sun-glasses but kindly, saying she looked pale and feeling her head for a fever. Sergeant Milhaus or one of her team.

Mark turned out to be clear. He'd worn gloves that morning, slightly ahead of the cold weather, and a muffler. In full winter, I realised, with frost masks in use, the SPU would have to do their tagging legally: house visits with the rigmarole of a magistrate's order. Poor things.

As well as scanning her for tags, we'd told Anna about the Minister, and what we planned to do and why, and what it meant for her, and then laid the choice before her. I think we did it fairly. I hope we did it fairly. But, as Mark had said, for an idealistic girl who loved and admired (heaven help me) her mother, it was no choice at all. She instantly caught the sense of what I wanted, and wanted it too.

'The frontier?' I looked at him. It was a tempting thought. 'Couldn't we – ?'

Mark shook his head. 'Even if we did, the SPU has a long arm. And could you get your research material together in time?'

I couldn't. I hadn't even started. Of course I couldn't. It was a crazy idea.

Anna came downstairs soon after, hair wet from the shower, face scrubbed and shining. She was beautiful. She'd pulled on a long wide-necked shift, and I had a sudden unspeakable mental image of Sergeant Milhaus's knife against her golden skin. I got up from the table, displacement activity, and urged her uselessly to eat a decent breakfast. Would Moma could have heard me. Patterns, patterns. At fifteen, as I had done, Anna favoured coffee, black, and a low-calorie rusk. I had survived, and so would she.

'What was all the shouting about?' she said.

I glanced at Mark. 'Shouting? We weren't shouting. We were talking about – '

'You were shouting, Moma.'

'Not at all. You mean the telephone call I had from the Asgeirsons?'

'I mean the shouting, Moma.'

'So we were shouting. That's not the end of the world.'

'I never said it was. What were you shouting about?'

Mark laughed. 'The implacability of the young . . . We were shouting, Annie, about the best place for your hide-out.'

'I'm premenstrual,' I put in. I'd suddenly realised I might be.

'Oh, you're both so stupid.' Anna joggled the coffee-pot,

testing it for a second cup, then poured. 'Why didn't you ask me? I've been thinking about it and I've had the best idea. A nunnery. One of Granna's Motherist places. Not her own, on Great-Granna's island – that would be too obvious. But she could easily organise another. And even if I was found, I'm sure they have right of sanctuary or something.'

The best idea. Yes indeed. What better place to hide a girl than in a nunnery? And she was right – houses of the Sacred Order of God the Mother *did* offer legal sanctuary. It was one of the many concessions – lesbian co-parenting rights were another – that their founder, Margarethe Osterbrook, had been able to wring from a government running scared, for the first time facing an election with an electorate in which women hugely predomin-ated. Even the Minister would think twice before sending Sergeant Milhaus into a nunnery with all guns blasting.

The matter was agreed. All that remained was for me to get Moma to fix it. That would entail a trip out to the island – telephoning was out, and the Order had no need of a secure computer link – but a visit was overdue anyway. I hadn't been to see Moma in nearly a year. I was a busy lady. I couldn't be a perfect daughter and save the world from the Syndrome too.

Apropos of which, I told Mark I had to spend the morning at the Institute, beginning to sort out my research papers. The sooner that was done, the sooner I could write my piece, the sooner we could fax it off to *Natur*, and the sooner Anna could be put out of harm's way. My impulse was to send her now, immediately, but that would signal my intentions, and even a nunnery could only be expected to remain secure for so long. I didn't underestimate the opposition: there were surely pressures they could bring to bear on Osterbrook, once – as was inevitable sooner or later – they had traced Anna to one of her Houses.

Anna asked if she could come with me to the Institute, and of course I agreed. The ova-harvesting work of the clinic fascinated her – the lab technicians knew her well – and if she wanted to help me I'd be able to find her something at the computer. With two scientist parents, she'd been born keyboard-friendly.

There was a small group of reporters – women and very junior – waiting at the bottom of the path down to the road. They asked the conventional questions – had I been asked by the Minister to resign and was I satisfied with the progress of my

Syndrome research – and took video footage as I gave the expected conventional answers. Irritation was in the air, but not at me: at unreliable ministerial leaks rather, and at the gullibility of their editors. They soon let Anna and me go.

A tram arrived and we boarded it. The morning was cold but bright, with no signs of an overnight frost. Anna was subdued. She sat by the window, staring out.

'I hate men.'

'What say?' I'd been planning my morning at the Institute, and looked up only just in time to see a magazine shop with a screamer about last Thursday's killing of Janni Wintermann. 'That's silly, Anna. Just because – '

'It's not silly. Have you ever heard of a woman serial murderer?'

I thought about it. 'Lucrezia Borgia? No – her reasons were mostly political.'

'That's what I mean. Only men have this sex and violence thing.'

I had to admit it was hard to imagine a woman killing just for kicks.

'I hate hormos too, Moma.'

'You're hating a lot this morning. I thought I was the premenstrual one.'

'I do hate them. There's a couple in my class. Growly voices. Hair on their chests. They give me the creeps.'

'That's more like it. You don't hate them – you're scared of them.'

'Isn't that the same?'

I sighed. 'Sometimes you're just too smart to live.' The tram rolled on. I turned to Anna: I had a TV program on hormos in production and my clinical curiosity was roused. 'So tell me about these hormos. Seriously – how are they managing?'

'They still sit down to pee, if that's what you mean.'

'I was thinking more about their sense of identity. Hormone treatments must be disorientating . . . How do the other girls regard them? How do they regard themselves?'

'They think they're the greatest.'

I doubted that. 'Is there any dating?'

'Any sex, you mean? Most of the other girls think they're gross. It must be pretty vile for them really.'

94

It was outside my field, but that was what I'd feared. Perhaps there should have been legislation. But if parents genuinely believed their children would gain a competitive advantage in this sad old world by some sort of testosterone-based cocktail, there'd always be doctors willing to provide it. And as a scientist I'm opposed to government intervention in areas which are basically matters for the individual conscience.

'No great glory for them in athletics either, I suppose?'

Anna shook her head. 'Not since the Olympics people hived them off. They just compete among themselves. I mean, who cares? Like I said, Moma, it's pretty vile.'

So why the hate/fear? I didn't ask that obvious question. Boring mothers have to know when to stop.

And besides, I was uneasy with hormos myself. Even *Homo super-sapiens* had trouble with the alien.

At the Institute two more reporters were waiting, stamping their feet. More video. Different questions – did I know that Unikhem were rumoured to be close to a cure and how would I feel if they pipped me – but the same unhelpful answers. And the same lack of general enthusiasm. It was a story, thank God, that was dying on the vine.

I took Anna round to the clinic. Saturdays produced a flood of donors, mostly women who could only get away at weekends. I wasn't needed in any medical sense – Karen's people knew what they were doing – but a visit from the Director went down well, made donors and staff feel appreciated. And I was on TV often enough for new donors to recognise me without heavy introductions. Anna was an asset, of course. A little of my glory rubbed off on her and she blossomed, and a little of her radiance rubbed off on me and I blossomed.

We *noblesse oblige*'d for maybe an hour, then retired to my office. I don't apologise for saying that: if people are going to have heroes I'd rather they were scientists than soldiers or pop singers. I called up a list of computer files, set Anna to printing out the relevant ones, and sat down at my desk to get my thoughts in order. Mark had established his study at home, linked electronically to everything he needed. I did my writing and thinking work here, close to the people and laboratories that gave me my raw material. And close to the stainless-steel vacuum flask on its plinth on my desk, the flask from Erzurum, and before that from the Biberian Research Centre near Tbilisi, that was our mascot.

It still contained traces of the thirty-five-year-old sludge that Mark had paid a lot of euros for. It was our lucky charm and it did a pretty good job.

I began to lay out a research sequence, weeding out the merely ornamental. I read enough German to be aware of *Natur*'s house style – it was a clever compromise, not entirely academic but much less populist than *Science News*. It didn't mind offering its readers what Mark called a wow-factor, but it liked them to work for it. I was lucky to have *Natur* interested, it was the most serious of the European non-university journals. If I couldn't go public at the World Health Organization's Paris seminar, then *Natur* was a fine second-best.

The morning passed. I was scanning a sheaf of radiation test results – a blind alley, as things had turned out, but part of the research story – when I realised it was twelve thirty, time for my daughter's lunch. Just then Gusso Polder looked round the door.

"Morning, boss.'

I'd forgotten he'd be in the building. The poor man was catching up on the RNA breakdown I hadn't got round to, on account of Dr Marton.

He nodded to Anna. "Morning, boss junior. I see you've been busy.'

She was wrestling with mounds of print-out and didn't know what to tell him – they were for my paper, which I wasn't supposed to be writing.

I improvised. 'We'll be needing data in ready-access form, once the human test program gets going.' I hurried on. 'Your RNA give you what you wanted?'

'Another bit.' He shrugged. 'To add to all the other bits . . . ' He looked at me sideways. 'Were you serious about a full-scale human test program?'

'It's got to come, Gusso.'

Anna was bent over her print-out, separating it and putting it into folders. Gusso pointed at me, then at her, and raised his eyebrows. I shook my head. My family didn't yet know I'd done the classic mad-scientist thing some weeks back and I was now my own one-woman advance test program. No one knew

96

except Gusso – he'd had to fake me the lab time and an excuse for a sample vaccine therapy from his head technician. I'd offered to sign him a waiver – obeying instructions, against his advice, all that – and he'd told me, balls. When the therapy proved effective (not if), he wanted his share of the glory.

The secrecy wasn't fair to Mark, but I particularly didn't want to make any big deal about it. Having babies is a nine-month business, and often fraught. And having male babies was something else. So I wasn't saying a word, just enjoying our sex *au naturel*, and if we clicked I'd tell him I was pregnant and that'd be great.

If the foetus turned out to be male, that too would be great. And if I carried it to full term, and if the birth went well, and if the baby was normal, that would be world-shaking. But it was a lot of *ifs*, far too many to start gabbing about.

And now, if I was premenstrual, that meant a wasted month, and a series of very difficult tests to find out if the vaccine had failed to prevent a rejection or I simply hadn't conceived.

Gusso moved on smoothly. 'The way you came out with the human program yesterday, I thought it was busy work.'

'Busy work?' How right he was. 'You ought to know me better than that.'

'I do know you better. That's why I also hate your reasons for the changed combinations too.' He looked at Anna again. 'Maybe you don't want to talk about it.'

'Maybe I don't.'

I didn't. But not on account of Anna. I saw him, his gentle, clever face, the wide-apart eyes I'd always associated with honesty. Why was I lying to him? If he was the guilty one on my team he'd have guessed the truth anyway. And if he was innocent, what harm would the truth do? And in any case, what possible motive could Dr Gustav Polder have for sneaking about with pilfered papers? What motive could any of them have?

Money? Disregarding the possibility of secret vices – I knew my people too well for that and worked them too hard for them to have energy left for such luxuries – our virologist Liesl Wronowicz was the only member of my team who might have difficulty managing on her Department salary. Like many those days, she was co-parenting – not lesbian, sharing with another woman the upbringing of her IVF daughter as if in a marriage –

and the other woman had got sick, so there were bills for her as well as for child care and education. But I couldn't imagine Liesl, eye over her shoulder, raiding my safe.

A conflicting loyalty? What to, for heaven's sake – another country? They were scientists, every one: I couldn't imagine nationalism playing much of a part in their iconography.

No, the most probable motive was blackmail. Its permutations were subtle and disgusting, and if that was the situation here, I felt for whoever it was and I didn't want to know.

But I couldn't go on not trusting them. I'd been handling this all wrong. Lies begat lies; openness begat openness.

'I'll tell you about it on Monday,' I said. 'I'll tell all on Monday.'

He came forward into the office. 'You're in trouble,' he said. 'Poor boss.'

I felt sad, this was a sad business, and he was so dear that if Anna hadn't been there to jump to all the wrong conclusions I'd have kissed him.

But she *was* there, and finished with her papers, and apparently feeling neglected, looking up at him pathetically. 'Poor me too, please sir. I'm starving. I never get decent breakfasts. My mother's always busy painting her toe-nails and eyelids and that sort of stuff.'

Gusso adjusted. He had three daughters of his own. 'It's called parents' rights, boss junior. After twenty thousand years of decent breakfasts, at last mothers can – '

Behind him a man cleared his throat and knocked on the open door. It was the NatSekur guard from Reception.

'Sergeant Milhaus for you, Dr Kahn-Ryder.' He leaned forward, lowered his voice. '*Special police . . .* '

Sudden. A nightmare. She was close beside him, in uniform today, police cap tucked smartly under one grey-blue arm. She came past the NatSekur guard and Gusso, into my office. My office.

'Morning, Dr Ryder. Sorry if I intrude. Shan't keep you long. This is entirely a routine matter.'

Her manner was pompous and crude, and I didn't believe in her routine matter. Were we going to acknowledge Thursday? Anna had retreated, joining me behind my desk.

Sergeant Milhaus smiled. She spoke to me via Gusso, looking him up and down. 'A confidential matter, Dr Ryder.'

No way. The guard had gone, presumably back to Reception. I wasn't losing Gusso too. 'Professor Polder is my right hand, Sergeant. We have no secrets.'

'Anything you say.' She had a little swagger-stick which she beat rapidly on her trouser leg as she looked round the room. She spotted the flask on my desk, then passed on and settled, predictably, on Anna and her papers. 'Your daughter's been helping you. What exactly is your daughter's security clearance?'

She was faintly ridiculous. She'd been faintly ridiculous last time, to begin with.

'You spoke of a routine matter, Sergeant Milhaus.' Saying her name made me sick. I was so angry, and so afraid for Anna, that I could scarcely breathe. Anything was possible. With Sergeant Milhaus anything was possible.

'Security, Dr Ryder. Your daughter, your papers, your office. The Minister feels as how – '

'Are you the person who killed my cat?' Anna's eyes were wide, her knuckles white on the arm of my chair. 'Are you? Are you?'

Sergeant Milhaus wouldn't be hurried. 'You're Anna. We haven't met. I'm Sergeant Milhaus.'

'We *have* met. You were wearing dark glasses and you stuck a tag on my forehead. Did you kill my cat?'

'Cat's die, Anna. If not today, then tomorrow. Cats and other animals. If not tomorrow, then today.'

'You're hateful.'

'I do my duty. Now, as I was saying . . . ' She moved across in front of Gusso to the printer unit, lifted a folder with the end of her stick. 'Your security, Dr Ryder. The Minister feels as how it could be tighter. The work here is of national importance. The Minister wouldn't want it straying.'

'My security is excellent.' If Anna could fight back, so could I. 'But that's not what you're here for. That's only an excuse. Professor Polder is my witness. You're here to threaten and intimidate me.'

She didn't argue. Couldn't be bothered. 'This is the age of bio-engineered surveillance – microphones, cameras the size of an insect's eye. You should have this room swept.'

Gusso came forward. 'May I see your warrant card, Sergeant? Or is that bio-engineered too, and insect-sized? And your police

99

number? It's only fair to say I intend to lodge a complaint with your superiors.'

I felt better. He was so sarcastic and so formal. Sergeant Milhaus gave him her card, waited while he made notes on a pad from my desk, then took it back.

'Cameras the size of an insect's eye. Microphones too. All the offices should be swept.'

Between the windows there was a picture in a chromium frame, a wide stylish black-and-white photograph of the midnight sun behind fir trees. Sergeant Milhaus inserted the end of her stick, lifted it away from the wall, and peered behind it. She went on lifting it away from the wall until its fastening came free and it fell on to the low slate table beneath it, and from there to the floor. The glass smashed noisily into long daggers on the corner of the table, and these daggers smashed again as they scattered across the tiles. The wall where the picture had hung was clean and very smooth. Not even a camera like an insect's eye.

Sergeant Milhaus didn't mind. Didn't seriously look. She was here to break things. To break me.

'Cameras are often hid behind pictures.' She looked out of the window, at the tranquil stone garden. 'Directional mikes could catch every word spoke in here from the surface of this glass. The Minister's concerned.'

She went briskly to the open door, paused in it, turned. I expected her to tell me where to send the bill for the broken glass.

'I'm a servant of the state, Dr Ryder. So are you. We do what we can, don't we?'

I hadn't corrected her over my name so far today and I didn't now. I waited for her to go. Replacing her police cap on her head, she went. She didn't hang about. She was good at going, good at everything she did.

Beside me Anna was crying. Gusso lowered himself into a chair.

'You *are* in trouble, boss,' he said. '*Vraiment.*'

I rang the Minister. Saturday lunch-time and I rang the Minister. I had to get Sergeant Milhaus off my back. Gusso took Anna up to the canteen and I rang the Minister. She wasn't out to lunch, she was away in Rome, and I got Oswald Marton instead. Men like him worked lunch-times and Saturdays. To keep down women they worked every day there was.

'What do I have to do,' I said, 'to convince you that I'm not going to try to publish?'

He wasn't slow. 'You've had a visit from the SPU.'

'I've had two. Today the officer broke a valuable picture. On Thursday she killed my cat.'

'That's a serious accusation. Do you have witnesses?'

'To the picture, yes.'

'It's unfortunate, but pictures do get broken. I meant, witnesses to the cat.'

'That was unfortunate too.'

'I'm sure it was. But if you don't have a witness – '

'Dr Marton, what do I have to do to convince you that I'm not going to try to publish?'

'I'll see if I can get the SPU to keep their distance.'

'You mean there's nothing I can do?'

'Look at it from our end, Dr Kahn-Ryder. You're tagged and your phonecard's referrable. But we can't reach your husband's computer.'

'What happened to trust, Dr Marton?'

'I like you, Dr Kahn-Ryder. I'm not going to answer that.'

'Would the SPU really harm my daughter?'

'What a preposterous notion.'

'Goodbye, Dr Marton.'

'Goodbye, Dr Kahn-Ryder. And enjoy tomorrow's boat trip. Mrs Asgeirson's spreads come highly recommended.'

Of course the SPU would harm my daughter. Myself I would risk. Perhaps even Mark. But never Annie . . .

For their Sunday yacht party on the Lakes the Asgeirsons had put together an interesting and prestigious group of people. I was surprised that Dr Marton, showing off, hadn't given me the guest list over the phone the previous afternoon. It was so prestigious that it seemed to prove the last-minute nature of our inclusion. Personally, I was outside the important world of art and politics that Magnus, with his age and wealth and gender, made a good shot at living in. Mark's writing had brought him respect within the profession, and an international following, but he was nowhere near the league of, for example, the controversial young French novelist Paulette Something in horizontal blue-and-white woollen stripes on the foredeck, or of the Arts Minister's aide, Helga Chavas, who had clearly been at the imported Brennevin for hours before we were introduced.

I'm sorry. I was feeling bitchy then, and the feeling's still around. But I was there under protest, doing Mark's bidding. Magnus was an old friend, but he was too much an establishment figure, and too high in Brandt International, ever to help me evade the Security Protocol, and mere curiosity about the connection between his invitation and my failed application seemed poor reason for accepting. Particularly since there were things I'd rather be doing.

Typically, the Asgeirsons were lucky with their day. The fine weather held, the temperature climbed a little, and as we walked down the pontoon at the lakeside Knolle marina brilliant kingfishers flashed by low above the water, hunting the last of summer's midges. Anna led the way. She'd come because she liked Jenny Asgeirson, they were ski rivals, and because the Sunday alternatives were homework or tidying her room. I'd encouraged her because I wanted to take her mind off Sergeant Milhaus. The rest of yesterday afternoon had been difficult. Gusso did what he could, but the woman's coldness had bitten into Anna's bones.

'Annie, Harrietta, Mark – how good to see you.' Magnus spread his big arms at the head of the gangplank, his usual welcoming self, in his usual ragbag of clothes. Today he wore running-shoes, loden trousers, a quilted parka and, in honour of the occasion, a last-century yachting-cap. If this gives the impression he was phoney, that's wrong. He was cultivated, an able scientist, a comfortable family man, and he didn't care a damn for appearances.

'Come aboard. Gila's below somewhere, slicing cheese, I think. Jenny's down in the saloon, playing some ridiculous board game with Chuck. There's only Michael to arrive, and then we'll be off.'

We knew Michael well. He was an old friend, the archaeologist husband of my Natalya. Without the two of them there'd have been no Dr Fateya, no Erzurum, no vaccine. Natya'd been invited, but was pleading work. Housework, I thought, for

102

there was little doing at the Institute. Chuck, we discovered, was an elderly visiting stage director, American of course, at the State Opera.

Magnus introduced us round, then settled us up in the wheelhouse with drinks and Helga Chavas's girlfriend. I felt sorry for her. Even in those days being a homosexual spouse was somehow a still smaller identity than being a hetero wife or husband. Annie went below to find Chuck and Jenny. Gila passed her on the companion-way, bringing plates of smoked cheese and crispbread. Then Michael arrived and we were off.

Knolle was on the smallest of the lakes. Within half an hour we were through the rocky channel at the far end and out into the big water. The day was perfect. What little wind there was came from astern, and the Asgeirsons' cat ran in virtual silence, as smoothly as if on silk. She was a graceful craft, in traditional white fibreglass with imported Huon-pine fittings: a panelled deck saloon flowed back elegantly into the all-weather wheelhouse, and raked masts hung with colourful club ensigns gave her a stylish, old-fashioned air. We travelled up the centre of Lake Marandel, the tree-lined shores on either side no more than distant blue-green blurs, the mountains ahead reflected with startling exactness in the glassy water. For a while we were the only movement, the only twenty-first-century intrusion in the whole vast panorama. Then a covey of little boats with tall white sails appeared round a headland, dipping prettily in the breeze.

When Gila went below and started serving lunch, I followed her. Women's work. Even if the Attrition continued, men and women would be role-playing up to the bitter end. Roles were nice. They gave shape to the shapeless. Shades of Helga Chavas's girlfriend, identity to the unidentified.

The food, as Dr Marton had promised, was excellent. We ate up in the deck saloon, evicting Chuck and the girls and their board game, and people served themselves. Conversation was desultory. I think we were dazed by the beauty and, if not by the warmth, then by the lack of cold. In a country with so long a winter as ours we cling to the mind-set of summer. So we sat outside in our woollens and parkas on the Asgeirsons' fore-deck, and ate the Asgeirsons' wonderful food, and drank the Asgeirsons' wonderful wine, and watched the lake go by.

And, in my case, ceased to remember Sergeant Milhaus, Dr Marton, and the Minister. I hope the others, if they needed them, had similar remissions.

Someone, our young French novelist I think, mentioned the coming election. Helga Chavas's girlfriend said that Helga Chavas would be standing, and was sure to succeed, and got glared at for her pains. Since we had no pundit, Chuck chipped in: he had a charming accent and he told us that in his country there was a disappointing sameness to politics even after forty years of the Attrition. The US Congress was seventy per cent female, but really all that had changed was the pitch of the voices.

Our archaeologist suggested that this was inevitable: gaining power within the democratic process required masculine qualities of ruthlessness and personal ambition (nobody, interestingly, questioned this classification), so obviously the women who made it work for them would be ruthless and ambitious.

We motored on up the lake. At the far end the frontier was marked by narrows, spanned by a swing-bridge and a village of bright-painted houses, and beyond them the water opened out again, with eroded sandstone cliffs on the shoreline.

As the only journalist present, Mark felt obliged to point out that Michael Volkov's view was a simplification. It wasn't the democratic process that required those masculine qualities, it was the men who still ran the democratic process.

Helga Chavas, defensively, thought it wasn't so much the men who were responsible – they were such a minority – as the male world-view. Habits of thought, women's as well as men's, were hard to change. She recognised this in herself. Time was needed.

It was great electioneering, nobody wrong, everybody right, and herself rightest of all, but no one applauded. Ungenerously, Chuck wanted to know how much time. Someone in his own country had calculated that the longer the Attrition lasted, the less likely the US was to elect a woman president. He could imagine a situation in which only one man remained alive in the United States, a janitor one hundred and ten years old and senile, with flat feet and halitosis, and he'd be elected by a landslide. And they'd change the Constitution to give him a third term if – the Lord be praised – he lived that long.

Magnus protested, and Mark joined him. Politics didn't only belong to politicians. He quoted the recent upset in the Philippines. The US President, ignoring his Congress and Senate, had committed American troops to a shooting war in defence of US interests. A million women went to Washington. They didn't do anything. There were agitators and they squashed them. They didn't do anything. A million women. The President changed his mind. The silence was killing him.

It was nearly three o'clock, and the end of the lake was to be our turn-around. Mark nudged me unobtrusively and pointed: two high-speed police launches were idling along, patrolling the swing bridge at the entrance to the narrows. Their bows were reinforced for ramming and they had missile launchers on their foredecks. I wished he hadn't shown me. I'd been ceasing to remember: now my tags burned on neck and hand, playing the national anthem and giving off sparks.

'I expect it's a regular patrol,' he murmured. 'The drug trade would love a place like this.'

I nodded. Any other thought was paranoia. Young drug baronnes, though less violent than their male predecessors, were just as active. According to Mark, whose job brought him police contacts, they ruled their empires with a fair wage rather than guns: everyone, down to the humblest street hack, was properly paid, and they offered a career structure . . . But *two* patrol boats, in broad daylight, guarding one exit point? Well, Sunday afternoon, in broad daylight, with visibility for ever, maybe they got together for the company.

The conversation rambled on. Gila Asgeirson wondered if hormos would prove more electable. Michael thought not. They were playing the after-lunch game. Even if I could have told them about my cure for the Syndrome, I wouldn't have. Not then, there on Magnus's yacht on Lake Marandel.

I wasn't ready. Wondering why, I realised what a moment that would be. The end of my life. Beyond it, chaos. Beyond it, fame I didn't want, money I didn't need, pressures that could destroy me.

I got up quietly and went aft, leaned on the stern rail. I was galloping towards publication because I was afraid of it. Publication now, at any cost: the excuses for delay were beguiling and I was my mother's daughter. Moma was a stern lady: not for her *a little of what you fancy does you good*. I dreaded publication, the media hype, the carping from my fellows, the world saved for humankind, the end of my life. Like the Minister, as Natalya had said, I did not know, or did not care, what every month more meant to village women. As I had all along, I thought only of me. Publication now. Nasty medicine was good for you.

Magnus turned the boat. From the foredeck the murmur of voices continued. Rugs were distributed. Already the sun was low and the snow on the mountains above the end of the lake was golden in its light. Mist was rising from the water. By the time we reached Knolle, night would have fallen.

The police launches faded behind us. Magnus set our course, then wandered aft and leaned beside me. Aha. My spine prickled. There was a reason for my last-minute inclusion on this trip, and its time had come.

My spine was right. Magnus yawned too casually.

'How's the work going?'

'Can't complain. How about you?'

'I complain all the time.' He laughed.

Below us the water chinked and muttered as the engine drove us forward. Magnus raised his eyes. He was a big man, broad, his wild blond hair greying, with the Icelander's open, raw-boned face.

'What a view,' he said.

I looked at it.

'You warm enough, Harrietta?'

'Fine.'

I wasn't going to help him. He recognised this, took several deep, appreciative breaths of the pine-scented evening air.

'I'm glad you were able to come with us on this trip, Harrietta. I wanted to talk to you.'

'I know.'

He wasn't going to apologise. We knew each other too well for that.

'There are rumours, serious rumours, that you've made a breakthrough at the Institute.'

'Aren't there always?'

'The thing is, Harrietta, you'll be in need of a manufacturing base . . . You've worked with us – you may not always have agreed with what we were doing but I don't have to sell you Brandt's facilities.'

That was a nice way of putting it. At one time I'd virtually closed down their primate operation with my TV campaigning.

'I still don't like what you're doing with your dolphins, Magnus.'

'It's a difficult area. I'm sure we could meet you.'

'I'd hold you to that.' If I'd been brought all this way for a sales pitch I might as well make the most of it. At Brandt's Windstrohm outfit I'd heard there were dolphins strung up on PTG research that broke your heart.

'In the field of culturing micro-organisms, Harrietta, I'd say we're unbeatable. Submicros too. Parasitics. Which are what I gather you'll be looking for.' He leaned towards me, lowered his voice. 'We've built a new block. Up in the hills. Self-supporting environment. Guaranteed security.'

'I heard you were having staffing problems.'

'Not up there, Harrietta. Only low-grade and only in the PTG centres. Can't get lab technicians for weekend shifts at places like Windstrohm, specially nights when the scientists go home and they're on their own. Frankly I can't blame them – these bombings just don't stop.' He gripped my arm. 'But that's nothing to do with our new complex. Outstanding facilities. Excellent personnel relations. Running like a dream. Twenty-second-century stuff. Parasitics are only the beginning. If you can think of it, Harrietta, we can do it.'

I let him run down. He was trying hard. Another minute and he'd get out the company brochure. The evening was too beautiful for this. Magnus was too nice.

Was he? Could he be? His job title these days was Vice-President Marketing. Could a Vice-President Marketing be *nice*? And how the hell did he know I was using parasitics?

'Rumours, Magnus? What are these rumours? Where did they come from?'

'You said it yourself, Harrietta. There are always rumours.'

'No, Magnus. I'm sorry, but no. When I hired out your primate facilities you maybe deduced a lot, but not that much. What made you come up with parasitics? I'm not even sure what you think it means.'

'It's true, then? Engineered parasitics? You've broken it?'

He knew a lot. Brandt was where the leak from the Institute must be going.

'Nothing's true until the order's in your book, Magnus. You know that. There's a long road ahead. Field tests, ministerial approval, competitive tender, Act of Parliament for all I know . . . I won't be going bulk for months. Years.'

'But when you do?'

I looked down at the water again. As a foretaste of my post-publication life this was nothing.

He prompted me. 'You'll need a reasonable level of production for field tests,' he said. 'If it looked good, and I put it to the board, we'd carry you on that.'

Which only showed how badly their own line of research was going.

I made up my mind. He *was* a nice man, a Vice-President Marketing could be, and I'd've gone to Brandt anyway.

'A deal, Magnus. You tell me where this serious rumour of yours comes from, and I'll promise you first sight of the spec. When we have one. Always assuming the Minister doesn't have ideas of her own.'

For all its caveats this was the greatest business opportunity in the history of capitalism, and he knew I'd keep my word. Two people leaning in the dusk on a yacht's stern rail. As easy as that. Wealth beyond the dreams of avarice, I think the phrase is.

Magnus didn't hesitate. 'We have a friend on the Unikhem board,' he said. 'A contact . . . ' He cleared his throat and shrugged. 'A spy. And the word is, your security's down and they're getting information. Intermittent, but it's coming in.'

'Unikhem? Not you? Are you sure?'

'Would I be here now if it was us? Why not wait until I had enough to give to my own research people?'

A nice man. Also a realist.

'Then it's incomplete so far?' He nodded. Thank God for that. 'What's missing?'

'It's hard to say. These are general board meetings and our contact is a money man, not a scientist. They discuss the nature of your work, nothing specific.'

And now, thanks to Oswald Marton, damn him, the leak was stopped. Otherwise, the coming weeks before the Paris seminar could easily have let Unikhem in first. I thought of the people I'd quarrelled with at Unikhem before I left: it made sense that one of them should go all out to get me.

I asked Magnus, 'How long have you known this?'

'Too long. Several weeks. I'd have spoken to you before but some guys in my department wanted to wait and see.'

'Dangerous. If Unikhem got the whole picture, then your only hope would be to act on it first.'

'That's what I said, Harrietta. It was safer to cut off their source, then try for a deal. That's why I'm here.'

I laughed aloud. He wasn't here to warn me, one scientist to another. Such an honest man. He was here to do a deal.

I straightened, took his arm. 'Thanks for the tip, Magnus. And thanks for a wonderful afternoon.'

As we went forward along the side of the wheelhouse the wind caught us, now chilly, coming from straight ahead. The party on the foredeck was breaking up, gathering their blankets and making for the shelter of the saloon. Mark was among them. He caught my eye interrogatively and I nodded. He'd been right to insist we come. I had the destination for the leak at the Institute, and evidence that I'd stopped it in time. And, as a bonus, I'd had a delightful time out on the water.

I squeezed Magnus's arm. Wonderful boat, wonderful food, wonderful wine. He was a dear good man. Gusso too, and Mark and Dr Hannes and Chuck and Michael . . . they were all dear good men. And Daniel, on his better days. Perhaps that was what had made up my mind for me all those years ago, in our little house by the Windstrohm River: the discovery, sitting on Dada's knee, that I did like men.

CHAPTER SIX

The Attrition. Year 23: late July.

Leaning against the wall at the back of the sunlit lecture hall, Daniel yawned, and glanced unobtrusively at the clock above the platform. Eleven thirty. The two-hour presentation had another thirty minutes to run. As if two hours, or four or forty, would prepare these girls for the realities of life in a Muslim sheikhdom. He knew. He'd spoken to NCOs who'd been there. Thank God he was Military Police now and didn't have to worry about foreign postings. They needed all the MPs they could get, here at home. The wisest move he ever made.

He'd been getting nowhere – coming up five years and he was still a fucking squaddie. The company commander'd never liked him. A poncy, egghead git, he'd blocked his applications for course after course, and rigged the results on those he did go on. Made him out like some sort of half-wit. He'd been heading down the tube, only his long service to keep him from mucking in with the girls. And he'd have been on this Gulf draft sure as shit.

Now, an MP for only six months, he'd put a stripe up and was staying at home, permanent staff at training HQ. The blue capband had given him back his pride. MPs were a breed apart: they belonged to the old army, when it was a place for men, tarts barely tolerated. There were MP tarts now, a load of fucking lezzies, but they recognised a shine on a pair of boots when they saw one, and a regimental haircut, and a bearing that looked the world in the eye, no fucking about.

Training HQ was in a city a couple of hundred k's north of the capital. It was ancient and classy and he liked it. He wasn't all a boots-and-gaiters man. Growing up with Dada and Harri, there was room in his life for cobbled streets and fancy architecture, and the occasional concert if it wasn't too heavy. And Harri was off at State College in the capital now, which wasn't far. He'd been up on the train to see how she was getting on. College, for fuck's sake – but she was still the same Harri.

She'd got rooms with another girl, Liese, in a tall house close by the castle. Liese liked being the boss, which was what Harri needed. No late nights, and meals properly cooked. Moma had been up too, a couple of times, and she'd taken to Liese – the stupid bloody woman'd left her a stack of her God-the-Mother books. Liese wasn't Daniel's type, but few tarts were. He reckoned he was picky.

He straightened his back, heaving himself away from the wall. In spite of the air-conditioning his shirt had stuck to his shoulder-blades where he'd been leaning. That was the one thing wrong with this place: the city was in a valley and it could be fucking hot. Bad for UV too. He fanned himself with his cap. The lecturer's voice droned on. Not a quarter as hot as the place these poor bloody girls were going to. The army was hiring them out to one of the oil companies, them and a lot more like them, as protection for the Muslim tarts working its oil wells. Their menfolk, thin on the ground now, couldn't make the grade and they didn't like it. And they'd rather score own goals shooting up the buses bringing in the tarts than just get on with getting out the oil. Daniel couldn't see it. If women could do the job, then let them. It was happening all over the world.

Still, as far as the army was concerned, this Muslim thing was good for business. It paid for a lot of hi-tech gadgets no taxpayer would sanction. Their concerns were shrinking population and recession. And the Syndrome. His sister'd have to hurry if she was to get to it.

The telephone rang on the table behind the lecturer. He broke off, pointer poised, apologised to his audience, and moved back to answer it. He was a civilian, an Arabist who'd come in white desert robes and keffiyeh head-dress, to help the girls get used to the idea. Ninety-five minutes into his presentation a lot of them still hadn't. They shifted in their seats, giggling behind their hands. Daniel shuffled his metal-studded boots and cleared his throat warningly. The giggling died.

Looking up from his telephone, the lecturer asked, 'Is there a Corporal Ryder present?'

Daniel sprang to attention. 'Sah.'

The lecturer peered at him, spoke quietly to his caller, replaced the receiver. 'You're wanted in Company Office, Corporal. There's an outside call for you. I gather it's rather important.'

Daniel frowned. 'By rights I'm here till midday, sah.'

'I've told Provost-Sergeant Breitholmer you're on your way, Corporal.'

Daniel left the hall. He hoped the man knew what he was doing. A civilian, trying to control seventy-eight army tarts on his own – it didn't bear thinking about.

He jammed on his cap and proceeded at the double, down the path past the officers' mess and across the parade ground. By the time he reached Company Office he was sweating. He paused to check his turn-out in the mirror by the door, straightened his lanyard, and marched in.

A girl private second class was at the desk. He kept his breathing steady. 'Lance-Corporal Ryder, miss.'

She smiled and pointed to one of the small interview rooms. 'I'll put you through. It was your mother, Corporal. We said we'd call her back.'

He removed his cap, crunched it anxiously. 'Any idea what's up?'

'A family matter. She didn't say what.'

He nodded, went into the room, closed the door, sat down at the table. It didn't look good. Bloody woman. A room to himself – ten-to-one the girl knew and wasn't saying. Outside on the parade ground the guard was assembling for the midday salute. The single window was high up and small, but it was open and through it Daniel could hear the men muttering together and stamping their feet. He wished them luck – today's orderly officer was a right bastard.

He waited, palms flat on the table. The telephone rang. He picked it up.

'Moma?'

'Daniel? It's your bloody father, Daniel. It's your bloody rotten lousy father.'

'Harriet? It's your bloody father, Harri. It's your bloody rotten lousy father.'

Harriet stared at the yellow jasmine in blossom on the wall outside Karl's window. 'I don't like you saying that, Moma. You know I don't.'

'You always stick up for him. See if you can stick up for him now.'

'What's he done?'

'What's he done? He's bloody killed himself. That's what he's done.'

Harriet closed her eyes. What could she say? She believed her mother instantly.

'He's made a mess of it too. Stole a jar of stuff from Brandt and went up in the woods above the river. But he got something wrong and burned his rotten lousy throat out.'

Harriet leaned her forehead against the cool glass of the window. 'I'll come at once, Moma.'

'They've only just found him. I've told Daniel. Your father was on night shift, signed off the same as always. Quiet, the man says, but that's nothing out of the ordinary. But he didn't come home. I was sick with worry.'

'I said I'll come at once, Moma.'

'They've only just found him. Nasty. Looks like the stuff never reached his stomach. I've told Daniel. They say he'd've been a while dying.'

'I'll be there as soon as I can, Moma. Danno's coming?'

'What d'you think? You know your brother. Nice excuse for a bit of free leave. Compassionate, they call it. That's a laugh.'

Harriet screwed her eyes up tighter. *Shut up, shut up, shut up . . . Take out your guilt and your grief on someone else, you cow!* She relaxed. *No. Take it out on me. Danno'll have had his share. Who else is there? Gran? No, take it out on me.*

'See you this evening, Moma. Around six, probably. Depends on the trains.'

'A woman walking her dog found him. Threw up all over her shoes. And he'd left a cheque for her. No letter for me, just a cheque. In an envelope: "To cheer up whoever finds my body." Dear God. Not much, but I reckon she's earned it.'

'I'll be on my way, then.'

'I haven't seen her yet but I've talked to her and she says it isn't pretty. Trust Johan to make a rotten lousy mess of it.'

'It's just after twelve, Moma. I'll get over to the station soon as I can. Pecker up, Moma. 'Bye.'

'I'll get a woman to come down from the Church to take the funeral. Our founder, if she's free. That's Margarethe Osterbrook. And don't tell me it's not what he'd've wanted. He's out of it, the bloody bastard.'

'Mum, I've got to go. I'm putting the phone down now. 'Bye.'

'The local vicar won't mind. She lets all sorts use her premises. Ecumenical, the word is. Not that she's got a congregation of her own worth spitting at, from what I hear.'

'That's right, Moma. You talk to her. I'll see you at six. 'Bye.'

She dumped the receiver, turned from the window. The books on Karl's cool white shelves were still in their places. His pictures looked out at her calmly. His pen was still on his scratch pad in front of his keyboard on his desk. Nothing had changed. The antique longcase clock still ticked by the door.

Parents went on for ever. How old had Dada been? Twenty-four years older than she. Forty-three. *Forty-three . . .*

Why?

She knew why.

She sat down, instantly got up again. She had to leave for the station. Throw some things into a bag. Thank God she was getting her phone calls transferred over from Liese at the Haldanes'. Otherwise, God knows when she'd have heard. Karl. She must contact Karl. Perhaps he'd come with her. She couldn't go alone. He had to come with her.

How long would they be away? Who would feed Gnasher? She must contact Liese, get her to catsit. Liese didn't much like him, but that was tough luck. Love me, love my cat.

What else? She had to call Danno. No. Getting through to him at the base took for ever, and he'd already have left. So what else?

Black. Moma would expect her to wear black. What had she got? Something conventional. The Church of God the Mother was very conventional.

She realised she hadn't moved from the chair by the window. She forced herself forward into the room where nothing had changed, taking her change with her. They called it a death in the family. She stooped over Karl's desk and picked up his telephone. She called Admin, asked them to page him, and waited, staring at the telephone.

What if he didn't call in and she had to go without him? She found his pen, wrote on his scratch-pad, *Darling Karl . . .* Where was he? His lecture that morning ended at eleven. Even with questions he should be back. *Darling Karl, I have to go home. There's been a death in the family.* She couldn't write that. Shit. She ripped the sheet off, crumpled it, tried again. *Darling Karl, I have to go home to my mother. Dada's killed himself and –*

Her writing-muscles fused. Her writing-muscles in her fingers and in her head. She picked up the scratch-pad and wandered round Karl's study with it, looking for places to put it where he wouldn't miss it. Finally she brought it back to his desk.

She read it. '*Dada's killed himself.*' She'd written '*my mother*'. Shouldn't she have written '*my father*'? No, it wasn't unfair. It was because of her mother, of the row there'd have been, that she'd never told Dada about Karl, and suddenly his not knowing was the most terrible thing. The most terrible thing, dead now and not knowing that his daughter was in love with her beautiful black professor, and he with her. Another guilt to add to her mother's list, to the list her mother didn't know she had.

It wouldn't have altered anything, of course. She'd already been so happy and he'd known it – so lucky, at the college of her dreams, the best student of her year, on the course of her dreams – that the extra happiness Karl brought, the extra luck, wouldn't have made any difference. She'd known of his sadness, but refused the responsibility. She refused it still. He was older than she, a big grown-up man. Parents were not their children's responsibility. He had committed suicide because nobody needed him and he didn't need himself. Poor Dada.

No. That was yesterday. Today it was *poor Moma*. And *poor Danno*. Perhaps it was *poor Danno* most of all. Dada was dead and, Dada was dead and, Dada was dead and . . . The clock by the door struck half-past twelve. And what?

She didn't know. Except that she had to go into the bedroom and throw some things into a bag.

Karl called in at twelve forty-five.

'Honey, I was gloved-up in the lab. What goes?'

She ran her fingers through her hair. 'Lab? You weren't supposed to be in the lab. You had a lecture. You shouldn't have been in the lab.'

'You're in some tension, honey. I had that DNA thing to follow up on. You forgot. People do. Tell Karl now – what's winding you up?'

His voice was smooth. It mended her. 'My father's killed himself.' She could say it. 'I have to go home. Will you come with me?'

'Killed himself? What a terrible thing.'

115

'It is. Will you come with me?'

'Your poor mother. You too. Has someone told your brother?'

'Moma did. She rang him first. Will you come with me?'

'I'm trying to think, honey. There'll be a funeral?'

'Moma's fixing it. I didn't ask when.'

'Of course not. When're you leaving?'

'Now. As soon as I can. Will you come with me?'

'What time's the train?'

'I really don't know. They leave every hour.' She listened to the silence. Karl was thinking, and she realised she was making things very difficult for him. 'You can't come. What could you tell your students? It could be days.'

'I don't have to tell them anything. This is an emergency.'

'And then there's the Dean. No Karl – I shouldn't have asked.'

'You should, you should. This is us, honey. This is what we're about.'

'No Karl – you have an entire summer school depending on you. I can quite well manage.'

'Of course you can. But I want to come.'

'You can't. I shouldn't have asked.'

'Well . . . '

'I'll call you when I get there.'

'Losing your father's a terrible thing. Don't underestimate it.'

'I must go, Karl.'

'Maybe I should tell you goodbye at the station.'

'Station goodbyes are horrible.'

'You're right.'

'I'll call you when I get there.'

'I insist. And I'll be with you all the time. Right?'

'Right.'

'Love you, honey.'

'Me, too.'

She rang off. She wasn't stupid. He hadn't wanted to come and she didn't blame him. She herself was only going because of Moma, and he hadn't ever met her.

She phoned Liese before she left, but she wasn't answering. Harriet wouldn't have been home that morning either if she hadn't decided to skip a genetics workshop and write up her notes. Gnasher wasn't around – a shady bed of catmint down the road claimed him in the hot weather – so she left his food out on Karl's terrace. Then she took a tram to the station.

There was a diversion. Some anti-parthenogenesis group had flung a bomb through a window of the research centre in the middle of town. It hadn't exploded, but the area was cordoned off while NatSekur dealt with it. The police no longer handled bombs. There was a lot of feeling against cloning, against what the gutter press called virgin births.

In spite of the delay Harriet caught the one-thirty train.

Beyond the city outskirts the fields of the central plain were dusty, bleaching under the midsummer sun. This was the third hot summer in a row. Hot summers and scourging winters. People talked about sunspots, the ozone layer, changes in the jetstream. Harriet's interests were microbiological. She had no opinion.

As the train rolled south towards the coast she had a sudden thought: her father was dead and she hadn't wept. The books said weeping was a healthy reaction. Therapeutic. She decided to wait for the funeral. It sounded as if her mother was going to have Dada buried. Even with Margarethe Osterbrook and the Church of God the Mother, Harriet decided to rely on the funeral to crack a tear or two. That was what funerals were for.

She changed at the junction, caught the shuttle down the steep Windstrohm Valley. The tide was out, the mudbanks steamed in the heat. As the shuttle passed Brandt International Harriet gazed steadfastly out at the river, away from the dark loom of the forest above Brandt's spiky roof-tops. Not that he'd still be there.

Her bag was light, she hadn't been able to find anything black, and she swung it easily as she strode past the New Century Café. She'd told her mother she'd be there by six. She was there by ten to.

Daniel had beaten her to it. When she opened the front door she could hear Moma and him quarrelling down in the kitchen. She went downstairs, dumped her bag noisily in her bedroom across the passage before she joined them. They'd heard her. Danno was leaning quietly by the window, looking out, and Moma was putting things away from the dishwasher, clashing them and banging cupboard doors. She looked terrible, a dead cigarette, bent and soggy, hanging from her bottom lip. Danno was dressed in civilian slacks and T-shirt: he hadn't worn his uniform home since his very first leave. Some things he learned.

Moma went on clashing. 'Harriet. Thank God you're here, child. Someone sensible at last. You must tell me what to do. They're trying to wriggle out of your father's pension.'

Shit. 'Not now, Moma. We'll talk about it later.' Danno's back was still turned. He hadn't moved. 'Hullo, Danno. Hi there.'

'Hullo, Harri.'

He didn't look round. He was weeping. On her and Moma's behalf. It was a therapeutic reaction.

She heard herself. Christ, what a family they were. What a family she was, what a sister, daughter. She crossed the shadowed room, leaned beside Daniel, put her arm round his shoulders. He gripped her hand painfully.

'He's out of it now,' she whispered. Daniel didn't answer. His whole body shook.

'Why talk about it later, child? Why not now? Don't you go starry-eyed on me, too, Harriet. These things are important.'

'Of course they are, Moma. I just meant – '

'Life goes on, Harri. Or is that too ordinary a thought for you?'

She squeezed Daniel's shoulders, reached round awkwardly to kiss his cheek. Then she turned back into the room.

'About Dada's insurance.' Moma too had her needs. 'Brandt may wriggle but I'm sure they'll cough up. They're hot on the caring face of capitalism these days. It wouldn't do that much good, beggaring a poor innocent widow woman . . . '

Daniel couldn't bear it. He hunched his shoulders as their talk went on. *A poor innocent widow woman* – sweet weeping Jesus, she was dancing on Dada's grave.

He looked out at the harbour. How could all this end? The little boats down on the water leapt up at him, each one bright and precise. The houses on the far side were so close he could touch them. This was real. Death wasn't real. Dada couldn't end. It made no sense.

She was dancing on his grave – phoning Gran, phoning the vicar, phoning Brandt, phoning a lawyer, phoning for flowers, phoning about the funeral, phoning the hospital, phoning the police, phoning the local newspaper. Somehow he got through the rest of the evening. Harriet produced a meal from the freezer. She went to the Pelikan for his beer. They ate together at the kitchen table, food like sawdust, beer like piss. He couldn't face it. He wanted TV but Harri shook her head, glancing sideways at their mother.

The provost-sergeant had given him a week's compassionate leave, saying his mother would need his support at this difficult time. Standing to attention in Company Office, Daniel had believed him. But distance, as he'd read somewhere, lent enchantment. He'd be leaving straight after the funeral.

His mother had fixed the funeral for eleven tomorrow morning. There wasn't a great clan of relatives and friends to gather, only Mrs Hand from next door, who'd been with his mother when he arrived, and Gran who was already on her way. And someone from his mother's stupid church to take the service. Soon as that was over he'd be off.

He persevered with the beer, found it grew on him. By bedtime he was gone. Harriet helped him up the stairs to his room. He felt bad about that – Harri'd lost her Dada too, and she was only a kid.

In the morning, when he woke up, his father was still dead.

Gran arrived from her island soon after breakfast. She'd been travelling all night but she took charge of the three of them, even Harri who'd started the day clapped-out, hardly able to open her eyes. Gran had Daniel rearranging the sitting-room, and his mother and Harri making salad and seafood dips in case anyone came home with them after the service. She cancelled the motor hearse. Dada's body was up at the hospital, on the rise above the cemetery, so they could use the old hand-wagon on its high thin wooden wheels. Gran was from the city, but she was old-fashioned: if there was a traditional village way of doing things she'd choose it.

Daniel knew he'd have to steer the wagon and probably do most of the pushing, but he didn't protest. Gran didn't put his back up the way his mother did. He hadn't seen her since joining the army and he remembered her as a lot older. The first thing she did when she arrived was tell him how sorry she was, and how sad it was that his father didn't have any family to be at his funeral, and then she asked him if he knew his father's wishes. When he said that as far as he knew his father hadn't had any wishes she glared at his mother as if she wasn't surprised. He reckoned the kids on her island were lucky, with her to teach them.

When the time came for the wagon he was glad Gran had insisted. The sun shone on Dada's coffin and the flowers and the bright black wheels of the gold-lined wagon, and he was proud to push it. Harri walked beside him, one hand resting on the wagon rail. His mother walked behind with Gran: it was part of the tradition.

She'd had her victory, though. Margarethe Osterbrook, the founder of her church, wearing blue, led their little procession. Another bloody woman. He didn't care – somebody had to tell them what to do. She'd been waiting for them outside the hospital morgue. She shook his hand and asked him if he wanted to say a few words at the graveside. He told her he didn't. He'd have liked to but he couldn't. His heart was broken even worse than yesterday.

Harriet, who remembered Margarethe Osterbrook from break-fast TV, was agreeably surprised at her. The sugary preacher's voice had been a put-on, or maybe she'd been schooled out of it. She was stoutish and seemed sensible, with a strong face and gentle hands, a recommendation for God the Mother. Everything poor Moma wasn't. And she'd given Danno his due as man of the house, which was a curiously last-century gesture for Margarethe Osterbrook.

Also she was willing to acknowledge Dad's suicide and accept it. 'Your poor father had problems he couldn't face,' she said briskly. 'For God to add to them would be unloving, I think – not what She leads us to expect. And in any case he died ultimately at Her hand, not his own.' She smiled. 'As we all do.'

Harriet walked beside the wagon, one hand lightly touching its rail: and through the rail, the spindles supporting it, the heavy wagon boards and the coffin, touching her father. She hadn't looked at him up at the hospital, hadn't wanted to. Through her medical studies she was already used to the dead, and they were so much less than the living that she didn't see the point. She had pictures of Dada in her head that were far more. Touching the rail of his wagon was more. She could feel the weight of his body which was now a corpse. It was heavy. He'd been a biggish man and now he was a biggish corpse.

She could hear her mother and Gran behind her, talking

quietly, an old woman and a younger. They sounded now what they were – Moma was Gran's daughter. It hardly seemed possible. Harriet had been out to Gran's island last summer, before starting college. The numbers were shrinking at the school Gran taught at and it might have to close. She'd not seen Gran very much in her life, but she loved her probably more than anyone, even Karl. They wrote letters, and perhaps not meeting helped. She'd written to Gran about Karl straight after the second time they'd slept together. How she was nineteen, and he was forty-five and black. Gran hadn't pretended she approved, but she'd sympathised. If there weren't any men of your own age to learn sex with, what were you to do?

She was learning sex with Karl very well. When she was younger, Dada had talked to her about men's and women's similarities. Karl showed her their differences. His blackness helped: she liked it against her whiteness. His muscled neck excited her, his big pale hands, his amazing penis. She liked the idea of its blackness inside her and she wanted to have his baby very much, especially now that Dada was dead, but she was only nineteen, too young, and she didn't know what he'd say. She didn't think he liked babies.

Mrs Hand from next door was waiting at the graveside. So were the Stollmans, Julius and Anka. She acknowledged them, smiled, but didn't go over. She couldn't remember when she'd last played the piano: not at all since Karl. She hadn't asked them to be there, which was a pity, many things were a pity. Neither, she felt sure, had her mother. But they lived only a step away, in the square called the Eckett, and everyone in the village knew what was happening.

Crowds of them, with little dark darting eyes, were looking over the low cemetery wall. Had she ever belonged in this village? With them but apart, as curious as they, the local minister in a broad-minded flowery dress. Harriet recognised her only because she was carrying, rather visibly, a small black leather book with a gold-leaf cross on its cover.

At the hospital morgue there'd been a porter to help with Dada's coffin. Now there was only the family, and Moma was useless. Julius Stollman came forward, and Anka. They slid the coffin out between the wagon's spindled sides. Margarethe Osterbrook kept herself aloof, riffling through her own black leather book. Harriet was glad. Margarethe Osterbrook was a stranger.

The grave had been dug in the traditional fashion, one narrow end a slope down which they slid the coffin, restrained by a broad black braid. Margarethe Osterbrook told them, 'Humankind that is born of woman has only a short time to live, and knows much sorrow . . . '

Seagulls wheeled overhead. Children were in the school playground just down the road, and their cries mingled.

' . . . We come up and are cut down like flowers, brief in our joy but precious. In the midst of life we are in death: whom may we look to for comfort but you, Almighty Mother?'

There were shovels leaning against the long pile of earth. She gave them out to the two men and the five women standing round the grave, gently, like tokens of remembrance: like roses. Harriet drove hers into the dry gravelly soil. The first shovelfuls to fall on the coffin made a hollow ringing sound.

'Now that it has pleased Almighty God in Her great mercy to take to Herself the soul of this Her dear son Johan Ryder, we therefore commit his body to the ground: earth to earth, fire to fire, water to water . . . '

The sun was high, the cemetery without shade, and Harriet sweated. The others laboured around her, Moma's little pecks strengthening as she found the rhythm. Danno was in a sort of frenzy. The grave soon filled.

Harriet swung her shovel like a farmer: *and in the midst of death*, she thought, *we are in life*. And, sweating and stooping, stooping and shovelling, shovelling and patting down the soil in a long narrow mound that promised the corpse beneath it, she wept. She hadn't believed it, but that truly was what funerals were for.

Daniel had stumbled, and one of his shoes was full of gravel. He stood on the other foot while Margarethe Osterbrook finished her praying.

'We give You thanks that it has pleased You to deliver our brother Johan from the miseries of this sinful world, and we beg You soon to accomplish the number of Your elect and to hasten the fulfilment of Your purposes here on earth . . . '

There were local television people now, late, but they hadn't come to see Johan Ryder buried: the bastards' cameras were on

Margarethe Osterbrook. Daniel waited till she'd finished praying, then limped away. Behind him he could hear her answering questions:

'I'm here because I'm needed and because there was a lucky gap in my engagement calendar.

'No, I didn't know Johan Ryder personally, but Bess Ryder has been a member of the Motherist Church now for fifteen years.

'Yes, I do believe that suicide is a sin, but God the Mother teaches us to hate the sin and love the sinner.'

Daniel left the cemetery. He limped past the school, which was quiet now, and along School Lane to the village playground. He sat on the bronze plinth of the statue of the two children, took off the shoe that was paining him, and emptied the gravel out of it. He sat with the shoe in his hand, staring out at the ocean.

He wouldn't go back down to the house, to seafood dip and his mother making up to her tame celebrity. He'd go straight to the station, catch the first shuttle out and an express back to camp at the junction. He had brought very little with him, a few things in a bag, and Harri could post them to him. He didn't like leaving her like that, they hadn't talked at all, but it wasn't his fault: half the time Harri seemed to be on the side of that woman. Maybe because she was still a kid she took her mother's part.

He put on his shoe again and leaned back against the bronze legs of the children. His head fitted under the boy's outstretched arm. Against the children's strength, their unchanging years in the wind and rain and snow and ice, his bones felt dangerously fragile. Shovelling the earth on to Dada's coffin was the most difficult thing he'd ever done. His bones were made of glass and if he jolted them they'd break. Christ Almighty, he wished he could be back in barracks now, with none of the hassle of getting there.

'Daniel? Daniel son, why did he do it?'

Daniel closed his eyes. He turned and embraced the children's bodies, hanging on. Hanging on.

'It's not fair, Daniel. Was I really so terrible?'

Yes, Moma. Yes, you were terrible. You are terrible. Women are terrible. You're the worst.

'You don't blame me, do you Daniel, for what your father did?'

He opened his eyes. It was like a dream, just as if he were looking down on the playground from far away, on himself by the statues, his mother standing alone on the yellow summer grass, his sister away by the entrance to the playground, watching, then School Lane and the school and beyond it the cemetery, the tiny television people and tiny Margarethe Osterbrook in her blue dress. He watched himself let go of the statues, moving very carefully, and stand up. If he jolted his bones they'd break. He walked round the statues and up to his mother. He saw himself look at her, really look at her, at her hateful clothes and her hateful face.

'It was his work that made him unhappy, Daniel. It wasn't me, it was his work. And the terrible Attrition.'

'Of course it wasn't you.' The dream ended and he was back inside his head, looking at her, at her hateful face. 'It was his work. He talked to me about it once. It was his work.'

'You don't blame me?'

'I'm going back to camp now. Of course I don't blame you.'

'When will we – when will I see you again?'

'Very soon.' She'd reached out a hand to him but he avoided it. He could lie to her but he couldn't touch her. 'I don't know. Very soon.'

She seemed to accept this. If there'd been a God, Mother, Father, any sort of God, she'd have been struck down where she stood, blasted, shrivelled, the skin flayed from her body.

'Pecker up then, Moma. See you soon.'

He walked round her, past her and on to Harriet, watching by the gate.

'You tell her, Harri,' he said. 'I can't.'

'Tell her what? You want things simple, Danno. They aren't.'

'If she'd been different, he'd still be alive. Isn't that simple?'

'If she'd been different, if Brandt had been different, if you'd been different, if I'd been different, if he'd missed the bus to work that morning. For God's sake, Danno, if *he* had been different.'

Harri was only a kid. She took her mother's side. She didn't understand.

'I'll be off, then. You can manage fine without me. Give my love to Liese.'

'Take care, Danno. *Take care . . .* '

She hugged him, her skinny arms right round him, and he didn't want to go. She mended him. There was nowhere else he wanted to be. She released him and he walked away along School Lane, turned right between the safety rails and went down the long alley of steps. At the bottom, on the Parade, he passed his mother's house without pausing. There was a black ribbon nailed to the door.

He caught the shuttle, and the express at the junction, then a tram from the station out to the camp. He moved with care, keeping shocks out, the noises and sharp corners.

Booking in at the guardroom, he was seen by the provost-sergeant. Sergeant Breitholmer came out of his office. He'd always had his eye on Daniel, and since Daniel's promotion to lance-jack he'd tried to keep him out of trouble.

'You shouldn't be here, Lance-Corporal. I sent you on leave.'

'I came back, Sergeant.'

'Can't keep away. Is that it?'

'That's it, Sergeant.'

'I rejigged the whole fucking duty roster because of you, Corporal Ryder. Now I'll have to start again.'

'Put me on kitchens, Sergeant. There's always room there.'

'Don't tell me my job, boy. You'll go where you're fucking put.'

He returned to his office and Daniel went on into camp. He took a shower, changed into his uniform. Tiny bits of gravel fell out of one of his civvy shoes. He hadn't felt them there: they'd been caught under the insole. He gathered them up, stared at them in the palm of his hand, then flung them across the room. He checked the money in his wallet and left the camp, aware that the provost-sergeant was watching him go by.

The city streets were airless, sweltering in the last of the day's sun. The city was in a valley ringed with low pine-forested hills, and the July heat lay over it, trapped and crackling with pollution. He entered the first bar he came to and tried to get drunk, but his mind was too careful and the alcohol couldn't get into it. He left the bar, found the city park, and sat on a bench by the artificial waterfall. The ducks in the pool at the bottom were busy and noisy and didn't feel the heat.

A girl in a pretty summer dress was leaning over the footbridge across the top of the waterfall. He watched her lose her hat and watched it drop into the water, drift away, then scurry down between the rocks of the fall, into the pool at the bottom. The ducks pecked at it, then swam off. The girl came down by the path, found a stick, stood on the grass at the edge of the pool and reached out, but her hat floated quietly in the middle and her arms were too short.

Daniel watched her. She looked a decent young woman, not showy. These days there was about a seven-year back-up of women without their year's men, so he'd had no lack of opportunity, but he hadn't done them the favour. He couldn't see wasting his sperm on some condom or the inside of someone's fanny: he saved it for the donation centres, three times a week, where it did some good. He chose the state centres where you delivered for nothing, on your own in a little cubicle. Private centres charged and offered facilities, games rooms, hot baths, helpers of either sex, but he'd never cared to spend his money.

The girl took off her sandals but the water was too deep for paddling. Her hat floated just out of her reach, visited by ducks. He decided he was letting his uniform down, not helping her, so he got up off his bench, went forward, took the stick from her, and retrieved her hat. She stood beside him on the grass, shaking it and laughing. Then she put it on, green algae dangling from its wide brim.

They started talking. She was glad to have her hat back: it had been given to her by her boyfriend. He was in the army, like Daniel, and when he asked her his name he recognised one of the radar corporals. They walked together round the park. Dusk was falling. He told her he hadn't eaten since breakfast and asked her if she'd like to join him in a café. He mentioned one she didn't know, it was on the other side of town, and she agreed. When she wondered what he'd been doing, not eating since breakfast, he told her he'd been to a funeral. She looked up at him, concerned, but she didn't ask whose.

Then, and afterwards, if he'd had to say why he chose that particular café, he couldn't have. He liked it, but not that much. It was cheap, but he had plenty of money. He knew a short cut to it, down two quiet back-streets, but he wasn't in a hurry.

The back-streets were delivery areas behind big shops, hardly more than alleys, deserted and already dark. He was still shut away, scarcely there, and she trusted him in his uniform. When

126

he paused in the second of the streets she turned and looked up at him again, expecting him to kiss her. He'd seen her white neck before, how thin it was, and now he struck at it, his fingers stiff like rods, the way the army'd taught him. She choked, and stared up into his face while she died, and he held her to stop her from falling. He was there now, back in his body, and his bones were strong.

Behind them footsteps crossed the end of the street. Quickly he carried the girl into a loading-bay and round behind some crates. The street was silent again. He put the girl down carefully and arranged her skirt. He still felt sad for her. She wore two nice rings and he didn't want them stolen, so he hid them in one of her sandals. He hid her purse too, underneath her body. He stepped back. He realised with disgust that, striking her, he'd ejaculated into his underpants. A phrase came to him: *wicked waste*. The camp doctor'd said there were a million sperm in every offering.

He listened to the silence. He'd been crazy, risking this. The girl's head lay back on the tarmac, her eyes staring at the sky, and there were bruise marks on her neck. He looked at his bitten nails and the tips of his fingers. Fingerprints? He got out his handkerchief and stooped over her, rubbing at the bruises. The broken cartilage of her windpipe squeaked loudly beneath them. He straightened his back. The front of her pretty summer dress would have fibres on it from his uniform, where he'd held her while she died. He frowned, then relaxed. Army fibres, easily from her boyfriend corporal.

He left her and walked quietly back to the entrance to the loading-bay. The street was empty. He returned to the main road. Not a car or a tram in sight. The pavements were deserted except for one man, a soldier, walking towards him. It was the provost-sergeant.

He approached, stopped close in front of Daniel.

'Corporal Ryder,' he said. 'So it *is* you. I thought I saw you, and then I fucking didn't.'

Daniel nodded down the street behind him. 'I went for a quick piss, sergeant.'

'Did you now? That's the sort of thing that gives the army a bad name, Corporal Ryder.'

'Yes, Sergeant.'

'Lucky you wasn't caught.'

'Yes, Sergeant.' If he saw me, Daniel thought, then he saw the girl. Was he following me?

Sergeant Breitholmer moved in closer. 'You all right, Corporal?'

'All right?'

'You look fucking awful to me. Like you seen a ghost.'

'I'm fine, Sergeant.'

'That's what I like to hear. Stick to *I'm fine, Sergeant* and you won't go far wrong. Let me buy you a drink, Corporal.'

'Thanks Sarge, but – '

'No bullshit, Corporal. Just a drink. I mean, pissing in alleys, it's lucky you wasn't caught.'

'Just one then, Sarge. Ta.'

They had several, still not enough to signify, in a basement bar, spotlights and fish-tanks, just down the road. Then they walked back to camp in the last of the daylight, discussing the bad state of football and the Socialists' chances in the next election. Daniel didn't get his supper – he scrounged some smoked ham and bread in the cookhouse after he'd left Sergeant Breitholmer at the sergeants' mess. The sergeant didn't mention any girl Daniel might have been with. The murder was big in the news for a week or two but Daniel kept his head down and Sergeant Breitholmer never said a word.

They became friends.

CHAPTER SEVEN

The Attrition. Year 40: early November.

Monday was the first day of the new month. Ice month, we called it. The cold had not arrived when I woke in the morning, but already Sunday's mellowness had been scourged away by a driving east wind and mean, gale-shredded clouds. And when I got up I was greeted by a dismal torrent from the PIPS unit in Mark's study.

In those days I maintained a profile with the local Professional Information Print-out Service – anyone in my position had to – and twice a week they voided the accumulated technical garbage into my home. It spared me ploughing through the medical journals.

I parked my bum on the corner of Mark's desk. There was the usual mass of serious research data that I put on one side, along with Syndrome social-impact stories and the usual dozens of anecdotal cure claims – everything from an Inuit TV shaman promising the help of the Big White Spirit to a Milan advertiser who guaranteed viable male foetuses from his secret regimen of diet and New Age sexual practices, particulars despatched in secure print-out on receipt of 25,000 euros.

The swindles were numberless: simple peasants gulled by female infants with crudely implanted plastic male genitalia, sophisticated socialites gulled by plush health-hydro operators and their expensive chimpanzee-gland therapies. Gaians spoke of restoring the world's Natural Balance, and one Indian sect sacrificed virgins at the full moon in the hope of appeasing Shiva.

One item of slight interest that Monday morning was a United Press report of a spontaneous remission in a civil-war zone in North Africa – three male infants born to a Bedouin tribe somewhere between Murzuq and Al Qatrūn, in what had once been Libya. The report was unconfirmed, from a single Red Cross aid worker, and the tribe had moved on by the time she returned to the area, but there seemed to be no commercial or political reasons for her to lie. Personal reasons were another matter: women tended to see male infants simply because they wanted to so badly. A fold of fabric, a congenital deformity, the parent's finger in the shadows at the back of a tent, many things could be interpreted as penis and scrotum if the need was great enough.

Trashing the junk and leaving the UP report for later reference, I wandered through to the kitchen with the serious published research data. Mark and Anna were eating breakfast. Yvette was reading a long letter in French from her mother: she had been an IVF child and they were very close. We couldn't have our usual weekday planning session till she'd done, so I poured myself coffee and leafed through my print-outs. There was frightening work coming out of South America, male genitalia transplants that seemed to be taking on their female hosts, which suggested a new industry: ageing men willing to sell their equipment, others parted from it forcibly. Big money. Fortunately, if I was right and the vaccine therapy was effective, they wouldn't be needed.

The therapy . . . was it effective? Had it been effective for me? I'd no idea. Mostly I didn't think about it. A terminal leukaemia sufferer once wrote that you couldn't spend your life permanently frightened – other matters got in the way. Similarly, I didn't spend my life brooding over the state of my ovaries. Two days ago, as my standard excuse for shitty behaviour, I'd said I was premenstrual. My period still hadn't started, so maybe I wasn't. Maybe I really was pregnant. It did happen to women like me, with enthusiastic husbands. If it had, then in two weeks' time we could sex the embryo, and there was a sixty– forty chance of it being male.

I shuffled print-outs, wondering if I'd carry him to full term, if he was a him. Bring forth the only male baby in the world, a wonder of science, a media event, a freak. I thought not. At a couple of months the proof would be there. Full-term births could wait on the extended field tests. There'd be a group of them then: safety in numbers. I didn't need the glory and my little boy didn't need the hassle. I was thirty-six years old. I had plenty of time to bear Mark's son later, in obscurity.

Yvette finished her letter, dried her eyes. Her mother's letters were always happy and they always made her cry. Mark and Anna roused themselves from their workday breakfast torpor and we went over the day's plans. Mark's material from the

Bristol UV symposium had come in the post, so he was back on his project. There was nothing he could do for me until I'd written my *Natur* piece. In the morning he'd sort through the British stuff and in the afternoon he'd probably need the car to go back to the farmers, take up where he'd left off on Thursday. I hardly ever used the car – it was Mark's work that got us the methanol.

Anna would be at school all day, and had a music lesson afterwards. I hadn't been able to find her anyone quite like Julius, there wasn't anyone quite like Julius, but she was happy with a woman in town who cared about technique. Fingers were coming back, and discipline, after many years of pianos you waved at. Women respond to discipline, if they can see the point.

Yvette had her morning's work around the house, and the afternoon for her course at the City University. She planned to teach when she returned to France, and she'd come to our country to study the language and our education methods. We've been among the first to face up to the ball-less half-culture being taught in our single-sex schools. It didn't matter that I hadn't told her how close I believed I was to curing the Syndrome – even if it was eliminated tomorrow, she'd be fighting a female educational mind-set for at least another twenty years.

As to my own Monday, I had my piece for *Natur* to work on so I was going to the Institute. I'd be there all day, getting my stuff in order. Also, as I'd promised Gusso, I had to come clean to my people about the leak. I could tell them now where it was going, Unikhem, and we could assess the damage. Presumably one of them already knew all this: perhaps I'd be able to spot her from her reactions.

Her . . . I'd ruled out Gusso, you see, and was choosing between the women. He had wide-apart eyes and a friendly smile and I'd worked with him closest of all.

Maggi Frik, then? My secretary simply wasn't clever enough to be that devious. Also she and her lover were considerably left-wing and hated everything Unikhem stood for.

Natalya Volkov? My project director was transparently honour-able. Also her husband Michael was respected and successful and she had no possible need of the money.

131

Karen Bakst? My clinic manager cared only about her patients.

Liesl Wronowicz? My virologist was above all a perfectionist, in her work and certainly in her dealings with me.

That completed my team and none of them was a thief. Which left only friendly Gusso, and I'd ruled him out. He didn't have a cheating nature.

For me, therefore, a difficult day at the Institute. Anna would be away at school and music lesson, Mark and Yvette would be out in the afternoon, and dinner would be late. I suggested a menu and no one objected. Whoever was home first would get it out and zap it.

Anna and I left the house together, she for school and I for the Institute. No reporters waited: for the moment, as a story, I was dead.

Waiting in the tram shelter with Anna, I was reminded of our Saturday conversation. I'd told her man-hating was easy. For some of us man-loving was easy too. Long long ago Julius Stollman had asked me if I found young men beautiful. I'd answered something smart-alecky – I couldn't remember what, but I was a smart-alecky child – but Anna was growing up in a world where the question didn't apply. If my therapy was effective and she had a son, how would she treat him?

'I've been thinking about what you said, Anna. About men and sex and violence.'

'Crikey, Moma – where did that come from?'

I didn't tell her. 'I want you to remember women torturers. Brutal wardresses. Women can be violent too.'

'They're men. Look at horrible Sergeant Milhaus with her little stick. She's a man.'

'OK. Look at your father. He doesn't have a stick. Is he a woman?'

'Of course not.' She frowned. 'Well, perhaps . . . It depends what you mean by . . . Oh, I don't know.'

'I don't know either. But I don't like labels.'

She held her fibreglass school-case against her chest, her chin resting thoughtfully on the top. The tram shelter creaked, buffeted by the wind.

She began slowly. 'The thing about Dada is . . . the thing about him is, he's not as big and important as you, but he doesn't mind, and he keeps us all going, and maybe that makes him bigger.'

I eyed her sharply. It was a remark with a will of its own, something she'd wanted to say, probably for a long time. Bigger? I'd never looked at Mark in terms of our relative importance. Perhaps I should have. If Annie did, perhaps he did too.

I realised something else. Where one observer saw 'dictatorial ways', another saw 'keeping us all going'.

Her tram came down the hill. Hers went into town, where the school was, mine came later and went round the ring road to the Institute.

'You distracted me, Annie. I was thinking about my vaccine. If it's effective there'll be millions of little boys growing up all over the world without men around. Somebody's going to have to stick up for them. For their man-ness.'

The tram drew up. Anna's friend Jessica Simpson from along the road was waving at one of its windows. Anna kissed my cheek.

"Bye, Moma. I'll stick up for Dada-ness, if that's what you mean. Looking at history, though, I feel safer with women.'

The tram doors opened and Anna was gone. She left her youthful chauvinism with me, like the slight moisture on my cheek from her kiss, cold now in the wind. Being an enlightened lady, I brushed it off. Too easily.

Enlightenment's great. Ancient truths can be great too. The trick is to know t'other from which.

At the Institute the broken glass in my office had been swept up and the picture cleared away. The empty space between the two windows where it had hung remained, a reminder of the person (how's that for a weasel word?) I least wanted to think about. I took refuge in the work she'd interrupted on Saturday, distilling the significance of a sheaf of early radiation-test results. The aim had been to duplicate, and so begin to understand, the process of embryo rejection involved in the Syndrome, and we'd used a heroic group of volunteers, subjecting them to a number of uterine assaults, including carefully measured and shielded radiation. The tests were significant now because they had eliminated many possible mechanisms, and so had narrowed the line of our enquiry. As such they merited maybe a paragraph in *Natur*, nothing more.

As I was polishing my paragraph Maggi came through on the inside line.

'Dr Volkov to see you, boss.'

'Send her in.' An opportunity to tell her how sorry I was she'd missed the Asgeirsons' party.

'And I've just had Dr Marton on, boss. He says the Minister's back from Rome and she'd like a word with you. I said you could be there at three this afternoon.'

'I can't possibly, Maggi. I'm supposed to be on holiday. Why didn't you put him through?'

'He said not. He was in a filthy mood, boss. He started off wanting you there now, at once. When I told him you were on holiday he said he knew you were in your office. And when I put him off until this afternoon he said he supposed it would do, but the Minister would have to take time off from an important debate in the House.'

'Any hint what she wants?'

'No, boss. But it didn't sound friendly.'

I sighed. 'I'd better be punctual.'

The fact was, I felt found out. There I sat, working on the piece she'd specifically forbidden. It seemed shabby. I decided that this afternoon's chat was a good thing: it would clear the air.

If Oswald Marton was difficult, so was the Minister but in a different way. He was difficult because, as a civil servant, he was jealous of his power: she was difficult because, as a career politician, she was jealous of her reputation. This was a clever observation on my part – smarty-alecky, some would say – but it didn't help much. I hadn't a clue how to act on it, face to face. But I'd got on well enough with the Minister in the past – if I could give this political lady political advantages for early publication she might even change her mind. Were there any?

I glanced at my watch. Mark was the one for political advantages and he'd be at home now. It was a good moment to call him.

'OK Maggi, so it's the Minister at three . . . And Maggi, I'm having one of my meetings later, so could you ring round the family? Apologies, and could they make it here in my office in about half an hour?'

I rang off, started to dial my home number. A movement made me look up. Natalya Volkov was standing in front of my desk. I cancelled my call – I'd forgotten Maggi was sending her in.

'Natya – good to see you. Sit down. Park your bum.'

She didn't move. Behind her, unusually, the door to the outer office was closed. Presumably she'd closed it.

'Is something the matter, Natya? Are you ill?'

She looked ill. She was pale, and her hands, clasped at her waist, were actually shaking.

'You should've stayed at home. Is that why you didn't go to the Asgeirsons'?'

She shook her head. 'I did not go to the Asgeirsons' because I was not ready to see you, Dr Harriet.' Her Russian accent made her very solemn this morning. 'I had not made up my mind.'

'Dear Natya – don't look so glum. Whatever's the matter?'

'Your research is the matter. I am the matter.' Her voice broke. 'Have you not guessed?'

'Guessed?' Now I had. I sat back, dismayed. 'Oh Natalya – why?'

She made tiny embarrassed movements, standing in front of me with painful solidity, an old woman.

'It is not a betrayal. My mistake is not to tell you. But now you change the access codes and I see the folders on your desk and I know you have discovered that your work is being stolen.'

'*Our* work, Natya . . . So you spent the weekend deciding what you would do. I appreciate your coming to tell me.'

'You asked me why. It – '

'I'm sorry.' I held up a hand to stop her. 'I shouldn't have. You're a good friend, Natya. A dear friend. There'd have been no cure without you, in any case. I don't need to know your reasons.'

'It is not a betrayal, Dr Harriet. I hope you do not think that. We and the Minister, we are on the same side. We – '

'I don't like talk of sides.' I didn't understand what she was getting at. And I didn't have to sit through a full confession – I'd been put upon enough already. 'In any case, no great harm has been done. Unikhem are still a long way off a vaccine. Why don't we leave it at that?'

'*Unikhem?*' She put her hands to her face. 'Unikhem are not involved. Never.'

'Of course they are.' Forgiveness wasn't an issue, but I didn't want her to lie to me. 'I was talking to Professor Asgeirson yesterday afternoon, and he told me – '

'Never. What sort of traitor do you think I am?' She gestured fiercely, freed by her indignation. 'I report to the Minister. Never to Unikhem. I keep the Minister up to date in the progress of our work. Dr Marton says this will help with our funding.'

'Marton said that?'

'He said . . . ' She hesitated, spread her elbows, apologising very Russianly. 'He said you are a brilliant woman, but a very troublesome woman. He said he wanted to avoid misunderstandings between you and the Minister.'

A troublesome woman . . . Plausible, I thought, from my difficult man. And I didn't imagine my previous employer had delivered me with a glowing reference in terms of my tact.

'So you've been keeping the Minister supplied with details of our progress from the very beginning?'

She shook her head. 'Dr Marton came to me about a year ago. He said he sensed there was a breakdown in communication. The Minister feared you were, in her words, being "less than honest".'

I thought back a year or so. Less than honest? I'd have been back from Erzurum by then, and I'd certainly told her about that.

'So you started then.' I remembered the folder. 'And you've been filling in the background ever since.'

'I believed it was the right thing to do.' Natya glared at the wall above my head. 'She is the Minister.'

A Russian attitude. I'd wondered about a motive and this was what I'd got. Even after many refugee years, a Russian attitude from a Russian lady with Russian elbows. It would have helped the Institute's funding greatly.

I didn't bother to ask why she hadn't let me in on the secret. I was a troublesome lady with troublesome elbows – I'd have been pissed off.

'But you don't believe it's the right thing any more?'

'Yes and no. Scientific freedom is important also. I have spoken to Dr Marton as I promised. I have pleaded with him. But the Minister still refuses to allow you to publish, and I don't like her reasons.'

'Her reasons?' Perhaps Natya'd been given different reasons.

'Your research is not complete. Dr Harriet, that is not so.'

She'd been given the same reasons.

Everything fitted. Almost everything. 'What about Professor Asgeirson and his Unikhem information?'

'The professor is wrong. I know nothing of Unikhem.'

I doubted if Asgeirson was wrong. In some areas Vice-Presidents Marketing were never wrong. But I believed Natalya about her and Unikhem. With her dogged sense of socialist justice undented by fifty years of the ex-Soviet Commowealth's version of free enterprise, she'd never have betrayed me to such an ultra-capitalist enemy.

'Well, that's that then, Natya. I'm very glad you came to see me. Now we can – '

'No.' Her solidness had returned. She shifted her feet heavily, and tugged an envelope out of the pocket of her doctor's white coat. There's something about resignation envelopes – you can tell them at a hundred metres.

I stood up, matching her heaviness. 'Please put that away, Dr Volkov. I won't accept it. The clinic needs you. The project needs you. For God's sake, Natya, *I* need you.'

I didn't mind if she'd seen the movie – it was a good line, and I meant it.

She fingered her envelope warily, as if it were likely to explode. Then she came to a decision, stuffed it back into her pocket, and held out her hand across my desk. I shook it.

'Good.' She fetched a chair and we both sat down. She leant forward, her Russian elbows on my desk. 'Tell me about Unikhem, Dr Harriet.'

Penance had been offered, now she could move on. Sensible Natya. I told her what Professor Asgeirson had told me.

'So there have been two spies here at the Institute.'

I said that was ridiculous. They'd have been bumping into each other.

She nodded. 'Certainly I never saw anybody. But what else is possible?'

'I'm having a family meeting in half an hour. Maybe we'll find out.'

'I do not believe one of us is selling to Unikhem.'

'Nor do I. But who else has access?'

I'd been round the same circular questions with myself and Mark. Now I was going round them with her. Soon I'd be going round them again at the meeting. I had to remind myself that half an hour ago I'd have laughed at the idea of Natalya as a spy. So nothing was impossible.

My people arrived. I'd been dreading this all night. I told them about the leak to Unikhem and that I believed my access-code changes had stopped it before Unikhem had enough data from which to produce its own therapy program. More importantly, I told them why I was telling them. All of us were under suspicion, including myself – perhaps especially myself, if I'd guessed that the Minister might block my publication. If they had any ideas, I'd love to hear them.

I didn't tell them about Natalya Volkov and the Minister. There was no point. It would have distressed her and it didn't rule out the possibility that she was supplying information to Unikhem also. Once again, nothing was impossible.

It was an appalling speech to have to deliver. I tried to meet their eyes, each one of them fondly and fairly. They were my friends. We called ourselves the family. When I'd done my office was silent for a while, heavy with the six shared years of our endeavour.

Gusso spoke first. 'Ideas? I don't have any. Theoretically anybody could hack into the Institute's computer, but safe combinations are safe combinations. We're far on from the old three-to-the-right-two-to-the-left bit. There's no way an outsider could read them.'

Karen ground out her cigarette. 'There has to be. I refuse to believe that one of us . . . ' She gestured dismissively and there was a general mutter of agreement.

Liesl stood up, went to the window. As our virologist, much of the basic slog had been hers. 'You say Unikhem doesn't have the whole story . . . ' She was scanning the grey boulders of the garden for watchers, listeners, the people she knew were always invisible. 'How can you be so sure?'

'My contact has a friend on the Unikhem board.'

She had spread her hand against the window glass. Now she removed it, leaving a condensation outline, like a cave painting. It quickly faded. 'I can see you trust your contact. But can you trust his friend? Do you know his friend?'

Good questions. The bias in my life, in most people's lives, was towards trust. It was a difficult bias to overcome.

Maggi caught my eye. At meetings like this she never spoke. She felt she was only a secretary, and secretaries didn't. She was a great deal more, of course.

I raised a finger. 'Maggi?'

'Isn't the real point of all this that it gives you a soddin' good argument for making Herself let you publish? It doesn't matter how much Unikhem have got – anything is too much. They won't be sitting on their backsides with it. Give a scientist a ball and she runs.'

'So it's up to us,' Gusso said, 'to run faster.'

They were right. I'd never wanted to get into a race – one of the many reasons why I'd left the private sector – but I'd spent a great deal of the taxpayers' money and they should get something back on it. If my vaccine tested out, the licence fees for its manufacture belonged to them, not to Unikhem's stinking-rich shareholders.

I said, 'I've got an appointment with the Minister this afternoon. I'll see what I can do.'

Karen got to her feet. 'We should all come. Form a deputation.'

'I hope that won't be necessary. We'll keep it in reserve.' I sat forward. 'But it's agreed, then, that I press for immediate publication? Not wait for the Paris seminar?'

'With Unikhem breathing down my neck,' Gusso murmured to his neighbour, 'I wouldn't wait to wipe my ass.'

The meeting broke up. I was grateful to Maggi. Our priority now was to publish, file patents, and establish a human test program monitored by the WHO. Other, more corrosive questions could wait. Of the people now leaving my office, had one of them looked guilty? Had one of them avoided my gaze, fussed with clothes, shifted feet, protested too vehemently? Of course not. They were my friends.

Even so, *someone* had leaked to Unikhem, someone who stood to gain millions, probably billions, if Unikhem filed patents first. This was an ugly thought, for it left me – and through me Anna – desperately vulnerable. If Sergeant Milhaus, no great genius, had seen that the best way to influence me was to threaten my daughter, obviously the Unikhem side of things would see that too. And with billions at stake, would they not be equally evil?

I rang Mark. My hand on the telephone was shaking. I didn't care how many listeners were on the line, or what they heard, I had to talk to him. And anything I told him I'd be telling the Minister myself that afternoon. Political reasons for immediate publication were no longer needed: money spoke far louder.

Mark was reassuring. Even his voice on the phone reassuring.

When we'd discussed Unikhem's involvement in the car on our way home from Knolle he'd concentrated on the source of the leak: we'd both failed to see the race this put me in. But he pointed out now that if Unikhem was itself running with the ball, the pressure on me personally had eased. I could even back out – my team at the Institute could publish and file for patent without me.

He paused . . . perhaps to draw breath and perhaps giving me time to notice my delusions of grandeur. In either case, I took the point – the Institute could publish without me: why hadn't I thought of that before? Then he gently moved on, calming my fears for Anna. There was only one Sergeant Milhaus, he said. Any shift away from her jurisdiction must be for the better.

As for the magazine *Natur*, once the Minister had agreed to publication our deal was off and they'd have to be told. For the sake of the listeners neither of us mentioned this, but it was in both our minds.

'Mark,' I said just before ringing off, 'don't do anything until I've seen the Minister.'

I was at the Science Ministry early. I confirmed my appointment with the Minister's secretary. The name on her desk was Branka Golbchek.

She looked doubtful. 'The Minister's still in the House,' she said. 'Dr Marton is expecting you.'

'My appointment isn't with Dr Marton.'

'The Minister's still in the House.'

'I'll wait. My appointment is with her. She specifically requested it.'

'The Minister's still in the House. I'm sorry.'

She wasn't sorry. Branka Golbchek was a politician's secretary, deaf and blind but with a fine nose for anything to her employer's advantage. It had told her I was trouble. Even so, she accepted my coat and showed me into the Minister's private office, which I took to be a good sign. I'd been here before on Institute business, annual meetings, progress reports, funding surveys. It was green and silky, modern fluid spaces, calm: I'd happily wait here till the Minister was ready.

Then, far away across the expanses of ministerial privilege, I saw Dr Marton behind the Minister's desk. Being a large desk for a large woman, and he a small man, it did him no favours. The

Minister had gone for body-contour seating, free-flow work areas, a huge light-responsive armoured glazing unit looking out across the park. She'd told me it was alarmed against audio-tapping. She enjoyed hi-tech and used a personal communication net: there wasn't a telephone in sight. The desk reminded me of a TV newsreader's workplace.

Away from his antiques and his power paraphernalia Dr Marton lost impact, added up to less. I was not reassured. He came quickly forward and we shook hands.

'Dr Kahn-Ryder. In the middle of your holiday. How good of you to come.'

I'd been given little choice. No point, though, in starting on a sour note.

'Holiday, Dr Marton?' Man to man. 'When do civil servants like us ever have holidays?'

He inclined his head and perched handily on the curved front edge of the desk. He registered better there.

'Do sit down.'

I sat. From the low chair he registered better still.

'The Minister sends her apologies. The Opposition are staging one of their little melodramas and she can't get away. They're pushing it to a vote and she'll be needed to wind up for the Government.'

'I'll come back later.'

'It could be an all-night sitting.'

'Tomorrow, then.'

'Dr Kahn-Ryder, on holiday or not, you're a busy woman and so is the Minister. I know her mind. She has asked me to convey to you her feelings.'

This wasn't last Thursday. I wasn't going to grovel. 'That isn't good enough, Dr Marton. There's been a development – '

'Certainly there has. I spoke to the Minister about the threat to your daughter. She was very concerned.'

'I think that's over. Since I spoke to you from the Institute we've discovered that – '

'The Minister was also concerned at the recent high volume of computer traffic between your husband and a certain German scientific journal.'

Coming from nowhere, that stopped me dead. *'What?'*

He raised his hands, smugly calming me. 'The Minister and I

141

realise, Dr Kahn-Ryder, that Mr Kahn is a journalist. He has every right to communicate with whatever journals he cares to. But – '

Some worm-cans were best left unexamined. 'I think you should listen to what I'm telling you, Dr Marton. Things have changed. All this argument about publication – we no longer have any choice.'

'You're referring to the Unikhem leak?' He folded his arms. He was intolerable. 'It's really very minor. They're a long way from anything meaningful.'

I lost my temper. The games he played, the surprises he kept up his sleeve, his pleasure at my humiliation. I leapt to my feet.

'Is this how you treat all your heads of department? If you knew about the leak, why the hell didn't you – '

He tried to take my arm. 'I'm sorry, Dr Kahn-Ryder. I really am.'

I shook him off. The last time the bastard had touched me it had been to plant a tag.

'If you're innocent,' he went on, 'you have every reason to be angry. But you must see our difficulty.'

'Innocent?' Again he'd stopped me dead. 'You mean you really thought I might be capable of selling my research data to – ?'

'I repeat, Dr Kahn-Ryder, you have to understand our difficulty. Asgeirson isn't the only one with friends in Unikhem high places. We have an excellent contact there. With your people, however, we – '

'You have Dr Volkov, don't you? She was doing so much for you already, why not have her spy on her fucking colleagues?'

'I'm sorry?'

'I said – '

'I know what you said.' He stood up from the edge of the desk. His blandness had slipped away. He was as angry as I. 'You suggested that the Russian woman is in some way connected with this office. You suggested that – '

'For God's sake, Marton, Dr Volkov's been giving you our work for the last year at least. She admitted it to me this morning. She's been borrowing records, wiring them out to – '

'I deny it.' He slammed his fist down on the desk. 'I categorically deny it. Ask the Minister. Ask anybody in the Department.' He strode away to the door and wrenched it open.

'The Minister's secretary would know. Ask her.' He called through the open doorway. 'Branka – come here a minute.'

I stared at him. His denial was horribly convincing. Why would he bother unless it was true – the method, using an informer, mightn't be strictly ethical but the Minister had a right to be kept abreast of progress in her own departments.

Branka Golbchek appeared in the doorway. I waved her away. She checked with him, a raised eyebrow, a nod, then left.

'I believe you . . . ' My anger had chilled, leaving me tired and depressed. 'Natya lied to me. She must have done. I believe you.'

Dr Marton closed the door. 'I'm sorry.' He spoke quietly. 'I know the trust you placed in Dr Volkov. In all your people. It's very hard, to have your trust betrayed. But I promise you, if she said she had supplied the Minister with confidential information from your records, she lied.'

He returned soft-footed across the silky green carpet. If he was going to offer me his sympathy I didn't want it. Of all people's, not his.

Sympathy? From Oswald Marton? I should have known better.

His silvering hair had been disturbed by his anger. He smoothed it. 'At least we now know the source of your leak,' he said briskly, rubbing his hands. 'Presumably Dr Volkov believed she was about to be discovered, and made up this story to – '

'Presumably nothing, Dr Marton.' I sat down wearily. 'I shall ask her. She won't lie to me again. And in any case – ' I hurried on, not letting him interrupt ' – in any case, none of this alters the fact that we must publish now, at once, before Unikhem can file for patent.'

'On the contrary, Dr Kahn-Ryder, this makes it all the more essential that our research is unimpeachable before we do publish.' He circled the Minister's desk, sat in her chair. I watched him limply. Whatever he said, he knew I was beaten.

'Dr Kahn-Ryder, I didn't speak lightly last Thursday when I said we in the Ministry have our ears to the ground. Unikhem aren't the only people with a start along your path. If pressed, several firms may think they can put together something, steal a march on us. But you must believe me when I tell you they can't. Crucial steps are missing. Believe me . . . ' He rested his chin on his steepled fingers. 'Which is why we let this thing with Unikhem run. We could stop it by tightening security at any time. But there was no real danger, and there was always the hope that your spy would reveal herself – as has now happened. And meanwhile . . . '

I let him run on. Soon he'd get round to reminding me that I still must not publish, that the Minister was concerned that I should not think of breaking the Security Protocol, that I should go meekly back to the laboratory, do my homework, resubmit in six months' time . . .

Dare I break the Protocol? There was a safe place for Anna, but we still had to get her there. And why should we bother? If Marton was right about the opposition, was a six-month delay so terrible? Scientific freedom? These fucking farm women in their fucking fields?

' . . . So for the time being the Minister suggests protective custody.'

Marton's words dragged me back. 'What did you say?'

'Protective custody. For your daughter Anna.'

'Protective from what?'

'I've already made that clear.'

'Make it clear again.'

'For heaven's sake.' He shook his head. He'd been in lecture mode and I'd jolted him. He'd been reading the news. 'You raised the matter of the SPU yourself, Dr Kahn-Ryder. And all this computer time to Germany doesn't look good . . . I make no accusations, I just say how it looks.' He paused, gathering my attention. 'And there are exceptionally loyal elements in the SPU.'

I smiled. 'Over-zealous.'

'I'm sorry?'

'Over-zealous.' He'd lost his edge. Earlier he'd had me beat. Now my anger was fighting back. *Protective custody?* 'Over-zealous was the word Sergeant Milhaus used. Officers in the SPU. Over-zealous, like herself.'

'Was a Sergeant Milhaut the officer who threatened you?'

'Haus. Milhaus. Sergeant Milhaus.' A poor try at innocence – I didn't believe a word of it. The bastard. 'The officer you sent, Dr Marton. The officer who killed my daughter's cat. Cut its throat.'

He laughed lightly, spun the Minister's chair in a disarming fashion. 'I assure you, Dr Kahn-Ryder – '

It was as if I could feel my rage actually swelling. Tumescing. 'What you're trying to tell me, Marton . . . what you want me to believe is that the Minister plans to take my daughter Anna into protective custody because she can't guarantee to control Sergeant Milhaus.'

'That's not what I said.'

'Isn't it what you meant?' Give the Minister my daughter as a hostage. Isn't that what he meant?

He stilled the chair, tried sweet reason. 'It's a violent world out there. Young girls are very vulnerable.'

'You're sounding more like Sergeant Milhaus every minute.'

I was on my feet again. I'd just had one of those extraordinary mind-shifts after which the impossible suddenly becomes absurdly easy. Getting Anna to sanctuary was absurdly easy. Fate, supposedly unkind, had been trying to help me for days. I'd simply been too busy to notice.

'I don't need your protective custody, Marton. Anna doesn't need your protective custody. And I warn you, Marton, if you try coming to enforce it you'd better bring big legal backing with you. We aren't dumb peasants, Mark and I. And I tell you something else – there are no dumb peasants, they went out with the Millennium. The next to go will be dumb civil servants. Good day.'

I was making for the door. He waited till I reached it. Oswald Marton was a man who knew how to lose battles but retain options on the war. He waited until I'd reached the door and opened it.

'Good luck with Natalya Volkov,' he said, speaking so softly that I had to strain to hear – which, fuck him to hell and back, I did. 'If she claims she's given us all this material, ask her how it's supposed to have reached us. If by wire, then to what number. Ours is ex-directory. So try the number she gives you.'

I closed the door on him. I didn't know what he was up to but of one thing I could be certain – his intention was not generous. It was not gentle. It was that of an enemy.

On Branka Golbchek's desk a screen was showing the debate in the House. The Minister was on her feet and Branka was watching and making notes. The Minister was a handsome woman, a natural dealer, always well-prepared, successful in what was still, as Mark had pointed out, tenaciously a man's world. In the few seconds I saw her as I passed Branka's desk I wondered what had happened to make her my enemy. For she was Marton's God. However Jesuitical his worship might be, however purse-mouthed and judicious his relationship with his deity, she was ultimately the fount of all his goodness. If he was my enemy then she was too.

I gathered up my coat and took the elevator down. In the echoing foyer I was reminded of my last time there and my call to Danno. It stopped me, drove thoughts of Marton, Natya, the Institute out of my head; the sad, familiar puzzle of Danno and me, two people with shared parents, a shared home, shared TV, shared Christmases, shared school, sixteen years of growing up together, that terrible fight with the lad Brak, all this and yet the identity hidden away in my brother's head, in his heart, was uncomprehended by the identity hidden away in mine. So uncomprehended that for months on end he dropped out of my thoughts, was no part of my concern. He no longer *was*, until conjured by a phone booth, sibilant feet. I stopped and stared. How could that be?

People jostled me, muttering. I obstructed trodden life-paths across the vast marble floor. I hurried out, gasped at the cold, flagged a blue-chequer taxi. It was four o'clock and darkening, and I must return to the Institute before going home. I sat very straight on the tired upholstery.

It was Dada's funeral that had started the rot. And Moma. Of course Moma. He thought I took Moma's side. Maybe I did. He who is not against me is with me. But we had good times after that, so why the break? Was it something I did?

The taxi out from the old city centre to the Institute on the ring road took twenty minutes, time enough for me to tidy away the Danno puzzle, to tidy away Danno. He'd looked fine on Thursday's phone screen. We were grown-up people. If I needed him he was there, if he needed me I was here. So why the fuss? The fuss was that for years now, and I didn't know why, he frightened me. My brother frightened me.

At the Institute I returned to the real world . . . There's a laugh. Was that what it was, the nightmare four-day farrago of spies, informers, deception, secret havens, fear – was that what it was? There's a laugh.

I went in search of Gusso first. He was in his office, a glass-walled cubicle adjoining the first-floor general laboratory. I went in search of him because on Saturday, and again today, a kindly Fate had been showing me radiation-test data, rubbing my nose in them, demanding that I make the connection, and at last – in the middle of abusing Dr Marton – I had. Where there's clinically applied radiation, there's shielding. There has to be, to protect the surrounding tissue. Scientists use a lot of shielding. It used to be lead and cumbersome but now it's far lighter, spun carbon and metal-fibre alloy in square two-metre sheets you can cut with scissors.

To lift our electronic tags with solvent was a serious step – it would destroy them and provoke the opposition. But with radiation shielding . . .

Gusso rang up his inventory, found shielding, radiation, eleven sheets. I said I only wanted one and he took me down to the basement store. My sheet folded into a neat package. He didn't ask me what I wanted it for and I didn't tell him. It wasn't that I didn't trust him, I simply felt that using it to mask our tags and fool the SPU seemed squalid. Cowardly. Travelling secretly about the countryside, conspiring with *Natur*, fixing for God the Mother to give my daughter sanctuary, it all made me feel like, look like, be . . . a sneaky sort of person which I didn't want to look like, feel like, be.

Next I went in search of Natya. She wasn't there. It was nearly five o'clock and she'd gone home to her Michael. Maybe that probability was why I'd gone to Gusso, the easy one, first. I could hardly phone her at home with her Michael for the sort of conversation, the sort of accusation, Marton's denial demanded. It would have to wait till tomorrow or even, if I was out of town as I thought I might be, the day after. Thank God for that.

When I arrived home with my package, Mark was waiting for me. He'd come back early, shattered, from the windswept farmlands. The first family he'd visited, following a tip-off, had been so destroyed with skin cancers he'd got no further. He'd sat in the car afterwards, weeping.

I'd told Marton there were no dumb peasants. Wrong. But, dumb was a dumb word – these farmers were simple, and

147

obstinate: they'd cultivated their fields in this way and that way down fifty generations and they hadn't been about to change.

Mark was grey. The state health people were doing nothing, he said. All the money went on fucking Syndrome research. Women were dying in the fields not 200 k's from the capital. It wasn't them you heard from, only AI clients who had to wait half an hour at the clinic, or PTG subjects who complained that the treatment was intrusive. Always assuming they could find a PTG clinic that hadn't been terrorised . . . I let him sound off, respected him for it. He cared about my work, and me, and Anna, but he cared about his work too, and other people. The piece he was researching would be important.

Yvette came in from college and we started fixing dinner. Mark stayed in his study, punishing his keyboard. When I returned to him I showed him the shielding and we tested it with the scanner. It masked the tags. Anna and I could disappear at will, and reappear with the tags undamaged. There'd be nothing to say the watchers hadn't lost us through their own equipment failure.

With scissors I cut a pad I could wear unnoticed beneath a high collar, and another to fit inside a glove. Anna's forehead tag would be less easy to mask unobtrusively. A hat pulled low might do the trick . . . and in any case once we got Anna disappeared we hoped she'd stay that way until the danger was over, so permanent removal with solvent would be the answer. By the way, where *was* Anna?

Mark and I discussed my latest interview with Marton. He'd met the Minister's aide, and if it came to choosing between him and Natalya Mark knew which one he'd believe. As for protective custody, he said they didn't have a chance – whatever the threat they needed parental consent. By the way, where *was* Anna?

I asked if we could discover the recipient of Natya's information from the wire-service number. Mark said the company never supplied names from numbers, but he had a police contact who might help. In any case, knowing Natya, she'd almost certainly tell me the truth if I pressed her, especially if it would help with the threat to Anna. She and Anna were old friends. By the way, where *was* Anna?

Dinner was ready. I'd been determinedly not worrying. Now it was a full hour after the end of Anna's piano lesson, which was a twenty-minute tram ride away. I rang her teacher. Anna had left on time. There'd been no question that she wasn't coming straight home.

I was sensible. We were talking about forty minutes late. It wasn't long. She could have missed her tram. Anything could cause a delay of forty minutes.

The forty minutes stretched to an hour. Yvette knocked on the study door: should she serve dinner? I shook my head and rang Anna's friend just up the road. She couldn't help. I covered my eyes. The lights in Mark's study were unbearably bright. The colours jangled and the drawn curtains kept out terrible secrets.

I suggested calling the police. My child was an hour and a quarter late home from her piano lesson. It wasn't enough. Mark offered to get out the car and drive somewhere. There seemed to be nowhere he could usefully drive – if someone had taken Anna, if Sergeant Milhaus had taken Anna, she'd be far away.

I waited for the telephone to ring. *You can't publish now, we've got her.* Anna was an hour and a half late home from her piano lesson. It still wasn't enough.

I was on the vodka now. Mark was measuring it anxiously. I remembered Liese. Perhaps Anna had gone to visit her sensible Aunt Liese. I rang Liese. Nobody answered. It was ridiculous. If Anna had been there they'd have called me.

An hour and three-quarters late. I was out on the pavement, looking up and down the road. Mark agreed that at two hours he'd call the police. He didn't remind me that Anna's lateness mightn't have anything to do with Sergeant Milhaus, that the city was violent, that she might have been raped, might have been murdered. He didn't need to.

At one hour and fifty-five minutes late a tram came up the road from the city. It stopped, the door hissed open, and Anna dismounted. Her clothes were neat and clean and she waved to me brightly.

'Sorry I'm late, Moma. Have you been waiting?'

I saved my rage for when we were in the house.

She left her school-case on a chair and went slowly through into the big sitting-room. She was very pale. Her brightness had been a sham.

'Honestly Moma, it was ghastly. This poor man did it on purpose. He threw himself under the tram.'

149

'You could have phoned.'

'He was caught between the wheels. They put up screens. It was ghastly.'

Mark was stirring the logs in the stove. He agreed with me. 'You could have phoned, Anna love.'

'I couldn't. They wanted statements. Names and addresses. They took ages to come. It all took ages.'

'I've been worried, Anna. They'd have let you phone.' I grabbed her arm. 'I've been worried out of my fucking mind.'

'In the middle of the street? Phone?' She shook me off. 'There were ambulances. Police. The tram had stopped so suddenly passengers were hurt. It was ghastly, Moma.'

'That's no excuse. Police have radios. You could have got a message through. You know how things are. You've behaved appallingly. I shall never be able to trust you again.'

'That's not fair. There were dozens of us on the tram. People really hurt. Bleeding. Just because you're a raving neurotic, that's no reason for – '

I nearly struck her. 'Shut your mouth. You cruel little monster – don't you realise I've been waiting here for two whole hours, imagining – '

'And what d'you think I've been doing? There was blood, Moma. Maybe you wouldn't have minded. Being a doctor and all that, maybe you wouldn't have minded. I did mind. The man had killed himself, Moma. He'd chewed himself up under the tram . . . '

She was crying and so was I. Mark came between us. 'Annie. Annie love, you've had a terrible experience.' He put an arm round her shoulders. 'An ugly thing happened . . . but it isn't neurotic for your mother to worry when you don't come home. We both – '

'All this screaming at me? Isn't that neurotic? The classic I'm-going-to-punish-you-because-I've-been-frightened – isn't that neurotic?'

'Not again, Annie. You've been frightened too, remember.' He spoke very gently, waiting for her to understand. 'We do both know now that you really couldn't have phoned.'

He held out his other hand to me. Had I screamed? Christ.

I took his hand. 'I'm sorry, Annie love.'

'Me too.'

'And I'm glad you're safe. That's all.'

'I'm glad I'm safe too, Moma.'

The two-hour delay hadn't completely ruined our dinner. It was pretty bad though.

CHAPTER EIGHT

The Attrition. Year 25: mid-August.

'An excellent female embryo, four or five weeks old, firmly implanted.' Dr Vrieland looked across at her over the top of his glasses. 'You're pregnant, Harriet Ryder.'

'I thought I was.' His matchboard office in the City Hospital was tiny: the chair in front of his desk stood sideways to give room for patients' knees. 'That's wonderful.'

He smiled. 'Once more, my dear, this time with feeling.'

'No – it really is wonderful.' It was. She'd wanted Karl's baby for years, now she was having it. 'It's just that . . . '

'It's just that you're twenty-one years old, you have your studies to finish and an important job waiting for you, and you do not think that the man in the case is interested.'

'You get a lot of that.'

Dr Vrieland shrugged. 'Maybe he is married. Maybe he is running multiple families and cannot afford another. Maybe he is a nice man who does not like children. Maybe he is a nasty man who likes children too much. Maybe he has forgotten you. Maybe he never knew you. Maybe – '

She laughed. Which one of these was Karl? 'I don't want a termination, Doctor.'

'My dear Harriet, I never thought you would.'

'I was in love with Karl once and I want his daughter.'

'And if we do not terminate, that is what in eight months' time you will have.'

Silence settled between them, ruminative, letting in the life of the hospital outside the thin partitions. She sensed Dr Vrieland's reservations. She realised also that he had sprung her into an admission she had previously avoided making even to herself. She was living with Karl, having unprotected sex with him, but she was no longer in love with him.

Knowing Dr Vrieland, and the world twenty-five years into the Attrition, that fact would be no part of his reservations.

'I've done my ward work, Doctor. And my gynae. I'm within months of graduating.'

'Indeed yes. And in the shortest time of any student in the history of this hospital.'

'You don't think I should have this child.'

'I think you should consider very carefully. I think you should remember that true excellence is not divisible.'

'You're saying that my work will suffer.'

'No, Harriet. I am saying that your daughter will suffer.' He allowed a long pause, his eyes fixed on hers. '*Suffer* is a big word. You are a healthy woman, you will have a healthy daughter, and you will look after her well. I am saying that in the event of any conflict between your work and your daughter there will be only one possible outcome.'

She stood up briskly. 'Then I'll just have to make sure there aren't any conflicts, won't I?'

Hannes Vrieland was a broad man, tousled, forty-something, not at all old, with large hands and a gentle, fatherly manner she found irresistible. She saw that she'd hurt him. He'd told her an unwelcome truth and she'd come back flip at him. It brought her, on that overwrought day, almost to tears.

'I'll be careful, Hannes,' she whispered. 'Don't spoil my baby for me. I'll be careful.'

She turned to go. One pace, her hand on the door latch, and he was beside her. He could be surprisingly nimble.

'I am your doctor, Harriet.' He gripped her arm. 'We will both be careful. All right?'

'All right.'

She nodded and he released her. 'See my nurse for an appointment at our clinic. Not even the Ryder baby can be allowed to miss being prodded, photographed, scanned, cross-examined on her political affiliations.'

As she left the gynae wing Harriet was listing in her head the people she could tell. First she looked in on the junior staff common-room. 'I'm pregnant,' she announced to its only occupants, two frazzled interns she scarcely knew. 'With child, in the club, *enceinte*, expecting . . . Isn't it wonderful?'

She left before they could agree with her. Then she visited her course professor. 'It's not going to interfere with my work,' she told him, leaving again before comment was possible.

The canteen girls cheered her news. The porters, always

lugubrious women, gave her a slow handclap. The laundry staff promised little vests.

She rang Liese, with a sociology degree now and a job in parent management, still living with the Haldanes, but Liese was out most afternoons with her problem families. Harriet didn't leave a message. She didn't know what to say. She'd try again later – the chances were, in the months ahead she was going to need Liese.

Harriet rang her mother. They communicated regularly but incompletely. Bess was still in the same little house down by the Windstrohm harbour. She hadn't met Karl but she knew he was black. This she didn't mind. His crime was maleness – she couldn't understand why Harriet hadn't stayed with sensible Liese. She was claiming to be homo these days, which explained a lot.

'It's me, Moma. I'm pregnant.'

'That's nice, dear. Do you know the father?'

She wasn't being funny, which was why you had to laugh.

'I'll finish my degree work, Moma. Then I've got an application in with Unikhem. They'll pay me while I get my doctorate.'

'Plus a baby? Not if they're men, they won't.'

'They'll have to. I'm the best applicant.'

Bess had her doubts. 'I talked to your brother last week. He's doing well for himself.'

'Moma – what shall I call your granddaughter?'

'Call her Anna. Your gran would like that.'

Harriet rang other people, friends, but they were all out working. She got round to Daniel. Karl could wait. It was time she moved out and she might never tell him at all. He answered none of Dr Vrieland's descriptions. He had no wives and no known children, and he said he'd welcome both or either. But he was a games-player by nature, what he himself would have called a 'free spirit', and his various women had recognised the signals in time, Harriet included. That was why, now, she was having his daughter: unlike her father Johan, he asked no questions of life and wished to be told no lies. He was safe. Ultimately he'd defend his free spirit with whatever it took.

She picked up the telephone to call Daniel, then put it down. Four years ago, at their father's funeral, he'd walked away from her and Moma, away along School Lane, the loneliest person in the world. They'd called each other and written since, he sent her a traditional gold bracelet for her twenty-first, hideous, but they never met. She had her work, away in her city, and he had his work away in his.

Moma was wrong to say he'd done well for himself and she knew it. The small promotions that had come to him in the army had gone again. There were fights, apparently. Harriet never questioned him and he never did more than hint that his CO was an Easterner with a hate of Westerners. A few months ago, at the end of his nine-year contract, he'd quit on the advice of a friend called Breitholmer and joined one of the private security agencies. He was based in the city now and had an address, 17 Pike Street, no great distance from the hospital. She decided her news would make a good excuse to visit him.

She didn't ask why she needed an excuse to visit him. Neither did she ask if the excuse was to give him or to give herself.

The hospital was in a shabby area of the old town. Pike Street, a ten-minute walk away, was shabbier, not helped by the August heat and dust. January wouldn't help Pike Street either. Small shops on one side, many of them boarded up and scrofulous with shredded viscera-coloured posters, and on the other side a derelict car-repair yard, two raw-ended houses held up with timber braces, a wine warehouse and an old people's day centre. Cats watched her from doorsteps and window-sills. A vandalised delivery truck rested on its hubs outside the warehouse. Some girls hung about outside the repair yard, kicking the blue plastic fence. Otherwise nothing moved.

It was a street where trust buttons might still be an issue. They died hard. Girls hereabouts, loyal to traditional role models, might well run gangs demanding buttons, but jokily, with a lot of bad language and little action. Male gangs, middle-aged now and heavy-duty, were rarer but a problem – policewomen on the beat found them hard to deal with, and policemen, older and higher in rank, preferred to stay in their patrol cars. It was not a street that Harriet would care to visit after dark, alone.

Danno lived above the shops: his doorway was between a launderette and a hologram rental firm. Harriet hesitated. She should have telephoned ahead. The chances were he'd still be out at work.

Reassured, she rang the bell. A camera inspected her, a speaker gave her Danno's voice, words she didn't catch, and the door opened. There was a staircase inside. She had no alternative but to climb it. He was wearing a crisp grey NatSekur shirt and pants, and his boots gave off sparks.

'Harri. This is great. I just got in. Long time no see.'

'Yes. Yes . . . it is.' He was bigger than she remembered, and more army. 'You're looking good, Danno. Your new job suits you.'

He was in good shape, one of those men at their best in a uniform.

'You're not bad yourself, Harri. Not bad at all. Well . . . what d'you think of it?'

He stepped back and gestured at the room. She'd already seen it past him and been amazed. It must have extended over several of the shops downstairs and it was magnificent: rich oatmealy fabrics, a floor of the latest polished pine-needle terrazzo, a traditional blue-tiled wood-stove, the best electronics, velvety high-definition black-and-white photographs, sexy, on the walls, a brown glass drinks area, the lushest responsive seating. It explained the fancy security arrangements at the door. It had nothing to do with what she knew of Danno.

'It's super, Danno. Did you win the lottery?'

'Not me. It's Bert's. The guy I share with. I told you. Kitchen, two bedrooms, two baths, study, sauna, all this . . . and a roof garden out the back. Done well, haven't I? Bertholt Breitholmer. Captain Breitholmer. I told you.'

'You told me you shared. Not his name. You said he was with NatSekur.'

'That's right. Bert got me in. We met in the army. He left first, made NatSekur captain after only six months. He says I'll do the same. Us being Military Police helps.'

'It obviously does, Danno. I'm impressed.' She removed her floppy hat, went in, sat down. She'd heard you had to wait a few seconds for these seats to take up on you but the one she'd chosen took up instantly. The room was air-conditioned. She found such luxury shocking. The old Danno would have found it shocking too. Perhaps that explained his nervous chatter.

He crossed to the drinks area. 'What can I get you? Coffee, tea? We don't have alcohol. Orange juice, grapefruit, iced milk?'

She laughed. 'Coffee'll do fine . . . No alcohol, Danno?' She should have liked that but she didn't. 'What *has* your Bert done to you?'

'It's not him, Harri. I do what I like.' He drew the coffee. 'There's a bar just down the street. I go easy, that's all.' She felt reprimanded. He brought her a cup, and one for himself. 'And how's the world treating you, old girl?'

He sat down opposite her, attended to the crease in his uniform trousers, leaned back, the chair accepting him.

'I'm fine.' She crossed her legs. 'Graduation in a couple of months, then a research job lined up.'

That was all he was getting. He wasn't nervous, he was loving it. Cups of coffee, old girl . . . any minute now, lovely weather for the time of year.

Danno drank his coffee. 'Where are you off to for your holiday? Or have you been?'

She should have known. Hols were better than the weather any day. 'I don't bother much with holidays,' she said stuffily. 'I suppose I'm lucky – work's my holiday. I might go down, see Moma for a couple of days.'

'Yes. Well . . . I won't be getting a holiday this year, not with changing jobs and that.'

And what? She heard her silent carping. She'd been carping ever since she got there. She reached out to him. 'We might go off together somewhere, Danno. Just for a weekend.'

'Would you like to? That'd be great.' He sat forward, creases forgotten. 'Really great. Moma said you had a bloke last time we talked but I told her you couldn't have . . . Maybe we could go up to the mountains. Find a state camp.'

'I'd like that, Danno.' The last summer before her baby.

She didn't correct him about not having a bloke. She wasn't sure if she 'had' Karl or not.

Danno sagged. 'I can't do weekends. I forgot. It's the shift-work and that.'

And what? *Shut up.*

'It doesn't have to be weekends, Danno. If I'm not on at the hospital we can go any time.'

'That's all right, then. That's fine.'

She could see it still wasn't. He was no actor.

They talked about where they'd go. One of the cushy places,

easy to reach and no mosquitoes – they weren't outdoors people. Danno got out maps. There were tilt-rotor ferries to get them there, or they could hire a car. Danno said he liked the idea of roughing it in the car. Car or tilt-rotor, she knew they'd never go. What had Danno remembered? Not his shift-work. Captain Bertholt Breitholmer?

She changed the subject, coming at him sideways.

'Last time I was down with Moma she was pretending she was homo. Did she tell you?'

He gaped at her. 'That says it all, Harri. I always knew it. That fucking says it all.'

She persevered. 'I don't think it's true, though. It doesn't feel right. I think it's part of the God the Mother thing. I've known lots of homos and it doesn't feel right.'

'Trust you, Harri.'

'What d'you mean?'

'Trust you to fucking stick up for her. Christ Almighty, if she was shagging donkeys you'd stick up for her.' He'd lurched up out of his chair and was back at the bar, stabbing buttons.

'Stick up for her? What's there to stick up for? I wasn't – ' She stopped, watched his anger as he gave himself more coffee, spilling it on the brown glass counter. She'd tried for a reaction, now she didn't know what it meant.

He mopped up the spills with a cloth. 'You're only a kid,' he muttered. 'You wouldn't understand. More coffee?' He didn't wait for an answer. 'I said, would you like more coffee?'

She stood up also. She'd buggered this whole visit. 'I ought to be going.' She gave him her cup. She'd been totting him up like a patient. She had no right. 'Great coffee, Danno.'

'Yeah . . . Bert likes his coffee . . . Look, you can't go. You must stay and meet him. He's heard all about you. He'll be back any minute.'

'I have things to do, Danno. I really can't – '

'You must. He's heard all about my little sister. You're my *family*, for fuck's sake.'

'I'm sorry, love.' Love? Yes. Yes, she loved him very much. And she was his family. But she wasn't his little sister, not in the way he meant, and possibly never had been. 'I've got to go. I'm on duty at six.' Any lie would do. 'I just thought I'd pop in, see how you're getting along.'

'Getting along?' His eyes glazed briefly, then he slipped back into the social and the possible. 'Landed on my feet, Harri. See for yourself. Always was a jammy bastard.' He was at the head of the stairs, easing her out. 'You really got to go, then?'

He couldn't wait. If she wasn't his little sister, and if she wouldn't stay to be shown off to Bert, he couldn't wait. So that her pregnancy, which she'd been afraid to tell him about, could be lost in the babble of her going.

'I do have one bit of news, Danno. I'm pregnant. If all goes well I'll be having the baby in April.'

'Hey. Congratulations. I'll be an uncle . . . ' He peered at her sideways. 'Congratulations in order, are they?'

'They're in order.'

'That's great. Great.'

Not too lost. 'I'll be calling her after Granna.'

'Hey – Anna after Granna. Does she know yet?'

'I'm ringing her tonight.'

She'd expected him to ask about a father but Danno's eyes were flicking past her, down the stairs.

'I'll be on my way, then.'

'You won't change your mind?'

'I can't.'

'I know. Duty calls. Thanks for coming by, Harri.'

She looked round the room. For an ex-army security captain Bert had done very well for himself. 'I'll call you about our camping trip.'

'Do that. And Harri – look after yourself. You're eating for two now.'

She went down the stairs. They hadn't touched so far and they didn't touch now. He released the remote latch, she opened the door, waved, jammed on her hat, and went out into the street. The door closed expensively behind her. Opposite, the girls were still kicking the repair yard's plastic fence. It was stronger than they, but not for much longer.

Danno was a mess. Everything about him was a lie, his reaction to the baby most of all. He'd hated it. She didn't know why she was so certain, but he'd hated it. *Hated it* . . .

As she went back along the street a man in the uniform of a NatSekur officer was walking towards her, his studded bootsteps ringing loudly. He was upright, well built, dark close-cropped hair showing beneath the leather binding of his wide-brimmed summer cap, his strongly lined face suggesting fifty-plus years in command of himself and others. They observed each other openly. Harriet realised that living on Pike Street presented no problems if one had the presence of Captain Breitholmer – it had to be he – or the muscles of her brother.

As he approached, Captain Breitholmer stepped off the narrow pavement into the roadway, not breaking his stride, saluting jauntily and giving her the smallest twitch of a smile. She returned both smile and salute as he passed. For a man old enough to be her father, and a man who had done suspiciously well for himself, he was extraordinarily attractive. Glancing over her shoulder, she saw him stop at the door to number 17, dig in his pocket for keys. Their eyes met again, then she went on her way.

Dr Vrieland hadn't spoiled her baby for her. Danno had. But then, he'd wanted to. She set about putting together her happiness again.

At the top of the stairs Bert Breitholmer removed his cap and accurately lobbed it on to its hook. He loosened his tie and as he crossed the room he was taking off his jacket.

'Christ, what a fucking awful day. The city's been like a fucking oven.'

He disappeared into his bedroom, reappeared without shoes and shirtless, undoing his trousers.

'Those poor bloody anti-PTG guys. They haven't got a clue. Fix an iced coffee for me, will you Corporal, for after my shower?'

He removed his trousers and socks and underpants, tossed them through the open doorway behind him, and went into the bathroom.

'I mean, we knew they were coming. Their security's pathetic. We were waiting for them. And when they finally turned up – '

His voice was drowned by the noise of the shower. Daniel had been sitting with his feet up, an unopened fashion magazine in his lap. He rose, went to the bar, drew cold black coffee, added ice. No cream – Bert had to watch the calories.

Daniel put the mug on the end of the brown glass bar-top, wondered what to have himself, decided not to bother. He'd soaked up enough coffee while bloody Harri was here. He opened a can of pine-nuts and took a handful, leaning on the bar to eat them, spitting the husks into his hand. He thought about nothing.

Bert Breitholmer came in from the bathroom naked, individual drops of water like beads on his skin. He stood by the bar, drinking his coffee.

'I mean, it was slaughter. Or it would have been, if I'd let it. They came marching in like it was some fucking high-school treat. Three guys in dinky face-masks, no flanking, no feints, no cover, just straight in up the middle. Their bombs clear as day on my scope. We could've detonated the lot of them remote. Minced the poor fucking idiots.' He finished his coffee, turned to Daniel behind the bar. 'You're very quiet, Corporal. Anything wrong?'

Daniel wiped damp husks off his palm, into the bin. 'I'm fine. You were saying about the PTG guys?'

'I told you yesterday. We had this tip-off, so we were waiting for them. Not that I'm a PTG-lover – you know that. Frankly, Corporal, I'd have been out there with the bombers, given the choice. And I'd have made a better job of it.'

He stalked about the room, back very straight, sniffing the air. His feet were already dry and made no marks.

He said, 'Something's happened. You're not yourself, Corporal. I can feel it.'

Daniel shrugged. 'I hate bloody PTG. It's not natural. Who do women think they are?'

'Cloning is genetically unsound, Corporal. It limits the gene base. It's also unreliable and very expensive and diverts funds from finding a cure.'

'So what happened?'

'This afternoon? At the city PTG centre? Shot the knees off one, paragassed the others. When will they learn?' He stopped in the middle of the floor, legs apart, arms folded, waiting till he had Daniel's full attention. 'There's an atmosphere. You're not telling me something.'

Daniel gave in. 'My sister was here.'

'Tall? Sexy smile? Walks with her feet turned out? Yellow hair in a straggly bun?'

Daniel stared at him, not answering. Usually Bert knew when to leave well alone.

Breitholmer laughed, flung himself down on a sofa. 'I saw her. She was leaving as I came by. Very nice, Corporal. I'm surprised you don't have her picture. Up in your room, I mean. I'm surprised you don't have her picture.'

'She didn't stay. Caught me up on the family news. I gave her a coffee.'

'Fine. That's what it's there for. You pay your share. So why the atmosphere?'

'There's no atmosphere.'

'I mean, your beautiful sister comes to call, she doesn't stay, and you give her a coffee which you've every right to. So why the atmosphere?'

Daniel grinned at him desperately. 'There's no atmosphere.'

'No? No . . . ' Breitholmer nodded and lay back indolently, eyes half-closed, one hairless leg over the sofa arm. 'Christ, it was hot in the city. We could have minced those pathetic bastards. Where were you today?'

Daniel tried to remember. Harri came in between and made remembering difficult. 'Today? Today I was down at the meat market, and – '

'The meat market was yesterday, Corporal. Today you had a cushy inside job in the provincial bank headquarters.' The reminder was gentle. Breitholmer yawned. 'And you still say there isn't an atmosphere?'

'I'm new at NatSekur. My jobs are all the fucking same. How the hell do you expect me to remember?'

Breitholmer slowly straightened the leg that was hanging over the sofa arm, looked along it at his foot which he turned from side to side, spreading his toes. 'I had a sister once. I don't think I told you. She went off to Africa to do good works. The local blacks thought she meant on her back. Maybe she did, the silly cunt, but not like that. Not for the mass market.' He laughed harshly. 'She didn't last long.'

Daniel had nothing to say to that. Breitholmer came to a decision, swung his leg off the sofa arm and stood up. 'So. No atmosphere. How was your sister?'

'Fine.'

'I'd say she looked fine. Very fine. Nothing else?'

'For Christ's sake, what d'you want me to say? Nothing else.'

'OK, Corporal. OK . . . ' He came to the bar, leaned across it, the edge of brown glass digging into his muscled belly. 'So I push you sometimes. You pay your way here – you can tell me to get the fuck to hell. There's no rank here, Corporal. But we go back a bit now and I know there's something bugging you.' He put a hand on Daniel's shoulder. 'I'd like to help.'

'There's nothing bugging me. Harriet's fine. There's nothing bugging me.'

Breitholmer's grey eyes stared into his. The hand tightened.

'It's nothing much. She says my moma's gone lezzie. She's come out of the fucking closet.'

Breitholmer's hand continued to tighten. Daniel sweated with the pain. He lasted it out and the hand relaxed. Breitholmer cuffed him lightly.

'You see, Corporal? We mustn't have secrets. I was right to push.' Daniel knew he wasn't believing him. 'Just look at it this way, Corporal. Remind me – how old are you?'

'I'm twenty-seven.'

'So look at it this way. Be glad she didn't find she was homo twenty-seven years ago. Else you'd've been nipped in the bud before you'd fucking started.' He cuffed him again. 'I'm fifty-two, incidentally.'

He padded away, across the bright pine-needle flooring, into his bedroom. When he returned, dressed in shirt and slacks, Daniel had just got round to tidying away the maps Harriet and he had been looking at. He stopped tidying them and spread them out instead.

'I've been thinking,' he said. 'Why don't you and me get away? Have a weekend up in the mountains. Book a camp.'

Later that night he went out on his own, into the city. Breitholmer looked up from the TV but didn't try to stop him. He would worry, though, until Daniel got back.

After her time with Danno Harriet didn't return to the hospital. She didn't go home to Karl either. She found the nearest tram stop and rode out to the Haldanes'. Liese was in from work now and they had a long talk. It was agreed that they'd find somewhere to live as soon as possible, and after the baby was

163

born Liese would give up her job. It was the obvious solution. They wouldn't set up a formal contract but Liese knew about co-parenting from her work, and Unikhem would be paying Harriet enough for the three of them. Always assuming that the job offer still stood, and it would. There weren't that many Harriet Ryders in the barrel.

Going home from the Haldanes' late that night, Harriet had to change trams in the city centre. Despite the hour the square was hot and dusty. Its sex supermarket days were over but a few prostitutes still paraded beneath the trees. The world's oldest profession was on hard times. Harriet was surprised that the females among them could still earn a living – with so many women glad to give it away, were there enough men left who wanted a commercial element in their sex, the remote, non-judgemental, naughty transaction that only paying gave them? She thought how lucky she'd been to have Karl, and wondered what she'd do about sex after the baby. Go without? She sure as hell didn't want to join the frantic meat market the Attrition was causing.

As Harriet waited for her tram Danno walked by in the shadows on the other side of the street. She saw him and waved, but he didn't notice. He was out of uniform, oddly insignificant in a decent grey shirt and decent trousers. A nice young man. He couldn't have hated her baby. She'd been overwrought.

He walked by quickly, obviously going somewhere. She called to him but a tram was approaching and drowned her voice. And when it had passed he was round the corner and gone. She was glad she'd seen him. It showed he had a life apart from that creepy flat and Captain Breitholmer.

The next morning's news report led with pictures of a young woman murdered in a back street a mile or so from the city centre. Harriet was understandably shocked, but made no connections. The young woman, a piano-tuner working for one of the big stores, had died of a fractured windpipe. She hadn't been raped. The TV station reminded viewers of a similar crime, two years before, which had remained unsolved. Harriet still made no connections. She had no reason to.

In the flat on Pike Street Daniel had left for work and Captain

Breitholmer, who didn't believe in taking chances, was burning a decent grey shirt and decent trousers. Daniel missed them a couple of days later but he didn't say anything.

CHAPTER NINE

The Attrition. Year 40: early November.

I was at the central railway station by eight that Tuesday morning, carrying the statutory small overnight bag. The routine we'd planned was as old as a last-millennium spy movie – Mark had worked out this particular variation with the help of Yvette's train timetable. Foreign students are useful for items like train timetables that no local resident ever has.

At the ticket office I bought a cheap day-return – loudly but not ostentatiously – for a place up north where there was a major experimental IVF centre and therefore a reason for my visit. The train there was standing at the platform, smouldering, ready to leave. I boarded it, locked myself in a toilet, took the two radiation shields out of my overnight bag and put them on my neck and hand. Then I went along the corridor until I found a compartment with few, and female, occupants. I screwed myself up, entered it hurriedly, muttered that I was fleeing a lover, and left it on the far side, climbing down on to the track. Faces peered down at me. It wasn't necessary that the women should believe me, only that they shouldn't raise a fuss. They didn't. There'd have been no point.

Climbing up into the next train over was harder. The door handle was out of reach above my head and the side of the carriage was smooth, but there was an exterior step at floor-level and I made it with a jump and a bit of a struggle, closing the door behind me just as the train I had left rolled out. I crossed my new train, found the local I needed on the next platform, and stayed on it, buying my ticket from the collector when he came round. Finally, three stops on down the line, I got off, waited a few minutes, and boarded a train to where I was really going, the South Foreland, again buying my ticket from the collector.

I sat and watched the world go by. If all had gone to plan I had vanished. Assuming I was being tracked, I had dropped off their scopes. I had bought a train ticket, entered a train, and disappeared – a local effect they could attribute to interference, the masking of the metal carriage. If they were trusting and called ahead for someone to pick up my tag at the other end they were in trouble, and if they were untrusting and immediately set up a search they were still in trouble – I'd given them the whole country to search in and no tags to follow.

I spell this out because I sharply remember the pleasure fooling them gave me. I couldn't imagine why I'd thought it would be squalid. The mechanics were delightful, this door and that door, this ticket and that ticket – also the simple fact of being vanished. I was nowhere. I didn't exist. The illusion was marvellous, exciting, a new start. I sat and watched the world go by, feeling uniquely free.

It didn't last. The world as it went past my train window was suburbs, then huge flat fields ploughed in great clods as far as the horizon, grey with frost under a greyer sky. I had a three-hour journey ahead of me, and the Minister on my return, and Marton, and Sergeant Milhaus. I was uniquely unfree.

We were keeping Anna home from school. After yesterday's false alarm I was taking no chances. Mark was staying home with her – he had his UV piece to work on. Until we could move Anna to a safe place she wouldn't leave the house and she'd never be on her own. I'd wanted to stay with her myself and send Mark on this trip, but he hadn't spoken to Moma since our wedding, which was seven years ago, and in any case he scarcely knew her. Also, the island I was going to hadn't been called Nomansland for nothing: although it didn't mean entirely what it said – there were male community members teaching in the school – unknown men arriving at the gate stood a good chance of being turned away.

Moma had been there ten years or so. Granna, who'd taught in the convent school but never became a nun, was dead now. She hadn't been old and she'd died last year, of nothing in particular. The doctor's stand-by, heart failure. I still missed her badly, especially when I had good news to share, but if she'd had her reasons I respected them. At seventy, after nearly forty years of skewed Attrition living, maybe she'd had enough. On the other hand, hearts did fail for their own secret diastolic reasons.

Moma was a full nun now. Poverty, chastity, obedience . . . I didn't see the first two bothering her – she'd never valued things as property, and sex had been so confused for her that doing without it, on holy grounds, would be a relief (I was sure the homo phase had just been ideological) – but obedience must come very hard. That she'd stuck it, and prospered under it, was a tribute both to Moma and to the Order's founder. At my only brief personal contact with Margarethe Osterbrook, at Dada's funeral, her robust spirituality had impressed me. She'd come a long way from the unctuous vehemence of my childhood. Even TV preachers could grow.

She'd not so much founded her order as had it thrust upon her by popular demand. There were convents now for the Daughters of God the Mother in twenty-seven countries. Not a monastic herself, Osterbrook gave the convents total self-government as she got on with her preaching, travelling constantly. On the rare occasions when I bumped into clips of her on TV I got the impression that, while she undoubtedly loved her people, she didn't like them very much. This gave her words a refreshing edge.

I wasn't expecting exactly a fulsome welcome, as Moma's famous daughter, on my arrival at Nomansland. Convents are never flabby places – it takes steel to keep people living even half-way peaceably together – and a convent backed by Margarethe Osterbrook would be as bright and sharp as any.

The train made good time across the flat southern plain – 500 k's in just over two hours – and then climbed briskly through the mountain passes of the coastal divide. Up there November had taken hold and the treeless north-facing ridges were streaked with snow. The train leaned on steeply banked curves, with only space rushing beneath my window, and hawks circling, and a tiny river winding in the distant valley bottom. The grey overcast thinned, letting a white sun show through. The train reached the highest pass and swooped on down the other side, zigzagging. Ahead of us and far below, the islands off the South Foreland – Nomansland the nearest and largest – were ringed with ice-white foam in a black sea. They flashed on and off between tree-trunks, steep rocky outcrops, the gables of old hunting-lodges, then disappeared as the train descended.

At the station there was a bus to take me out over the bridge to the island. The town on the mainland, an ancient fishing community, was prosperous now that sound design had brought the hard physical labour down to womansize and women's international agreements had restored fish stocks in northern waters. The town's road surfaces were heated and drained now, and my bus passed a huge domed athletics stadium and swimming-pool that hadn't been there on my last visit. The Attrition had been hard on team sports but individual competition was as hot as ever.

Nomansland was the only island off the South Foreland still with a bridge and still inhabited. Falling population levels world-wide had emptied the others. When my grandmother first came to Nomansland – then called Pakke – there were farms, a large private boarding-school, and a year-round village. Now only the school remained, extended to accommodate ninety-odd nuns as well as the girls and school staff.

The bus left me outside the convent gates, on the turn-around at the top of the cliffs on the island end of the k-long bridge. I was its only passenger, and when it had departed for the mainland I stood for a moment on the chiselled red-black rock of the roadway, dazed by the silence, my legs still buzzing from wheels and engines. Only the wind hissed in my ears, and small sounds of the sea on rocks far below. Wintry sunlight shone through the overcast, sharpening the white arrow-flight of the bridge and the orange dot of the bus as it diminished to invisibility.

I turned to the gates of the convent. They were ribbed glass in slender frames, lit internally so that on a grey day such as this the archway in the original high wall of the school was welcoming – despite the glum legend *Nomansland* carved above it. And beyond, above the wall, loomed the roofs and turrets of the ancient convent building, once a royal summer retreat. The gates might appear fragile and ineffective, but with modern materials and electronics they were surely neither. Not that there was much for them to keep out – and they kept in only the few schoolgirls randy enough to face the long walk to the mainland (no bus driver would take them) and the rough and ready, very rough and very ready, lovers they would find there. No, the gates' function related to the letters carved above them. They approved. *Nomansland*: God was in Her heaven and all was right with the world.

Why then was I planning to send Anna here, I who accepted neither of those proposals? I shrugged. Because I'd no fucking alternative.

I stepped forward. On my last visit to Moma a little wicket-gate had opened automatically at my approach and a recorded voice had invited me through to a beefy nun behind a reception desk inside. Today, when I arrived at the gates, nothing happened. The wicket was still there, and beside it now a discreet bell-push. I pushed it. After a suitable pause the gate was opened by a pretty, noticeably unbeefy nun. Convent policy had changed. No more dazzling with science. Technology was out, the human face was in. This had to be aimed at parents. They'd long fallen out with technics, and this was importantly a school.

A label on the nun's left breast identified her as Daughter Annika. She gently took my arm and led me to the reception desk, where she asked my name and business. She walked on her toes, with the coiled grace of a judo black belt. Under the new order few risks were being taken.

Moma worked in the kitchens and video/hologram library. My experience was that she could easily be prised loose for a fifteen-minute break to talk in an interview room with her daughter. More than that and you had to write or phone ahead. I booked Moma for my usual short meeting, then asked Daughter Annika please to contact the Convent Superior's office as it was important that I talk with Her Reverence. Moma could advise me on presenting Anna's case for sanctuary, but only the Convent Superior could authorise it.

Annika frowned delightfully – her skin was exquisite, with the bloom of angel faces painted on silk – and told me that requests given at such short notice were unusual but she'd do what she could. She tapped buttons, spoke, listened, reported that I was in luck – the Convent Superior would see me during the after-lunch rest period. I was welcome to eat with the teaching staff in the school refectory, and before that – she rang a small brass handbell – a novice daughter would take me to one of the interview rooms where my mother, Daughter Elizabeth, would quickly join me.

I thanked her. The convent murmured about me; rustling feet, and voices, and occasional bursts of children's laughter. Distantly a piano was played, accompanying a cello. The nun who answered the bell was a handsome young woman, sexuality undimmed by her shaven head and drab brown shift. In a

170

world where she'd probably stay celibate maybe she was offering it up to God the Mother. I hoped she made it to ordination but the boisterous length of her stride and the moist fullness of her lips promised trouble. And the longing glances she cast upon the clothes under my topcoat, the grey suede-textured suit and simple high-necked jersey I'd thought meek enough for the Convent Superior. I had to keep my topcoat on, and at least my right-hand glove: they masked the shielding over my tags.

The novice led me away from the reception block, across a paved quadrangle to the main convent administrative complex, and left me in an interview room I hadn't seen before. It was entirely pre-Millennium, chintz and dark oak tables with turned legs, a good Canaletto print above the period fireplace and a fine view out to sea. There was a recently installed coffee-dispenser, however, and the novice had said I could help myself, so I did. I stood by the window with my cup, looking out at the sea. At freedom. I remembered the decisive click of the ribbed-glass gate behind me and my impulse to turn and beat my fists against the glass. Presumably there were minds in here that found the gate's click comfortable.

I had resisted the impulse. I was on a short visit. Anna, very like me and on a short visit too, would resist it also.

There was a tap on the door, I called something, and Moma entered. She was shining.

'Harriet. What a lovely surprise. How good to see you.'

'Moma . . . you're looking great.' She was. She needed the gate and its click. She left her anger outside, its corrosions. The click told her she was home. Moma, laughing, was the girl my father had fallen in love with. She was the happiest woman I knew. She belonged here, where she served and was never disappointed. God the Mother and Jesus, through the wise agency of the Convent Superior, had checked her flailing, established boundaries for her, given her self-respect. Visiting her was a pleasure.

She was also a little crazy. Not Alzheimer's crazy, at fifty-eight, just crazy crazy.

We embraced. 'Harriet – I've got so much to tell you. And how is little Anna? Starting school soon, I suppose. My good-ness, how they grow.'

I moved her on whenever we met, but she always slipped back. The outside world had stopped for her on the day she renounced it for Jesus and God the Mother. Psycho-engineering could have sorted her out – that was my neighbour Peter Simpson's area – but the convent doctor saw little advantage and I agreed with her. Moma needed to disconnect. Maybe, having long felt she was in the world's driving-seat, she couldn't accept the idea of it moving on without her.

'And Mark – how is he? Has he found you all somewhere proper to live yet?'

We'd been in the apartment last time she'd seen us. She'd never thought it 'proper', she who'd had a house to raise her children in.

'Mark's fine, Moma. He sends his love.' We sat down at the table, held hands across it. 'We have a big house now, Moma, with a garden and a garage. And a nice French student to help us with the housework.'

I was impressing her for her sake, not mine. I did so on every visit and she was always pleased.

'An au pair, Harri? Are you sure that's wise? Mark's not like other men, I know, but he *is* only human.'

I told her, as always, that I trusted Mark completely, and that if he wanted to stray he wouldn't need Yvette – what with AIDS and the Attrition there were a hundred women for every man in the city.

'Don't I know it, pet. Sex is all the videos for the library seem to be about these days. I ask the Convent Superior if I've any doubts. She's a sensible woman.'

I didn't tell her, as always, that I once warned Mark that I felt I should loan him out, as a gesture of female solidarity, unless he did his duty by the sperm banks. He did, of course, so my solidarity was never tested.

'Anna's been at school for a while now, Moma. She's fifteen, and so beautiful you wouldn't believe.'

'Fiddle. Mothers always think their daughters are beautiful.' She looked at me sharply. 'It's not always a recipe for happiness, Harri.'

This was new, and amusing. It suggested she found me so middle-aged now that she could imagine me being jealous of a beautiful daughter. I moved on quickly.

'It's about Anna that I've come, Moma. I'd like her to spend some time here in the convent. Are there any snags? Paying, for example – does the community accept donations or would the Convent Superior be offended?'

'Anna? Down here? When do you want her to come?'

I cleared my throat. 'Tomorrow,' I admitted.

'In the middle of term?'

'If that's all right with the Convent Superior.'

'And for how long?'

'I don't know.'

I shrugged apologetically. I'd explain if I had to, and truthfully, but it wouldn't be easy and Moma'd be no better for knowing.

Apparently, uncrazy on some important level, Moma understood this, for she asked no questions.

'It does happen,' she said. 'Parents who suddenly have to go abroad . . . I don't know about the school side of things, but the community never says no to a donation.' She leaned towards me, lowered her voice. 'Tell her Anna needs to come on a retreat. That's something she can never refuse.'

She laughed awkwardly, and looked round as if she thought the interview room was bugged. I doubted that. Trust was important in a place like this.

'I'd rather not start with a lie, Moma. I – '

'Of course not, dear.' She patted my gloved hand. 'I was naughty to suggest it. Just tell her you have family reasons.' Again she whispered. 'Then she'll think it's to do with saving your marriage . . . '

She sat up straight, glared at me, said loudly, 'It's *not* to do with saving your marriage, is it?'

I laughed. 'No, Moma. I promise. Mark and I are fine . . . '

'That's all right then.' She relaxed, patted her brown-robed chest in what, for a shaven-haired nun, was a curiously matronly gesture. Then she settled herself expectantly, elbows on the table.

'So how're you doing, Moma?' I said. 'How's Daughter Pasquale?'

Daughter Pasquale, working in the kitchens, was the cross Moma bore. She was a fat, jolly person with no idea of the right way of doing things. She stacked the washers incorrectly and Moma had to go along behind her, restacking them.

173

'Pasquale's not been well, Harri. She's losing weight. I worry for her . . .'

I listened to her symptoms, the treatment prescribed, and the prayers being said for her. From the sound of the first two, the prayers were her best hope. Poor Daughter Pasquale, and poor Moma . . .

Our fifteen minutes came to an end. A tactful warning bell reminded us and Moma stood up. We embraced again and she went quickly to the door. There she paused.

'Do you have any news of your brother, Harri?'

I thought how often, as a doctor, I'd seen the most important question masquerading as an afterthought.

'Not much, Moma. You know how he is. I called him last week. He seemed fine.'

'No, Harri.' She turned and faced me. 'He didn't seem fine. He never seems fine. You come here, and you think I'm silly, and you tell me everything's fine. Everybody's fine. But I'm not silly, and everybody's not fine.'

She dismayed me. Her back was against the door, her hand ready on the knob. Only that way, I think, did she feel safe enough to say these things.

'Daniel's not fine. You think I don't remember but I do. Every day I remember that I sat on your father's knee, Harri, and you sat on the other, and your father sent Daniel up to his room, and I saw his hurt, and I was happy. It was in our kitchen. It's a long time ago now, but I was happy. He'd hurt you, something or other, and I was happy seeing him hurt in return.' She shifted her gaze, staring past me at the window and the sea beyond. 'Daniel's not fine. Never. Never.'

'That's nonsense, Moma.' I was angry. I could see where she was going, and it was towards much too big a guilt. 'Everybody *can* be fine. Listen to me, Moma – it's up to them. It really is up to them.' I believed it. I still do.

Moma's eyes refocused. 'You're hard, Harri. You're my daughter, and I love you very much, but I have to say it. You're hard.' She fumbled behind her, opened the door. 'I hope the Convent Superior agrees to have little Anna. I shall like seeing her. And Harriet – next time you talk to Daniel, say I was asking after him . . . 'Bye now. God bless.'

The door closed on her. I flung myself down in my chair,

amazed. What the hell had brought that on? Moma'd gone stir crazy. Of course I was hard. Life was hard. Bloody hard.

I wasn't amazed. Amazed was the word I chose, but really I was destroyed. Reconstruction took time.

Soon afterwards the refectory bell rang for lunch. I stayed where I was. The novice came for me. Normally I'd have enjoyed talking to the teachers but I told her I wasn't hungry. Moma'd gone stir crazy and anyway I couldn't sit at the staff dining-table in topcoat and glove. It was unlikely that the SPU down here would be scanning for my tags, but I saw no point in taking the risk. For all I knew, there might be a nation-wide alert. And Moma'd gone stir crazy.

I stayed quietly in the interview room, opening the window for fresh air and coolness in my outdoor clothes. The wind had died down and the air was still, the sound of the sea gentle. And I was hard. No. But Hannes Vrieland had thought so. *In any conflict between your work and your daughter there can be only one outcome.* I sat at the table. Like Moma I remembered that moment in the kitchen above the harbour. She could still shake me. What the hell was I to say to the Convent Superior?

She came to me in the after-lunch rest period.

'Dr Kahn-Ryder – welcome to our small community. And forgive me for keeping you waiting.'

'Waiting?' I was dazed. 'I haven't been waiting.'

'How sensible. Always so much rush and hurry. I tell my nuns to read the old creation story. An omnipotent God who allows Himself a whole day just to make the light and the darkness. And who rests for all of the seventh, even though there must have been a million other things needing His attention. It's a lesson to us all.'

I gathered my thoughts. She had a point. But omnipotence had always worried me – it left so little to the excitements of chance.

'So to business. Your mother has explained why you're here, Dr Kahn-Ryder. Perhaps we could talk in my study . . .'

I followed her. Moma's explanations might be anything. The Convent Superior moved briskly in her blue woollen robe, pointing out historic features of the building as she went. I smelt incense, and cold stone-dust. She was old, a large plain woman with a heavy jaw and deep eye-sockets. She moved her jaw constantly when she wasn't speaking and there was a mole on the side of her nose that she could have had removed. But her gaze was attentive, and her conversation was both gentle and commanding, and I respected her.

We reached her study: bare white walls, ironwood crucifix, scrubbed elm desk, large-print screenlink to the convent library. The tiled wood-stove was popping hot and she offered to take my coat. I hesitated, then agreed. She had a right to the whole story.

When I had told it, its essentials, I hope honestly, she was silent for a long while, watching me and champing slowly. Then she took up her pen and made a small mark on the clean sheet of paper on the desk in front of her. She stared at the mark.

'You believe you have discovered a cure for the Syndrome?'

'Developed. "Discovered" sounds too . . . visionary.'

She nodded heavily, drew a circle round her mark. 'Why should our government wish to suppress this cure?'

'Not necessarily suppress. Certainly delay. There are any number of possible reasons. Most probably – '

'I apologise, Dr Kahn-Ryder. That was not a useful question.' She drew a careful box round the circle. 'Governments seldom have reasons you or I would recognise as such.'

She examined her box, drew a short line out from the centres of each of its sides. I waited.

'I imagine,' she said finally, 'that you have devoted a great deal of time to the . . . the development of this cure.'

I nodded. 'One way or another, my entire adult life.'

'And now, because of it, your daughter is in danger?'

'No. Not because of the vaccine, because of the Science Minister's reaction to the vaccine.'

'A fair distinction.' She joined the ends of the short lines, making a second, larger box at forty-five degrees to the first. She observed the effect, then laid her pen down thoughtfully and got to her feet. 'Come with me, please.'

There was a narrow, pine-planked door in one corner of her study, and beyond it a circular stone staircase ascended what was clearly an exterior turret. We climbed steadily, the Convent Superior in front, her purple-veined feet visible in their sandals at my eye-level beneath her robe. At regular intervals we passed narrow windows, once naked by now glazed, giving ever wider views of the cliffs and the distant mainland. The turret was cold, and smelt of spiders.

My companion's breathing laboured. I hoped that she made this climb often, preferably daily, so that her heart was accustomed to the effort. The stairs went up and up. I wished I'd counted them. I'd no idea how far we'd come but my own heart was busier than I'd have chosen.

At a dark segment of the tower the Convent Superior stopped, fumbled lengthily, and then a hatch above me opened, flooding us with light and cold bright air. She went on up and I followed her, out on to the flat leaded roof of the turret, surrounded by stone battlements. It was a circular area possibly five metres in diameter. We were enormously high up. When I leaned on the stonework and looked down I might have been flying. I might have been in a balloon, flying far above the island, far above the steep perspectives of the copper-green convent roofs and chimneys.

The Convent Superior leaned beside me. We were both, suddenly and very powerfully, women. Two women, together. The air, unusually at such a height, was still. The Convent Superior took my arm and walked me the full circle of the battlements, not speaking, gazing always outwards. I saw more ocean, more cliffs, more towns, more mountains, than my mind could encompass. We arrived back where we had started.

'I brought you here,' she said, 'to look and to listen. But more especially to listen. And when you have listened I shall tell you what you can hear.'

Her eyes were bright. Beneath the unknowable dome of her thoughts her big old ugly face was radiant. I obeyed her. Closing my eyes, I listened. Vast emptiness. Nothing stirred. No bird cried. No sound rose from the earth below. No sound. Only the blood singing in my ears.

I opened my eyes. 'You mean the silence?' I didn't understand. 'Is that what I'm to hear?'

She shook her head. 'You hear peace, my dear.' Her voice trembled. 'Peace. For the first time in humankind's life on this planet, peace. There are no wars. No wars, anywhere on this earth.'

'No wars?' I still didn't understand. 'You mean that literally?'
She smiled. 'Oh yes. No wars. Quite literally.'

I looked past her, out again at the seas and mountains. What was she saying?

'The news came through yesterday.' She was matter-of-fact now, blowing on her bony hands to warm them. 'Our church has been monitoring the world-wide situation. Yesterday agreement was reached in the last known organised armed conflict – a dispute over water rights in central Africa. With the signing of that agreement all officially sanctioned bloodshed in the world ceased. The silence you hear is the silence of peace. No battles, no maiming, no mourning dead heroes. Peace.'

There were tears in my eyes. But a disbelieving voice asked, why no media event? The end of war, and no cameras, microphones, reporters?

Obliquely the old woman answered me. 'In the fortieth year of the Attrition,' she said, 'we haven't yet run out of men to order wars. We've run out of women to fight them.'

I nodded. A development men would fear, hence no research to establish it. It wasn't only wars that men still ordered, they ordered ultimately much of what we did. No media event, therefore.

I turned away. Hard? Was I hard? I looked out over the worn stones of the battlements, listening to the silence, listening to the peace. I felt free. It was as if a monstrous tyranny had crumbled. War had ended. Women had defeated war.

My happiness chilled, like sweat on my skin. Had the Convent Superior brought me here simply to share her joy? We'd been speaking, down in her study, of my cure.

'You want me to justify my vaccine.' My tongue felt leaden. 'The Syndrome has given us a falling population, and now the end of war. You want me to justify my vaccine.'

She looked at me sharply. My heart faltered.

'You're very earnest,' she said. 'Only a very earnest woman would try to spoil my silence with justify and mustify . . . ' The phrase pleased her. She chewed it, relented, smiled, became a kindly bald old woman with big teeth, wearing a shabby blue robe.

'Your mother tells me she might once have been an actress. I too. That's why we came up here, for the theatre of it. Not for a catechism.' She leaned towards me. 'But I like your intention. You're earnest, but I like your intention. And of course we'll

178

offer your daughter sanctuary. It is our duty. If you had been a monster we still could not refuse.'

She patted my hand with its taped-on shield. Bracingly, as a mother will encourage a muddled child – you can do it. And, whatever it was, for just that moment I could.

I thought we'd be going down, but she hadn't finished with the silence. She returned to it, I'm sure forgetting me. I kept my spoiling to myself but it grew. Not peace, I thought, but rather an absence of war. Even so, quite something. I stood with her – what if my vaccine produced wombs bursting with eager little soldiers? What then? I didn't know what then. I was being earnest again.

We went down the circular staircase to the Convent Superior's study. I arranged for Anna, brought by Mark, to be accepted at the convent the following day at noon. I was sending her with Mark because the sooner I got in a full day on my piece for *Natur* the sooner they'd publish and the whole affair would be over. Also because he'd be a better minder for her on the train.

In my coat and gloves again, I asked for a tour of the school. Anna didn't expect to get much out of a few weeks of classes in a strange school but she'd sensibly said she'd rather take lessons than sit round twiddling her thumbs. The school was very orderly. Clearly it believed in the New Authoritarianism – indeed had never quite fallen out of belief in the old. It had, after all, employed Granna, who'd never been of the let-it-all-hang-out, last-century persuasion.

The tour over, I paused to write the Convent Superior a cheque, then took my leave. I didn't see Moma again. She spent her afternoons in the video library, and the Convent Superior said she took her work very seriously. Her work in the House of Illusions. Little changed. Except that for Moma things had got immeasurably better. She'd managed to become just a little crazy – north-north-west, like Hamlet. She'd stepped outside but she could step back in again when events demanded her presence. Events like truthfulness. Which was tough on the untruthful but great for Moma. Lucky Moma.

Hard? Was I hard?

It was three thirty, and dusk, when I boarded the train home. Frost already sparked its roof. Night fell as we climbed up through the mountains. I looked back once, saw lights out on the island. If I was pregnant, with a male foetus, I'd keep it. Mark's son would never be an eager little soldier and we'd need all the non-soldiers we could get.

I took a taxi from the station, removed the shielding from my tags on the way. I'd stepped outside too, like Moma, and now I was stepping back. Sergeant Milhaus would be glad to see me.

Dinner was laid in the dining-room, a send-off for Anna if my news was good. I told them the Convent Superior had agreed to everything I'd asked. Mark opened a celebratory bottle. This time tomorrow Anna would be safe in Nomansland and Mark would be home again from taking her to the island.

We believed it. I actually said it to them. 'This time tomorrow,' I said, 'Anna will be safe in Nomansland and Mark will be home again from taking her there.'

CHAPTER TEN

The Attrition. Year 29: early May.

Captain Breitholmer had been right when he told Daniel that in NatSekur promotion came quickly for men with their army police background. Within four years of joining Daniel had moved up to full lieutenant, in charge of security in four major firms. Breitholmer was now a commander, the top NatSekur rank, one of the command group responsible for overall on-site company policy. They were still stationed in the capital and still lived on Pike Street.

Daniel would have been content, but Breitholmer was quickly bored with his office-bound position. Stuck most of the time behind a desk, with nowhere to go in his profession, he'd looked around for some other outlet, ideally one that included Daniel. Given the two men's shared basic views on life, the solution was obvious.

Breitholmer was a planner. Also, his interest in the mechanisms of violence, and the coldness of his courage, complemented Daniel's simpler nature, his instinctive rage at what was happening to the world, and gave it direction, purpose, respectability. Daniel understood this and was grateful. Now that he was older he no longer believed that the army had made a man of him. Nine years in the army had made him a soldier. It had taken four years with Bert to make him a man.

Daniel had other rages; rages that Bert did not share. There was a dark area in his mind. He forgot it so completely that it didn't exist. It wasn't there. He never had to explain it or justify it because for him it wasn't there. Except that suddenly, sometimes, it was.

The good thing about Bert was, he didn't have a past. He started at their first meeting, he a provost-sergeant, Daniel a newly joined trooper. The years before – and there were many, Daniel's whole life and then some – didn't count. He started at their first meeting. It was a trick Daniel still had to learn.

Today they had a gig planned, their third. Gigs took time to set up. Bert had a reliable explosives source, but he worked through a cut-out for absolute security, which added weeks to any deal, and there was also Daniel's duty roster to be accommodated. Bert liked to set up gigs for when he himself was officially working, to avoid any pattern of shared off-duty time that might link them. He took no chances: their uniforms gave them easy access to the gigs but also made them prime suspects if anybody started thinking that way. Bert bought in ammunition too, again through a cut-out. It would have been easy to fudge NatSekur's records – book out half a dozen test rounds on every trip to the range and you soon had a store – but Bert said NatSekur's rounds carried a tracer and Daniel didn't argue. Bert knew best.

Today's gig was up north, in a town close to the frontier, a four-hour drive from the city. They travelled separately, Bert by car with the equipment, Daniel by motor bicycle, both vehicles with false plates. Spring was well advanced, the weather mild, the evenings long. It was a mid-week gig, Daniel on a rest day, Bert getting off after a meeting he knew would end early.

Daniel and Bert, Bert and Daniel. That was the way things were.

Daniel rode up in the afternoon, by a roundabout route, wearing civilian clothes, his uniform in a sports bag in one of the panniers, an empty briefcase in the other. He passed the gig slowly, checked the entrance for any obvious changes since their assessment visit, then went on to a restaurant on the other side of town. He parked down the road from it, packed helmet and goggles in beside the briefcase, went in for a drink and something to eat. He was good-looking, Bert said, and there was no way he wouldn't be noticed. But that was fine, provided nothing connected him with the motor bike or the gig. The gig was a NatSekur contract. They all were – that way Bert and Daniel got in without question, and could check architects' plans and manning levels ahead of time from the computer.

Today's gig was a clinic only – no research facility, no scientists wandering in and out at all hours. Hence the nine-o'clock off. Lab technicians were long gone, once the bloody patients were bedded down they stayed there, and the night nursing staff were writing up case logs at their stations. Nine o'clock too because the first two gigs had been in the early hours and Bert said patterns were dangerous.

Daniel ate a leisurely meal, paid cash, left the restaurant and looked in shop windows for a few minutes before returning to the bike. He rode out to a previously chosen men's toilet on a quiet square with a bandstand, close to a bus stop, and changed into his uniform in one of the cubicles, putting a light summer civvy raincoat on over it. He returned the sports bag, now containing his civilian clothes, to the pannier, took out the briefcase, put his NatSekur cap in it, then left the bike and caught the first bus going in the right direction. Motor bikes and men's toilets went together with gays in police minds – no policewoman would think of reporting the bike, even if she noticed it. Homo men were quick with harassment suits.

Daniel arrived in the area of the gig with twenty minutes to spare. He stayed away, walking purposefully round twenty minutes' worth of city blocks, swinging his briefcase, attracting nil attention. It was a pleasant town, a clever blend of old and modern, terraces of smart arcaded shops, trees, narrow pink-stuccoed apartment blocks with winterised balconies, wooden boardwalks above heated cobbled streets, and the clinic was in a classy district, a small last-century office block expensively converted for PTG. Daniel swung his briefcase. Bloody women, it made no sense – each visit to a place like this cost a small fortune and the chances of clicking were still terrible. Some tarts came back three and four times and still didn't pop. More money than sense. What were they fucking proving? Against nature, the whole fucking business. It was men that made babies. What PTG clinics proved was that some fucking lezzies couldn't wait to give men the needle. They deserved what they got.

The sun was low, the light golden. Most citizens were home in front of their TVs. Daniel took off the raincoat on a deserted stretch of road and swapped it in the briefcase for his NatSekur cap. He was outside the clinic at five to nine. A glance up and down the street revealed no sign of Bert. This was fine – they must never be seen together on gigs by people who might remember. Daniel checked his reflection in a shop window, straightened his cap, drew in his stomach. His bowels griped and he winced. This was always the worst moment. Like jumping off the edge, knowing how cold the water was.

Up to this moment only one of them ran any risks if stopped. Bert carried the guns and the explosives. He wanted it that way. Daniel was in the clear. He carried no weapon, had broken no law. Now he committed himself. This was the worst moment, and the best. He pulled smartly on the hem of his uniform jacket and strode in through the double armoured-glass doors to the clinic, past the NatSekur girl lounging inside. He acknowledged her hasty salute, went forward to the reception desk.

Four sets of doors led off the clinic foyer, two elevators, and a curved open staircase hung on fine carbon fibre threads. Daniel ran the architect's plan in his head. Behind him the doors to the street, on his left the staircase, ahead of him the elevators, then the entrance to the patients' waiting room and wards, to the right of that the reception desk and the staff entrance, and in the foyer's right-hand wall a door to the maintenance area and the building's rear access. The elevators and staircase went up to the clinic's administrative centre, and above that were floors of rented office space, empty every evening after seven.

The foyer was decorated in shades of dusty blue, thickly carpeted, with a big light-responsive abstract backing the staircase. At present there was enough daylight to keep the picture shimmering between yellows and whites. Soon artificial light would take over, changing in slow random sequences to avoid institutional monotony, and the picture would respond in tactful purples. It was an expensive outfit, for expensive customers.

Daniel clicked his heels in front of the reception desk and smiled at the receptionist.

'Good evening. Hi. My name is Ryder. Lieutenant Daniel Ryder.' He produced his NatSekur warrant card and showed it to her. 'You can tell Commander Breitholmer I'm here now.'

They used their own names. It kept things simple.

The young woman's pin identified her as Marie. She wore green eye-shadow and a very tight blouse. She checked her screen.

'I'm afraid we don't have a Commander Breitholmer.'

Daniel looked slowly round the foyer. It was deserted, the NatSekur guard sprucing herself up by the door, hand on her radio alarm as specified in the manual. He returned to Marie.

'Commander Breitholmer. Of NatSekur. Would you check that please? Breitholmer.' He spelled it for her.

Marie waited politely. It wasn't a name she could easily miss. 'I'm afraid there are no NatSekur officers on the premises. Only the guard behind you, and the mobile guard somewhere round the building.'

'I see.' Daniel frowned. 'My orders are to rendezvous here with Commander Breitholmer at twenty-one hundred.'

The receptionist looked up at the clock. 'It's that all right.'

It was two minutes past.

Daniel caught her eye, smiled again. 'No Commander Breitholmer?'

'No Commander Breitholmer.'

'I expect he's been delayed.'

'I expect he's been delayed.'

She was a sporty young woman, and she'd decided she liked the look of him. Silly cow.

'I'd better wait. It's not like him, though . . . ' He tipped his cap back a shade, leaned on her desk. 'Anybody working late?'

'Only the nurses. After visiting-time this place is like a morgue. I watch TV mostly.'

She indicated her screen, pressed buttons so that a program switched in, did a quick jiggle to the music. Daniel looked at the clock again, then out through the glass doors. There was a bank opposite, its doors and windows shuttered. The street was quiet. He turned back to Marie.

'I'd better call in, I think. May I use your phone?'

She cut the TV and pushed the telephone across the desk with one sporty finger. He lowered his voice.

'We do these spot checks. It keeps our young women on their toes.'

'That's nice. I'm off at ten. How about you?'

'Depends on Commander Breitholmer.'

'Fuck Commander Breitholmer.'

'I don't think NatSekur would like that.'

'Would Commander Breitholmer?'

The doors behind him flapped open. 'Lieutenant Ryder?'

At last. Thank God for that. Daniel turned smartly. 'Sah.'

'Sorry I'm late. Bloody traffic. Let's get on with it.' Bert came forward to the desk. 'I'm Commander Breitholmer, my dear.'

Marie smothered a giggle, looked at his warrant card.

'NatSekur area controller. I'm here to inspect your security arrangements.'

He was carrying a small attaché-case. He put it on the desk, opened it, took out the two silenced handguns. Daniel kept his eyes on the glass doors meanwhile, and the empty street beyond. Bert gave him one of the guns, holstered the other himself. Marie watched interestedly as he closed the attaché-case and looked keenly round the foyer.

'Everything in order, Lieutenant?'

'Two guards on duty, sir. One mobile, one static.'

'That's what the book said. I'm surprised there aren't more, Lieutenant. PTG's a high-risk area.'

'That's in the big cities, sir.'

Also, NatSekur didn't come cheap. But Bert and he had dealt with three times that establishment on their first time out.

Bert grunted, strode back to the guard at the door, asked her name, nodded. 'Let me see your radio.'

She gave it to him. He looked it over, nodded again, did not return it. 'And your gun.'

She gave him that too. He checked it, gave it back to her. Meanwhile Daniel had beckoned the receptionist out from behind her desk, away from its alarm bar. Employees of firms protected by NatSekur were not allowed to carry their own alarm systems: they could interfere with NatSekur frequencies.

'Marie – would you show me the elevator emergency cut-out, please?'

The box on the wall between the two elevator doors was clearly marked but she humoured him. They examined the box together, her hand on his arm.

Bert had finished at the door. 'Keep an eye on things out here, Lieutenant. I'm taking the guard with me to inspect rear access.'

They went out through the door into the maintenance area. Daniel crossed to the staff entrance door and nudged it open. He carried the handgun Bert had given him casually, down the side of his leg.

He asked Marie, 'What about the lab technicians?'

'They don't work nights. They've all gone home.'

He looked sideways through the door and pointed. 'Who's that, then?'

'What d'you mean? Is there someone?'

She went to him, looked curiously out into the passage beyond, and he shot her behind her left ear. The round was of a low-impact type that left a small entry wound, expanded catastrophically within her skull, and did not exit. There was no blood, the sound was soft, hardly more than a fart, but she'd need more than a psycho-engineer to put her mental processes back together again. He eased her dead body through the door and closed it on her, locking it with the passkey NatSekur provided. Then he crossed to the patients' entrance and locked that also. If a nurse tried to come through the double entrance doors now and couldn't, she'd return to her station and ring reception. Reception wouldn't answer. The nurse, puzzled, would call the charge nurse, who would come and try the doors also, and then decide to activate the alarm. But they'd both be dead long before it got to that. They and most of their patients.

Daniel leaned against the double doors. The pupils of his eyes were dilated and suddenly his pulse was racing. Women in a place like this deserved all they got.

Bert returned, alone, from the maintenance area. 'Have you fixed the alarm?'

'Not much point. We'll be out in a minute.'

'Do it.'

Their eyes locked. Daniel broke contact first, went behind the reception desk and switched off the alarm.

'Good. That's the way.'

Bert walked forward to lock the main doors. As he reached them a woman arrived on the other side, pushing the handle, wanting to come in. He opened them a crack.

'Can I help you, ma'am?'

'I couldn't get away.' She was distracted. 'Is visiting-time over?'

'Visiting-time ends at eight, ma'am.' He opened the door wider. 'But we could make an exception.'

Daniel watched, intrigued, as Bert let her in. She was a flashy woman, fortyish, in expensive clothes. Bert's attention was on the empty street.

'Would you help me please, Lieutenant? This lady is hoping to visit a patient.'

He turned to the woman now and smiled at her, and as Daniel hurried forward he shot her in the chest. Daniel was ready to catch her but she didn't fall. She staggered and stared at Bert, amazed.

'How dare you,' she said. 'How dare you.'

He shot her again, finding her heart at this second attempt. Daniel dragged her behind the reception desk while Bert was locking the doors, fumbling with the keys. Then he hurried back to his attaché-case, still open on the desk. He was sweating. Watching him, Daniel felt suddenly anxious and uncomfortable. Bert never fumbled, never hurried, never sweated.

'Move it, Lieutenant. We're getting out.'

'What about the other guard?'

'That fucking woman . . . Fuck the other guard.' He was setting the timer. 'She's upstairs somewhere. Has to be.' Now he slammed the case shut. 'Two minutes, Lieutenant. Stay if you like. I'm getting out.'

He strode away towards the maintenance area and the rear exit. Daniel hesitated. Bert was never like this. Everything went to plan. Suppose the guard had been on the stairs, suppose she had seen them? They always dumped anyone who had seen them before they left. Bombs might leave survivors and the success of their gigs relied on nobody saying they were NatSekur afterwards.

Two minutes. The elevator lights caught Daniel's eye. Had they flashed? He backed away, grabbed his own briefcase from where he'd left it on the floor in front of the desk, and hurried after Bert.

Who had waited for him.

He'd switched out the rear-access alarm and was waiting among the waste bins just inside the open door, leaning against the wall. The dead NatSekur girl was piled in a corner. Bert was a mess. He was trembling violently, his hands over his eyes. Daniel had never seen him like this before.

'It's a fucking farce, Lieutenant. That fucking woman, that fucking woman . . . It's not a gig, Lieutenant, it's a fucking farce.'

Daniel got one arm round his waist, helped him out through the door and down the alley. This was wrong – they ought to be leaving separately. Security guards were like postwomen: nobody saw just one. Luckily the alley led into an old multi-storey car-park, hardly used.

They struggled on. Bert was recovering, getting his breath back. 'Plans, Lieutenant. You make them and you stick to them. If there's one thing I fucking hate, it's fucking make-and-mend.'

Two minutes soon went. The explosion was enormous, shaking filth down on them from the car-park floor above. They leaned together for a moment, relieved, overjoyed, embracing. There were tears in their eyes. Then they straightened up and went on out into the street.

'I can manage, Lieutenant. I'm not a fucking cripple.'

Dusk was well advanced. There was, in any case, no one out in the street to see them. They walked briskly – running attracted attention. They were supposed to return immediately to their separate vehicles, not meet again till Pike Street, but Daniel didn't think Bert could drive yet. By the time the police had set up road-blocks round the clinic, Daniel had found him a basement bar, ill-lit, half a kilometre away. They were in their shirt-sleeves now, carrying their jackets and caps, which they put on the chairs in the corners of their booth, their handguns under them.

Bert, who never touched alcohol, drank straight vodka. 'A fucking farce,' he said. 'If there's one thing I fucking hate, Lieutenant, it's fucking make-and-mend.'

Daniel wasn't fooled. 'You knew that woman,' he said.

'Remind me never to do an evening gig again, Lieutenant. Rushing around like a fart in a bottle. Give me the small hours every time, and fuck the pattern. At least there's no interruptions.'

'That woman didn't know you,' Daniel said, 'but you did know her.' For once he had the edge on Bert. The woman gave him it. He'd never wanted it but now that he had it he used it. The edge was like that. 'You knew her. You've been shook up ever since.'

Bert had been restless, smoothing the table-top, scratching, shifting on his buttocks, peering round at the beer adverts. Now he was still.

'Knew her, Lieutenant? I'll tell you something – I thought I did. I'll tell you something else – for a moment I thought she was my daughter. Grown up, I mean. But she wasn't anything like her.'

'Your daughter?'

'When I first let her in. But she wasn't anything fucking like her.'

Daniel was puzzled. 'So we dumped her. That's all right then.'

'It's not all right.' Bert closed his eyes wearily. 'The things we fucking do. Think about it.'

Daniel tried. All he could see was that the edge the woman had given him was slipping away. 'You've never said you had a daughter.'

'I don't.'

'But – '

'I did have but now I don't.' He opened his eyes and regarded Daniel painfully. 'We just dumped her.'

'But you just said . . . '

'Think about it.'

There was an uncomfortable silence between them. Daniel didn't like the contradictions Bert was throwing at him. Was he playing some sort of game? Did he have a daughter or didn't he? Had they dumped her or hadn't they? He was losing his edge and he didn't like it.

He went doggedly back to the beginning. 'You had a daughter, that woman was nothing like her, we dumped that woman, and now you say you don't have a daughter. It doesn't make sense.'

Bert emptied his glass, leaned across the table, suddenly venomous. 'The tarts *you* dump, Lieutenant. On your nights off. Do they make sense?'

Daniel gaped at him, blasted by the savage violence of his assault. By the cruelty. The blood pounded in his face. The roots of his hair pricked like hot needles. His mind fused. He couldn't speak. Couldn't move.

Bert leaned closer, baring his teeth. 'Last year's tart, Lieutenant. This spring's. *Oh Bert, I was upset, Bert. Oh Bert, I couldn't help it, Bert. Oh Bert, the nasty world did nasty things to me* . . . Sense, Lieutenant? Don't make me sick.'

Still Daniel couldn't move. He gaped at Bert's ugly, spit-wet teeth, at his tight, ugly lips. He'd never said any of those things. He denied them. He'd never said anything. Neither of them had. Not ever. Those nights were something else.

Bert had no right. Those nights were something else. Someone else.

Bert had no right.

Those nights were someone else.

Bert eased away. He relaxed, looked Daniel over, smiled, spoke softly. 'A word in your pearly, Lieutenant. You're stupid. Bone stupid. You mustn't worry, though. I do still love you.'

Behind them news of the explosion was coming through on the bar TV. The clinic was wrecked. Casualty figures were incomplete, but two NatSekur guards had been killed for certain. They'd been identified by their uniforms.

Daniel listened to the TV. He was greatly relieved to hear about the two dead guards – whatever the second guard might have seen, it didn't matter any more. And he didn't have to listen to Bert. Maybe Bert had a daughter and maybe he didn't. That didn't matter either. It certainly wasn't worth making a fuss about.

And as for the other . . .

He suggested another drink, to celebrate the two dead guards, but Bert said no – they had to start back for the city, it was a long drive, especially for him after his day in the office and the drive down and the gig, and they shouldn't take any chances.

Daniel didn't argue. One more drink wouldn't touch him, but he still didn't argue. He might be stupid, he reckoned he *was* stupid, but he understood enough to do as he was told. The whole business of the edge had been a mistake. There wasn't a daughter. Bert started in the MPs, a provost-sergeant. There weren't any years before that. The thing about Bert was, he didn't have a past. It was a trick Daniel still had to learn.

Harriet heard news of the latest clinic bomb next morning, over breakfast.

'We're going to see a lot more of that sort of thing,' Liese told her, competing doggedly with Anna's spoon-bashing on the tray of her high chair. 'The Attrition's really beginning to bite. People can't coast along any more, pretending it isn't happening. They'll be wanting to hit back.'

'People?' Harriet looked up from mixing Anna's cereal. 'Men, you mean.'

'Not just men.' Liese folded the morning's news print-out and propped it behind the teapot. 'I was reading yesterday about girl-only street gangs in Paris. They're bashing anything and everything. It's Cohn-Bendit, sixty years on.'

'Cohn-Bendit didn't last.'

'Cohn-Bendit's support wasn't being reinforced all the time by the Attrition. It's like a group neurosis. A hysteria, and it's building up right across western society.'

'That's media talk, Liese.' It was also social anthropology talk, Liese's degree course catching up with her. 'This idea that societies – ' she raised her voice to be heard ' – this idea that societies behave like individuals hasn't really been . . . oh, shit!'

She gave up, defeated by her daughter's racket. Anna was three now, and perfectly capable of talking if she wanted attention, but bashing things was more fun. Harriet slopped cereal crossly into a bowl and stuck it in front of her. The bashing continued.

'She likes banana in it,' Liese said.

'She didn't yesterday.'

'She did last night.'

'Why the hell doesn't she bloody well say so?'

'She's been learning from those girls in France. Nobody listens unless you make a noise.'

'I listen.' Harriet was chastened. She sat down beside her daughter. 'I listen, Annie-poo. I listen.'

She reached for a banana from the bowl by the sink, disturbing old Gnasher to reach it. The cat shifted huffily, settled again. Harriet peeled the banana, wincing at Anna's continued racket. She'd worked late last night and it was one of those mornings. She didn't mind Liese interpreting for her daughter – no, to be honest she hated Liese interpreting for her daughter, hated Liese co-parenting the child all day, five days a week, knowing everything about her. But that was the way things were. She'd have hated a househusband co-parent just as much. Babies were for momas to know about . . . it wasn't the way things were but it was the way, in some Arcadian dreamworld, they ought to be.

She sliced half of the banana into Anna's bowl and the drumming stopped.

'And what's my Annie-poo going to do today? You're going to school today, aren't you pet?'

Anna had dropped her spoon and grabbed a handful of banana. Harriet prised the fist open, scraped the mush back into the bowl, mixed it in with the cereal.

192

'We're going on a trip,' Liese said. 'If the weather holds the school's organised a forest ramble. We're collecting ferns.'

'A ride on the tram out to the forest, Annie-poo? That'll be fun.'

Harriet removed Anna's banana-smeared fingers from her mouth, wiped them, and folded them back round the handle of her spoon. She guided the spoon into the bowl. Anna could feed herself perfectly; this was one of her mornings for playing baby.

'Why don't you come?' Liese said. She poured herself more tea. 'Take a day off. Parents of all sorts are invited.'

'Oh Liese, I wish I could.'

'You could, Har'. Just one day. Unichem could survive one day without you.'

Anna loaded her spoon, concentrated, found her mouth with it. She was an enchanting child, velvety golden skin, dark bright eyes as round as a black baby's, her father's easy smile. She removed the spoon. Much of the banana mixture came out with it, slipped down her front. Harriet scooped it up and put it back.

'Phone in,' Liese said. 'I will, if you like. Tell them you're ill, Har'. Annie'd love you to come.'

'Liese, don't. It's such a temptation.'

Liese drank her tea, made no comment. She was an unexceptionable woman, sensible and kindly. The tea she drank epitomised her: sensible and kindly. She loved Anna, and in the best way loved Harriet too. And the comment she didn't make was in itself a comment.

It wasn't fair. She'd given up her work because she wanted to. She liked their apartment and keeping it clean, tidy. She liked arduous but simple tasks with quick, clear rewards. She liked pleasing. In another age she'd have made a wonderful husband, wife, butler, housekeeper, gardener, lady's maid. Harriet would have made none of those. Harriet drank raffish coffee.

She guided Anna through her breakfast, washed the child, set her out with her tricycle on the balcony. Anna rode it earnestly the three metres to and fro, puffing. The sun slanted in across the south-east-facing balcony.

Harriet collected her notes from the night before off the top of the piano and stuffed them into her case. How often did she get to play these days? Almost never. There was amazing new music out there, but Liese liked her to stick with Chopin.

'It's going to be hot,' she told Liese. 'You'd better take some anti-bug stuff.'

Liese had been making brioche sandwiches filled with cream cheese and salami. She handed them over with an apple. 'Home as usual?'

'Can't think why not.'

'Good luck with Fovas.'

Harriet held up crossed fingers. 'I'm keeping my head down.'

Professor Andrea Fovas was Harriet's boss, head of Unikhem's Syndrome research. A woman in terms of her bodily orifices, but not much else.

Harriet went back out on to the balcony. ''Bye now, Anniepoo. Be good with Auntie Liese. Have a lovely day.'

Anna didn't look up, went on puffing. Harriet returned to the kitchen, gathered up her case, kissed Liese's cheek.

'I'll be good too,' Liese said.

Unikhem had a prestige block in the middle of town, close to the old walled city – mirror-glass cladding, atrium foyer with jungle foliage and a ten-metre fountain, the lettering SYNDROME RESEARCH in a cut-out ceiling-high screen you walked through to enter. Beyond it, and the reception area, and a final pair of chic automatic double doors, the carpets and showbiz detailing ended. No music: moulded-rubber floors, robot tracks for internal communications, clear bright colours coded to the different departments.

Harriet's – Molecular Genetics – was dark green, her own work area shading to pale beyond well-fitted doors, denoting a semi-controlled environment. Temperatures were low and at least the grosser detritus of life was excluded.

Harriet was working alone today, setting up human DNA snippets for computer scanning and microphotography. Gene-mapping as a basic research tool was out. The world program to map the entire human genome had long been abandoned, a victim of funding cuts in the face of escalating AIDS-related research expenditure, and of popular distrust of its aims. Genetic screening for crippling hereditary diseases (Huntington's, cystic fibrosis, haemophilia) was fine, but screening for mere tendencies (depression, schizophrenia, alcoholism) sounded too much like genetic discrimination. An underclass of the genetically unemployable was imagined, and support for the project withered away. At the other end of the scale, genetic profiles for aspiring presidents and top executives seemed endlessly contentious, just one more potential opportunity for muck-raking.

Syndrome research followed many different paths. Unikhem's approach was to assume an ultra-violet involvement, linked with the depletion of ozone in the stratosphere, and look for supporting evidence. UV's immuno-suppressive effect had made it a prime AIDS suspect for a while, but when that led nowhere the field for research into DNA changes was left wide open. Nobody knew for certain that the Syndrome was DNA-based and therefore hereditary – daughters of sufferers were invariably victims, but it might be through reinfection – but if comparative studies of pre- and post-Syndrome DNA were to come up with clear differences, then these would be strong evidence of a hereditary factor. Identification of the defective gene would then reveal the biochemical pathways through which it worked its havoc.

Harriet had been working for the last ten months with parings from one of the mouldier frosties from the nearest cryo-bank. Some of the cadavers optimistically frozen back in the nineties were in terrible condition, and singularly unloved by their surviving relations. Their DNA was reliably Syndrome-free, and Harriet was matching it with current samples. It was slow, exacting work, with maybe 100,000 gene pairs to be examined, but her post-doctoral had included molecular genetics and she was never bored.

It didn't matter scientifically that she herself had no great faith in UV as a precipitating factor. Finding a non-match, any non-match, would be a breakthrough. Personally, it mattered rather more. After ten months she was restless, felt that she was paddling up a tributary while the main river went on roaring by.

The thawed DNA had been cut by enzymes, the snippets trapped in gel and mounted on autoslides. A belt took the slides to the microscanner and on for computer analysis. This morning, in mid-program, the belt had failed, jammed sideways in its channel. Rather than call up the lab technician who would strip down the whole unit, Harriet was fixing it herself. The materials were at near-zero temperatures and she was easing the belt sideways, back on to its rollers, with surgical tweezers. The cold spread up the metal and she'd wrapped it in her handkerchief.

'You look as if you could do with another pair of hands.'

Harriet jumped, losing her grip on the tweezers but catching them before they fell into the dry ice surrounding the belt unit. Bent over the apparatus she hadn't heard Professor Fovas come in.

'Let me help, Harriet. I think I see what the trouble is. Hand me that metal rule.'

Together they levered the belt back on to its rollers. Harriet restarted the motor. The autoslides resumed their progress to the microscanner. She cut the motor again. The timing sequence had been broken by the hold-up and would need resetting.

Warily she turned to the professor. 'Thank you. I could've been fiddling for hours.'

Fovas laughed. 'Two expensively trained scientists, some of the most advanced scientific equipment in the nation, and we end up prodding it like farm-hands.'

Harriet didn't trust the laugh, the mateyness. She stuffed her handkerchief back into her overall pocket. 'I thought it would be quicker,' she said, 'than calling up a technician.'

Fovas laughed again. 'No harm done.' She paused. 'We *do* have a maintenance contract, though. Initiative is all very well, but we wouldn't want to invalidate the guarantees.'

Harriet didn't answer. Fovas was a po-faced cow. She'd been right to distrust the mateyness.

'Still, I'm not here to carp.' Fovas looked round Harriet's work area, blowing out her cheeks and speculatively drumming her fingernails on the rim of a glass measuring jar.

What *are* you here for? Harriet wondered. Andrea Fovas believed in leading from the top. She wasn't much seen at bench-level.

The professor drifted away, shifting things, opening drawers a few centimetres and flicking them shut. She was an elderly woman, thin and straight, wearing an immaculate white coat, her hair in a stiff brush-cut. Harriet expected her to find a ledge and run her finger along it, looking for dust.

At the door Fovas stopped. She asked the door-frame, 'How are you getting on here, Harriet? Any troubles? Are you happy?'

Suddenly Harriet caught up. 'I think what you really want to know, Professor Fovas, is what I was doing on the mainframe last night for nearly three hours.'

'Not at all. I see all the access codes. I know what you were doing.'

'You want to tell me not to.'

Fovas turned. 'This isn't a school, Harriet. I'm not your headmistress.'

Harriet leaned back, perched on the edge of her work-bench. 'Isn't it? Aren't you?'

'I refuse to let you make me angry, Harriet. It's too childish. I asked you a perfectly reasonable question.'

'You asked me if I was happy . . . ' Harriet folded her arms. 'Professor Fovas, in my first two years here, Unikhem had me sexing two- to eight-cell pre-embryos, picking out the males for disintegration tests. I was using forty-year-old polymerase chain because they were too mean to spend out on anything else. Work a second-year laboratory assistant could have done. Since then – '

'You paint a flattering picture of our technicians, my dear.'

'Since then, Professor, I've been on your gene-matching program. It's not the most fascinating work but I'm still quite new here and I'm certainly not complaining. But if you ask me if I'm *happy* . . . ' Harriet sighed. 'The point is, and I've said this before, the point is, I don't really believe any more in UV as a precipitating factor.'

'No, Harriet, I'm afraid that's not the point.' The older woman came forward, took Harriet's hands in hers, spoke gently, woman-to-woman. 'The point is, my dear, the research here is UV-based and you accepted that when you joined us. We start with the known depressant effect of UV on the immune system and assume a DNA involvement. And we also know the sort of damage UV can do to individual genes, so we know what to look for.'

Her hands were creepy. Harriet threw them off. 'This isn't herpes simplex, for God's sake.' She controlled herself. Professor Fovas knew that as well as she did. Professor Fovas wasn't foolish. Her problem was that she thought other women were. 'Look, if we want to establish ultraviolet as a trigger, why don't we look for last-century centres of heavy exposure?

In the UV surge that started all the skin-cancer scares? If one of those centres coincides with the spread pattern of the Syndrome, then – '

'Dr Ryder.' The professor had given her rope enough. Woman-to-woman was over. It was time to haul her in. 'Dr Ryder, it wasn't centres of exposure you were looking for on the mainframe last night. You were pursuing your own line of research. You've done it before. You were accessing Year 1 government health records.'

'World health records, actually.' Caught out, Harriet shifted ground. 'They're a mess. Thirty years ago many countries had no proper systems in place. And the information-gathering was terrible. But the Syndrome must have started somewhere, so – '

'No. *No* . . . ' Professor Fovas swung away agitatedly, took a couple of paces, turned back. 'If by "somewhere" you mean some single and particular place, Dr Ryder, then the Syndrome must *not* have started somewhere. Its spread was much too rapid. It must have begun more or less simultaneously in many different places.'

Harriet stared at her. It was an old argument. She didn't have an answer. Not yet. She simply knew in her bones that the multiple-origin people were wrong. 'I shouldn't have used the mainframe,' she said meekly. 'It's expensive. You must take the time out of my salary.'

'That's not the issue. The Department can afford to finance a degree of private research. The issue is one of commitment. If you don't believe in what we're doing here, then – '

'If you're dissatisfied with my work – '

'Not at all. Not with your work. Your *work* is excellent.'

Aha. Fuck it all. Three times round the mulberry bush and this was where bloody Fovas had been going all along.

'You don't like what I said on TV.'

A fortnight had passed since the program. She herself had moved on, more or less forgotten it. Not Unikhem. Unikhem, evidently, had needed the time to decide on their reaction. Now they'd sent poor old Fovas.

The professor clasped her hands primly at her waist. 'You have every right to your opinions, Dr Ryder.'

'And to express them in public?'

'That too . . . providing, of course, you neither slander Unikhem nor breach the confidentiality clause of your contract.'

'Which I didn't. My attack was on the *principle* of animal experiments. I made that absolutely clear. Absolutely clear.'

'You did.' She allowed Harriet a cold smile. 'I've been watching the tape. You made it so absolutely clear that viewers might be forgiven if they thought you were implying exactly the opposite.'

'That's their problem.'

'Not so. It's Unikhem's problem. And therefore, Dr Ryder, yours.' She reached inside her coat, brought out a news print-out which she spread on the work-bench. It headlined the successful bomb attack on a PTG clinic up in the north.

She leaned heavily on the bench. 'These are volatile times. It wasn't a Unikhem clinic, but it might well have been. There's trouble in the air, and not only in Europe. We have facilities world-wide and much local support. Your comments, Dr Ryder, will have gone out to cultures that will find your concern for animal rights deeply offensive in the context of threatened human male extinction. Even here at home your words were clearly inflammatory.'

'You want me to resign?'

'There's a profound social anxiety at work, Dr Ryder. Confusion. Often panic. Men are afraid. In this very city they are picketing sperm banks with women on their boards of directors . . . Your attack could easily have provoked a backlash.'

'I asked you if you wanted me to resign.' She knew she was pushing the older woman and didn't care. Let Fovas fire her. Firms like Unikhem had thrown their weight about for too long.

Professor Fovas considered her thoughtfully, moved away to the desk by her computer terminal, and sat down. She sighed, easing the violin-tight muscles in her neck.

'Some researchers are happy never to leave the laboratory,' she said. 'I don't think you are one of these. I've kept you at the bench and I've been wrong. I propose moving you to the clinical side of our work. To the wards of our medical facility over on Wehl Street.'

Harriet was relentless. 'And my television appearances?'

'I've already said it, Harriet. You want me to treat you like your

199

headmistress and I won't. I've pointed out the possible consequences of controversial statements to the media. The rest is up to you.'

A sharp reply. It stopped Harriet short. Was that what she wanted, a headmistress to keep her within limits? Someone she could rely on and hate? She'd never had one. Liese tried.

She moved on. 'And my new job?'

'It's a promotion. I want you to take charge of the embryo implant program. It involves working directly with members of the public, women volunteers.'

'And my predecessor?'

'Dr Hildebrand's past retirement age. We've been looking for his replacement for some time.'

As far as men were concerned, retirement age was a nonsense. Hildebrand was being eased out for other reasons. Did she want his job? She knew about Unikhem's implant program. They were fertilising donated eggs *in vitro*, implanting the male embryos in volunteer women, and seeing how long they could make them stick. With any luck it would give her a chance with some of her own ideas.

'The volunteers experience unpleasant side-effects,' Fovas murmured. 'They need a great deal of support from the program director.'

She'd take it. Fovas mightn't be the greatest scientist but she knew about personnel management. Harriet was a doctor, and doctors should doctor.

'If you're interested I suggest you go over there right away. Dr Hildebrand's expecting you. We can talk about terms of employment later.'

More money would help. Liese never complained, but life wasn't easy. Harriet had been pushing Fovas to sack her and she suddenly realised how bad it would have been if she had. Not just for the money – she needed Unikhem's backing. There mightn't be many Harriet Ryders in the barrel, but there weren't many Unikhems either. They gave her space. She was an ungrateful cow.

'I thought I was supposed to be lacking in corporate commitment.'

'That was the feeling in some quarters.' Fovas reached for the news print-out, folded it and put it back in her pocket. 'But

I think I can present your acceptance of the new position as a reassuring development.'

Harriet went to the door. 'I'll see Hildebrand. Then I'll let you know.' She looked over her shoulder. 'And thank you.'

Dr Hildebrand was old-school, smooth and spruce, with wavy silver hair. He ran ten four-bed wards, two theatres, and a large laboratory-support apparatus. His technicians conceived and selected male embryos *in vitro*, and a contract surgeon from the state hospital implanted the embryos. Hildebrand managed pre- and post-op, anaesthesia, and the subsequent immuno-suppressant therapies. These came down from on high and were frequently drastic. He hadn't had a patient die on him, but the word was he'd come very close. Any foetuses that survived the suppressants nevertheless suffered gross abnormalities and were terminated routinely at sixteen weeks.

Dr Hildebrand had fulsome praise for the courage of his volunteers: their stays could be for as long as four months, in conditions the equivalent of intensive care, and the suppressants' side-effects ranged from acute nausea to total hair loss. The women suffered cheerfully, believing in the cause.

Harriet asked him what progress had been made.

He flicked dust from his sleeve. 'Entirely negative, Doctor. We're gathering an impressive list of ineffective agents. We're learning a lot about foetal vulnerability. We can also predict the moment of breakdown for the membrane protecting the embryo . . . But the rejection mechanism, which is the object of the exercise, remains a complete mystery.'

'Who assesses results?'

'I do.' He eased his shoulders inside his expensive jacket. 'Under the supervision,' he admitted, 'of the program director.'

Harriet nodded. *Amour propre* was the issue here, a question of gender and generation. She, at twenty-seven, would be far happier with Andrea Fovas's supervision than Dr Hildebrand at seventy-plus.

'That must be difficult,' she said.

'Not at all. Fovas is the scientist. I'm only the humble doctor.'

Harriet nodded again. *Humble?* ' . . . May I talk to your patients?'

'Be my guest. Anyway, they're your patients now.' He glanced at his watch. 'Or they will be at seventeen hundred hours.'

She thanked him, smiling. He sounded military but he wasn't so bad. She realised that his age took him back forty years before the Attrition. It was an amazing span. Post-Attrition people tended to think that history began with them. What wars had he seen? He'd remember nuclear disarmament. It'd been men who negotiated that – they weren't all as rotten as Moma said.

She left Hildebrand and went down the long passage to the wards. Moma. Her brother Daniel she'd given up on, but she still saw Moma. There'd been her visit with Granna after Anna was born. They'd come from Granna's island: an Osterbrook community had started there and Moma was looking it over. Harriet had advised against it: she found God-the-Motherism shrill. Moma had ignored her. On Harriet's subsequent trips down to the island both Motherism and Moma had seemed progressively less shrill.

The medical wards of the Wehl Street facility were impressive. Harriet had a sterile head-to-toe suit to wear and an airlock to negotiate before she got to the nurses' station. The nurses, dressed normally, did three-day stints within the complex. Harriet couldn't see herself relating usefully to the patients through her plastic outfit, but most of the women were used to suited visitors. She talked to them.

Their main topic was the week they were in.

'I'm in my eighth, Doctor. Fifty-two days. Nurse says he's holding fine.'

'He?'

'The baby.'

This sense of a person in their wombs worried Harriet.

'I know it's silly, Doctor, but for as long as he's there I'm calling him Thomas.'

This worried her still more. 'You do realise,' she said gently, 'that you must expect a termination?'

'Don't say that, Doctor. There's no harm in hoping for the best.'

Harriet didn't answer. The remark wasn't phrased as a question, so she didn't have to. Part of good doctoring was knowing when the truth wasn't wanted.

She spoke to the charge nurse afterwards. 'Many of the patients seem to believe they may be allowed to go to full term.'

'I know.'

'They're never told that, are they?'

'Not precisely.'

'Not precisely?'

The charge nurse was an ostentatiously busy woman, her attention already on something that needed doing just over Harriet's shoulder. 'Our patients are volunteers, Doctor. They sign a release but few of them read it. They prefer to hope. We'd lose a lot of them if we didn't allow them that.'

'The dishonesty doesn't worry you? Doesn't worry your nurses?'

'It does no harm. And it's in a good cause.' She looked at her watch. 'And now, Doctor, if you'll excuse me . . . '

Harriet let her go. This was no time for arguments about the greater good. The patients were happy, the wards were immaculate, the research was running smoothly – what more could she ask? Hildebrand, and presumably Fovas above him, weren't troubled by their consciences. Harriet Ryder had an unpleasant need to flourish her righteousness like a banner. If she took the job and changes were needed here, she'd make them with the minimum noticeable virtue.

Would she take the job? She'd known she would from the moment Fovas offered it. It extended her work experience and would look good on her c.v. Also it would free her thinking by getting her out from under Unikhem's oppressive laboratory research program. She could take their money, and earn it fairly, and at the same time pursue her own ideas.

What ideas? She didn't like to say. She was looking for a virus. She wasn't a virologist, viruses were out of fashion anyway, retroviruses too, but something told her they were where the breakthrough would be made. Hence her work in WHO records. Show a single geographical birthplace for the Syndrome and the case for a virus became much stronger.

One odd thing. Knowing her delicate conscience, why hadn't Professor Fovas warned her about the volunteer's pathetic self-delusions? First the TV business and then this. Perhaps she was being tested. Perhaps Unikhem wanted to be rid of her but didn't dare sack her, and were hoping she'd leave on her own. She'd disappoint them.

She went home early, after a chat with Professor Fovas. She

had good news for Liese, and bad. There'd be agreeably more money, but no laboratory hours any more, nine to five. The contract surgeon fitted the implants in around his hospital work, often in the evenings, and he expected Harriet to assist. She'd learn a lot, but she'd lose the regular shape of her life with Anna, the bath, the bedtime story. Liese, with her parenting degree, thought such things important.

Also, full of her Unikhem news, Harriet had forgotten to ask about the forest ramble. And she'd had to have her attention drawn to the crumpled bundle of ferns in a pot on the kitchen table. Harriet, with no parenting degree, hadn't done very well.

Liese waited until Anna was in bed and settled.

Then, 'You must think very seriously, Har', before you take this new job.'

'I have thought.' They were in the living-room. Harriet had her feet up on the sofa. 'Very seriously.'

'We can manage without the money. You know that.'

She knew that. She wanted the job.

'Easy to say, Liese love. You're a hero. You work wonders. But – '

'Besides, in another year Annie'll be at a proper school.' Liese didn't argue with being a hero. 'Only a couple of hours, but I could get a little job.'

Harriet frowned. This getting a little job issue often came up. 'If you need time away from polishing the spoons you could have it easily if I was earning more.'

'I've never polished a spoon in my life.' Liese bridled. There was no other word for it. 'I just don't want you cutting down on the little time you already spend at home with Anna, just for more consumer durables we none of us need.'

Harriet reached across to where Liese was sitting. 'Don't let's quarrel, love. I want this job for *me*. You know that. But that doesn't mean you can't benefit.'

'I wasn't thinking of you and me.' Liese could be implacable. 'I was thinking of Anna.'

Harriet felt a paroxysm of rage, held her breath, counted to ten. Was Liese jealous of her work? It would be understandable if she was.

'The best thing, Liese, would be for me to get a part-time job.

Then you could go back to work properly. That's what co-parenting ought to be.'

'That's ridiculous. It's a way of shutting me up.' It was. 'You'd die if you worked part-time, Har'. You know I'd never let you.'

'I wouldn't die.' Harriet lay back, looked up at the ceiling. 'I might wilt a little . . . '

'And what good are wilted momas to their children?'

'Wilted momas?' Harriet looked at her sideways. Their eyes met. 'Wilted momas . . . ?'

Laughter often saved them. It did now. It grew from a grudged smile to gasping, and eye-wiping, and collapse in each other's arms. Wilted momas. It resolved nothing but there was nothing to resolve. Harriet would take the job. There'd never been any question.

The telephone rang. Liese disengaged, checked that its screen was off, and answered it. She listened, then covered the mouthpiece.

'It's for you. A journalist.'

'Tell him to go away. Journalists get me into trouble. I hate journalists.'

'He's from Science News.'

'They're the worst.' Harriet was on her feet and was on her way into the kitchen. Gnasher reared up from the sofa arm, followed her. 'They know more about my field than I do.'

'He wrote the piece about your TV appearance. His name's Mark Kahn.'

Harriet checked. 'I read that. It was flattering.'

The writer hadn't slavishly agreed with her, but he'd been pleased that at last a major scientist had spoken out. Harriet particularly liked 'major scientist'.

She turned back into the room. 'What does he want?'

'He's heard about your new job. He wants to congratulate you.'

'He wants me to say something indiscreet that he can quote out of context. I never will.' Harriet held out her hand. 'I'll talk to him. This should be fun. What did you say his name was?'

CHAPTER ELEVEN

The Attrition. Year 40: early November.

'This time tomorrow,' I told them, 'Anna will be safe in Nomansland and Mark will be home again from taking her there.'

I was in good shape. Peace had broken out, according to the Convent Superior, and I told them that too. I was in good shape.

Coping. Life had gone grotesque on me, gagged me, tagged me, cut my cat's throat, stolen my research, threatened my beautiful daughter, and I was coping. People do. We have obvious alternatives – breakdown, booze, hiding under the bed – but we surprisingly seldom take them.

We sat down to eat. I asked my family about their day. Anna made a face – apparently Mark had phoned the school in the morning and Jessica Simpson had stopped off on her way home with a pile of work for Anna to do on her unofficial vacation.

'That's nice,' I said. 'I've fixed up lessons on the island for you too. You really will be busy.' I helped myself to potatoes. 'Your Granna sends her love, by the way. She thinks you're still about five years old but otherwise she's fine . . . Anything else happen?'

Mark looked up from his plate. 'I wasn't going to tell you – not tonight. If your news was good. I didn't want to spoil it. And if it wasn't good . . . '

I froze. 'What now, for God's sake?' I waited. 'You can't just stop. *Tell me.*'

He drew lines on the cloth with his fork. 'I did what Marton suggested. I called your Doctor Volkov and got the number she's been wiring all the material to. She swears it's the number he gave her. Anyway, I passed it on to my police contact and he phoned back about an hour ago. He says it's one of Unichem's ex-directory lab inputs. She's been piping the stuff straight into their data bank.'

It might have been worse. Nobody was tortured. Nobody was dead.

'Natya? I don't believe it.'

'It's true, old buddy. I had a long chat with my contact. I'm afraid your Natya must be lying – Nils says not even ministers' aides have access to that sort of information. Marton can't have given it to her.'

'Come on, Mark – if you can go through this Nils, then so can Marton.'

'I know that. But every query's logged. There's no record anywhere of anyone from the Ministry asking that sort of question.'

Mark hadn't wanted to spoil my homecoming. I still believed Natalya wasn't lying. There was no way that Natalya Volkov, with her Russian elbows, would sell out to Unikhem, probably the most ruthless of the multinationals. Someone had fed her that number, swapped it with Marton's. Someone who was outside the Department. I liked that explanation. Not a member of my team, someone right outside the Department. Not easy to fix, but it wasn't impossible.

Mark was still telling us about his contact. He wasn't letting me brood on Natya's treachery. ' . . . The amount of stuff the police keep to themselves has always amazed me. One day I'll do a piece on it.' He glanced at Anna. 'I'll get *Science News* to print me a blank page, chock-full of all the things the police won't tell.'

She rose. 'If it's blank, how will people know what's on it?'

'I'll write a caption.'

'Blank pages are boring.'

'Very true. In any case, I think the police are often right.'

I laughed. 'That's not the man I married. What happened to the ruthless investigative journalist, the politician's terror?'

'That was someone else. I write solemn pieces about flu bugs and what happens on the other side of black holes. And I *do* believe there are times when the police are right to keep stuff up their sleeves. Murders, for instance – the police always hold back evidence on those if they can. It helps weed out the crank confessions.'

He chewed thoughtfully. I could see he was deciding whether or not to be indiscreet. Indiscretion won.

'The karate killer, for example – that guy they're still looking for. Nils told me the saddest thing. We all know the man never robs his victims. The fact is, he goes further than that – he seems to be afraid the girls'll have their few little possessions stolen after he's left them. He actually takes off their rings and jewels and hides them in one of their shoes.'

. . . *In one of their shoes.* I'd been reaching for my wineglass. Moma? My hand jerked, knocking over the glass. Moma . . . Wine spilled across the cloth and there was brief pandemonium as a sponge was fetched and salt was poured on the rich red stain. I didn't move. *He takes off their rings and hides them in their shoes . . .* Just like Moma. Christ.

I close my eyes. It has to be Danno. Only Danno would do that. It has to be my brother. He hates Moma. He always has. I remember how he used to frighten me. And the first girl who died, didn't she live in his town and didn't I hear of her death on the day after Dada's funeral . . . ?

'What's the matter?' Mark was leaning towards me. 'You look terrible, old buddy. Are you ill?'

Was I ill? Yes. I couldn't move. I couldn't breathe. I couldn't think. I felt I was dying. I shook my head. 'I'm fine . . . just tired. It's been a long day.'

He wasn't convinced but he didn't press it. He moved the conversation on, making plans with Anna for tomorrow's journey to Nomansland, giving me space. I wasn't ready to tell them. How would I ever be ready to tell them?

The fact was, the grotesquenesses of life had just gotten one too many. Gagged by the Minister I could cope with. Tagged too, my cat's throat cut, my research stolen, my beautiful daughter's life threatened. All this I could cope with. But coping cost, and my brother a serial killer was one cost too many.

None of the obvious alternatives appealed. Breakdown, booze, hiding under the bed – they'd get me out, but the price to my self-regard was unacceptable. What did I have, if not my self-regard?

One alternative remained. Unreason. Coping by not coping. Unreason. I couldn't cope but I coped . . . My recollections of the next day or so are sharp but disconnected, like a drug trip, people and events ballooning into my consciousness, enormous and over-real, then shrinking, losing my interest. I don't believe I behaved very well. I know I didn't.

That first night I didn't sleep. Doctors are used to patients who didn't sleep a wink last night, and the hour or so's sleeplessness that's closer to the truth, but I know I didn't sleep because I didn't go to bed. Mostly I didn't sit down. Mostly I didn't stop walking.

I don't know what I told Anna. She knew I was upset, she'd have been blind and deaf not to, and before she went to bed we must have talked about something, but I don't know what. My memory clears when she's in bed, and Yvette's in her room, and we're in the big living-room, and Mark's standing with his back to the stove, traditional back to the traditional stove, what a beloved traditional man he is, and I've just told him that my brother Daniel is the karate killer.

He doesn't believe me, of course, and when I explain about the rings he says it could be coincidence, and then I have to explain how the first date fits, how Daniel's a natural for the karate killer, the karate killer, and then I remember hearing about the second murder, and wasn't it on the day I told him about Anna, so maybe it's me he hates, not Moma at all, and then Mark says if I'm so certain I must go to the police.

I stop talking then, and stare at him, and after a while I say, 'The police? You mean, betray my own brother?'

And Mark says, 'Yes. If he really is the karate killer, you must.'

The karate killer. I know I must go to the police but I can't. Maybe I would go if Danno wasn't the karate killer, if he was something else, t'ai chi strangler, anything but the alliterative karate killer, because 'karate killer' is a phrase I've always hated, ever since it first came out. It's cheap. Cheap and nasty, like Moma used to say of things in the village shop. Cheap and nasty. I can't go to the police and tell them Danno's that.

Mark and I talk a lot. I tell him Danno's my brother. I tell him I can't go to the police. I tell him things I've never told him, about my childhood and Moma and Dada. He says if I don't go to the police he'll have to go himself. I ask him what we're going to do about my stolen research, and *Natur*, and protecting Anna. He says all that's already fixed, and if I don't go to the police about Danno he'll have to go himself.

'Don't do that, Mark. You can't do that. I won't support you. If you tell them about the rings I'll say you're talking nonsense. You can't go to the police if I say you're talking nonsense.'

'Be reasonable. You can't let him go free, old buddy, knowing what you do.'

'Maybe I'm wrong. You didn't believe me. You said it was coincidence. Maybe I'm wrong.'

'Then the police will investigate, and he'll have alibis or something, and no harm's done.'

'I can't do it, Mark. He's my brother.'

'The girls he killed were someone's daughters.'

Then I ask him what we're going to do about my stolen research, and *Natur*, and protecting Anna.

At some point Mark goes to bed. I've promised him I'll call the police but I've got to talk to Danno first. He's my brother and I love him and I've got to tell him what I'm doing. What for? For the pistol at the desk in the lonely room? Of course not. So that I can explain to him what I'm doing and why, and then he won't think badly of me? Of course not. So that he can get away, leave the country, murder girls in France? Not that either. Why, then? I just know that I must.

I ask Mark what happens to Danno when he's arrested and taken away and tried and found guilty, and Mark says he'll go for remedial psycho-engineering, and I ask what that entails and Mark says he doesn't know.

I stand at the front windows, looking out. At the side windows, at the back windows. I don't see anything, only the night. I'm afraid I'll see pictures of Danno putting gold rings into dead girls' shoes but I see only the night. I don't believe Mark when he says he doesn't know what remedial psycho-engineering entails. He's the science reporter. It's his job to know such things.

I'm the doctor, isn't it *my* job to know such things? Well, I know about neural-network computers. I know about equalising wave generators. I know about psychogenic drugs and laser brain surgery. But my knowledge is incomplete, wilfully so, an unattractive course that was a required subsidiary, and it's twenty years old. Psycho-engineering is sharp-end technology. I go to the medical books on my shelf and they're thirty years old. I stand at the windows, looking out.

Perhaps I sleep a bit after all. I remember Mark appearing, the middle-of-the-night quality of the lights as he switches them on. I remember him reaching out. 'Come to bed, old buddy.'

I think I'm standing in the kitchen. 'No, Mark.' They look like the kitchen lights in my memory. 'No.' I'm deciding what to do about Natya. I'm sure she hasn't sold out to Unikhem.

'Leave it till the morning. Come to bed.'

'I've got to find Danno. I've got to talk to him. What are you doing?'

'I'm phoning Doctor Vrieland.'

'I forbid you. He's an old man. It's the middle of the night and I forbid you. I don't need a doctor. He'll want to make me sleep. Too much fuss is made over sleeping, you've said so yourself. And I need to think. I forbid you to call him.'

I believe Mark and I had other such talks. God knows how much sleep he got, up and down the stairs. But he was out of bed and dressed at six, waking Anna. They needed an early start if they were to catch the good morning train straight through to Nomansland.

Another memory. Mark's study, Anna standing by the desk and Mark on his knees in front of her. He's wiping her forehead with a cloth and her eyes are watering. There's a strong smell of solvent.

'What on earth are you doing?'

'Removing Anna's tag.'

'What's the matter, Moma? You mustn't worry. It's what we agreed, isn't it?'

'I'm sorry, pet.' I'd forgotten her tag. 'It's . . . just the smell. I don't know how you stand it.'

'It's not too bad . . . Thanks for packing my case, Moma. I was expecting to have to do it.'

Apparently I've packed her case. 'Yes . . . Well, I just hope I've forgotten nothing vital.'

Anna grins. 'I've checked. You forgot my snow hat.'

I always forget her snow hat. It's a blue fur monstrosity and I hate it. Mark finishes with the solvent and gets to his feet, wiping his hands on the cloth. He corks the bottle.

'You're sure you want us to go?'

'Of course. Why ever not?'

'You'll be all right?' He looks at me so anxiously.

'I've got my piece for *Natur* to work on. I'll be fine.'

We're at the door. I say to Anna, 'Don't forget your practice. Come back Rubinstein.'

'I'll do my best.'

'Take care, Mark.'

'And you. I'll call when we get there.'

'I'll miss you, Annie-poo.'

'It's not for long, Moma.'

'I'll miss you.'

The taxi's waiting and they go off down the path. We must have hugged: I can feel Annie's cheek against mine, the softness of her skin. Keep her safe, Mark. God. Somebody . . . It's a cold grey windy morning. A little rain falls, mixed with sleet. The taxi drives away. Once the disappearance of Annie's tag is noticed, I wonder how long it'll be before someone comes round to investigate. I decide to tell Oswald Marton the moment I know she's safe.

A picture. The telephone in the kitchen is hanging from the wall, torn off its fixing screws. I phoned NatSekur, needing to know where I could find Daniel. I had to talk to him but nobody answered. It was eight o'clock, for fuck's sake. When do these fuckers get in for work?

Another picture. PIPS have sent my mid-week report and it's spilled out of the rack in zigzags all over the floor of Mark's study. I collect it up, glance at some of the stuff, get hooked. Two thousand five hundred traditional tribal communities have been declared extinct by UN experts, including the village-dwelling Inuit – AI was getting to them but their life-style was too harsh for women only. In Spain groups of men are calling themselves Male Liberationists and raping women with gun barrels. Men are so wicked. Danno never raped anybody. Unless the police are keeping that secret too.

How soon will Anna be safe in Nomansland? It's only eight thirty. I ought to be working on my piece. What are we going to do about my stolen research, about *Natur*, about protecting Anna . . .

Half a million Gaians are planning a convocation in America's Grand Canyon. Four more male infants have been reported in North Africa, this time by a Motherist missionary. One could hardly accuse her of wishful thinking. That makes seven. The Pope has held out against male masturbation unless medically supervised in collection centres, with procreation the purpose.

What will happen to Danno when he's arrested and taken away and tried and found guilty and sent for remedial psycho-engineering? They won't turn him into a cabbage. They'll leave him some joy, won't they? It was men who fought remedial engineering. We women were the tough ones. Behind all their arguments the men were afraid for their libidos. Getting it up. We women cared less about murderers and rapists getting it up.

I voted *yes* in the referendum. I didn't ask the details. Did I leave Danno any joy? I didn't ask.

Nine o'clock. Time to call NatSekur again. The kitchen telephone doesn't work and Yvette is embarrassed. I ring NatSekur from Mark's study and an idiot girl answers who hasn't heard of Colonel Daniel Ryder. Then she says perhaps he's with Headquarters and I say yes he is, and I realise I've called NatSekur's city office and I ask her, can't she put me through, and she says no, and starts to give me the Headquarters number down in the South Forest and I ring off because I've already got it, and try again.

'Colonel Ryder isn't available at this moment in time. Perhaps you could call again later. NatSekur thanks you for calling.'

I've got some fucking computer. I scream into my mouthpiece, anything to alert the circuits.

'Good morning. NatSekur Incorporated. Can I help you?'

'Are you a fucking computer?'

'No, ma'am.'

'Are you a fucking computer programmed to say you're not a fucking computer?'

'No, ma'am.'

'How can I fucking believe you?'

'I don't know, ma'am.'

' . . . My name is Harriet Kahn-Ryder.' She'll know this from the voice-match and my eurocard, but I tell her all the same. 'I want to speak to my brother, Colonel Ryder. That's Colonel Daniel Ryder. Your computer says he isn't available.'

'I'll check that, caller.' Keys mutter. 'Colonel Ryder is out of the office. He's on a tour of the south-west.'

'I spoke to him at your number last Thursday.'

'Colonel Ryder left on Monday, ma'am. He's inspecting NatSekur establishments. He'll be gone a week.'

'How can I reach him?'

'I don't know, ma'am. He could be anywhere.'

'I must speak to him. It's urgent.'

'He sets his own schedule. That way establishments are kept on their toes. He could be anywhere.'

'Anywhere in the fucking south-west, you mean.'

'Anywhere in the south-west.'

'Give me a number. For God's sake, give me a number. Any number.'

'I can't do that, ma'am. I'm sorry. We don't want establishments forewarned.'

'I've got to talk to him.'

'Try his home on Sunday, ma'am. Do you have that number? It's – '

'I do have my own brother's home number, you pusillanimous little shit. I have to talk to him now. Now. Not Sunday. Now . . . Hallo? Are you still there? Answer me. For Christ's sake, answer me.'

'I really cannot help you, caller.'

'Then connect me with someone who can. Connect me with someone who can.'

Silence.

'Good morning. Customer Relations. Can I help you?'

I sever the connection. I know about Customer Relations. At Unikhem, at the Institute, anywhere, Customer Relations is where the run-around begins and ends. They never give. They're well trained.

I sever the connection, grab the pile of unread PIPS print-out from beside the telephone, stuff it into Mark's stove and light it. I lean on the stove, feeling the paper roar in my veins as it burns. It burns away quickly, leaving the blue Delft tiles of the stove cold. I ring Danno's home. I saw Bert Breitholmer once but I've never spoken to him, perhaps he'll tell me how I can reach Danno. His telephone rings. Bert and Danno are very close. Does he know my brother's the karate killer? His telephone rings and rings. I fling mine down. It falls on the floor and I think I chase it, kicking it round the room.

Another telephone rings. I stand at the front windows, looking out. I'm afraid I'll see pictures of Danno putting gold rings into dead girls' shoes but I see only the night. Another telephone rings. I run to answer it in my little sitting-room. Cats with their throats cut, beautiful daughters. I'm smashing the telephones and soon there won't be any left. It's eleven in the morning.

Maggi is calling from the Institute. The TV people want to fix a date for me to sit in on a rough cut of the hormo film, in case

I'm needed for bridging voice-over. I tell her to tell them to call back next year some time. She thinks I'm joking and tells me I'm free next week and I can't think as far away as next week so I don't argue, but the hormo film is ridiculous and irrelevant, and I want nothing more to do with it.

Maggi says Dr Volkov is hoping to hear from me about the fax number she gave Mark yesterday. I tell Maggi to tell Natya everything's fine and she's not to worry, and I'll call back later, which I won't. My brother is the karate killer and I can't wait for Maggi to get off the line because I've thought of something I can do that might prove he isn't the karate killer. So I get rid of her and I use Mark's screen to call up the news-print-out reference library.

If my brother isn't the karate killer perhaps I'm wrong and the dates and circumstances of the crimes will prove he couldn't have committed them. They prove I'm right and he could have. The first murder took place in his garrison town on the evening of the terrible day in July when we buried Dada, and the next is here in the capital in August three years later, which I know for certain matches with the day Dr Vrieland told me I was pregnant. Betrayals? Is that it? First Dada betrays him, by dying, then I do, by growing up? And now I'm supposed to betray him again? Christ.

But there are three more murders with dates I don't recognise, so maybe that's simplistic. So I wonder instead what happened last week to make him kill Janni Wintermann. I talked to him on the telephone from the Ministry only a few days after. He looked so ordinary. Maybe that's the secret. He *is* ordinary.

A picture. Yvette's face, pale and frightened, close to tears. Silly cow. I've been playing the piano, Prokofiev, fingers, fingers, fingers, and by now she must know better than to come with her vacuum cleaner. I know these days that Julius was wasting his time, trying to make a musician of me. It's for the fingers that I play the piano, for the cleverness of the fingers. Problem-solving. The wail of Yvette's vacuum cleaner makes me mad. She turns the cleaner off, takes it away, puts it back in its cupboard.

The telephone rings again. I haven't smashed one for hours. It's Mark, calling to say he's safe where he was going with Anna. He doesn't mention Nomansland, as if it mattered. How am I doing? Have I called the police yet about Danno? I tell him I'm doing fine, and I'm more glad than I can say that Anna's safe, and no, I haven't yet called the fucking police about Danno. Mark says he understands how difficult it is, but I must. He's talked to Moma, and I mustn't worry about her finding out about Danno because he thinks her craziness will protect her. She uses it as a buffer all the time, he says. He seems inclined to chat. I tell him to get off the line and back home here ASAP. I tell him I'm glad he has Anna safe in Nomansland. I say the word, Nomansland, because not even Sergeant Milhaus's SPU card will get her in there. I sever the connection.

It's one o'clock and Yvette has cooked me lunch. I can't think why – she sees the mess I'm in – but she'll cry again if I don't eat it, silly cow, so I eat it. Moma's craziness won't protect her. It's only north-north-west and this is south-south-east, and already she's on a guilt trip about some fucking knee she sat on. *I must talk to Danno.* Moma said the next time I talked to him I should tell him she asked after him. 'Moma asked after you, Danno, and now I'm going to turn you in to the police because you're the karate killer.' I've got to. Mark says so. I say so.

Yvette has screwed the telephone back on to the kitchen wall. She's a capable little person and it's working again. I stuff in my card and I'm talking to Oswald Marton.

'Anna's safe,' I tell him. 'I won't be needing your protective custody.'

It's the gloat I've been looking forward to, and he spoils it. 'Nomansland's a good idea,' he says. 'I imagine you've sent her there.'

He's spoilt my gloat but I'm still feisty. I say, 'Of course. Where else?'

'Where indeed. Nomansland was always your most obvious, indeed your only option.'

'Aren't you worried?'

'Me? You mean, the Minister? My dear Dr Kahn-Ryder, the Minister was only concerned for your daughter in so far as *you* were. If you're content then so are we. Publication is a separate issue.'

'A separate issue. I'm content. You're content. That's nice.'

'Apropos of which – I've been checking police staff records and I can find no SPU officers by the name of Milhaus. You did say Sergeant Milhaus, didn't you?'

'I did say Sergeant Milhaus.'

'I can assure you there's no Sergeant Milhaus in the SPU. No Sergeant Milhaus in any branch of the police force. Are you sure you got the name right?'

'What you mean is, am I sure I didn't make her up.'

'I mean what I say, Dr Kahn-Ryder. It's the best policy.'

I sever the connection. I don't need him clever-dicking me.

This isn't good news, Sergeant Milhaus a freelance. Her warrant card looked official, with a hideous photograph, but it didn't mean anything. Who's behind her – Unikhem? She's got good government contacts, turning up on my doorstep like that two hours after Marton gagged me.

Sergeant Milhaus. Natalya. The patent office. *Natur*. Danno. *Danno* . . . I've got to turn him in and I don't know what they'll do to him. I think I can stand it if I know what they'll do to him. There's a laugh – *I* can stand it, what about Danno, can *he* stand it?

I'm going up the Simpsons' front path. It's a twenty-minute walk away, two stops on the tram, and the day's windy and grey and miserable, but it's not actually raining and waiting at a tram stop I couldn't do. So I walk and a stream of trams pass me. I give them two fingers.

Peter Simpson's house is a bit like ours, but bigger. Running multiple marriages, as well as a consulting-room, he needs it. He has two wives and six daughters here – Anna's Jessica is his youngest – and he has another wife and a family I've never met, in an apartment in town – she doesn't get on with the two wives here, she'd rather have him on visiting terms but all to herself. He manages his relationships surprisingly well – he was a psychiatrist before the profession joined aroma therapy and the tarot, marginalised by the nuts-and-bolts men – but they cost a lot and he boosts his psycho-engineering practice with various consultancy jobs with Government. He's pompous, and English, but a worker. One of these government jobs, I remembered back at the house, is with the prison remedial service. He can tell me what they'll do to Danno.

Two doors lead off the Simpsons' porch, PRIVATE and CONSULTING ROOM. I've never tried the latter but today it seems suitable. There's a waiting-room inside, and a receptionist. I tell her I don't have an appointment, she says will early the week after next do? and I tell her early the week after next will not do. Early the week after next will intrude upon my Christmas shopping and I do not allow visits to the psycho-engineer to intrude upon my Christmas shopping. She gives me this assessing once-over – a dollar to a dime she's a better diagnostician than her boss – has another look in her appointment file, and discovers that the doctor happens to be free at just this very moment.

The truth is, he likes a nap after lunch and he's told her, on pain of death, never to disturb him before two thirty, but there's something about me today that makes her prefer death to it. This guess is borne out when he isn't in his consulting-room as I enter, but he appears a moment later through the door obviously leading into the house, and he's buttoning up his psycho-engineer's jacket.

The receptionist never asked my name, she must have thought I'd bite or go off bang or something, so Pete's surprised when he sees who I am. I tell him this isn't a proper consultation, I'm perfectly well, never felt better, I just want some expert information. He invites me through to the house for a drink and a chat, I say I'm sorry, I really don't have the time, and we sit down in his consulting-room, me in the patient's chair.

He too gives me this assessing once-over. 'So, Harriet,' he says in his charming English accent, 'how can I help you?'

'You can tell me about remedial psycho-engineering.'

'The legal requirements or the techniques?'

'The techniques.'

'The techniques derive from the intention. The intention, basically, is to produce an offender who does not reoffend.'

'What are these techniques?'

'They are not widely advertised. Government likes to spare people what might be seen as painful details.'

'Yet Government authorises these techniques on our behalf.'

'Very true. But there's a collusion. Government believes the people don't want to know these details, so it doesn't tell them.'

'So a free hand is enjoyed by all.'

'Not precisely. The medical council employs a watchdog. And in any case – '

' – In any case I'm people and I do want to know the details.
I'm also a fellow doctor. I have seen an opened brainpan.'

'Very seldom practised these days . . . ' He smiles. He hasn't
asked me why I want to know. He hasn't asked me anything.
He's handling me. He's seen I need handling and he's handling
me. 'What's the criminal tendency we're aiming to eradicate? I
take it we have a particular case in mind? So what is it? Child
molestation? Arson? Homicide? Habitual theft? Drunk driving?
Adult rape?'

'Homicide.'

'With excessive violence? Or simply sufficient to the crime?'

'Sufficient to the crime.'

'For personal material gain?'

'No.'

'A sexual motive? We *are* talking about a male offender, I
imagine?'

'No rape, if that's what you mean.'

'But a male/female offence . . . difficult. There'll be motiva-
tions here that are beyond our reach. An ancient enmity. Fear.
Power. Fascination. Man/woman, white/black, Gentile/Jew. A
passionate distrust . . . '

I don't need poetry. 'Then there's nothing you can do?'

'There are always things we can do.'

'Castrate the bastards?'

'Certainly castration could eliminate sixty per cent of crime,
but the legislation forbids it.'

'The legislation was framed by men.'

'Very true. But why use the blunt instrument approach when
a microtransducer in the right place does the job just as well?
We're not after punishment or deterrence. Both were tried for
millennia and didn't work. We're after offenders who don't
reoffend.'

'And my homicide?'

'Treatable.' He sits back. 'Aside from the underlying trauma,
three basic malfunctions are involved. Failure to compensate,
resulting in anger. Failure to inhibit, resulting in action. Failure
to moderate, resulting in violent action – in this case, murder.'

He runs on. And on. He tells me he can block the brain's
surface excitation that's required in the build-up to the performance of an act of violence. He tells me he can identify and

stimulate with microlaser therapy what he calls the brain's conscience centres. He tells me he can control with drugs and bio-engineered synapse separation the onanistic spiral that produces anger.

I'm impressed. Bio-engineered synapse separation. Onanistic spirals. I ask him the effects of this fucking bio-engineered synapse separation.

He spread his hands. 'An offender who doesn't reoffend.'

'Cabbages don't reoffend.'

'Certainly not a cabbage. Some of the sparkle will be lost, undeniably. But – '

'Do you leave him joy?'

'Does he have it to begin with?'

I experience two of his three failures. Only the battered ruins of my brain's conscience centres hold me back. Amazingly, he notices something.

'I get a sense, Harriet, that you're personally involved in this. Shouldn't you tell me about it?'

'We all have joy, Peter.'

'Is this man somebody you know well?'

'Until you psycho-engineers get at us.'

'Has Mark killed some woman?'

'Some of the sparkle, Peter – what did you mean?'

'That's a sentimental question. The legislation grasped that nettle eleven years ago. Of course there are losses. We opted for offenders who don't reoffend.'

'So it's what I said – anything goes.'

'You're upset, Harriet.'

'I'm a woman talking to a man. I'm a black talking to a white. I'm a Jew talking to a fucking Nazi.' I've come to like the idea. It explains a lot. The ancient enmity. 'Of course I'm upset.'

He glances at his watch. This is the bedside manner he got rich on? 'I've a patient in five minutes, Harriet. Look – why don't you go through to the house? Let Janey get you a drink. I'll join you as soon as I'm free.'

I go through to the house, straight down the passage and out the front door. Janey's the meekest, happiest, most non-existent of his wives. I sever the connection.

I'm riding the tram. Rain has swept in across the city on a bitter wind and it's lashing the streets between the Simpsons' house and ours. The tram's nearly empty. I sit in a damp fug. It's only for two stops.

What will they do to Danno? Did Natya sell out to Unikhem? Where is Sergeant Milhaus? What about the patent office and my piece for *Natur*? Bio-engineered synapse separation. Danno has joy. We all do. Don't we? Doesn't he?

Two men, neat office suits, are sitting opposite me, across the gangway. One of them nudged the other when I got on. They smile together now and look at my legs and breasts, and say quiet things to each other that I can't hear above the tram noises. One of them widens his eyes and puffs out his cheeks and they both laugh. They're open about their interest and I think I'm supposed to feel flattered. I don't feel flattered. I feel like a Yid, a Nigra, a Woman.

I shout at them, 'You killers.' It's not dignified and I don't care. Yids, Nigras, Women don't. I shout at them, 'You fucking karate killers. You fucking karate killers . . . '

I'm hitting at them and one of them has blood on his cheek. I'm kicking them and pulling at their neat office suits, tearing the cloth, and one of them is trying to get round behind me and hold down my arms, and the other is huddled in the corner of his seat, protecting his face.

'Killers . . . killers . . . ' A limited vocabulary, but oh Christ, the ancient enmity. 'You fucking karate killers . . . '

I shake off the man behind me and the man in the corner of the seat somehow gets his foot up and kicks me in the stomach. I think I vomit. But I'm still fighting, and other people on the tram join in and they hold me and the tram stops and I'm still fighting.

Stillness next, a sweet gentle pressure in my ears. My cell door has closed and the stillness is a sweet gentle pressure in my ears. It drives out thought and leaves me with my bruises. I have a lot of bruises. Between the tram and the police station and this cell, a lot of bruises. I'm strong but policewomen are selected to be stronger, and it's well known that they don't go easy on their own. I deserve no deference and receive none. The two men receive deference. The master race. No – not fair. The aggrieved parties. I finger my bruises. The stillness drives out thought.

Not for long. A tall smart policeman comes in, a senior inspector. He tells me my victims aren't preferring charges. How dare they be so generous? But I like that *victims*. I hope they really were my *victims*. I hope they have bruises now that are worse than mine. The inspector tells me there's still the offence of Creating a Disturbance in a Public Place (I can hear the capitals) but he says he's confirmed my identity and if I can get my husband to apply for bail he can have me out of here before nightfall. He says he's rung my home and spoken to my maid (no wonder he's so polite, after speaking to my *maid*), but my husband isn't available.

I explain that my husband's away on business. He won't get home till after seven. The inspector's concerned: by then, he says, the magistrate's office will be closed, ruling out the possibility of bail until the morning. I'll have to spend the night in jail.

My night in jail clearly worries him more than it worries me. I'm Dr Kahn-Ryder and he doesn't think it suitable for a woman in my position. Also I'm Dr Kahn-Ryder and he doesn't want the media getting wind of my incarceration. To be honest, I don't give a shit, either about a night in jail or the media. Handled right, the facts of my incarceration would gain me sympathy. There's a snag, though – who'll do the handling? Not me. I've got to find Danno, I've got to talk to Natalya, I've got to deal with Sergeant Milhaus, I've got to write up a patent application and write my piece for *Natur*, and I've got to sleep. I'm incredibly tired. It's only four o'clock, and I've got to sleep, and a night in jail is just the ticket. The inspector will keep our little secret. He doesn't want the place knee-deep in media any more than I do.

He asks me if I want to see my lawyer. I tell him I don't have a fucking lawyer and if I did I wouldn't want to fucking see him. He says he really would like me to see a lawyer, for his sake if not for my own, to establish that he's acted in full accordance with the law, and I tell him to take a running fuck at himself. I've never said so many fucks before in my life. They'll make a man of me yet.

I sever the connection. The inspector goes away and an orderly brings me food I don't need. I'm incredibly tired but my head is buzzing and I was tired last night after my journey to Nomansland with Anna, and I didn't sleep then, and there's a woman in a cell somewhere near who's singing and sort of screaming, no, screaming and sort of singing, and in any case, whichever it is, she's not going to help me sleep, to say the least, and now there's daylight coming through the window and my bladder tells me it's morning and I've slept.

At nine o'clock Mark arrives. He looks terrible. He hugs me and kisses me and tells me arranging bail will take about an hour. It takes less. He goes away, comes back, hugs me again, I collect the contents of my pockets from the policewoman at the desk, sign for them, and we go out into the street. He has a taxi waiting.

We're inside, on the back seat, and he hugs me and hugs me. He's very glad to see me. I think I hug him back. I smell the damp dusty smell of the plastic back seat and I look at the shiny rolls of red neck-flesh above the fat taxi-driver's collar. I listen to the gnashing of her old engine and the clunks of her old suspension. Outside the taxi it's another cold grey windy day, rain falling, sleet mixed with it. I'm afraid Mark is going to ask me when I plan to tell the police about Danno, for he's obviously guessed that I haven't yet, but instead he says, 'You've got to be very brave, old buddy.'

He pauses and I wait, being brave was yesterday, being brave isn't today, and then he tells me, 'Harriet, they've taken Annie away. The Convent Superior rang me early this morning. They've gone in with guns and taken Annie away.'

I drag my eyes away from the rain and the fat taxi-driver's neck, and I look at him calmly. At last, calmly. They've taken Annie away. How simple. At last, simple. I like things to be simple.

CHAPTER TWELVE

The Attrition. Year 35: late October.

'You really do have a nerve, Har'. I hope you realise that.'

'And you're an angel, Liese. I hope you realise *that*.'

Liese did. Which was partly what made this week off work worth the inconvenience – that and her love for Anna. She'd just arrived. They were in the entrance hall of Mark and Harriet's large third-floor flat down by the river, on the outskirts of the city. Three years earlier this meeting wouldn't have been possible, but Harriet was now well established as Mrs Kahn-Ryder, and with the passing of the years Liese's pain had eased.

Harriet took her friend's arm and led her through into the living-room. South-facing, on this late October afternoon it offered only grey banked clouds above leafless trees and the dull dead river. Harriet sat Liese with her back to the window.

'Let me get you something. Annie-poo won't be in from school for a while yet. Tea? Coffee? A drop of the Forester's Friend?'

'Tea, Har'. The day I resort to vodka at three in the afternoon I'll know it's time I found myself an expensive lover.'

Harriet laughed. 'Nothing doing otherwise . . . in that department?'

'Don't be coy, dear. I'm nudging thirty, a virgin, and likely to stay that way. Mark Kahns don't grow on trees.'

'No. Well . . . I'll get the tea.' Harriet gestured at the hi-fi. 'Choose us some Chopin. I'm coming round to him.'

She drifted out into the kitchen. Asking Liese about her sex life was a mistake. It pointed up her own good fortune. Asking Liese about almost anything was a mistake, and for the same reason. But they were sensible women, and if most of what they shared these days was Anna, Anna was a lot.

Harriet boiled the water, made the tea. The energetic young woman who kept house for her and Mark had already left, off for a week's holiday at her mother's house, up in the mountains. She was hoping for some skiing. A Chopin nocturne wafted in from the living-room. Helped by Mark, Harriet was at last coming round to Chopin.

Liese. Mark. She hadn't known she could be so ruthless. She'd known she could be ruthless, but not *that* ruthless. Custom had been on her side, which helped, but the consigning of one love to a less important level than another was never easy. Custom assumed, in its anti-feminist way, that the love between woman and man outrated all other. A dodgy assumption. It worked in Harriet's case, for Mark possessed all Liese's better qualities – gentleness, loyalty, intelligence, tolerance – plus a readier sense of humour and a penis too, but in many cases it was an assumption that simply pandered to the hysteria of sexual infatuation.

The day she moved out on Liese, actually packed her bags, and Anna's, and left, was one of the worst in her life. Liese helped her carry down the things to the waiting taxi.

'Of course you must go.' Dismantling five years of family, the books, the records, the potted plant, Anna's toys. 'Of course you must go.'

They stood on the emptied balcony. Harriet bit her knuckles, borne down by happy memories. 'You'll come and see us? Annie'll miss you. You'll come and see us?'

The skin of Liese's face had shrunk upon the bone. 'Of course I'll come and see you.'

Anna did miss her and she did come. At first the visits had been a minefield. Anna went to a minder after school now, till Harriet got home from her job at the Institute. The minder was the sort of friendly silly woman to whom Harriet and Liese would never in the past have given care of their daughter. Mark worked irregular hours and wasn't always in the best of tempers. The apartment was small. Harriet had left Unikhem, was putting together a team at the government research institute, and brought home papers to read that sometimes meant Anna saw more TV than was good for her. Liese's visits were a minefield of avoided subjects and unspoken criticisms. Worst was her way of always finding something nice to say.

Liese acquired a full-time job in family care again, and gradually her own life. Harriet and Mark got married, and felt brave enough to take on the responsibility of a larger apartment and live-in help. The stress between them and Liese eased, Liese was still Harriet's best friend, and the enormous efforts that had kept their friendship going were no longer necessary.

Liese turned from the record shelves as Harriet carried in the tea-tray. 'When exactly does your plane leave?'

'We've got to be at the airport by eight tomorrow morning.'

'And you're still flying straight to Ankara?'

'I think so. The consul there says it's fine – the fighting's been over for more than a week now.'

'Crazy women. What do they think they'll gain?'

'Apparently they've gained it.' Harriet poured two cups of tea. 'The fundamentalists are out. The chador's been declared illegal.'

'Massacres gain nothing, Harriet. Not in the long run. The Muslim countries are already chronically short of men. Hacking thousands of them to pieces will hardly help the situation.'

'There speaks your typical non-Muslim woman.' Harriet passed Liese her cup. 'Personally, I can imagine it helping a lot.'

'That's one of your poses. You're the least militant woman I know.'

'That's because I've had things so easy. It lets me disapprove of militancy, call it male and reprehensible.'

She offered biscuits and Liese took one.

'What are massacres then,' Liese asked, 'if not male and reprehensible?'

'That particular massacre was a thousand years in the making, and thoroughly female . . . In any case, it's over now and the consul says Turkey's safe. We're leaving Armenia and Azerbaijan until we get there. With any luck we can give them a miss. If this old chap's got the stuff Michael Volkov says he has.'

'He will have. He has to have. That's why I'm taking Anna – to advance the cause of science. Behind every successful woman there's an unsuccessful woman.'

It was lightly said. Harriet looked at her. It was lightly said, but no – behind every successful woman there was a woman successful in different ways. Liese certainly believed that – did she want to be told it now? Harriet was spared a decision by the banging of the outside door and Anna's arrival in the living-room. Eight years old, dark hair long and wild, school satchel swinging, beautiful and precious.

'Auntie Leez . . . I knew you'd be here. I knew you wouldn't forget me.'

'I don't know about you, child. It's Elvis I'm here for. And you haven't greeted your mother.'

'Greet, greet, Moma.'

'Greet, greet, Annie-poo.' How desirable it was, Harriet thought, that Liese'd had to remind her.

'Only Elvis, Auntie Leez? What about me?'

'Let's look at you, then. Stand up straight. You aren't very big, I must say. If you promise not to eat too much I expect I can fit you in somewhere.'

Liese was quite right – Harriet *did* have a nerve, asking her to look after Anna and Elvis for a week while she and Mark went off to Erzurum in eastern Turkey, looking for Dr Aku Fateya. But it was strictly a business trip – according to Professor Volkov, who'd been there and ought to know, *nobody* went to Erzurum for pleasure – and Anna was delighted to be left with her aunt, and Elvis's opinion wasn't asked, and Liese would be able to get Anna to and from school every day, and in the last three years Liese's pain had eased, and it was altogether the ideal situation. Also, it let Liese be an angel.

Mark arrived soon after. He'd been over in *Science News*'s office, tidying his desk. He had a piece in the pipeline on women's changing expectations in the professional workplace, and he'd wanted to be sure it wasn't subbed to death. Now he was free and was flying to Ankara and on to Erzurum for a story that, if it came off, he wouldn't be able to write up for a very long time, years, as long as Harriet's follow-up research took.

He flung himself down on the sofa, reached out to feel the cold teapot, groaned. Harriet saw and heard and stayed where she was. She'd been at the Institute till noon herself, and since then she'd done Anna's packing. Liese observed the impasse, but Anna was showing her one of her history essays – 'Life in a Viking Village'.

Mark linked his hands behind his head. 'How's Liese, then?'

'I'm fine.' She didn't look up from Anna's book. 'And you?'

'Perking. You know . . . perking.' He stretched his legs. 'This really is extraordinarily good of you, Liese.'

'Not at all. Anna and I will have a fine time.'

He glanced questioningly at Harriet. She shrugged. Muttering continued between Anna and Liese. Mark closed his eyes. Apart from making friendly bracing noises at arrival and departure, he claimed he found it best to leave Liese to Harriet. There were uncomfortable overtones, he told Harriet, of a ménage à trois.

Suggestions that she knew his wife better than he did. He was sure Liese did her best to avoid them (which meant he wasn't sure at all), but they hung around all the same.

Finally it was time for Liese and Anna to leave. Harriet fetched Elvis, and Mark Elvis's basket, and he was put in it. He protested, providing a general distraction from whatever emotion the parting might have entailed. Anna talked to him, without effect, all down the stairs and out into the taxi. Liese joined them. Mark put Anna's cases in the back. Harriet leaned in, kissed her, and the taxi drove away. A bitter wind blew down the street. Harriet stood on the pavement, waving. This would be the first time she and Anna had been apart for more than a few hours.

Mark put his arm round her waist. 'Annie's big now,' he said. 'She'll be fine. It's you I worry about.'

Harriet fitted herself against him. 'We're both big now.'

They went back upstairs together. The flat was very quiet, and their plane didn't leave till the morning. Mark fetched his folder on their coming trip.

'Help me with the notes my researcher made for me at the office,' he said, spreading papers on the kitchen table. 'It'll be our last chance before chaos takes over.'

Harriet wiped her eyes unobtrusively on a dish towel. He was shuffling his papers and didn't see.

'Don't be so north-European, Mark. I'm sure chaos doesn't really begin the moment you cross the Danube.' But she could see what he was up to, keeping her busy. 'Still, your notes are your notes. And I expect now is as good a time as any.'

She filled the coffee-maker. She didn't want coffee, Liese and she had only just had tea, but at moments like this coffee was what one did. Coffee, and Mark's notes . . . These were genuine – he might never write the piece, or in this case not for years, but he was a man who liked everything down on paper. How can I know what I think, he said, until I see what I've written?

She leaned against the counter, waiting for the coffee. 'So where do we start?'

'The Turkish garrison town of Erzurum.' He selected a sheet of paper, tapped the others into a neat stack, read from the sheet he'd chosen. 'We're going to Erzurum because . . . because that's where your friend Professor Volkov says we'll find Dr Fateya. And Dr Fateya is our prophet in the wilderness. So how does a Russian archaeologist come to put us on to an Azerbaijani virologist?'

'Probably not a virologist, nothing so grand. Certainly Michael had no great opinion of his doctoring. They were on a dig in the area – there are Hittite remains all over north-east Turkey – and Michael fractured his left tibia in a rock fall. The expedition doctor was herself badly concussed in the same rock fall, so they had to look for local talent in a hurry.'

'And the talent they came up with was this Dr Fatty?'

'That's right. The overseer recommended him – everyone's someone's cousin in that part of the world – so they shipped him out to the site. Apparent the expedition's mobile X-ray equipment baffled him completely. He did his job in the old way, sensitive fingers, a splint, gallons of plaster. It worked, incidentally – Michael's as good as new. Anyway, it was a long trip back into town so Dr Fatty stayed the night. And after a drink or two, or maybe ten, the reminiscences began. He started boasting that once, long ago, when he was a young man, he'd been working in his own laboratory and he'd discovered a cure for AIDS. Then there was some story about a missile attack, and he didn't have the cure any more.'

'That figures. But they took him seriously?'

'Of course not. But in the morning he modified his story. He'd worked in the Biberian Research Centre, and *they'd* discovered the cure.'

'Biberian Centre . . . that's what I thought you said. My researcher couldn't find it.'

'I'm not surprised. Rudolfo Clarence Biberian was a millionaire Armenian – shipping, oil, yacht marinas, you name it. Drugs, probably. Anyway, at the end of the last century he coughed up some of his millions for a research centre that he built in what was then southern Azerbaijan. He attracted some distinguished people, Professor Woodruff from Harvard med school among them. Nobody knows exactly what they were working on, but they certainly never published anything about a cure for AIDS. The place was razed to the ground in the civil war. As Fateya said, a missile attack. A lot of senior people died, including Woodruff.'

'Wars are like that. But why the interest now? How did Michael Volkov make the connection between all this and your work at the Institute?'

'He didn't. But he talked about Dr Fatty to our Natalya when he got back, and *she* made the connection – mainly because of where the Biberian Centre was, the sticky end it came to, and the date of that sticky end.'

'So let me guess – the Centre received its quietus a few months before the beginning of the Attrition.'

Harriet nodded. 'Nearly a year before – and in pretty much the area our research into the spread of the Syndrome had finally settled on as the most probable starting-point.' Mark scuffled a map out of his stack of papers and handed it to her. 'We'd pinpointed Tbilisi . . . here . . . in Georgia, and the Biberian Centre was only a few hundred k's away, near the small town of Kamo . . . here . . . up in the mountains around Lake Sevan. All this used to be northern Armenia and it suffered horribly in the troubles. According to Dr Fatty the people in the Centre were warned again and again, but hung on. They hung on too long. He was one of the very few who escaped. He was badly injured. He fled across the border into Turkey and he's been there ever since.'

The coffee was ready. She poured two mugs, pushed one across the table. She glanced at her watch, hesitated.

'D'you think Liese's got home with Annie yet? Perhaps we should phone. Make sure they're safe.'

Mark put a hand on hers. 'They're safe, old buddy. It's a ten-minute taxi drive. They're safe.'

'Maybe Annie's forgotten something.'

'Then they'll call and say so.'

' . . . I'm going to miss her, Mark.'

'Of course you are. So am I.'

'A week can be a long time.'

'We'll try to get back sooner.'

She eased her hand away, shivered slightly, pointed at his notes. 'Where had we got?'

'We don't have to do this.'

'Yes we do.' She shivered again. 'Chaos threatens.'

'Ah. You're right . . . Well, we'd got to Lake Sevan and AIDS research . . . which interested you because you've always believed that the MER Syndrome, like AIDS, is the result of a viral infection . . . ' He frowned. 'I have to say, Harriet, that the connection here still seems a bit far-fetched.'

She made an effort. 'I agree it's far-fetched, Mark. But at least it's something . . . We're chasing our tails – thirty-five years of the Syndrome and we're still where we started.'

'AIDS has been with us longer than that. Cancer for ever. Maybe the mistake is to assume that science can always find cures for everything.'

'Of course it is.' She picked up his pen and handed it to him. 'Write this down, Mark – it's a *very* dangerous assumption, one that has misused more resources, and soured the relationship between more doctors and their patients, than even the greed of surgeons.'

He wrote obediently. ' . . . *Than even the greed of surgeons.* And that's saying something.' He looked up. 'Yet you keep on trying. As far as the Syndrome's concerned you still believe there's a cure out there.'

'Yes. Yes, I do . . . ' She drank her coffee, looking at him thoughtfully over the mug, steam wetting her eyelashes. 'The Syndrome is different. It's special. It's so mysterious, Mark. Almost as if – ' she looked for the words ' – almost as if it had been intended.'

'Intended?' Mark flung down his pen and pushed back his chair. 'You're not going Gaian on me, are you? The universal organism? Men being phased out because they're bad for the environment?'

'Just as plankton die off when the DMS they produce seeds too much cloud cover for their own good?' She shook her head. 'Not exactly. But there is a *rightness* about it. A symbolic quality. It's as if – '

'You're talking like a woman, old buddy. As a man, I don't see much *rightness* about my own extinction. It's too wholesale. Just a long-winded way of getting rid of the species.'

'That's what I mean, Mark. Extinction *is* too wholesale. That's why I believe there's a cure out there. Something for us to find.'

'Put there by God the Mother?'

'Don't cheapen me, Mark.' She stood up abruptly. Her anger didn't last. She returned to her thought. 'Something put there,' she went on, now staring past him, her eyes unfocused,

231

'maybe something put there by whoever, whatever put God the Mother there . . . ?'

She didn't expect him to understand. But he didn't rush in; he allowed a long silence, as if the idea had penetrated even his armour-plated rationalism.

Then, 'So what are you doing this for? God or mankind?'

She frowned. 'That's much too heavy. I'm not doing this for either – I'm doing it for me. I'm problem-solving. Being clever among clever people. I love it.'

'Helping the world doesn't come into it?'

'Don't interview me, Mark.' She turned away. 'I'm not one of your victims.'

'I was interested.' He picked up his coffee-mug. 'I'm sorry if I sounded like an interview.'

She thought about it. Maybe she was the heavy one. No, they both were. She sat down at the table again. 'And I'm sorry I sounded like a victim.'

'And I'm sorry you're sorry.'

'And I'm sorry you're sorry I'm sorry.'

They nodded at each other solemnly. It was a family joke – his family, not hers, a behavioural psychologist father and a lawyer mother, both living now in Italy. Family jokes were handy escape mechanisms.

Mark's coffee was cool and he finished it in one. 'Where were we?'

She told him, 'We were believing there was a cure out there.'

'That's it. A cure for a virus.' He found another of his pages. 'So what's so difficult about a virus?' He answered his own question. 'A virus is an independent genetic system capable of transferring itself from one host cell to another. It varies its morphology to suit its host cell. Many are so tiny as to be unfilterable.'

Harriet laughed. 'That too. The largest is a tenth of the size of your average bacterium. Electron microscopes cope, though. And I'm not so sure about your "independent genetic system". They're pretty primitive. Some virologists consider them non-living unless in a parasitic relationship.'

'So?'

'So they're hard to study. Purifying and concentrating progeny viruses for study can be a bastard. Sometimes we know them best from the antibody production they stimulate.'

'But the Syndrome doesn't have any antibodies.'

'Not that we've found so far.'

'If you can't identify it, and it doesn't have any antibodies, perhaps it isn't a virus.'

'Perhaps it is. You're talking like bloody Fovas.' She could see he didn't approve. 'I'm not just being obstinate. Viruses *do* produce non-specific responses. And there are others – many cancers, for example, and herpes simplex – inapparent infections that wait around until they're activated. Fever, maybe, or stress. Menstruation. Intense sunlight.'

'Menstruation?'

'That's what I mean.' She leaned forward eagerly. 'A reaction that's female-specific. If it can happen there it can happen somewhere else.'

'But you haven't yet found where.'

'No.'

He underlined something in his notes. 'So how's this Dr Fatty going to help you?'

'I've no idea.' She smiled apologetically. 'I know that sounds feeble, but – '

He hushed her. 'A mysterious laboratory, a big bang, the right place and the right time, a lone survivor . . . of course it's tempting.'

'The right area of research too, Mark. Woodruff was brilliant – a geneticist with a long history in AIDS research. And there has to be an AIDS involvement. It can't be coincidence that the Syndrome gives women HIV immunity.'

'So a cure would take the immunity away?'

'We don't know that. Most immunities outlast their pre-cipitating factor. It's one of those things we'll have to deal with when we get there.'

He nodded, turned another page. 'I've got a big question mark here. Could a Syndrome cure equal an AIDS cure?'

'No. No way. They're connected but they're different beasts.' She hesitated, shrugged. 'All new knowledge helps. I'd put it no stronger than that.'

'I see. Pity.' He wrote briefly. 'So now it's all up to this Dr Fateya and what he remembers after thirty-five years. Let's hope he's friendly.'

'Michael says the answer there is UK whisky. Preferably one

called Johnny Walker. I've a half-litre bottle in the kitchen. It's squalid, feeding an old man booze, but – '

The telephone rang. Harriet's eyes flicked sideways. Anna?

'But indeed.' Mark capped his pen.

Harriet answered the telephone, carefully not rushing. Anna came up on the screen. Aunt Leez had had a surprise for her, a boy doll with hair you could brush in a pony-tail. She was calling him Sam. Elvis hated Aunt Leez's apartment. He'd peed in his basket and he'd been under the bookcase ever since they'd got there. Aunt Leez said cats were territorial animals and they'd have to give him time to get used to it. Aunt Leez sent her love. Annie did too.

Mark had put his papers away. Harriet felt better after the phone call. Liese was managing the change from co-parent to courtesy aunt as well as she managed everything else. Annie was fine. The trip to Erzurum would be Mark's and her first time alone together.

They finished their packing. Northern Turkey would be chilly in late October. Erzurum, in the mountain foothills, might have snow, and if they went on to the ruins of the Biberian Centre they'd be up around 4,000 metres. The packing done, Mark took her out to dinner. They ate well. Michael had warned them that, away from Ankara and the fishing villages of the Black Sea coast, they should expect goat pretending to be mutton, and *yogourdi* – pungent local yoghurt – with everything.

They went to bed early – they'd booked a taxi to the airport for six thirty in the morning. They made love. Harriet hadn't expected to want to, but Mark's presence beside her in the bed was persuasive. She felt herself opening to him and didn't resist. He made her safe. Together they shared starbursts, music, peace. Afterwards, as she was drifting off to sleep, she thought of Liese. She wondered how Liese could bear it. The only difference between them was that Liese was plain and she was pretty.

The morning's flight to Ankara was uneventful, three hours in a methanol-burning airbus. From Ankara they took a tilt-rotor to Erzurum. Ankara airport, though Muslim, was a typical Attrition public place, women running everything, not a chador in sight. They didn't leave the building, saw no sign of the recent bloody riots.

Erzurum airport, 800 k's away to the east, inhabited a different century. The law against the chador hadn't reached this far. Women fetched, carried, swept, served in the buffet, were robed from head to foot. Armed men stalked among them, smiling, directing their work. There was no chance of the riots in the regional capital being repeated here. Erzurum was an army town. The Turkish army accepted women but only the men, ageing officers, sergeants and corporals, had guns.

Harriet had come prepared. She wore long loose trousers, a quilted coat, and a large headscarf swathed under her chin, and she hated herself. This wasn't courtesy towards local custom, it was gutless compliance. It was collaboration in systematic oppression.

It was raining in Erzurum. They had flown in low, up a steep mountain pass with feathery leafless trees and houses under low-pitched roofs with wide eaves, oddly like a traditional Chinese print. That delicate, faded impression died as they left the aeroplane. The city was approached from the airport along a ruler-straight mud road between mud-walled hovels, the mud running off them in the rain. A thunderous diesel taxi took them to the town's best hotel. Mark had insisted on the hotel. They were there on business, needing somewhere to stay that offered the minimum disease and discomfort. Unique local life-styles could wait on another trip.

As they entered the town their driver pointed to a ruined concrete tower and told them it had been a Hilton. Harriet didn't ask if the damage was due to subsidence or bombs. She knew the Muslim world had been hit hard by the Attrition but she hadn't expected this. She was used to order, in her relationships, in her work, most of all in the physical structures of her tidy north-European life. Erzurum seemed to be returning to its primal elements of earth and water as she watched. And fire too – smoke rose from countless mud-brick chimneys and tents and open street braziers. It drifted at roof height, acrid and grey in the steady drizzle.

They were taken to the Paradise Hotel in the centre of town. Puddled filth seethed in the street outside. The minimum disease and discomfort? Harriet and Mark avoided each other's eyes. While a porter, mud up to her waist, carried in their luggage, an ancient French-speaking Turk in a greasy tarbush offered to weigh and measure them for 300 euros. If she'd been staying longer Harriet might have agreed, for the sake of future ancient francophone favours.

The man at reception was ancient too. In any other decade he'd have been worrying his worry beads by some daughter's fireside. He offered them toothless French or German or Greek – probably with Farsi for his swarthier guests – and Mark chose German. They booked in, and a heavily robed bell-hop, whom they were forbidden to tip, showed them to their room. Mark tipped her all the same. The hotel building was third-millennium, with glass lifts and TV surveillance in all corridors, but recently installed wood-stoves heated its bedrooms. The makeshift iron chimney-pipe of Mark and Harriet's was cracked and it leaked. Mark opened the window, letting in drizzle and the sudden blare of the evening muezzin.

It had been a long day. They ate a passable dinner in the hotel restaurant – Mark suspected the rabbit stew of being cat but Harriet was too tired to care – and went to bed. In the morning the stove was out, the curtains were sodden, and the muezzin roused them earlier than they'd have chosen, but they'd slept well. Breakfast was American cornflakes and Turkish *yogourdi*. Tea came milkless in little belled glasses, with lumps of sugar. It was good.

The rain had stopped. They fetched coats from their room and Mark put the Johnny Walker discreetly in his pocket. Outside the hotel male taxi-drivers drove aged diesel Volvos up and down, leaning out and beating on the door panels with short sticks. Mark and Harriet consulted. Michael Volkov had warned them that the taxis operated on the bus principle, gathering and shedding passengers as they went along, suiting their destinations to the most vociferous. Pedal taxis were surer for foreign visitors, but were ridden by haggard girls, skinny grey legs and feet, black robes billowing. Harriet checked the alternatives and wanted to walk. Mark told her they'd never find Dr Fateya's house on their own. They took a pedal taxi, Mark showing its rider the address Michael had written out for him. A lot of passengers were fatter than they, Harriet thought, anxiously sitting very straight and thin, as if suspended.

Dr Aku Fateya lived in the suburbs at the edge of a group of army barracks on the opposite side of town from the airport. The mud was drying now but its colour was pervasive. The pedal taxi dropped them off outside a row of low two-storey open-fronted shops with sodden awnings. The street was crowded but oddly quiet. Men everywhere, in dull resentful groups among the food stalls, the tailors, letter-writers and fortune-tellers. Mark queried the place but their driver insisted, pointing at a screened-off shop beside a seller of vivid green and pink drinks from tall, scum-encrusted glass jars on a worn plastic counter. A large piece of cardboard was pinned to the screen, announcing, in English, *Dr A. Fateya, Doctor of Health and Medicine*. Mark approached it warily, fingering the half of whisky in his pocket. He paid the taxi-girl in advance to wait for them and she hunkered down against the wall of Dr Fateya's house, disappearing into a heap of rags. The sky was clearing but the acrid city haze still lingered.

The screen was slatted bamboo, with a narrow gap in the middle by way of entrance. Harriet followed Mark in, avoiding the iridescent puddles. A dividing wall inside blocked off most of the shop, leaving a small area at the front as waiting-room, with three rusty folding garden chairs. The wall was of faded, bluish-pink plaster, decorated with contraceptive advertise-ments and a portrait of the last-but-one American president. A further opening, hung with a nylene chenille curtain, led into what was clearly Dr Fateya's consulting-room.

Mark was nonplussed. Harriet watched him look for a door to knock upon. She would have gone straight in, except that the doctor might have a patient. She prodded the curtain.

'Dr Fateya?' Taking the lead from his signboard, she called in English, 'May I come in?'

There was no response. She looked at Mark, who shrugged. This trip was becoming increasingly improbable as the source of unique research material.

She raised her voice. 'Dr Fateya?'

She pushed the curtain aside and went in. The room was silent and in darkness. She fumbled for a light switch and two enormously bright neon tubes flickered on, illuminating a desk, two chairs, a moulded-plastic examination couch and a large padlocked glass-and-chrome-steel cabinet filled with bottles. Cockroaches fled with a sharp little pattering sound. She shaded her eyes. Framed professional certificates hung on the walls, in languages Harriet couldn't read. It seemed unlikely that many patients here would be able to read them either. There appeared to be no washing facilities.

Mark joined her. 'And this is a doctor?'

'We're not here for his doctoring.' She was being sturdy. 'Michael did warn us. And Fateya did fix his leg, so he can't be hopeless.'

There were sounds of movement, footsteps descending stairs, then an elderly man, in heavy woman's make-up, put his head round the door at the back of Dr Fateya's consulting-room. Seeing them, he ducked back, then reappeared, only his large bright kohl-rimmed eyes showing above a spangled crimson shawl. Harriet felt sudden sharp rage, at the shawl, at the cockroaches, at Turkey, at someone who accepted the veil as his price for being a woman.

She smiled at him very gently. 'Dr Fateya?'

The old man rolled his eyes upwards, then pushed out past them, through the curtain into the waiting-room and away. He moved nimbly, not looking back.

Harriet went quickly through the door, found a narrow staircase, called up it. 'Fateya? Aku Fateya?'

There was a distant groan. She told Mark, 'I'm going up.'

'D'you think you should?'

'I think that was what passes for Mrs Fateya and I think she invited me up. I think she invited us both up.'

Mark laughed softly. 'I'm sure she did.'

The room upstairs was as dim and cluttered as the consulting-room was bright and bare. A fake marble-topped dining-table, assorted dining-chairs, a wardrobe with the clothes bursting out of it, two maple-veneered sideboards, a gilt-scrolled china cabinet, a large Swedish-style TV set, nesting coffee-tables in green onyx, many cardboard boxes, a greasy glass chandelier hanging from the ceiling, and in one corner – its egregious shiny pinkness seeming to generate what little light there was in the place – a bulbous double divan bed with a towering heart-shaped quilted satin headboard. An even older man, presumably Dr Fateya, dressed in a sombre European double-breasted suit with over-square shoulders, lay on the bed, propped against a number of pink satin pillows, regarding them with neither surprise nor curiosity. He might once have been handsome but now, in old age, his deep-set eyes were ringed with brownish-purple, he had several days of grey stubble on his hollow cheeks, and his stringy neck was many sizes too small for the formal collar and tie he wore. The whites of his eyes were bloodshot and his lips were crusty. He was either very ill, Harriet decided, or suffering from a terrible hangover. Or both.

She hesitated in the doorway. She'd come a long way for this, for a professional interview, doctor to doctor. Michael Volkov had warned her not to expect too much, but he hadn't prepared her for *le vrai* Dr Fateya. Was this Dr Fateya? He looked too old. Dr Fateya would be in his sixties – perhaps this was his father. She cleared her throat, glanced over her shoulder, ready to run. There were glasses, and three empty bottles, on the table.

'We're looking for Dr Fateya,' she said uncertainly. 'Dr Aku Fateya – '

Mark pushed past her. 'Good morning, Doctor. Good morning . . . ' His voice made the ornaments on the sideboards jump and jingle. 'My name is Kahn. I'm a journalist. How d'you do. My wife is sick and we've been recommended your services by a friend of ours, Professor Volkov. You may remember him. He speaks of you most highly.'

The blood-rimmed eyes widened slightly.

'Most highly. You see, my wife has been having severe abdominal pains and we fear she may be suffering from an appendicitis. We're strangers in your beautiful land and we urgently need your advice.' He approached the bed, one hand outstretched for shaking. 'I'm sure you will not fail us.'

Harriet was impressed. Appendicitis? The strategy was good, to flatter the man through his profession. The choice of illness too – under palpation she knew exactly the places to produce pains that would indicate wind and not an inflamed appendix. She hoped Fateya knew them. She didn't relish his hands on her lower abdomen, but they'd be a small price to pay for his confidence.

Dr Fateya had sat up on the bed. He shot his cuffs, then flexed his fingers like a pianist limbering up.

'Forgive me, Mr . . . Kahn, was it? Mr Kahn, Mrs Kahn . . . I was resting. I . . . the truth is, I have not been well.'

'I'm sorry to hear that, Doctor.' Mark retreated a step. 'If you don't feel up to examining my wife, then of course – '

'No, no, no . . . ' Fateya was on his feet now, straightening his tie, discreetly tidying his mouth with the slippery white handkerchief from his breast pocket. 'After resting, behold – I am quite recovered.' He bent his arms like a professional strong man and grinned cadaverously. His teeth were the most expensive things about him. 'Quite recovered. So let us concern ourselves instead with the little lady . . . '

He dodged between them and turned. 'Please, shall we descend to my consulting-room? You should not be here, of course. That blithering boy should have sent for me. She is a thorn in the flesh. A cross to bear. Truly.'

He gripped Mark's elbow. 'But you are people of the world. For people of the world it is not so shocking to see an old man resting?'

He was gone, briskly down the stairs, before Mark could reassure him. They followed, avoiding each other's eyes.

'That was quick thinking,' Harriet whispered.

'First lesson at reporters' school – never start by asking what you really want to know.'

The consulting-room was empty. Dr Fateya appeared a moment later, drying his hands – to Harriet's relief – on a disposable towel. He waited politely till Mark took the hint and went through to the waiting-room. Dr Fateya's examination was light on clinical sophistication but heavy on old-world tact. He let her keep her briefs. His bony old hands probed delicately, his eyes closed, his head on one side as if listening. Harriet gave little brave cries when appendicitis was counter-indicated. He tutted, then thanked her and went outside to talk with Mark. She'd receive his diagnosis, properly, through her husband.

The two men returned. Mark told her everything was fine, she had nothing to worry about. He wasn't so indelicate as to mention wind. Dr Fateya unlocked his glass cabinet and presented her with a dusty tube of charcoal tablets. She accepted them humbly. She'd heard of charcoal tablets in her first year at med school. She took one. The instructions on the tube were in a language she didn't understand, presumably Turkish.

The men murmured together and money changed hands. It looked like a lot. Then Mark took the Johnny Walker from his pocket and diffidently asked if a small toast to the good news about his wife's appendix would be against Dr Fateya's religious principles. It wasn't. Mark was so happy to have his mind put at rest about his wife's condition that he offered a second.

Noises out in the waiting-room suggested another patient. Dr Fateya put his head round the curtain, spoke at length and sharply, and the patient went away. The three of them returned upstairs, where Dr Fateya said they would be more comfortable. As he held a chair for Harriet he asked her if the charcoal pill was taking effect. She told him it must be. She felt better already.

They were up in Dr Fateya's room for two hours. Near the bottom of the whisky bottle Dr Fateya had shown them an old-fashioned stainless-steel vacuum flask from a locked box at the back of one of his cupboards. Even at that late stage in the Johnny Walker he made no firm claims for the flask. He'd snatched it from a lab refrigerator in the few moments between the first and second missile strikes on the Biberian Research Centre. He believed it had been one of a batch containing experimental vaccines. He'd never opened it; he was a responsible scientist. It was a memento, nothing more, and he'd take it with him to his grave. He'd left instructions. Harriet could see its importance to him. He handled it reverently. Stamped with the logo of the Biberian Centre, still tagged with its batch reference number, it was his glorious past.

His past had a price. Prompted by Harriet, who felt bad about picking the old man's brains, Mark bought the flask from him for 30,000 euros. Such a figure had a totemic significance. Dr Fateya reminded them that Mr Kahn was a respected journalist, a serious person who would make sure that the flask was treated responsibly. Dr Fateya blessed the day that Allah had sent him.

He led them cheerfully down the stairs. The whisky bottle was empty and Harriet felt slightly blurred from the little she'd drunk. Dr Fateya, with more than half of it in him, was as steady as a rock. There was no sign downstairs of the blithering boy. Fateya fetched himself an umbrella, set a shutter to his consulting-room doorway, locked it, bundled Mark and Harriet out into the street, waved to them and hurried away, dodging neatly through the sullen crowds. He was on his way, Mark said, to the nearest *bankası*.

The pedal-taxi driver hadn't moved. Mark roused her and they set off back to the Paradise Hotel. Hunched beside Harriet on the basketwork bench beneath its flapping roof, he showed her the flask.

'I hope you know what you're doing, old buddy. You're surely not expecting an identifiable vaccine after thirty-five years?'

She took the flask from him. 'Not a chance. We might learn something from the medium, but if it needed refrigerating I'm not even expecting that. For all we know, Professor Woodruff used this flask for his lunch-time tomato soup.'

'So the money was for the other stuff.'

'Of course.' She held the cold metal of the flask to her cheek. She was excited as well as blurred. 'He's given us treasures, Mark. Couldn't you tell?'

'I could see the idea of the carrier got you going.'

'Pick-a-back, Mark. It's a revelation. A door opening. Not exactly a parasite, not exactly self-sufficient. A virus that's engineered to ride as it were *on* another, lipid to lipid. Reaching all the same host cells.'

'Undoing all the first ones' dire work?'

'It's not as simple as that. More like a transduction – that's when viruses mediate exchanges of genetic information between host cells.'

'Very nice. Remind me to ask you about it some other time.'

A stall selling baskets had overturned in the street ahead. As their pedal taxi slowed and stopped a beggar with no hands leaned in, and on the other side a man selling Korean wrist videos. Mark took the flask from her, pocketed it safely.

'Anyway, the vaccine didn't work.'

'No. We always knew Fateya's talk of finding an AIDS cure was the tiniest bit of an exaggeration.'

'How much of the work was his anyway?'

'The original research? None at all. The project was Woodruff's. Very brilliant and innovative. He'd have shaken things up, if only he'd lived.'

The beggar thrust his stumps at her. A bag hung on one of them and she stuffed euro notes into it.

'Listening to Fateya, I'd say he was a lab assistant at best.'

'Not even a paramedic?'

She shook her head. 'Anything he knows now he's learnt over the last thirty-five years, by doing. He probably worked in a hospital when he first escaped here after the missile attack on the Centre.'

The beggar had been replaced by three others, and a seller of powdered rhinoceros horn had joined the video man. But the block ahead was clearing. They sat out the wait. Harriet thought about a society in which women weren't allowed even to be beggars.

They moved on. 'So if this paravirus didn't work for AIDS,' Mark said, 'then what's the big deal?'

Harriet gathered her thoughts. She hated these streets. 'Two big deals, actually. First, Fateya said it migrated. That means there was another virus that matched its carrier requirements. He didn't really know what he was talking about, but he mentioned the common cold. That contradicts a lot of stuff we know, but it's a fascinating path to go down . . .'

She tailed off, going down it.

Mark dragged her back. 'And the second big deal?'

'It was an *engineered* virus – that means it was totally new, with no family or friends, which would make it particularly hard to find. And we know it was designed to work on the immune system, boost it as an AIDS counter, so it fits in with theories of over-active immune reactions as a Syndrome causation. So you see what that adds up to.'

Mark stared at her. 'It adds up, old buddy, to that missile attack releasing a common-cold epidemic that was carrier for an engineered virus designed to boost the human immune system.' He clenched a fist, opened it, blew across his palm. 'Hey presto. The way people moved about then, in a year's time the virus and its pick-a-back friend were everywhere, boosting up women to reject the alien male . . . It's so obvious I can't imagine why nobody ever thought of it.'

'Too many strands needed joining. Nobody knew them all. It's the old story . . .'

'So what now?'

Harriet didn't answer. What now? She didn't know what now. She couldn't think. Too many strands, she'd said. It was up to her to draw them all together. The implications of what Fateya had said were still bursting around her like firework stars. Incredible, a man like Fateya with such wonders in his head. After Erzurum everything was possible. She needed vision, she needed grasp. There were experiments to be designed, projects for each member of her team, priorities, equipment to be found, back-up staff, someone with a paravirus speciality. Everything was new and everything exciting.

The pedal taxi lurched, balked for a gap by a yellow Volvo. Far ahead, above the listless crowds filling the street, was the flashing neon sign of the Paradise Hotel. She sighed, drew in a huge joyful breath of the stinking city.

'What now, Mark?' She hugged him. 'The first flight out of here, the first flight home. Three years' hard grind. Maybe four. Maybe five. Then a stable vaccine. Patent rights. Health Ministry approval. Happy Dr Marton, happy Minister. Plain sailing all the way to millions and millions and millions of healthy boy babies.'

He struggled, laughing. 'Are things ever that easy?'

'Never. But they will be this time.'

That afternoon Daniel was late getting away from the office. He strode down the hill as quickly as its steepness would allow. He was stationed at NatSekur Headquarters, and he and Bert had been given company housing, a ground-floor apartment – on account of Bert's condition – in a handsome modern block backing on to the forest. It was after five and lights were coming on all over the complex spread out below him.

A woman, thick-cloak nurse's uniform over her, came out of the block and started up the hill. She was a new girl but he thought he'd seen her around.

He stopped her. 'I'm Colonel Ryder.'

'I know. I'm Nurse Elmer. Good evening, Colonel.'

He looked down past her. 'You shouldn't have left him.'

'It's late. I saw you coming.'

'You shouldn't have left him.'

'He's asleep.'

'That doesn't fucking matter. People wake up.'

'I know.' She lowered her eyes. 'I'm sorry.'

'I ought to report this.'

She worried at a loose thread on her cloak. 'I really did see you coming.'

He was tired. It had been a long day. She wasn't worth the fucking bother. 'OK. Fine. I believe you.' He walked a couple of paces, then turned. 'Are you our new afternoon shift?'

'Yes, Colonel. Nurse Elmer, Colonel.' She paused, then added defensively, 'I've specialised in residential care.'

'Good. Good . . . We'll talk some time.' He stamped his feet, looked back down at the apartment. 'Just one thing, Nurse. You're new on the case. Commander Breitholmer caught this thing with women. He'd want you to know that.'

'Yes, Colonel. It's very sad.'

With women, with men, with fucking ostriches – Bert wouldn't give a damn. It was he, Daniel, who wanted her to know that.

'How's he doing?'

She waited till he met her gaze. 'Not good, Colonel.'

'No. I see. He never is, these days.'

He went on down the hill. At the door to the apartment block he glanced back. Nurse Elmer was still under the streetlamp, watching him.

He let himself in, flung his cap on a chair. Bert slept too much. For the dying, sleep was a waste of time. He called out loudly, 'I'm home.'

He fetched himself a beer from the kitchen, then went through to Bert's room. 'Those fucking girls in the transport pool. They've ballsed up the requisitions. Nobody told me, of course. I had to find out for myself. That's why I'm late.'

Bert's room was at the back, looking out on the forest. Daniel went to the window, switched on the floodlights. Ranks of fir trees sprang up out of the darkness, their trunks white in the brilliance, climbing the hill in stiff lines behind the apartment. An owl dropped out of one of them and swooped low and away, escaping the light.

'I met the new girl up the road. Nurse Elmer. I had a word with her. She should have waited.' He leaned his head against the window. 'Idle cow. I'll go and see if she's done anything about dinner.'

He circled the room, was stopped in the doorway.

'She's not a cook, Colonel. She's a nurse.'

Daniel raised his eyes, looked at how Bert was doing. He was doing fine, propped up in his contoured bed-rest.

'They're none of them cooks. But they still help out.'

He went back into the kitchen. Nurse Elmer had left a salad, very decorative, on the counter. Soup was warming, chicken by the smell, and something in foil was in the oven. It looked like the trout Daniel had bought on his last trip to the NatSekur market.

Noises came from Bert's room. Bert was calling. Daniel looked for potatoes to go with his salad and couldn't find any. All these fucking nurses were the same. He got out the bread and cut thick slices. What business was it of theirs the way he ate? The Elmer cow hadn't even seen him – she'd got the tip from the one before. For Christ's sake, if he wanted a belly on him he'd fucking have one.

The noises from Bert's room were repeated. Daniel leaned round the door. 'You said?'

'I said I had visitors this afternoon. Two of them.'

'That fucking useless doctor. Who else?'

'Not the doctor.'

'Who then?'

'My wife and daughter.'

'You don't have a wife and daughter.'

'Ex-wife. You think you know a lot about me, Colonel. You don't.'

Daniel went back into the kitchen. There *was* a daughter – Bert would have dumped her if he'd had to, that night at the PTG clinic. The night they'd gone to the bar. Daniel didn't understand at the time but he worked it out afterwards. Bert was upset because he knew he'd have dumped his own daughter if he'd had to. Bert thought about the things he did.

Daniel stirred the soup, then returned to Bert's room. 'What did they have to say for themselves?'

'Not much. They did their best. They asked me how I was. They asked me what was wrong with me.'

'Pneumocystis pneumonia.' He knew Bert's condition by heart. The doctor loved just saying the words. 'It's an opportunist infection.'

'Thank you, Colonel. When I want prompting I'll ask for it. Pneumocystis pneumonia. I told them that.'

Daniel looked at how he was doing. He was doing fine. Wouldn't Nurse Elmer have said something if there'd been a wife and daughter?

'What's your daughter called?'

'Chantal. Not Breitholmer – Chantal Hakkensen. Her mother married again and Chantal took her stepfather's name.'

It sounded good. 'How old is she?'

'Hakkensen was a civilian contractor at my first camp. Fresh vegetables, that sort of thing. I caught them at it in the back of his van. I didn't kill him but I nearly did. She left me and – '

Daniel stopped him. There were things he didn't need to know. 'How old is this Chantal?'

'She left me . . . and she and Hakkensen hooked up . . . hooked up the day he got out of hospital.' Bert was gasping. This was too much talk. The doctor said his lungs were solid.

'You'll wear yourself out. How old is Chantal now?'

'Eight? Nine?' Bert's head jerked. 'I'm not good with children's fucking ages. Eight or nine.'

'I'll get your soup.'

Back in the kitchen, Daniel poured the soup into Bert's plastic bowl with the spout. The daughter'd be his own age. Thirty-six at the least. He tested the soup with his tongue. Bert was remembering the girl from the last time he'd seen her. How old was Bert? Sixty-two? Roughly sixty-two . . . Did NatSekur know about the daughter? Maybe someone should get in touch. He took the soup through to Bert.

'They brought me candies,' Bert said. He groped on his duvet cover, 'I must have eaten them.'

'Here's your soup.'

Daniel fetched a napkin from the nurses' table, squatted down by the bed, held the bowl to Bert's mouth, inserted the spout between his lips. He tilted the bowl and soup trickled down Bert's chin. He wiped it with the napkin. Bert coughed and shook his head from side to side, forcing the bowl away. Bert coughed some more and his blue tongue stuck out, straining. Daniel eased him forward and patted his narrow back.

The tongue retreated. 'Filthy muck.'

'No it's not. I tasted it. It's fine.'

'I know one thing, Colonel. It's her I should have gone for. Not Hakkensen, *her*. Like you. With a short sharp one, like you.'

His hand moved again, poked the air with stiff knuckly fingers.

'Drink your soup.'

'Cunt. I gave you an alibi, the one time they came for you.'

'I said drink your fucking soup.'

The plastic spout clattered against his teeth. He drank his soup. As much as he'd drunk in weeks. Daniel leaned him back against his bed-rest and took the bowl out into the kitchen. He opened up his trout and decided it was cooked. He put it on a plate together with the slices of bread he'd cut, and buttered them liberally. Then he filled a tray with the plate, the salad bowl, cutlery and a can of cold beer, and carried it into Bert's room. Bert was asleep again, his head back, his mouth open, snoring. Daniel sat down by the window, the tray on his knee. Bert slept too much. Daniel cleared his throat but the snoring continued.

Daniel separated the trout's backbone, peeled it away, and arranged it on the side of his plate. He took a forkful of fish and a large bite of bread and butter. He chewed.

'I was thinking,' he said, 'about your daughter. About Chantal. Maybe someone should tell her.'

The snoring continued. There was a smell in the room that told him Bert needed changing. He glanced at the clock – the nurse had been gone for less than an hour and she'd have left him clean. Poor old Bert.

His snoring had altered. He whimpered now and woke, and his blind eyes rolled, and his body thrashed on the bed. Daniel got up, spilling his supper-tray across the room. He tried to lean Bert forward but Bert's body was rigid and jerking, and his feet danced under the hospital duvet. He was stronger in his dying than he'd been in the last many months of his living. Daniel held him till he was still.

'That's it, then, you stupid fucker.'

He'd never called Bert by his name, never dared, and now he never would. The stiffness had relaxed so he removed the moulded bed-rest and laid Bert's body down. He went to the window, looked out at the floodlit trees. He turned the floodlights off. After a while his eyes adjusted and he could see shadows cast by the moon. He turned back to the dead man on the bed. He saw him too, now.

Bert had been dying, gathering the signs, for quite a while. His hair had been reduced to wisps that looked worse than being bald. He was famine-thin. His bare forearms above the duvet cover showed swollen wrists, then bone and a thread of muscle.

His closed fish-white eyelids glistened at the bottom of deep, wrinkled brown sockets. There were mottled sarcoma scars on his stringy neck and in the vee of his pyjama jacket. His cheeks sagged over missing teeth and his fingernails were grey . . .

Daniel returned to the bed. He touched his lips to Bert's dead, papery forehead. He cleared his throat, preparing. Then he went to the wash-basin in the corner of the room and filled a bowl with hot water, sprinkling it with cologne. He rested the bowl on the low table kept beside the bed for this purpose, and washed Bert's face, his flecked dead mouth, with a soft white cloth. He rolled the duvet down and put it temporarily on the window seat. Bert wore no pyjama trousers, only a diaper. Daniel opened the diaper, removed it, spread Bert's legs, lifted him and washed him. He weighed no more than kindling-sticks. Thin yellow shit had oozed up round his balls. Daniel washed them. His bush had been shaved for hygiene's sake.

When Daniel had finished washing him he put on powder and a fresh diaper, and replaced the duvet. Then he fed his card into the telephone and called the doctor.

CHAPTER THIRTEEN

The Attrition. Year 40: early November.

They'd taken Annie away, Mark told me. It made my life simple. At last, simple. I hope you can understand that.

'They' turned out to be a woman pretending to be SPU, and that too was simple. She'd got in on her warrant card and then produced her fire-power. I remembered that warrant card well. Every citizen should have a course in warrant cards – me, I'd have accepted anything that wasn't a dry-cleaning ticket. She'd shot a nun to death, and another in one arm, and another in both legs, the nuns were braver than me, I'd only needed to see Elvis die, and then she'd taken Annie away.

So my life was simple. It no longer mattered about the stolen research, the patent application, my piece for *Natur*, Natalya and her fax line to Unikhem. It no longer mattered about what they'd do to Danno. Moma had said I was hard. The Convent Superior had said I was tough. Hannes Vrieland had said, in any conflict between my work and my daughter there'd be no doubt as to the outcome. True, all true. Lies, all lies.

I asked Mark, 'What do the police say?'

He looked over his shoulder, out through the taxi's rear window. 'We haven't told them. Milhaus sent a message not to tell anybody.'

Not if we wanted Annie back alive. Of course.

'She said she'd be in touch.'

I told him, 'I talked to Marton yesterday. He said she isn't SPU. He's checked the records. She isn't regular police either.'

Mark nodded. 'So who's behind her? She knows too much to be on her own.'

'Presumably Unikhem.'

'Kidnap and murder? Could be, I suppose. It's worth billions . . . Not top management, they wouldn't want to know. Someone down the line.'

I shrugged. I'd worked for Unikhem. I'd never met that sort of Someone but I was sure she existed.

Mark frowned. 'Who told her Annie was down on the island? I wiped her tag. Unikhem didn't know. Who knew?'

'Marton said it was obvious. The obvious place.'

Mark covered his face. 'Christ. We thought Milhaus was police. We thought she'd respect the sanctuary.'

He was really upset. I put my arms round him. 'It doesn't matter, love. Whatever they want, we give it them. We wait until they call and tell us, then we give it them. And we get Annie back safely.'

The taxi was nearing our house. I could see it through the trees, and the steps where I'd stood and waved when Mark and Annie left for Nomansland.

'It's lovely to be coming home,' I said. 'How much bail did it cost you?'

'Nothing. The police withdrew the Disturbance charges.'

'What did you tell them?'

'I didn't tell them anything. They were very nice. Very understanding.'

Can you un-hug someone? I un-hugged Mark. 'I suppose they were sorry for me.'

'Something like that.'

'Bastards.' But it wasn't his fault.

'You're having a bad time. You've been – '

'They didn't know that.'

I remembered their raping eyes on me, the years of their raping eyes on me, the years of pretending not to see. Killers. Karate killers. *Danno* . . .

The taxi stopped. Mark opened the door and started to get out. I caught his arm. 'I didn't tell the police about Danno.'

'I know, old buddy. One thing at a time. Let's keep things simple.'

I love my husband. He cares, and he's clever.

He got out of the taxi and I followed. While he was settling with the fat driver I went up the path to the house. Yvette had been watching for us – she was waiting in the open door to the porch. She embraced me. I remembered shouting at her about the vacuum cleaner and maybe other things. It was a good home-coming, which somehow made its empty spaces worse. But Annie wouldn't have been there in any case. The silence behind Yvette would have been the same. At nine thirty on a Thursday morning Annie would have been at school.

No. No, the silence would not have been the same.

Mark came in smiling. 'I looked in the back of the taxi for your case. You'd been away for the night so I looked in the back for your case.'

Yvette didn't think that funny. Young people are conventional. The women she knew didn't spend nights in jail without suitcases.

'I've put good coffee waiting in the study,' she said. 'And little nut cookies.'

The study was a picture, the stove hot, lamps against the grey morning. What a wife she'd be, what a mother. Somebody had been out early and there were hothouse flowers. Mark's work-table had been cleared and laid with a cloth and our best hand-thrown pots. The telephone, back on his desk, looked none the worse for its kicking. Was that I? Had I kicked it?

Mark caught the direction of my glance and mistook it. 'They'll keep us waiting,' he said. 'Milhaus and whoever. They'll want to wind us up. They'll make nothing easy.'

I sat down, poured coffee, took a cookie. Took two. 'I've got all day. They can please themselves.'

He didn't believe me. 'They'll wear you down.'

'No they won't. I'm down already. I'll tell them, whatever they want, they can have it. My money, my research, whatever they want.'

'They won't believe you.' I worried him. He was re-membering yesterday's crazy lady. With Moma in the family he had every right. 'You mustn't give in too fast. They'll suspect a trick.'

'I'd rather keep it simple, Mark. No games. It *is* simple. They've got Annie.'

'So what are you going to do until they call?'

'I'll sort out my research. I've been meaning to all week.'

The telephone rang. My pulse-rate didn't flicker. It was too early to be them. Also, if they knew my line was tapped, and they knew everything else about me, they wouldn't use the phone. They'd come in on Mark's computer link.

The call was from Maggi, reminding me that I'd promised to talk to Natya. That was yesterday. Today I'd nothing to say to Natya. Today I didn't give a damn about Natya. I cheated. I told Maggi to remind her I was supposed to be on holiday, and to say if there was anything for her to worry about she'd be the first to hear.

I went upstairs. There'd been a shower at the police station, and a one-shot toothbrush, but I'd slept in my underwear and my other clothes were two days old and the long night in between. I showered again and washed my hair. I needed to feel in charge. I put on red, and higher heels.

Downstairs again and keeping things simple, I started on my research. I already had the stuff Annie had printed out for me on Saturday and I used Mark's equipment to access my computer at the Institute for the rest. I worked all morning . . . It was good for me – over the last seven days I'd got caught up in plots and lost sight of the incredible thing I'd done. My *team* had done an incredible thing. I built it up now, year by year, step by step. We were at the final test stage. A vaccine therapy, a vaccine we'd grown first on primate tissue then on human, a stable vaccine, a vaccine effective against the engineered paravirus that had been released forty years earlier, the result of a reckless act of war, from the Biberian Research Centre near Kamo, the paravirus we believed was responsible for the global spread of the Male Embryo Rejection Syndrome, the Syndrome that had brought us all to this fortieth desperate year of the Attrition.

It was a wonder. I spell it out now as I spelt it out then. Now it's a commonplace, then it was a wonder. My week away from it had sharpened the thrill. I forgot Annie.

, I worked all morning, and on into the afternoon. Mark tiptoed round me. He loved Annie too, lacked occupation, and worried. No word came from the kidnappers. He couldn't imagine their motive, what they would want.

I'd preferred to keep out of their evil minds, but as I built up the steps of my research, of our research, I began, against my will, to see.

I'd had a temp in a couple of years back. Maggi'd let her loose on the computer files. With an instruction so wrong nobody had believed it was possible, she'd lost me a whole raft of my research. Of *our* research. I was missing it now for the record of my research, of our research, and so – if they ever wanted to duplicate my results, let alone produce their own vaccine – were they.

(My research, *our* research – it's not a game I play. My cure, *our* cure; my therapy, *our* therapy. I didn't make the correction so often then, and when I did it was mostly only words. My research I meant, all mine. Mine to publish, mine to give away for Annie. But I make the correction here for accuracy's sake, and to show off the new unselfish me.)

What the temp had lost was computer copy. Getting hold of the original would take me back to where the work was done, back to the Windstrohm River, to Brandt, to my childhood.

A pattern? Fate? Orderliness? In the past, when I'd seen it in connection with the Syndrome, I'd talked about rightness. Mark accused me of going Gaian and I didn't have an answer. The fact was, I did have an answer but its banality fused me. The banality of patterns, a belief in fate, cosmic orderliness fused me. Everything works out for the best? Christ . . . Yet I was the problem-solver and problems were for solving.

The kidnappers came through at three in the afternoon. Mark's computer beeped at us. We gathered, opened the electronic gates, let the words come shuttling down the solid-state path in little digit parcels, to be flung at the screen thus: WE HAVE YOUR DAUGHTER.

I'd never doubted it but we were given a picture too: Annie sitting on a cheap sofa in a room I didn't recognise. No sound, just Annie in this room. They'd cut her hair, badly, leaving spikes. She pulled at the spikes, laughing, cheering me up. They'd let her cheer me up.

I typed in: TELL US WHAT YOU WANT.

The picture was eaten by neat little teeth. The next words were: WE'RE CONSULTING WITH OUR FRIENDS.

'They're stringing you along,' Mark said. 'They know what they wanted before they took her. They're stringing you along.'

I smiled at him. 'You said they would.'

I typed in: WHATEVER YOU WANT YOU CAN HAVE IT.

There was a pause. My words lay in a green line under theirs. Theirs were red.

Mark said, 'Ha. That's thrown them.'

Not for long. More red words. Not many, just: STAY TUNED.

The red words vanished. My green words had always looked silly. On their own they looked sillier. I sent them back to the green-word farm.

Staying cheered up wasn't easy. I went back to my research, step by step, year by year, sorting the tables, the papers, the results. I was sure now what they wanted. Everything else was here. I wanted it myself.

Mark was mending the towel rail in the bathroom. It had needed mending for months. He came down, screwdriver in hand, apropos of nothing, and asked me, 'When you were on the tram yesterday, where had you been?'

I rested my ruler to mark the line I was reading, and looked up. 'Peter Simpson.'

'Ah. Ah, I see.' It had been bothering him. Now he knew.

As he went upstairs I rewarded his restraint. I called after him, 'I asked Peter what sort of remedial therapy they'd give Danno. He said he'd lose his sparkle.'

Staying cheered up wasn't easy.

Around six o'clock a special-delivery girl brought a small parcel. No sender listed. It was very light and I knew what it contained.

Mark did too. 'Bloody sadists.' He tipped Annie's hair out on to the kitchen table. It was definitely Annie's. I swept it up and threw it away. I think Yvette would have kept it.

'What next?' I said. 'An ear?'

Mark took my hands. 'You worry me. You should let go.'

I disengaged. 'I let go yesterday,' I told us both. 'Next time they call they'll believe me. No police. No fuss. Whatever they want, they can have it.' I folded my arms. 'You agree, Mark? You think that's right?'

He sighed. 'They'd love to have us quarrelling.'

I knew he did agree.

It wasn't until nine that they came through again.

Beep. More red letters: YOU HAVE THE HAIR, WE HAVE THE HEAD.

Very droll.

More green letters: I told them, whatever they wanted, in exchange for Annie, safe, they could have it.

SAFE BUT SANS HAIR.

I agreed. One thing I knew – whoever I was talking to, it wasn't Sergeant Milhaus.

They said: WE WANT THE PRIMATE TEST RESULTS –

I typed it in unison with them.

— FOR THE C4 VACCINE.

The screen couldn't do surprise at my cleverness. Or it could but they didn't bother.

I told them they could have the results they wanted. They asked me when and I said I didn't have the results but I could get them for Saturday morning. They thought about it.

Today was still Thursday and I'd already worked out that I needed Friday night in between because the originals of the missing results were with Brandt International and I didn't want them to know what I was doing and from Friday nights on into the weekend they had staffing problems. Nice Magnus Asgeirson had admitted it.

The result of their thinks came up: WHY THE DELAY?

I could see Mark was wondering that too. I was sure they knew the answer and were testing me.

I typed a long one: YOU SHOULD THINK YOURSELVES LUCKY THE C4 RESULTS ARE STILL AVAILABLE. THE REST OF MY RESEARCH HAS ALREADY BEEN STOLEN BY UNIKHEM.

I too could be droll. I think they liked that.

They said they'd be in contact again early on Saturday to arrange the swap: results for daughter. I said I wouldn't fail them. They said they knew that.

The screen was filling up with our chat. They vacated it. Mark was sure he'd scooped them up and stored them somewhere but he hadn't. They'd put in a clever block. He pattered at the keys. It didn't matter — there wasn't much we could easily forget.

'What was all that?' he said. 'You knew what they were going to ask for.'

I felt exhausted. 'Must we?'

'Not if you'd rather not.'

I'd much rather have not. 'It's like I said, Mark. I've been checking my research. Everything except the primate material is on the Institute files so Natya will already have borrowed it and faxed it to Unikhem. But the primate results are important — anybody interested in the vaccine needs them.'

'Next question. Why Saturday?'

'I did the research down at Brandt's Windstrohm place. I needed to work with primates — it wasn't anything ugly, just a longish program of vaccinations — and the Institute doesn't have

256

primate facilities so I bought time off Brandt. They used to run a lot of primate research down there – it's a PTG centre now, working with dolphins.'

Parthenogenesis was still very hit-and-miss – everybody was trying to improve the success rates.

Mark frowned. 'It was your TV stuff that ran their primate program out of business. After the help they'd given you that wasn't very nice.'

'My work with them was *clean*, Mark. You should have seen some of the experiments they had going. Really ugly.'

'I saw your TV report.'

'What you saw was nothing. My producer wouldn't let me use the bad ones.'

I'd heard the dolphin research wasn't all that pretty either. That was another reason for waiting till Friday night and taking advantage of Brandt's staffing problems. Put baldly, with my anti-vivisection record my best chance of getting into the place was someone on Reception who didn't know her job.

'Anyway, Mark, I left the results in my safe there and I've never dared to go back for them. We had a working copy at the Institute of course, but we lost it in a computer glitch. I'm hoping now that if I arrive down there in the early hours I'll be able to sneak in somehow.'

'They can't keep you out, Harriet. The research is yours. Legally it's your property.'

'I wouldn't want to argue it. We don't have time for writs and injunctions.'

'I think you're over-reacting. Asgeirson was friendly enough on Sunday.'

'Magnus is Marketing. He'd never talk about it but I've a feeling he was glad to see Brandt's primate work go. In any case, Sunday was strictly business. Of course he was friendly – he wants the vaccine contract.'

'That's what I mean. You should try the open approach. Talk to Magnus. He wants your business. If he had a word with someone down at Windstrohm they could fax you everything you need.'

It made sense. But I went all the same.

Obviously, if I asked and was refused, Brandt would be alerted and I'd have no chance at all of sneaking in. But Mark was right. They wouldn't refuse, they wanted my business. In which case my sneaky middle-of-the-night approach could be disastrous. I might be able to talk my way past some twitty girl on Reception but there'd still be Brandt's staff computer, very possibly primed to ring bells at its first sight of my old freelancer's identity card. And if things went wrong at that moment they'd stay wrong. So why didn't I take Mark's advice and call up Magnus?

There's a simple answer. There were others, and I gave them to Mark, but this is the true one. I wanted to be a brave young mother. I wanted to dash through the night, and beat the odds, and save my beautiful daughter. This was *my* story. If I talked to Magnus, and he talked to Windstrohm, and Windstrohm faxed me the research, and I faxed the research to Annie's kidnappers, and they released her, I'd be cheated of my proper place. I needed to live up to my belief in the rightness, the pattern, cosmic order. The Windstrohm was where this had begun, the Windstrohm was where this should end.

That sounds dumb. It's not what I thought at the time. At the time I didn't think, I gave Mark answers. It's what I've worked out since. I mean, I must have had a reason.

I must have had a reason, too, for not letting Mark come with me.

'I'm coming with you,' he said.

'What for? You ought to be here, in case they want to get in touch.'

'I've a mobile link. You know that.'

I knew that. 'What can you do down there that I can't?'

'Two heads are better than one, old buddy. So are two pairs of hands.'

'Better at what? Better at taking a research folder out of a safe?'

'What if the kidnappers know where the research is? What if they're waiting for you?'

'What if they are?' I was getting desperate. 'You're not Mr Macho. In a fight between you and Milhaus I know which I'd bet on.'

'Would you do any better?'

'I wouldn't try. And if it gets to shooting then we're better apart. That way one of us survives for Annie.'

'I want to be there.'

'I want you here.'

'No, Harriet.'

'Yes, Mark.'

What could he say? A woman gotta do what a woman gotta do. I mean, I must have had a reason.

A reason: according to Liese it's a statistical fact that any woman/woman conflict is five times less likely to result in actual bodily harm than any man/woman conflict or man/man conflict. Look what happened to war.

I left in the car late next morning. Mark did what he could for me. He went out early and came back with an electronic gadget that scrambled the magnetic code on my Brandt staff identity card. He came back also with a knock-out nerve-agent aerosol, and protective capsules I was to take thirty minutes before I entered a situation in which I might want to use it. I asked him if he'd been reading the girls' book of spies. I knew what those capsules did to you and it wasn't desirable. But I took aerosol and capsules with me. It would have been ungrateful not to.

Mark also used his foul-smelling solvent to remove my tags. We no longer knew who was tracking them, Marton's lot or Milhaus's, but there was no point in taking chances. I couldn't be bothered with Gusso's shielding. Wiping the tags was symbolic. I could never go back. It sawed off the branch.

It was a longish drive down to Windstrohm and Yvette fixed me food to eat in the car. She was in on the drama and agreed with Mark that he ought to be going with me. He was, she pointed out quaintly, a man. Forty years into the Attrition, who taught her these things? Her Parisian mother?

Although the car was slower than the train, and the two-way journey would clear out Mark's November fuel quota, I chose it because there was no other way of getting to Brandt at two in the morning. It was a three-k walk from the station, and the shuttle to the main line didn't run between midnight and six.

I don't remember the drive down. If reality is only that which is derived from our senses, it didn't happen. I drove out of our garage and I drove into the Eckett. Teleportation. Yvette's food molecules combined into mine on the way.

The time was four thirty on a sad November day. The ornamental cherry trees that lined the Eckett were leafless, unornamental, and the smart privet hedges had wrinkled and drawn themselves in, like scrotums (scrota?), against the cold. I was there because I had decided that until two in the morning Julius Stollman would be my refuge. I hadn't asked him but he wouldn't turn me away.

Anka Stollman had died, her bio-engineered whisper turning predictably to cancer and silence, and Julius lived in the high old house alone. I think we wrote, and I'd visited twice since Dada's funeral, while I was working up-river at Brandt. He never came to the city. It wasn't much, for dearest friends, but that's what he was, my dearest friend.

I parked the car outside the house. The day was sad, the house too. The dusk hid much, but the bottom slab of the stone front steps had cracked and was held up in the middle on a brick, and the basement kitchen window was mostly covered with the bare stringy stems of some rampant weed. The curtains were drawn on the living-room window above, showing a fusty red glow from the light behind them. I heard faint, high, thin music. The stucco on the English Georgian entrance porch was falling off.

I rang the bell. It was an ancient arrangement of wires over pulleys along channels between the floor joists, that agitated one of a row of bells on springs high up on the basement kitchen wall, and from where one stood on the front doormat one had always heard the bell jangle, apparently under one's feet. Now, as I leaned lightly against the door, I listened and heard nothing save the music. The door gave slightly. I opened it wider and went in. There were smells of mould, and old cooking. In summer I always perched my sun-hat on the newel post. In winter I hung my quilted parka on the hatstand made of antlers. Today, arriving by car, a grown-up lady, I wore neither.

'Julius?' I called. 'It's me. Harriet.'

A chair shifted in the living-room. 'I'm in here.'

I went in to him.

'God-dammit, Harriet, you heard me put the kettle on.'

The day was sad, and the house, and now, to me, this room, but not Julius. He was sitting in the corner of one of the huge old velvet sofas, a tea-tray beside him, Palestrina coming from the record-player, the children's voices he loved. He heaved himself up, smiling warmly.

'My dear, how good to see you. I'll fetch another cup.'

We embraced.

'Shush,' I said. 'I'm spoiling the music.'

'Don't then.' He put a finger to his lips, motioned me to a chair, and went away down the familiar circular staircase to the kitchen. I sat down, fought briefly with the cushions, listened to Palestrina.

I've said the room was sad to me. That's nostalgia. Unlike the Stollman house, the Stollman living-room hadn't changed. There'd always been cobwebs. Twenty years, two old people, then one, the wear was minimal, change for its own sake unnecessary. That was where the sadness lay, my sadness. I'd pounded at Prokofiev here, now I was a grown-up lady. It wasn't an improvement.

The music ended. That too had been sad – that curious celebration of sadness that great art manages, but I'd heard only the sadness. I was trapped in my mood and I'd missed the celebration.

Julius reappeared, pink in the face with beaming. He carried a plate, a cup and saucer, the familiar biscuit tin. He fitted these on to the tray.

'You're looking wan, Harriet. Haven't you found that bloody cure yet?'

I shrugged. 'I think so. I know so.' My spirits didn't lift.

'Crikey, what a responsibility.' He lowered himself on to the sofa, punched himself a nest. 'Bloody thing . . . Not yours, a responsibility for their mothers. The first little boys in forty years. Crikey.'

I had other worries. 'I'm in a bit of trouble, Julius. I'd like to stay till after midnight.'

'Stay? As long as you like . . . The hard thing is, the first twenty years of them'll be brought up without any fathers.'

'I know.' It wasn't my problem. 'Till about one thirty, actually. You needn't stay up, Julius. I'll let myself out.'

'The men who'll make the future. My goodness . . . and better than last time if their mothers get it right.'

Not my problem. 'You're not listening, Julius. You never did.'

Not my problem? Christ. My heart stopped. For three clear beats, I swear. Christ, I hadn't bled. The calendar said I should have and I hadn't. I was pregnant. I pressed my legs together till my knees ached. A week late was nothing, a week such as this could have caused it, held up the flow, that's what I'd tell any

261

woman coming to me, but I knew I was pregnant. Women do. They don't, actually, but I did. And I knew it was a boy. The first, unless those Bedouin babies were genuine. Unless I aborted.

Julius was pouring tea. 'I always listen. It doesn't always look like that, but – ' He passed me a cup. 'You never took sugar.' He and Anka hadn't let me. 'You want to stay, Harriet, and leave at one thirty. Biscuit?' He offered the tin. 'I don't ask why. That's your problem.'

I laughed. How right he was. I took a biscuit. Shop-bought. Anka always made them. Sitting there, I missed Anka. How must he feel?

'Half-past one because I need every advantage and I want to get to Brandt at two, when their resistance is low. Hospital doctors call it the dying hour, but I swear it only seems that way because it gets them off their bums. Night duty should be performed exclusively in the staff lounge, playing poker.'

'You're chattering, Harriet.' He sat back, stirred his tea, observed me. 'You're chattering.'

I was, so I told him about Annie instead, enough to let him understand. I was interrupted by rusty clattering. We'd forgotten Polly. She was in her cage, beneath her green cover, and we'd woken her. She was protesting, bashing her perch against the bars. Julius removed the cover and she stopped. She was not visibly older, and just as repellent. She fixed me with one orange eye and creaked her beak.

'She likes you,' Julius said. 'She still hasn't laid an egg.'

I told him about Annie, and Oswald Marton, and Sergeant Milhaus, and cosmic order. He wished me luck of them and told me about a girl he was teaching from down on the Parade. She had talent but, like me, it was only fingers. He suggested I play for him and, after that, I said no, so he played instead. There were mistakes, but it wasn't just fingers.

We had supper from a store of convenience food Anka would have hated. I went upstairs to rest, chose one from several musty bedrooms, and instantly slept. I woke in a cosmically orderly fashion at one twenty-five, washed and peed, and went downstairs. I hadn't been taking the possibility of pregnancy seriously, or I'd've had a pee-test with me. Why hadn't I been taking it seriously? I should have been taking it seriously. Not that knowing or not knowing made a difference to the cosmic order.

Julius was in the sitting-room, listening to the Palestrina again. I looked round the door and he smiled and waved. He was an old man and alone, but he didn't seem lonely.

The Eckett crackled under a frost and a clear moonless sky. The mew of a little owl. Waves on the rocks below the school playground, but they were in my imagination. The girl and her brother, singing in the wind.

The car made a noise in the silence like cannons, screams, machine-guns. I drove slowly down the hill, coasting through the estate, down Harbour Street, left at the Town Quay and out past the New Century Café and the station. The town was a shopful of dolls, listening in their boxes. If I made too much noise they'd burst out at me.

Mark's knock-out aerosol was on the passenger seat beside me but I hadn't taken the protective capsule.

Brandt International was brightly lit: a four-metre glass-smooth wall, arc-lights, cameras, a single entrance, a guard-room with two husky NatSekur women. Behind me, a low parapet to the road, and in the darkness beyond it the river, faintly starlit. Brandt had come on since Dada's time. The Centre was built into the hillside, with a secure deep mooring, a tower with two floors of closed-environment PTG labs, roof-top glass for raising vegetable clones, a computer centre, underground dolphin pens, and a curved office wing along one side. The dolphin pens replaced Brandt's primate facility. Like it, they were underground. There was no scientific need – both primates and marine mammals benefit from natural daylight. But the primates had been buried and now the dolphins were.

I parked our Saab-Honda within the yellow lines of the staff car-park. I took up my briefcase – it had note-pads in it, charts, coloured pens, a convincing jumble of research impedimenta. I hesitated, then left the aerosol on the seat. The place was deserted – I didn't see myself nerve-gassing the receptionist. I got out of the car, walked to the NatSekur guardroom. The frost bit me and I shivered. I didn't lock the car: NatSekur guidelines forbade it.

The guards knew their job. One stayed inside, behind her armoured glass, eyes on her surveillance screens. The other isolated me in her 'airlock'. scanned me for metals, explosives, tempered-plastic weaponry. The name on her NatSekur ID pin was Renée. She let me through and I gave her my briefcase and my Brandt staff card. She wasn't like me, she had an infra-red lamp that threw out forgeries. My card passed and she laid it on one side.

'Nature of business?'

I told her, 'I have research to finish. It's a bloody awful time, but my people need it for Monday and I'd like to get it over.'

Renée nodded. I didn't think she'd worry, not recognising me: if she worked nights she wouldn't recognise most of Brandt's research people. She picked up my case and retired with it to her colleague. The disadvantage to two in the morning was bored guards with time to kill. They picked over my case and the junk in it. They looked at my card, then back at the case. They consulted, soundlessly, behind their armoured glass. Then Renée returned.

'How long do you plan to be?'

'I'm not sure.' All I needed was five minutes. How short a time could I get away with? 'A couple of hours?'

My card made me a senior consultant. I was good stuff. I was polite, and relaxed, and I was obviously a regular. I was good stuff.

She nodded. 'Fine.' She gave me my case, held on to my card. 'All I ask is, be out by six. That's when the new shift arrives and the captain's a stickler.' She held up my card. 'Most staff members with cards as old as yours get new ones. It's not a rule, just the way we like it.' She passed the card to me and I put it in my pocket. 'The captain's one of those women who like to make trouble. She'd chew us out. She's not doing her job if she's not finding something to bitch about.'

I said I knew the type. I thanked her and promised to be out by six. She saluted and I walked away up the drive to the main building. My consultant status had counted. Only senior staff members got salutes from NatSekur. And then only if the guards felt like it.

The area inside the wall had been cleared and levelled, and at two in the morning it seemed to gasp beneath the glare of the lights and cameras. The wide awning above the entrance doors was a blade of stainless steel and on either side the black armoured-glass cladding reflected no movement. Until, as I approached, it reflected me.

The guardroom had called up the NatSekur woman on the door: she opened it for me.

'Morning, ma'am.'

I peered at her ID pin. 'Good morning, Netta. It's cold out there.'

'Yes, ma'am. Nights like this I appreciate inside duty.'

I crossed to the desk against the back wall. The only decoration in Brandt's foyer was a huge, brilliantly coloured model of the DNA double helix which rose unsupported from the darkness of the floors below and disappeared into the darkness of the floors above. It turned slowly, catching highlights. Brandt's girl on the desk had pink painted cheeks and looked like a school-leaver. Her pin said she was Marie. I put my case on her desk, my card on top of it.

'It's cold out there.'

Marie read my card, compared the three-year-old picture. Her eyes wandered a couple of times to a place below her desk-top. My chances had improved. She had a TV set there, its volume killed, one of the all-night channels, sex or horror.

'I shall be along in the office wing,' I said, taking back my case and holding out my hand for my card. I didn't give reasons. My sort wouldn't.

Marie wrote my name in her book, gave me my card. I fed it into the slot by the staff entrance. It buzzed at me. I tried again. It buzzed again.

'The scanner's packed up,' I said. 'I told the girl about it yesterday. Press the gizmo for me, will you?'

Marie was back with her program. She reached out and pressed the override button under her desk. The latch slid back and the door opened.

'Thank you, my dear. It's happened before. I'm always complaining . . . Is Professor Sessions in his office by any chance?'

'Nah.' She didn't look up. 'You're the only one.'

'Thank you for your help.'

'Yah.'

The door closed itself behind me and I was in. The scanner'd been right to buzz at the mess Mark had made of my card, but what Brandt's central staff computer didn't know, its heart wouldn't grieve over.

The dim corridor of office doors curved round to the right, humming with automated functions. The place was busy twenty-four hours a day, caring for plants, embryos, bacteria, dolphins.

I'd never had an office of my own for my visits, just a shared work area, a locker, and a safe-deposit box. The boxes were down a level, in a medium-security vault. My key still worked. I turned on scourging overhead lights, accessed my box, and tipped its contents on to the central table. I'd forgotten how much I had. Most of it was from other experiments, stuff I'd needed for reference. I sat down and began sorting. The vault was quieter than the corridor one floor up, but still sang softly. I had ten minutes' work at most. Afterwards I could stretch out on the floor. I had at least an hour to fill if I was to keep Renée and her friend unsuspicious.

Daniel checked his car clock. Brandt was in sight and the time was fifteen past two. The dozy buggers wouldn't know what hit them. He swung the big NatSekur sedan off the road and stopped beside the only other car in the park, a small, late-model Saab-Honda.

He climbed out, locking the car door behind him. NatSekur rules didn't apply to NatSekur property. He marched across to the guardroom, boots ringing on the asphalt. He rapped on the armoured glass and one of the guards slid it back. She saluted. He drew his handgun. He could have shot her.

'You shouldn't have fucking done that, kid. You don't fucking know me from Adam.' He holstered the gun. 'Colonel Ryder. HQ inspections. You may have heard of me.'

The second guard joined the first, gaping.

'That's the both of you totalled. Christ on a fucking crutch, you still don't fucking know me.'

The first guard moved, shutting the glass. She pulled the microphone down on its swan-neck. 'Identification, please sir.'

'*Please sir*? Everyone's a terrorist till proved otherwise. You don't say *please sir* to fucking terrorists.'

He gave her his warrant card, fed it through the gas-proof slot, watched as she subjected it to infra-red confirmation.

'Now you salute, kid. Not before. Now. And the other one stays on the screens. Nothing – and I mean *nothing* – gets you away from those fucking screens.'

266

He waited till she was back in front of the bank of surveillance screens.

'Now you let me in. OK? Now you know who I am you let me in. OK?'

The first guard let him in through the 'airlock'.

'I see you're Renée.' He referred to his datastor. 'That makes the other one Dana. Netta's up on the main entrance and Karen's on mobile somewhere.' His tone was fatherly. 'You see, I know all about you.'

Renée stood to attention, her eyes wide. Daniel inspected her handgun, sighed, returned it to her. He didn't bother with her radio. He'd shook her up enough.

He swung round on Dana. 'Tell me about these screens.'

Brandt's perimeter was cleared and lit, she said, and under camera surveillance, back into the forest. Each camera turned in random arcs and had its own screen. The same occurred inside the wall. There were thirty-two cameras and thirty-two screens. They were a lot for one guard to monitor. The training taught guards to look only for movement.

Dana's mention of the forest had brought a tiny break in Daniel's performance. He covered it. The police had said suicide, but as far as he was concerned Dada had been murdered. By Moma. It wasn't important, after all these years, but Dada had been murdered.

He asked to see the guardroom log. 'No visitors?'

'Visitors, Colonel?'

'Visitors.'

'No, Colonel. No visitors.'

He thought about the hesitation, put it down to nervousness. He'd shaken the stupid kids up. It was the best way.

'Tell me about the river.'

Renée gaped again. 'The river, Colonel?'

'What's the security on the fucking river? It comes into the Centre, doesn't it?'

'Under the road, Colonel. There are double steel gates.'

He knew about the gates. 'Show me.'

He knew everything about Brandt International's PTG Centre. It was his job to know.

Renée let them both out through the armoured gate, locking it behind them. She led Daniel across the road and they leaned over the parapet. The night was very dark and they couldn't see the gates. He suggested that if they moved some fifty metres down the road, away from the guardroom, they'd get a better angle. When they reached this new position he said, 'You're a stupid fucking kid to work in a terrible place like this,' and he dumped her.

He shot her through the middle of her forehead with a soft-headed, non-NatSekur round, and tipped her body over the parapet. 'It wasn't your fault,' he said. 'Once you sign up with us you go where you're fucking sent.'

He returned to the guardroom. He rapped on the glass and Dana left her screens long enough to let him in. She was puzzled to see him on his own but she didn't say so.

'Call Netta, will you? Tell her I'm coming up?'

She called. As soon as she'd finished calling he dumped her too. She never knew what hit her. He left her body in front of the screens. In each one of them nothing moved. He got no pleasure killing these girls, but it had to be done as long as the fucking PTG people wouldn't learn, and dead was dead. It was their fathers he felt sorry for, always assuming they had fucking fathers. Half of them might be AIs and the other half PTG clones for all he knew.

He opened both sides of the armoured gate. Then he returned to the car and drove in, leaving the gate open behind him. There was always the chance he'd want to take off in a hurry. He parked the car between the lines beside the curved steel entrance awning, screwed round in his seat, and hefted his black moulded document-case out of the back. The guard Netta was ready for him and saluted. He inspected her uniform, her gun and her radio, and asked her about the building. She was smart and knew what she was talking about. Daniel had NatSekur's plan of the place in his head, and its workings, and she confirmed them. Also she contradicted Renée in the matter of visitors. She couldn't remember the name, she'd never heard it properly, but there was a scientist woman somewhere in the place. The guardroom had passed her, so had Reception. No other staff were around, just this scientist woman, quite young.

Daniel knew about Brandt's staffing problems. None of them worked weekends since Brandt had refused NatSekur's overtime rates for extra cover. This was why he'd waited till tonight, driving over from the far side of the peninsula after his official inspection there. Gigs were easier empty. One spare PTG woman didn't much concern him. If they met she'd have to die. If they didn't she'd probably die anyway. PTG scientists deserved all they got.

He asked Netta to put out a call for the mobile guard, Karen, wherever she was, to come to the foyer. Then he skirted the DNA mobile and reached the desk. The girl there had been watching him since he arrived. She was pink and saucy. A lot of girls went for a man in a uniform. She was a Brandt employee so he didn't know her name. He drew his gun and shot her. Then he turned, dumping Netta too, while she stared at him. It was no-fail. The rank and the uniform produced the time-lag that made the difference between a tidy gig and a fucking disaster. They always had done, back to when he was a lieutenant and Bert a commander. Gigs were harder now that he was on his own, some PTG places were impossible, but he did what he could. He never looked for outside help. Bert and him had been a team. In Daniel's head they were still a team.

Apart from the main entrance there was only the staff door into the foyer. It made for good security but it gave the mobile guard no chance at all. He dumped her when she'd opened the door and was still staring at his gun. He shot her in the mouth from a distance of less than two metres.

He was reminded, in a vivid ugly flash, of a day not long before when he'd been one of five or six people going down in a station elevator, and when the door opened at the bottom a man was waiting on the other side with his fly undone and his uncircumcised cock out, looking like raw pork, and he started pissing on the concrete floor at their feet. He'd have pissed in their eyes if he could.

Karen's moment when the door opened had been like that. The only difference was, they'd gone on out past this man not looking, and she'd died. He'd hated the silly fucker. He wouldn't be caught that way again. He'd kick his fucking balls in.

He went through the door, stepping over Karen's body, and along the corridor. There'd be lift doors then a staircase, the labs and the computer control room up it, a second level of offices below, and the dolphin pens below that. The dolphin pens. He was making for the computer control room, quick in, quick out, but the dolphin pens drew him. He'd never seen an actual dolphin.

The stairs led him down, through an armoured door, into a cool, dimly lit blue space filled with sighs and clicks and outlandish hooting. He was on an overhead gantry. His eyes adjusted. Below him were ten glass pens, maybe three metres by one and a half, arranged in a square beneath a grid carrying electric sockets, anchor points for straps, gadgets he couldn't guess at, with a central observation area and a surrounding access corridor.

He descended metal steps into the central area, treading softly, and rested the weight of his document-case on a ceramic-topped operating-table. It was backed by bright racks of surgical instruments. The narrow pens around him each housed a dolphin. They watched him, one eye each, unable to turn, motionless in the water save when one rose to breathe. They were rubbery blue-black creatures with smiley mouths. They'd been arranged head to head and tail to tail, so that alternate pairs faced each other. The clicks and hoots seemed to be their talking. Cameras scanned, needles jerked in dials on a console. There were screens showing rolling bands of letters and numbers. Intense lights shone down in cones on desks and work-surfaces. Daniel sniffed. The place smelt chemical, of hot plastic lightshades and sharp disinfectant.

He left his case and walked slowly round the pens. Some dolphins seemed to be hung from wires, others had incisions kept open by wide transparent inserts that showed pulsing movements inside. Still others were marked with what anywhere else he'd have said were radiation burns. The dolphins watched him, their mouths smiley.

Christ. Christ on a fucking crutch. He dumped people, OK, but this was something else. He'd asked Renée how she came to work in a terrible place like this but he'd meant PTG. This was something else. There were five dead people upstairs. With the scientist there'd be six. But dead was dead. This wasn't dead. This was something else.

He picked up his case and carried it out through a narrow passage between two pens, to the access corridor. The lift led off it, up to the computer control room, and he was in a hurry. He couldn't see any of the dolphins making it back to the ocean, but when he blew the control room they'd be out of their misery.

The corridor was dark, lit only by watery light coming in through the tanks. Blue patterns wavered. He located the lift doors and took a step towards them. Someone was standing at the end of the corridor where it angled to form the next side of the square. A woman was standing with her forehead against the glass and the palms of her hands, Netta's scientist woman, pressing into the glass as if she was trying to force her way through, the blue light around her. The scientist woman.

Harri.

She turned to him and he saw she was crying.

He put down the document-case full of explosives. Harri. It didn't matter how or why. Fucking Harri. Not four metres off. He didn't fucking believe it. All he could think of was Bert dumping that woman who might have been his daughter.

It's a near thing, which of us was more surprised. Danno, I think. In fact, after that very first second, I wasn't surprised at all. I'd been trying to meet Danno for the last three days and here he was. I'd been feeling so wretched about what I'd found down here. If I'd gone straight out I'd have missed him. If I'd decided not to come down, if I'd been a day earlier or later, an hour earlier or later, a minute earlier or later, I'd have missed him. But I hadn't, so here he was.

People meet by chance. They do it all the time.

He was drawing his gun.

I said, 'Hallo, Danno.'

The gun was still coming up. Quite slowly.

'Hey. Hey there. Danno? Danno, it's me.'

His eyes were wide and he was sweating. He was very frightened. I wondered why.

I said, 'I've been upstairs on a job. It got finished. I came down here to look at the research.'

He was going to fire the gun at me. Every muscle in his body was in spasm.

'Danno? Danno, it's me.'

Something reached him. His fear let go. He moved, breathed again. He tilted his gun barrel up and back, looked down it, and laughed.

'Harri. I don't believe it. It's so fucking dark down here. Long time no see.'

I too breathed. 'We must stop meeting like this, Danno.'

Off-the-shelf phrases, meaningless, for safety. I didn't remind him we'd seen each other on the phone a week ago. I didn't believe he hadn't recognised me, it wasn't that dark in the passage. I didn't know what had been going on and I was glad it had stopped.

He put the gun away. He was overweight but his uniform flattered him. Its tunic was loose in the right places. I went to him and he took my hands. We held each other off.

'What the hell are you doing here?'

We said it together. He hadn't heard me before.

He laughed again. 'You first.'

'No, you.'

'Ladies first.'

'Youth before beauty.'

'OK,' he said. 'I'm doing a surprise NatSekur inspection. Now you.'

I showed him my briefcase. 'I had to pick up some papers.'

'At two in the fucking morning?'

'At two in the fucking morning.'

'I saw a car outside. Yours?'

'A Saab-Honda? That's Mark's.'

'He's not here.'

'No. I left him at home.'

'How is he?'

'He's fine.'

We were marking time. The passage itself was a nightmare, flickering and watery, the dolphins watching us and suffering, making their talk. My tears for them were still wet and the promise I'd made them, to help, was still true. I'd been trying to contact Danno for days, and now he'd come within a heartbeat of shooting off his gun at me, no, of killing me, and I didn't understand. I was marking time because I'm a lady who likes to understand.

'How's Bert?' I said.

'He's dead.'

I thought I hadn't heard him. His face told me I had. 'Oh Danno, I'm so sorry. When?'

'Five fucking years ago. And ten days.'

I'd asked him about Bert over the phone last Thursday and Bert had been fine. If I could understand that, why Danno'd lied to me – perhaps he always lied to me – then maybe I could understand him killing Janni Wintermann.

'We've got to talk, Danno.'

He didn't want to. I realised – how had it taken me so long? – it was the last thing he'd ever wanted. He glanced at his watch. 'There's not all that much time, Harri. Come up with me to the computer control room. I've got work to do.'

He didn't wait for me, he didn't want me there, he didn't want my talking, he picked up his case and made for the lift. I followed him and we went in together, standing side by side, solemnly holding our cases. His was squarer than mine, and obviously heavier. The lift opened directly into the control room. He switched on lights, the tubes clicking and clenching across the wide white space, and went quickly forward. I followed him. I knew this room, and I wasn't afraid of Danno. I believed the time when he would have killed me was past.

He put his case on a desk, sat down at it.

I sat opposite him. Desks. Too much of my life was conducted across desks. 'Why didn't you tell me Bert was dead?'

He'd been opening his case. He stopped. 'I did tell you.'

'I mean, before.'

'I did. You just fucking heard me. This time ten days ago, five fucking years ago.'

I nodded. He didn't want to talk.

But this conversation had been my idea. It was necessary. I'd said to Mark, I have to tell him I'm going to the police. And this time ten days ago had been Janni Wintermann. Had been Janni Wintermann?

No. Nothing so crude. There'd been no other late October killings, the reference library'd said so, so I didn't have to believe in just an act of remembrance.

'I know you killed all those girls, Danno.'

I've tried to think of better ways of saying it. Gentler, wiser ways in which I might have told him. I've never found any.

He stared at me, shaking his head fiercely. I thought he was denying it.

'You took off their rings, Danno. Like Moma. And you put them in their shoes.'

'No.' Shaking his head.

273

'The police kept the rings secret. If they hadn't I'd have known it was you right the very first time.'

'No.'

'Did you want me to know, Danno?'

'No. No.' Shaking his head.

He wasn't answering me. His denials were deeper than that.

The control-room lights cast no shadows. Danno and I were without shadows. The room was so precious to Brandt that if fire was detected in it, the flame of a single match, its windows and doors snapped hermetically shut and inert gas was pumped in to replace the oxygen. So the fire went out and the people in the room died. It was a nice priority, and there were people, scientists, willing to work there. I'd worked there myself.

Cabinets lined the walls, calm white steel boxes that contained unimaginable unquiet. Among them tape disks whirled, checked, backtracked, whirled again. Information was analysed, instructions were issued. And in laboratories down the line gene clusters blossomed, plant clones, tissue cultures, bacteriophages, ten green dolphins. Blue-grey, really. Hanging on the wall.

Necessary? Was this conversation necessary?

'Bert knew, Danno. Didn't you ever talk to him?'

He was sitting at the desk, very upright, his forearms on it, the closed black case between them. His hands were spread flat, palms down, and he was staring straight ahead.

'Bert knew,' he said. 'He knew why, too.'

'Why, Danno? Tell me why.'

He hadn't heard me. He said, 'That Wintermann tart. She was asking for it.'

I waited, wanting to know what it was, but he was somewhere else. With the Wintermann tart, maybe. I wanted him back. Why didn't matter any more. I was just fascinated to know what it was.

'It, Danno?' Listen to me, Danno. Sex or death, Danno? Death or sex? Listen to me. 'It?'

His blank gaze didn't waver. 'Bert and me fitted. That tart was . . . ' he looked for the word ' . . . was disgusting. Didn't know a fucking thing. She didn't know it was the day he died, the stupid cunt, but I couldn't help that. Wouldn't have mattered if she had. Tarts are like that. Stupid cunts. Asking for it.'

274

I didn't repeat my question. He was quite right. That tart was disgusting. I was disgusting. My question was disgusting.

I wanted to touch him but dared not. 'If you'd talked to Bert . . . When he was alive, Danno, if you'd talked to Bert he'd have helped you.'

So talk to me instead, my dear. I'm alive. Forgive me, and talk to me, and I'll help you instead.

Slowly he lifted his head. He was bewildered now, as if from a trance, and had no defences. 'Bert died,' he said. 'All these people talking, what did talking do for him? What did talking ever fucking do for anybody?'

Muscles knotted in his jaw. Tears ran down his face. 'I've seen them. Clever people and their talking. It's what they do. They fuck each other up. Talking's what they do.'

I knew what he meant. But what else did I have?

'Bert and me talked, Harri. We talked a lot, but not like that. We were friends . . . Jesus . . . Christ Jesus . . . ' He shook his head. I'd never seen a man cry like that, like a child, exposed, not caring. 'Christ Jesus, Harri, what happened to friends?'

I put my hands on his. I dared that now. He took his hands away, my touch was too strange, but I followed them, insisting. I joined them together and folded them in mine. My options were limited: either the police or . . . the police. I had nothing to say. Would he have lots of loving friends, did I really imagine, after Peter Simpson's remedial therapy?

I faced him and now he was clutching my hands, begging me to help him. This conversation had been my idea. It was necessary. I'd said to Mark. I have to tell him. I have to tell him I'm going to the police. To which Mark had replied, Perhaps you'll persuade him to go himself. What a methodical conversation we'd let ourselves imagine.

Danno pulled me close. He pulled me forward across the desk and burrowed his face into the hollow of my shoulder. He was strong. Men are. I held him strongly too. He must have known then that I loved him.

A faint mechanical click-sound broke the room's stillness, and then a rumbling that for a moment I didn't recognise. The lift was going down.

Danno stiffened and wrenched away. 'Is this something of yours?'

He glared at me accusingly. I denied it and I think he believed me. I hope he believed me.

The lift's indicator lights followed it down to the ground floor. They paused there, then returned. The lift stopped at our floor and the doors opened, revealing Sergeant Milhaus, in her fake SPV uniform, a gun in her hand. So many guns. She saw Danno, then me, and smiled. Danno shot her.

I didn't move. I don't know which had been more shocking, her arrival, her smile, or Danno shooting her. I hadn't sensed him reaching for his gun. She should have got him first. She'd been standing there, her own gun ready, and the lift doors had opened, and still he'd shot her first. He was a man to know in a tight place.

She fell forward, blocking the lift doors as they tried to close. Lucky. Without the seal we didn't get the gas. Danno must have known about the fire precautions, but the lift door opened and he shot her. It was quicker than thought and I'd have a statistic for that if I'd paid attention on my psycho-engineering course.

Alarm bells were sounding. I went to her. Danno had shot her in the right upper chest, exactly through the heart. I looked back at him. 'You knew her?'

He was replacing his gun in its holster. 'Not her.'

'Then why?'

He thought about it. 'Others like her.' He actually smiled.

'I knew her, Danno. It was me she wanted.'

'Great. Then you owe me.' He stood up. 'I should bugger off then. She may have back-up, so go carefully.'

'This is crazy. What about you?'

He was looking down, carefully squaring his case on the desk-top. 'Fuck-off, I said.'

'Come with me.'

He thought about that too. He pointed at Sergeant Milhaus. 'I've got to make some calls.'

'I'll wait.' It was then that Sergeant Milhaus reminded me of Anna. I had the primate results on the C4 vaccine in my case. 'I'll wait.'

He sighed. 'Downstairs, then.' He dug in his tunic pocket and tossed me keys. 'Wait in my car. Just in case. If these girls have back-up it's usually very close. But the car's fucking bullet-proof, just in case.'

'You'll join me?'

'Wait in my car. You can't miss it.'

The bells were still ringing. I hesitated, not long, then did as he said. I too didn't think Sergeant Milhaus had a back-up. She'd been a loner, even at the convent. I left the computer control room and went down the stairs, taking with me my briefcase with the primate results on the C4 vaccine. I didn't hesitate long because my priority had become Anna and the primate results on the C4 vaccine. I think I knew I wouldn't see Danno again.

Daniel rubbed at the dry tear-runs prickling his face. He looked at the dead woman in her police uniform. She shouldn't have come alone – they were trained to work in pairs. He left her where she was, immobilising the elevator, and went to the double doors his sister had gone out through. He wanted to lock them but the only bolts were automatic and he couldn't make them work. The alarm bells rang like toothache. He returned to the desk and opened his case.

It had been a long day and he was very tired. The explosive came in two white, dough-like slabs wrapped in transparent plastic, enough to blow three bridges. The shortest delay the timer allowed was four minutes. Any less was considered suicidal. He set it to seven, making sure Harri'd be clear of the building.

The best trick he'd learned from Bert was not to have a past. Not to have pain. Harri was a good kid. He sat down at the desk, closed the case and rested his elbows on it. Across the room he watched the tape disks spin behind their glass panels. Fucking PTG. Who needed it? The bells went on ringing.

A NatSekur girl was lying on the carpet in the downstairs corridor. The alarm bells were louder here. The girl had been shot through her mouth, which had been open at the time. Sergeant Milhaus? If there'd been guards, Milhaus could more easily have waited for me outside. There was only one exit. Besides, I recognised Danno's marksmanship. I'd think about his reasons later.

I went past the dead guard and out into the foyer, prepared for more. One dead girl deserved another. And another. Logic, but no reason. If Danno was as logical as this, as crazy as this, why had he let me go? He knew I knew he knew I knew about Janni Wintermann. Et al. Should I wait for him in his car? I hugged my briefcase to my chest.

Two more dead girls, two more spot-on bullet wounds. When I'd called Danno from the Science Ministry he'd been instructing NatSekur girls on the indoor range. I was willing to believe he instructed them well. I'd always hated his job but someone had to do it.

I stepped over the body of the guard by the entrance doors to the foyer and went out into the night. The doors closed behind me, shutting in the worst of the bells. Thanks to Brandt's arc-lights the night was brighter than the foyer. I stood beneath the bright steel awning, looked left and right along the black bright walls. A bright black sedan with the NatSekur logo (Danno's?) was parked close by, and beyond it another car (Milhaus's?), commonplace blue and less classy. I thought I glimpsed movement between the two cars. If it was back-up it was very discreet. Maybe it had retired there when the bells started. There wouldn't be many Milhauses, drawn by the control-room lights, willing to go in over the bodies. I was glad she'd met her match in Danno.

I started walking. I was just another scientist going home late after a long day at the electron microscope. Perhaps Sergeant Milhaus's back-up wouldn't know me.

He knew me.

'Dr Kahn-Ryder? A moment of your time please, Dr Kahn-Ryder.'

It was Oswald Marton. Dr bloody Marton, Chief Secretary to the Minister.

'A moment of your time? Hmm?'

But he too had a gun. It was a curious mistake. His coat with its sleek fur collar was so urbane, his hair so silver, his scarf so chic, and his shoes were so immaculate – without the gun he could easily have fooled me. Without the gun I might easily have lowered my guard long enough to let him get his hands on the C4 research. Without the gun the truth would have dawned more slowly.

The Minister had never known of my application to publish. Marton had intercepted it, and had kept her and me apart ever since. My afternoon appointment with her, apparently with her, had been made by him and he'd kept it, knowing she'd be busy in the House. It was he who didn't want me to publish. He wasn't ready. Unikhem weren't ready. He'd promised them, in return for a euro or two, that they'd get there first, and their scientists were asking for more material. They were asking for the primate C_4 test results.

The moment he knew I had them in my briefcase, I was dead. I had to be. Anna too, we were both dead.

I stopped walking, stayed where I was, on the pavement outside Brandt's entrance.

'Give me your briefcase.'

'Anything you say.' I held it out. 'There's nothing in it.'

He didn't move. 'Of course not. Give it to me.'

'I mean it. The research goes back too far. Brandt clear out their safe deposits every two years. My stuff's in some central vault now. I don't have the access.'

'I don't believe you.'

I offered the briefcase. 'See for yourself.'

'Who's with you?' He was indecisive, afraid, keeping his distance. 'Why the alarm bells? Somebody killed these people.'

'Wasn't that your Sergeant Milhaus?'

'She's looking for you.' He glanced up at the building. 'There were lights . . . ' He looked past me, into the foyer, made up his mind. 'Stay still. Throw me the briefcase. Just stay where you are.'

I didn't move. I was trying to believe in Danno coming to my rescue.

'Do it.' He gestured with the gun. 'I'll only use this thing to hurt you, you know. I probably couldn't kill you with it even if I tried.'

That was true. I threw him the briefcase. I'd run out of excuses. I hoped it would hit him, distract him so that I could get away, but it didn't. It fell on the asphalt a metre in front of him.

The sky burst open in a shattering pulse of light. Marton thought the case had exploded and opened his mouth to scream – I registered this and can still see his tongue drawn back and his teeth gaping – but the sound was lost in the blast and thunder of the destruction three storeys above us, a splintered avalanche of glass and metal, wall tiles and jagged concrete lintels. I crouched instinctively, covering my head with my arms. The explosion was overhead and the awning protected me. The doors behind me bulged but held. When the roaring subsided the alarm bells had stopped. It seemed to me the silliest thing.

I stood up. Remarkably, the lights still shone. My briefcase was where I'd thrown it, littered now with broken tiles and daggers of glass. It had not been under the awning and neither had Marton. A beam had fallen on him, and a lot of glass. He was a mess. That sounds an unprofessional description. But he died as I reached him, blood spurting from his mouth and his eyes turning up, unmistakably a mess. I never saw the PM report but I'd say it was a mercy. I scuffled the glass off my case and picked it up. The top floors of the building were destroyed, stripped to carcass, smouldering. Small pieces still fell and charred paper drifted. Danno wasn't going to come to my rescue.

The cars too were a mess. I leaned on the nearest, Danno's. So much death. I wasn't that sort of doctor – I felt as if I'd seen more dead bodies in the last ten minutes than in my whole career. The windscreen of Danno's car was gone, the roof dented. Fires were gathering in the ruined central block above. I leaned on Danno's car. The guards at the gate would cope. It didn't occur to me that they might be dead also. My brother had had unimagined depths.

I'm still glad I loved him.

In the other car, Milhaus's car, Marton's car, a side window had gone. Inside it someone was crying. Not from pain, from fear, and sleepy. The door was locked but the broken window let me reach in and unlock it, and when I wrenched the door open Anna fell out against me.

Marton had run a tight ship. Milhaus his only employee, the minimum overheads, all his eggs in one basket. And convenient. Anna would have died with me, I'd no doubt of it, if he'd got what he wanted.

Her pulse was strong, her colour good. She was drugged but she knew me. Training helps at these times. I bundled her into the back seat of Danno's car. The front seats were covered with shattered glass from its windscreen but it started. I backed out, tyres crunching, and drove slowly down to the gates. The night air was icy in my face. The gates were open and I drove out through them. There were no guards.

I stopped the car by the river. Suddenly I was shaking too badly to be able to drive any further. I staggered out of the car and round into the back seat with Anna. I huddled down, hugging her and weeping. She hugged me back, in a dream, and smiled. I saw her smile in the light of the flames that were furling up into the sky from Brandt International's Windstrohm facility. They shone on the river.

Danno was dead. I didn't know how and therefore I didn't know why. I was still believing he'd been on a surprise NatSekur inspection. NatSekur had said he would be. The sufficient fact was, he was dead. He was better dead – he'd killed so often and I couldn't remember the joy Peter Simpson had doubted, or for that matter the sparkle. And Bert Breitholmer, who I thought might have remembered them, was dead too. So I hugged my little Anna and wept for Danno, for Danno's life.

When my rigor had passed, and I'd wept sufficiently, I used the NatSekur phone in Danno's car to call Mark. Lights were approaching from the direction of the town, and sirens. People had seen the fire in the sky. A helicopter burst over the hill. Mark's telephone rang only once before he answered.

CHAPTER FOURTEEN

The Regenesis. Year 1: early November.

It was the following January before our police had put together the forensic and ballistic evidence and formed the opinion that Daniel Ryder, and probably his friend Bertholt Breitholmer, had been sabotaging PTG clinics and research centres for the last ten years or more. By then, of course, parthenogenesis was no longer a burning issue. By then, also, I was three months pregnant with a male foetus, battling with morning sickness (boys were always worse for that, Moma said) and already crossing days impatiently off the calendar. The human gestation period is six months too long, any woman will tell you. But in any case I was glad to get out of the country on a research project while the media circus came and went. It was a small circus, one-ring if that, for by then Danno's efforts, like mine, were ridiculously out of date.

Who needs PTG clinics, or vaccines, now that the Regenesis has started?

Mark and I spent January touring the Mediterranean littoral. The births that had begun among the Bedouin, four here, three there, sketchily reported, were quickly up in the hundreds and thousands, first in north Africa and Egypt, then up through Turkey, across the Bosporus, Greece, Italy, southern France, Spain. The Syndrome was retreating outwards from the centre, the centre from which it had originally spread. It was nice, if pointless, to be proved right. It was far nicer to meet parents and their healthy little sons.

Forty years. It was a magical number. One thought of the biblical forty days and forty nights. Media people did, all the time. I didn't say a word. I liked the neatness of the pattern – our vaccine, the end of war, a spontaneous remission, such a coincidence – and Mark knew I did, but I kept it to myself. I was a woman crossing days off the calendar, no longer an oracular media person.

The Minister encouraged us to patent our vaccine, and Brandt persevered with a human test program in case the

Syndrome showed signs of advancing again, but it didn't so they quietly cancelled after six months. The Minister had needed to know about Marton. Bank accounts were traced, showing euro millions in advance payments, and a link to Unikhem, but they'd been careful and the link was never proved. In any case, if they wanted to pay Dr Oswald Marton millions, apparently because they loved him, that was their business. Outside the firm itself only Natalya and I, Magnus Asgeirson and his contact on the board, knew what they'd got for their money. A niece has inherited, a keen young social worker, quite deserving. She plans a hostel for the wretched hormo girls, misfits anyway, who are the Regenesis's only real losers. If she ever asked why her Uncle Oswald was visiting Brandt International's parthenogenesis research centre in the middle of a November night, I imagine the Minister thought of something to tell her.

Brandt International's dolphins died in the explosion. At least Danno's end accomplished that. The roof above them ruptured and they were crushed. PTG research on such a scale was no longer viable and Brandt abandoned it.

Nobody needed to know about Sergeant Milhaus. She wasn't even Sergeant – Marton had told the truth about that. She'd been police, but never sergeant, and she'd been sacked. Marton had hired her, and supplied her warrant card. She had no family and, unsurprisingly, no friends.

She hadn't been unkind to Anna. She'd kept her in a shack owned by Marton in the Lakes area. The roof had leaked and they'd both been very cold the short time they'd stayed there. She'd cut Anna's hair on Marton's orders, and filmed the video, but she'd cooked good big meals for a growing girl and she'd been hurt when Anna didn't want to play backgammon with her.

She was Marton's only helper. She and, unwittingly, poor Natalya whom he'd fed with Unikhem's fax number, saying it was the Department's. I don't know what he'd promised Milhaus but it wouldn't have been enough. Whatever his deal with Unikhem, he'd have ended up immensely rich. As I myself would have, if I'd got a patent application in first. Even working for the Government, there'd have been . . . a remuneration.

I haven't talked about money in this story. It's a serious deception. I wanted to be rich. I wanted other things more, but I wanted also to be rich. I find Mark did too. We admitted this to each other only after the possibility had gone away.

I'm on maternity leave from the Institute now, and our son Paulus is three months old. He's a wonder. A prodigy. Literally – there won't be another north-European baby to touch him for another seven or eight months. The Syndrome cleared Paris in June, Copenhagen in August. The French proclaimed National Fucking Night for midsummer.

It's the way of plagues to wither. The Black Death didn't last for ever. We don't know why.

Paulus is a wonder. He doesn't know he's the only C4 vaccine baby in the world and he never will. The media latched on to his parents' visit to northern Turkey as an explanation, the beneficial effects of Erzurum's post-Syndrome climate, so we fudged the dates and let them. But the Paradise Hotel had been no place for making babies. On our return there from Dr Fateya we found there'd been a mud slide and much of the hotel had fallen into the road. We spent the night in the airport lounge and flew home next morning.

Nobody here knows what happened to Dr Fateya. He isn't at the address where Mark and I visited him. I hope he spent his 30,000 wisely and is living with a blithering boy in a small retirement villa on the Black Sea.

I'm on leave from the Institute and Paulus is a wonder. He sits up, and screams, and sucks till my nipples feel like organ stops, and laughs, and urinates and defecates and sleeps. He also likes us.

He liked Moma too, when we took him to see her. Moma's fine now. Danno's death was a bad time. She wanted a funeral. She wanted to bury him in the graveyard beside Dada and nobody cared to tell her there was nothing to bury. Only my word said he'd been in the computer control room. My word, and melted bits of a handgun NatSekur recognised as his from the number.

We told her Danno had been cremated and I went with her to Dada's grave with some ashes. They were human ashes, I don't know whose, Dr Vrieland obtained them for me. Margarethe Osterbrook was there again, and read a service, and Moma scattered the ashes. I remembered Danno as a little boy, when he'd seemed to me so big. It was sad, Moma was sad, Danno was sad, and I wept as I had for Dada.

Julius didn't make the funeral. He had a stroke two days after the fire at Brandt and he's been in hospital ever since. He won't leave. His eyes move, but he's paralysed and deaf and dumb and, I hope and believe, mindless. They sometimes play him Palestrina.

Hannes Vrieland delivered the baby. More accurately, I delivered Paulus and Hannes caught him. A delivery in the English, cricketing sense. He was as pleased as we were. Anna was there too. She knows she's going to be jealous but up to now she's pleased. Maybe the sixteen-year gap between them will save her. She has exciting times ahead. After forty years of the Attrition there's nothing she can't do. In twenty more years some professions will be in effect entirely female and young men will enter them on sufferance. It's not just jobs, expectations have changed. Everybody can't do everything, they never could. But the chance is there. It used to be called positive discrimination. Thanks to cosmic orderliness, God the Mother, a random missile on an irresponsible genetic experiment, a little positive discrimination.

In three months' time my maternity leave will be over and I shall have to decide whether or not to go back to the Institute. Dr Vrieland is concerned for me. So is Mark. So are Anna, Yvette, Moma, Gusso, the Convent Superior, Julius's spirit, and the massed bands of the Presidential Guard. I'm damned if I do go back and damned if I don't. The Institute has switched to AIDS research, the C4 vaccine has interesting implications, and Natya is running the program. Bringing up Paulus, all the new Pauluses, is a useful occupation.

An understatement. Forty years of men are missing. Bringing up their successors is the most important job around. Past mistakes grew out of past pressures and do not need to be repeated. For the next twenty years most Pauluses won't have fathers: their mothers are already shaping them. Every eyeblink is important. Too important. We've got to calm down.

If I go back to the Institute will Paulus feel put down? If I stay at home will he feel portentous? I'm lucky, I have Mark, who is a good man. I also have work I love. I need precedent and there isn't one. It's what people have always wanted, a new start. He sucks and shits and pisses, and he's a wonder. So is Anna.